ROCKS

WITH A STORY

Published in 2021 by
Kinetics Design, KDbooks.ca

ISBN 978-1-988360-65-2 (paperback)
ISBN 978-1-988360-66-9 (ebook)

The editor: Matthew Godden

The designer: cover and interior design,
typesetting and printing by Daniel Crack,
Kinetics Design, KDbooks.ca
https://www.linkedin.com/in/kdbooks/

Contact the author at
lorneedy@hotmail.com

ROCKS

WITH A STORY

A NOVEL

LORNE EEDY

The Stories

*Downtown St. Marys in 1890. The Grand Central Hotel
is the third building from the right.*

The rock garden behind the Hotel in its 1930s prime, with Miss Marshall.
She will be the fourth generation to own the Grand Central Hotel building.

The Rock Garden

If the old spots have voices —
Garden, rock and well —
To welcome us,
     what memories they could tell!

Blooms woke up as we entered,
Murmuring somethin' nice
Told to each other, then said over
     and over thrice.

This rock garden holds memories,
Every stone a turn — so
In times ahead, stories we will know.

— Charles Wolfe Cruise
St. Marys, Ontario, 1927

PROLOGUE

**"Every rock in the
garden has a story."**

St. Marys, Ontario, 1996

"I like these little memories
That never fade or die.
They help to keep one smiling
When trouble clouds the sky.
Yes, 'tis strange how one remembers
Life's little moments gay,
While great events receding
Seem dim and far away."

— THE BARBER

The Grand Central Hotel, Queen Street East, St Marys, Ontario.
— Photo by Melvyn King

I am looking at the ass end of one massive building in the heart of downtown St. Marys. An old dowager, a once-upon-a-time hotel, stands up before me in dusty glory. The dirt of ages stuck to the faded yellow brick makes it hard to see, especially behind the imposing second-storey wooden porch. Pillars, posts and rails, stairtop pediment and pilaster flash out to the world, exposing a crazed and peeling paint job that stretches corner to corner. The only wood that doesn't need scraping is the porch staircase, worn to a bare finish.

The front end of the building shines brighter, three storeys with a main-street view. The two upper floors with the original four-over-four windows are stacked in rows above Queen Street. A small balcony with a decorative wrought-iron rail is an interruption in the middle of the second floor. The double French doors sealed shut add to the pretty façade. Partners in surviving details from a better time, all in need of new-owner TLC. High above, on the weather-worn sea-blue fascia, sits a faded lineup of gold-leaf letters: *GRAND CENTRAL HOTEL*.

Most citizens fail to look up to the name. They may wonder at the street level angel-stone facing which masks the original recessed wood trim. If you step back a few steps on the sidewalk you can see the upper tongue-and-groove pine that covers the original leaded lights. Between the worn wood and the misplaced angel-stone are two larger and one smaller display windows. Above the smaller window the faded sign reads *CARD SHOP*. The two larger display windows once belonged to a dress shop and a gift shop. The small entrance to the former card shop is overshadowed by the magnificent doorway at the centre of the hotel.

No one can build these classics today, and nothing can replace them. The glory of hand-kilned brick! I am grateful for the attractive forward face of this old queen, but as Stormin' Norman, the grey fox of real estate, states in his bible of sales: "Whether horse, hound or house, look the butt-end over before buying into the deal."

And so I'm standing out back with Virginia Marshall, the fourth-generation owner of the property, as I kick the bricks on this possible purchase. Virginia was the proprietor of all three stores on the premises, which I knew from the outside as a wide-eyed window-shopping kid. The gift and card shops were mall casualties, while the dress shop hung on for a while under new managers. Now this elderly landlord has tired of maintenance and renters.

A big pile of bricks has settled on an even bigger property. The double lot runs the full block length from Queen to Jones, a full sixty feet wide, while the hotel stretches side to side, matching the width with a sixty-foot-long foundation. A flagstone pathway runs between a former coach house and a blanket of green ivy smothering a long, low mound that runs a border the length of the property. An old and mouldy armless Venus stands up through the ivy, a solid witness to a dried-up pond. The garden mound reaches back sixty feet to a stand of junipers. The gravel widens at that point for a shared access to Jones Street. I turn my head left and right as I do the math: two hundred and fifty feet from street to street.

Virginia, her white hair coiffed to perfection as always, smiles at me. "Over a hundred years in our family. The Grand Central Hotel."

I can't help remembering another of Stormin' Norman's chestnuts about historic buildings. The real estate sage leaned in simple and direct: "Restoration. As soon as you pick up a nail and hammer, expect to add forty percent to your costs."

Never mind his dubious personal habits and shaky hands: Norman's weathered red face and wiry hair show off the experience of an astute horse trader. His laugh, omnipresent even in the absence of any joke, is a recognizable brand in town.

"*Aargh. Aargh. Aargh.* Better count on fifty percent, just to be sure."

But Norman balanced the bag-full of back-end costs with one magic word: cheap.

"Cheap," he repeated. "She's desperate to get it sold. Cheap makes a great deal." His grey-blue eyes lit up like the eyes of a wolf homing in on its target.

And I am the target, standing in the past glory of a dowager hotel. Anything above twenty percent in costs will hurt. Norman stands in the back of my mind, looking over my shoulder. "*Aargh. Aargh. Aargh.*"

Virginia brings me back to our tour. "I always tried to keep it the way he would like." Her soft voice rises up to the memory of her father and another past time. All I can do is just nod my head at her landscape confessions. "I left the junipers and the pea-gravel area." She points to the small, weed-infested clearing where Venus stands. "Father liked to have a smoke there."

Virginia waves her arms as she points out the various features of the property, pumping up the pride on her sales vision. She's building to an historic take-off. She sweeps her hands back in full sales flight.

"Three generations before me," she says, letting out a depth of breath. She looks down, deep down into her life. "Three generations before me, Great-Grandfather and Grandfather ran a hostelry."

I'm not quite with her on this flight into her family records. But I have to wonder about a possible connection between her family and my family. I do a quick roll call on my side. My grandfather probably knew her father, but it would be hard to verify since Charles Wolfe Cruise was dead before my birth.

The first two generations of Innkeepers,
the Marshalls and their families, circa 1890.

"Father ran the barbershop. He had just graduated from barber school. In order to work, he had to create his space. My grandfather, the innkeeper, helped him enclose the carriageway."

I knew about an open passage from the main street to the back of the hotel. Hard to imagine a buggy passage with the back of the space now blocked by a humungous maple.

"Grandfather was the second innkeeper. He settled the hotel business into room rentals with a coffee shop."

The thick blue file Norman gave me contains a photocopy of a hand-printed history and a stack of measured grid sheets showing off the skeleton structure of a hotel with three stores on the ground floor, three vast apartments on the second, and chock-a-block tiny single rooms on the third. The measurements go deep; even the basement is penciled in exact feet and inches. The transformed barbershop, now a defunct card shop, is marked as 11'9" wide. Empty tapered display stands are scattered along the full fifty feet of its length, everything covered in dust. On my tour of the interior I counted a dozen trips to the dump. Or one call to Frank's Scrap Metal might do it. The leftover hotel rooms are 8'6" by 9' square, the enamel door numbers marked in the centre of each room on the grid sheet, twelve in total. The scrap yard might recover some costs, but the parade of drip pails behind the upper set of rooms sets up a bad forecast on the state of roof affairs.

"Grandfather, the second innkeeper ..."

Her repetition is testing my concentration. There's a long history to process. I imagine a carriageway with a stagecoach pulling through the eleven-foot space of the no-card shop. The barn, or livery, is long gone, leaving a garden lined by a split-rail fence, trimmed in lilac trees and a leaning parade of cedars. Past the hedge the former paddock has transformed into a large area of manicured grass.

The garden area, apparently, has lived and prospered while the hotel died. As the new owner I will be taking no prisoners. I picture the garden trimmed and the cedar rail sold in the *Journal*'s classifieds. The grass will become a parking lot for new tenants and increased income.

I look up at the fascia detail, imagining the level of decay. My mind is in a state of rot over the cost of Terry, my finishing carpenter. That mind calculator is whirling away. I see the phone call coming. (*"Buddy, you may need to rent a lift truck."*)

She joins my upward gaze. "Just needs a good scrape, and two coats of Benjamin Moore heritage paint." She holds her hand up in the same direction, blocking the early morning sun. "Our family always took care of the old hotel."

What happened to the care in this fourth generation, I wonder? But she's on to me. "I can show you receipts for the front paint job. New metal roof five years ago."

It leaks, I want to say, thinking of the parade of pails on the third floor. You need to caulk the bolts.

"The receipts are in the file," she says.

She points back in silence to the long green mound acting as a boundary to the property. I may not be the constant gardener, but I know how ferns proliferate and those horrible junipers root for the centre of the earth. And that sea of ivy …

Dropping genealogy for geology, she sweeps past my limited ability to plant-index the property. "Yes, the family rock garden."

She keeps looking at the stretched-out mound until I am the one to force the words out. "Quite a site."

I'm about to get my deal. Half her opening list price and all the hotel furniture left standing. But she will get the final word in. She will not let the building go now without my little history lesson on the family record.

You can feel the garden suck right up into the soul of the woman. How in the world will this guy ever be able to keep up this landscape, she must be wondering. I can see her head wobble side to side. Not to be stupid, I move things along, making a dumb observation.

"Yes, a nice fountain."

The wet comment hangs dead in the conversation. She ignores me, arms stretched toward ivy and stone, that dry fountain clouded with weeds, and all those green humps. "It's a rock garden." Her hands are full sail forward. "Look close. You'll see dozens of rocks. The ivy covers dozens more great rocks."

Re-focusing now on the gathering point for her father's smoke, I can see it. It's not exactly Stonehenge, but there is certainly a lot of stone under those green humps anchored by the gravel spot and the junipers.

Some free rocks might work. My wife and I do enjoy all the pretty rocks in our home garden. Stupid is as stupid did before and now does again: out comes another dumb observation.

"A lot of rocks …"

"And you know what?" She steps in, real close. "Every rock in the garden has a story."

My mouth does it again. "Rocks with a story …"

My words fade as I face the breadth of the mound. I tune out the garden costs. She has my attention now. Stories are a huge part of my family life: Uncle Jim, son Jamie, cousin Sarah, not to forget my father, Charles Junior. A large family tree of full-monty raconteurs. And my war-bride mother …

"Yes," she says as a super smile widens on her face, "because each rock was special, a unique example. And my father the barber got most of them." She nods matter-of-factly. "He gave a free haircut to each customer who donated a great specimen. Mark my word, the rock had to be worthy of our garden."

My memory does contain records, indexed through family and friends, of some kind of haircut deal. Uncle Jim had this story of a cat stuck up in a tree, a cat tale that included some kid with a rock. Was there a connection there with the barber? A free haircut for the right rock is a classic bring-me-business. The most powerful word in marketing is "free." The story was a favourite post-Christmas-dinner request. He always finished by telling us that the cat tale was the origin of the expression "kitty-corner."

"Beautiful rocks!" she says. She makes eye contact, and I turn to follow her pointing finger. "Look, there's one that has to be petrified wood. That one could be a piece of an asteroid. This one beside Venus looks like a dog, and over there — sure looks like a pig."

My gaze sticks to one shaft-like piece. Did she describe it as petrified wood? She sees my half-dumb look of concentration. She is so past this point. "Can you see the dog?" she asks me.

I direct my attention to what appears to be a Scottie-dog profile and take it up a notch. "Yes, and the pig looks very porcine."

Her interest is historical responsibility. My interest is commercial. The rock-bottom price allows a freshen-up on the heritage façade. Then I'll freshen up the rent checks for higher-end office space. The freshened face forward to the main street will please Virginia. She will not be pleased, however, with her paddock paradise becoming a parking lot.

Slow down, I tell myself.

My father and grandfather had their haircuts with this barber, so I steady myself to listen with sympathy and respect — from his family to mine. I know something about the history of my town, being a descendant of another merchant pioneer family.

Did my father or grandfather as known customers put forward any stone nominations? Was there a haircut deal? Were there stories?

I can't help looking up again through the maple canopy, up to the downside of a major roof job. Those eaves, too, look worse for wear. The building has detail climbing up three storeys. Rocks do not pay for the finishing carpenter. They do not pay the rent. I am stuck on cost. This is a rustic queen.

"You can be sure that Mother, my sister and myself did not hear all the tales, but we did hear our share." Virginia fades into that cloud of memory again, then snaps out of it, laughing to herself. "Yes, we all knew that every rock had some sort of a story."

A few more questioning looks and an awkward pause bring our conversation that day to a close.

I buy the old hotel feeling splendid about the rock-bottom price. And it is a clean sweep. With a last little squeeze I have her include every display cabinet and every piece of leftover furniture the old hotel had hung on to for all those years. After Stormin' pushes a little on the family-record angle (*"The stuff should stay with the hotel"*), Virginia acquiesces, realistic about the cost of storage space.

"I'm not storing the stuff," she says, "so you might as well throw it into the deal."

The list goes on and on, including a massive unit of bevelled mirrors and walnut shelving trimmed with seventeen feet of brass boot rail.

Six months later

Tap. Tap. Tap, tap, tap, tap …

A rolling thunder of hammers resonates across the compact downtown.

Tap. Tap. Tap, tap, tap, tap …

The condensed historic core of our small town plays a loud beat. Surrounded by hills and contained between the wide Thames River on the west and a slow, misnamed creek on the north, it's a funnel that both contains and amplifies the sound. The confluence of water, earth and stone adds resonance. The tapping becomes sharper and more crisp as it moves up in elevation on the roof.

Yes, the hotel's best feature is the massive three-storey façade that pushes forward onto the main street, but again today the best view comes from the backyard. Here out back, a company of citizens have their heads up with their eyes towards the tap line. Overhead, by the sea-blue fascia and soffit above the second-floor porch, all under the shade of an umbrella maple canopy, a team of Amish roofers show their how-to in the modern age. None of the knock, knock, knocking of an air-pressure pump. Nor the stapling sound of a nail gun. Proper Amish do it all by hand, first-hand for the audience of locals downstairs known to them as "the English."

Bang. Bang. Bang, bang, bang, bang …

Fourteen sets of gloveless hands go at it under the leadership of Yost Roedden. He's the short dynamo talking into the phone. Yost and all hands look identical in sky blue shirts, suspenders, black denim trousers and stubby work boots. Their suspender clips and horn-rimmed glasses shine. The difference is the boss holds the flip cellphone, wears Ray-Bans and flashes a nice spring-water smile. His only piece of technology is well-used for order and organization among the English customers in this Amish enterprise. A God-approved tool to deal with modern neighbours and make the most of it. One phone call gets them out of Gomorrah with the pre-arranged white passenger van. The rubber-neckers line up, all eyes looking up above the sea blue fascia. And up, up and away those Amish go. The lineup of witnesses without suspenders melt into one conclusion:

My goodness, those Amish are a roofing machine.

Yost reminds all. "Ve're da Amish team. Youse Amish roofers." And that non-fluoride smile. "And remember." Every few minutes he offers his business card to the rubber-necker group. "Always Yost in time."

On the roof, it's a butt parade. Chrome suspender clips on black pants shimmer and shake, reflecting the cracks of sunlight through the canopy into zebra stripes. A dozen black boots shuffle along the edge of the tarp paper that forms their tap line. Stage west, a never-ending supply of asphalt shingles is shouldered up the ladder to feed the roofing machine. The younger lads scamper across the newly laid asphalt for a shoulder drop on the front line. All the workers' straw hats remain in place, a series of beige lines following a choreographed process row on row.

Bang. Bang. Bang, bang, bang, bang …

The Amish there on the roof, along with the rubber-neckers, Yost and the owner below are joint witnesses to changing technology. The Town Hall bell along with the Andrews Jewellery clock tower have simply rung out, now silent in the face of progress. They once were both marked sounds recognized by all. The bells no longer toll the standard times for work or break, school or lunch. Another God-approved reason for modern methods: the flip-phone has a clock. The cellphone-familiar audience join my amusement at the short, horse-driving man with Ray-Bans and a country smile, yelling into the device. We wait.

Yost is off his call now. He whistles. The audience heads crank from Yost to his team on the roof as the work site goes quiet. The suspenders rise, turn towards the ladder on the west side. All hats remain in perfect place as they reverse the shingle path. Yost turns to me, and surrounded by a half-moon beard, his lips spring into a full-bloom beam.

"Please, join us for our break, Mr. Cruise. Yost in time." His eyes twinkle with his laugh.

The lineup of bushy smiles guffaw at the pun, no matter how many times it's repeated. The players on the Amish roofing team form a long bench that's strung below the cover of the sea blue fascia of the Hotel's wide porch. It's an automated break. Hats come off and snacks appear out of white burlap bags. A large thermos of tea follows, to fill granite-ware cups.

"Mrs. Dunseith has made us a special treat," Yost says.

Mrs. Dunseith is a widow and perfect tenant, a carryover from the last owner. Yost is a man led by his sweet tooth. The English lady has struck the right chord. He's about to lick his clean-shaven upper lip in anticipation.

The irony tickles me. I point to the Boston cream pie being hoovered up by the Amish crew. "You know, lads. You know who Mrs. Dunseith is?"

Tea cups and cream pie stand still. All hatless heads and pairs of horn-rimmed glasses turn to my attention.

"She's the Presbyterian minister's mother," I say.

I picture the Amish cocooned from the world outside. It's an amazing feat, considering all their contact through "the English" in this small town. A world of us and them, and we are them. Head down go the Amish, shoulder to the wheel.

I hold back a smile. "You know she's Yost trying to convert you."

The roofers are watchful and quick. They absorb the good fun. All guffaws again with probable knowledge that they'll have a great story for their families to yuck about later by candlelight.

Fourteen kneeling and sitting Amish, Yost enjoying themselves. For my part, this group are a final addition to the big family of trades that have gathered here over the last few months. All parts are added to my tab.

This is the final bill, I repeat to myself. We needed the roof. Mac the plumber has been a small plunge here and there, and don't even ask about the upgraded electrical service by Handy Andy. I've limited the services of Mason Dunseith, the painter, to the sea blue fascia and soffit under the roof: a freshen-up on the makeup in front for a better face on the main street. Terry Wood, the finishing carpenter, hand-crafted replacement capitals to anchor the top corners of all three stores and the centre steps. Pictures for authenticity came from the Archives. Below the roof, the original hand-kilned brick begged for the spot services of Sandy Paynter, the master mason. (Yes, that's Wood on wood and Mason on the paint, while Sandy mixes sand and cement to make his point on the brick joints.)

My budget on this new purchase is exhausted, so in came the Amish. Cheap, efficient and hard at it. And Yost is up, always up on improvements to the job.

He starts with a chin wag, hat tip and head scratch. "Mister Cruise, my crew could be more efficient." More Amish efficiency catches my attention. "But we could not place the scaffolding or the ladder on the east side."

We both turn to stage east on the roof project, opposite side to the shingle ladder path. Nestled up against the east corner of the building-wide porch is the maple that reaches to the sky over the sea blue soffit and fascia, anchoring the neighbour's boundary wall.

"The maple?"

"No, Mr. Cruise, not the way you might think. There's room between the trunk and building. The tree could be an amazing anchor on that side. But an anchor still needs to be spiked down. Department of Labour regulations."

Yost turns a grim look to the corner. I am quick to answer with another question.

"The roots?"

"Not roots, Mr. Cruise. It's all in that mound," he says. "It's full of stones. We cannot pound the anchors to the scaffolding without hitting rock. We bent a bunch of spikes and broke two hammer handles."

Yost does not smile. "But the young lads are big and strong. We'll work from that side." He looks left. "No worries, they're upsy-daisy that ladder. They're tree rabbits."

My thoughts sink from the impressive canopy into the financial rabbit hole in front of me. My neglect of the garden is costing me. Touched by shame, I think of Virginia, the previous owner — now my tenant across the hall from the Presbyterian minister's mother — and our conversation which took place here in the backyard, on almost this same spot.

Yost turns the smile back on. I see him making a mental note to polish a little English on the invoice. Business is business.

Over the next few months, as bit by bit the hotel returns to a facsimile of its original form, the restoration reflects well on the downtown. The Heritage group provides a design map with faded photos of a former glory. Those details so alien to architecture here in the Stonetown, the fabricated angel-stone dressing and the worn pine that gave the building an odd barn-like appearance, both disappear. The cracked, paint-smeared windows are hand-replaced with leaded glass, bevelled pane by bevelled pane. I marvel at those three sections of five-foot bevelled lead mirror which prop up the reception area to a commercial rental.

Pressure washing, an unplanned and humbling expense that is softened by a government grant, reclaims the details of the yellow brick from underneath the dull grey paint. This full facial is a must for the massive hotel built 140 years ago, the first brick hotel in our town. Two new furnaces and air conditioning, which I can afford only by cutting to the bone on cost, add value with the infrastructure upgrades.

I never do paint the eaves, touch up the gold-leaf letters. A little high for Mason the painter. Terry Wood works lower down the ladder to get the trim ship-shape for a few more years — not much time in the life of a 140-year-old hotel.

But the longer I own the building, the more questions I have.

How little I know about the man they call The Barber.

It gets to be a cliché around town.

"So you bought the old hotel."

Not a question or comment, just a statement. I learn to greet it with silence and then wait for the story that follows. A story about their Grand Central experience. Rare early memories of good times over beer and contemplation. Somebody's grandmother pulling their grandfather out the back door while a gaggle of temperance ladies shake their gloved fists out front. The appearance of local magnate Jack Roger, and then his disappearance with the changeover to coffee. A period of tempered conversation only interrupted by the war years. The stories keep coming. The unfortunate Harold Ward who fell asleep smoking, woke up on a fiery mattress, and was known forever after as Burns Ward. Shakey the cat who disappeared into the attic walls; the coffee klatch downstairs swore they could hear the cries for months and months after. No stories of fights make the rounds, and no affairs that anyone would admit to, but there's a torrent of memories from my parents' generation. And then their sons, including me and most of my friends, finish with a first haircut.

Everyone seems to have had at least one haircut from The Barber. But most mention more than a cut: an *experience* in the big red & nickel chair.

In the end it takes ten years to turn my cheap buy into a restoration queen. After that, time permits me to begin following the property clues that have awakened my interest. What better place to start researching than my grandfather's C.W. Cruise Archives at the Stonetown Museum? (When Charles Wolfe died he bequeathed our family records to the town along with a donation covering a substantial portion of the museum's expansion.)

Further bits of information come together courtesy of the oral histories of my father and his friends. Most knew about the rocks. What is now the juniper circle beside that dry fountain and the pea gravel was once the smoke pit out back. Nicotine ruled back in that graveyard of granite, adjacent to what is now the maple's cool canopy of shade. The rocks just had to be part of the conversation. One farmer named Marvin, tipping the scales at over three hundred and fifty pounds, could lift over four hundred pounds of rock. Our neighbour George, during his own haircut, was witness to the arrival of the big man in his Mercury pickup.

Much of what's in the Cruise Archives is forgotten, filling row after row in the Museum basement. It's quite a pile of paper, print books and hand-printed diaries with copious notes, not to mention the hundreds of stereographs, copper negative photos, hand-coloured postcards, wax-paper surveys and local naïve art. But one photo of Charles Wolfe Cruise stands out. Grandfather, in a starched collar and bowtie, stands shoulder to shoulder with a man in a white apron. Together, Cruise and The Barber hold, in one hand each, a worn leather-bound book: the deerskin diary of The Barber.

Our curator general of the Stonetown Museum, Larry Smith, is quick on the track. "Wolfe, we have the diary," he tells me one day. "He had promised it to your grandfather, who insisted that he donate it to the Archives."

After my months of dry research, finding an extant firsthand record feels like unearthing the Ark of the Covenant. Perhaps this record will shine light on The Barber's contribution to his family's shady, ivy-covered mound and its maze of rocks.

After I hurry down to the Archives to pick up my microfiche copy, Larry calls it heads on. "Great stuff, Wolfe. Get this. He's a poet! The Barber writes poetry in a straight and steady hand-print." Larry can't contain his archival excitement. "In the margins he adds comic drawings. It's a puzzle to put a name to the pictures. I must confess that I've had some fun with it."

The curator of the Stonetown Museum is smirking. "There'll be quick entries for a few pages, with poetry, caricatures and notes. Then all of a sudden he'll fill three pages with his careful lines, describing in some detail an incident, event, personality ..."

"A story, Larry?"

"Yes, Wolfe. It's all recorded in that deerhide-covered diary. Check out the way it's embossed with a representation of a barber's pole. And what I thought were walnuts are supposed to be rocks. I had to put on my readers to discern that detail. The book is tied with a red ribbon with a letter of direction tucked in. The daughters found it after his death" — he leans in close — "under his freaking pillow!"

His eyebrows rise and fall. Larry is in full flight on a diary. "Wolfe, remember old George Sewell?"

More than just memories. I confirm the existence of a horrifying event without going into detail. "The voice of God," I say. "He was my Confirmation minister."

Again Larry's eyebrows are flashing up and down. "Wolfe, we have his diary too." He pulls his index finger to his lips. "It's like Emily Brontë behind a pulpit. Hussy fussy and the bitch tells all on St. Marys."

In me, Larry has found an ideal partner in research. "We can give you a microfiche copy of that, too," he says. "But you just have to check the two diaries out. Hold the history in your hands."

As it turns out, the diary of Rev. Dr. George Sewell, a dour, self-congratulatory epistle, will dovetail nice and tight with the other record of events. I now have two firsthand accounts, a self-described voice of God and a mimic of town life.

Slower than a tortoise I do research. I touch the originals on odd visits to the Archives. One digital copy covers a lifetime of desk drawers opening and shutting and key-strikes on an Underwood typewriter. The discs are uploaded onto my Mac desktop on my grandfather's work desk in my home office.

Ironic that I offered the big chuck of walnut to the Museum but its size ruled out a fit. My wife aligns herself with the opinion of the Museum:

"My goodness Wolfe, the size of the thing. Wouldn't one of those Danish computer desks give you more room for files and storage?"

"What? And send it off to Mike's Auction Barn? My grandfather's desk?"

"That's not a desk. That's bulky furniture filling up a room you have never used."

"It's a piece of history."

"History that a comfortable caster chair does not fit up against."

It takes me years to pull the stories together. My father advised me that in business you should "stick to your knitting." It seems that neither building restoration nor rental landlordship is my knitting. I continue moving on my own through the micro-disc in spare moments. When Virginia, the previous owner and The Barber's daughter, dies, all her papers, all the hotel files come to the Archives. She has kept a record of everything. The big red & nickel chair was her first memory. Father would place her on the booster board for young customers then give her a spin round and round. Her reflection was a blur held in the bevelled mirrors. As a child she found the back upper veranda a comfortable place to read. She wrote about how the sun, evening and morning, would play with light, turning the parade of stones into a jube-jube cake.

I never ever asked her about The Barber's stories. For heaven's sake, she joined the Presbyterian minister's mother as my tenant for twelve years. But I wasn't interested in the history, I was just looking for a distressed buy.

And so I remain, confronted by the longest yard with a mound of green humps fighting for air beneath an invasion of ivy, each one an indication of a large but hidden stone inventory.

I continue to read through the diaries of both men and more. My focus is on the shiny yellow-brick queen in the downtown and the former carriageway that morphed into a barbershop. My research, through a grandfather that I never met, in his vast personal archive of town minutiae, reveals lots of page turners on the characters of the town.

In The Barber himself we encounter two personalities. One is a private poet and pencil artist as revealed in his deerskin diary. The other is a public performer, a master mimic. The Archives have drawerfuls of playbills from the Stonetown Community Players. Most of these display his involvement — from principal roles in Gilbert & Sullivan to backstage carpenter or the chorus lineup. On the second-floor theatre stage at the castle-like Town Hall he performs in front of a packed house, then he returns two blocks down the main street to his big red &

nickel chair and a select audience in reflection. Here his skill as a mimic and a character actor reflect the magic of a busker's performance on a mirrored stage.

The Barber touches many more citizens in his role at the large theatre up the hill, but to the barbershop he brings a one-man show that's unseen elsewhere.

His first customers are probably mainly Protestants, including The Barber's fellow parishioners under the voice of God, George Sewell. But the barbershop chair is big enough to welcome a rainbow of St. Marys Citizens. The ground roots of pioneer merchant families grow to include the first generation of Italian cement plant workers and a bunch of Roman Catholic Irish farmers, followed by the Dutch and Germans. The Barber welcomes George Taylor, the Black school custodian, and once a month Mr. Lewis, the Chinese cook from the Innkeeper's café, appears, later joined by his son Phil.

With some of his irregulars, The Barber probably skips the mimic routine. But there's no denying that The Barber shepherds the largest and most interesting head count in town. A personal tale unfolds before each customer in the big chair. The seventeen-foot bevelled mirrors start to make complete sense.

The old Hotel continues to re-purpose itself in the 1950s.

CHAPTER 1

The Arrival of God's Messenger, George Sewell

1898

Before the advent of barbers in community evolution, a blanket of hardwood maple covers the fertile grounds of Western Ontario. The pioneers harvest these forests, pick from fields littered with stone. Material free and abundant for foundations, walls for boundary and building. A time for seeding new crops, planting, clearing, always to expand, make better. Grain for home, corn for livestock to milk and eat.

The best village site lies at the confluence of the Thames River and a creek named for a nonexistent fish. Unlike the surrounding lands, the small valley offers no value for sowing. It's water that powers the move to settle here. The Thames offers a nice drop in elevation: St. Marys where the waters meet has easy access to a ready supply of power, first for planing the timber by buzz saw and then for grinding grain. Water turns a sideways wheel that moves the gears and relays that push the heavy stone wheels. Decades later the unique wheel will be a landscape display next to the river walkway in the historic downtown.

Spring and stream develop into a municipal artesian well system in the mid-1800s. The crops grow with ample and timely precipitation. Cattle feed beside the many streams and rivers.

The water wheel grinds it out, and entrepreneurs in the building trades build it up. Scores of stone cottages crop up, scattered across Town. The builders of community are the self-employed stone masons whose cottage and quarrying skills were honed back in Inverness or Aberdeen. Here cottages sit adjacent to small quarries which grow from the well of construction projects and contracts. Each site empties of stone, morphing into a large basement foundation with back fill for yet another building site, and next time round a two-storey cottage goes up beside the earlier one-storey.

Stone, stone everywhere! The Presbyterian Scottish masons are contracted to build general stores and homes, farm supply and agricultural warehouses. They build for the southern Protestant Irish who dominate commerce: these are the pioneer entrepreneurs who take our Town to the next level of enterprise. They buy, sell, grind, saw and create. They mow the forest, moving on to establish four new grain mills. A lime kiln opens in Skunk's Hollow. Of the three busy door and sash companies, one will survive, using wood from out of town. Three wagon and barrel makers will in time combine into one multigenerational, national manufacturer of lawn mowers.

The first wave of the pioneers made do themselves, but soon tradesmen and craftspeople follow the open opportunities, from chimney sweeping to clockmaking, tinsmithing to candlemaking, metalwork to laundry service. Many of this itinerant group, along with the farm settlement in the Gore of Downie, fill the Catholic church for all three weekend masses.

The Town is blessed with the clay deposits necessary for making pottery kitchen and storage wear. Livestock render the opportunity to make candles from their waste. A German butcher offers a fine selection of sausage he advertises in the *St. Marys Journal*. Another German, the tinsmith, works with eavestrough and drainage pipe. (Both Germans are born in Berlin, Canada.) The shoemaker shows off his handcrafted boots and shoes in his display window. Shops selling ladies' fashions, men's work clothes, hardware, books and candy pop up in the downtown as the buildup starts to take the form more recognizable to residents today. Postcards show a downtown long, wide and wet. Two- and three-storey buildings appear, to face horse-drawn activity on a mud main street. Walking traffic sticks to the slab sidewalk.

The register in the Archives shows another influx too. The village becomes Town-like with the arrival of the teachers and preachers — as well as bureaucratic clerks, keep-it-legal lawyers, and first one doctor then more.

The professionals and showy entrepreneurs build a crop of larger homes that beg for the extras. One option is pricey copper drainage pipes from the German tinsmith. Others include cast-iron fences with fleur de lis, heritage gardens and large stained glass windows. The carved front door on Widder Street, for example, belongs to the first president of the Grand Trunk Railway, imported from their custom coach shop in Montreal.

A new way of travel begins with stagecoach then steams full ahead with railroad service. The two Ingersoll brothers, who arrive from the town named after them by foot and pack mule, are able to return home by train on the Canadian Pacific spur line less than twenty-five years later. Newbie arrivals foster an early room-and-board industry. At the pinnacle of hostelry, in my tenant's words, is her family's three-storey brick Grand Central Hotel, built in 1857. A big investment completed in time for construction business as the railway pushes tracks through Town.

The geography supports everything underfoot including agriculture, building material, water resources — even a dump and two new cemeteries. One undertaker tends to the Catholic flock while the other services Protestant needs. The latter also advertises in the *Journal* as a maker of fine furniture. (A small room in the front corner of the Stonetown Museum shows off a cherry sideboard, a small highboy and a cherry-framed oil as examples of his high-end sideline.)

The land produces, and produces. Seasons turn and turn again, yielding the largest per-acre harvests seen from sea to sea.

Yes, St. Marys is a special geographical Town.

The bed of the Thames River provides the biggest pieces of stone for the biggest projects. The fairy castle of a Town Hall, the massive misnamed Opera House, the overstated cube called the Box Castle, the arch bridges (including a triple for the Victoria Bridge), the towering churches, two railway viaducts, the phallic water tower — all show off the talent and prosperity of the residents. Their talented efforts change the physical community, a testament to the sophistication of the Citizenry of our Town. Who can't see those steeples for miles and miles? Just feel it in the air about you, the Citizen spirit arising, sitting up to take notice of a village that has become a Town. A sense of community aspiration aligns with higher purpose.

Look up!

A progressive breath pushes forward, invisible to eyes but proven on the ground by the proliferation of building projects. More than civic pride, a spiritual sense of reward and righteousness has permeated the air. The gusto of God back-winds all this prosperity.

Progress brings bigger houses, indoor plumbing, coal heat and house help, all of which belie a veneer of modesty. Who will justify God's presence in the heady development? Who will bring blessing on material gain? Who will be the messenger of God?

The crests of hills add a line of six steeples. The steeple chase runs along Church Street, from the north edge of Town to the cement plant in the south. The various Town groups of God's chosen ones authenticate their steeple heights with comparisons to European cathedrals (though perhaps Irish cathedrals would be a fairer fight).

The Methodist Church standing tall with its original steeple, before lightning strikes one Sunday morning.

The Methodist steeple boasts the highest elevation on a surveyor's report. The Roman Catholics across town claim their steeple is the tallest, their hall the prettiest and their own school the best. Who needs paper proof when the Pope is in charge, and the surveyor a heathen? The Presbyterians, two blocks over, remain determined in their height and resolution high up on Church Street North. The Baptists, in their tidy yellow-brick gospel hall, call it hubris; these Calvinists worship from their draughty stone perch under a narrow tower.

A second splinter group of disaffected Calvinists sit low across the street, row-on-row in their fat blob of a church, smarting from the size of their Protestant cousins, including the Norman tower of the Episcopalians across the street. One day on the entire year's calendar the congregation here cracks some smiles, over their Robbie Burns Supper. Happy times in dedication of the horrid Haggis by windy pipes and brogue prose. A time to ignore the pitch of their property, a marginal piece of Church Street. At least the craggy congregation enjoy very comfortable ash pews in an oyster-shell auditorium with a sweeping balcony.

Kitty-corner, the Methodists build the largest of auditoriums for miles around. The original one-room church becomes the pastoral office and parlour out back, now used for small funerals, family therapy and choir warmups. The second addition triples the space; the third addition just a few years later provides the glorious backdrop of the largest organ in Canada outside Montreal. All performers exclaim about the acoustics and the size. The unversed rave about the golden array of fake pipes that hide the nasty works of the real organ.

Four hundred parishioners can sit in their comfortable Wesleyan maple pews to study the imported stained glass windows that decorate three walls facing the outside. Their eyes follow the coloured biblical scenes that run all the way up to the faux bronze mouldings. Plaster medallions anchor the corners of a plain tile mosaic on the ceiling, an upside-down patio. Shamrocks, significant to the Irish parishioners, anchor the rosebud medallions which reflect the small but mighty group of non-Calvinist Scottish members.

On the north side, the cherry pulpit fronts the service diorama. The sloping floor shakes twenty-five rows back from the pedal bass on the

organ; Bach has never sounded better outside of Germany. It's a spectacular event on Christmas Eve, a big draw for once-a-year Christians,
when both side-wings of the half-shell choir pit fill up with sixty singers.

The first pastors have little impact, with little reference in the
Archives. The congregation is not listening. Perhaps they are waiting
for lightning to strike.

But the stage is set at the corner of Church and Elgin streets. For
over a year now, the carved pulpit has been in transition, occupied by
substitute ministers, but a star is about to rise in the east.

Three and a half hours away by train in the big city is an all-star
divinity graduate. He sees the big stage that fits his rising career, the
perfect nest in the west. The student learns from the library newspapers
of a large auditorium with perfect acoustics in rural Ontario. At school,
he's a bombastic and guileful braggart who dominates the debating
club. The gifted student is smart enough to realize that you can't be a
prophet in your own backyard. Greener pastures call.

An up-front, confident self-starter, he hops off the train, a big frog
in a small pond. The ink is still wet on his ordination diploma. The
Methodist Elders take a chance on the unknown, asking the newcomer
for a sample sermon. His imagination has practised this moment over
and over. It will be a walk-off home run.

The Archives hold the tattered clippings from the *St. Marys Journal*
where a parishioner-reporter glorifies the hired-on-the-spot graduate's
booming voice. She brands God's messenger neither a pastoral poseur
nor a glorious windbag, neither an ecclesiastic entertainer nor angelic
in manner. She brands him forever as "the broadcast voice":

No need to sit up front, or bring your hearing cone; nor does the
new Pastor at the Methodist Hall need a speaker cone himself. His
voice, along with his crystal-clear message, reaches the farthest
corner of the immense auditorium. The man has the cords to
whip the devil out of your week. He has a broadcast voice.

God's new messenger makes an immediate impression on the Town.
Few will deny his God-given talent to inspire breast swells among a
flock of bird-brains. The faithful, weak in the knees from six hard days

of work, get full restoration in an hour of power. He gives their under-belly of gumption a charge-up from the gut up. The right stuff in order to face the next week.

Spirit is in the air from the start. Their Methodist messenger delivers, taking up the righteous banner to lead his flock up from the river confluence, over from the surrounding neighbourhoods and in from the gravel concessions. They will come from far and wide to witness the host who holds an official audience every Sunday. He speaks in God's tongue before his jam-packed auditorium filled row upon row with Methodists and nosey parkers alike.

Never be shy with the man. Ask the messenger and he will give you his daily advice from God. On Sundays he glows with the glory of God's blessing. The apple is ripe, the future bright for the Pastor George Sewell. George preaches the right message at the right time in the arc of prog-ress for our Town. Every Sunday from the late 1800s through two great wars, not to forget the Boer conflict, the who's who of Town commerce gets a checkup from the neck up, right up to the end. A message from heaven above that ignites from the custom-crafted cherry lectern to churn in the guts of the massive Methodist Hall.

When it comes to the steeple chase, unwritten competition and backyard-fence oral conjecture will continue to percolate on who is closest of close to the highest of high.

These outsiders in other parishes, though, are quiet upon the arrival of the messenger. George is *the* show in Town. That Sunday in late July 1898, George is already in full stride as the new minister on the block.

"Sit yourself up! God is not your backbone. *You* are your own back-bone. God is your shining light. Sit up and let the light shine in."

His voice changes pitch from "broadcast" to "glory-in-heaven." The audience is filled with spirit and straight up in their seats. George is not shy about the volume or the repetition.

"Your backbone is *yours* alone to lift *yourself* off that seat of stagnation."

George picks the graphic bone of imagination to make his point.

"Smell it, folks. Can you smell it? That stink? It's you. You in your stagnation."

His voice shifts from a low growl of warning to a command, a command from heaven up above — or at least from the pool-deck tile ceiling. With George no one dares to look left or right, only dead ahead. A cough or sniffle, a tissue hack and honk, even a fart — nothing distracts his audience on their one-hour spiritual track.

"Sit yourself up ... by *lifting* yourself up! Then, and only then ..." (George lowers the broadcast voice again to a low, cautionary tone, looking out across the sea of faces. He reads their minds, feeds on their thoughts: *Give it to us, George. Give it to us!)* "... can you see God's path."

The still audience silently mouth their response.

(Show us the path, George. Show us.)

Let's be crystal clear: never ever does the Citizen parishioner stand up in Methodist Hall Church. Standing up is purely figurative. When soloist Fern Palmer sings "Jerusalem" backed by organ and double-wing-expanded choir, those gathered are tissue-dabbing. When prodigy Betty McKay stokes her eighteenth-century Italian violin with Mozart, smiles all around, but no applause. Anglicans and Roman Catholics stand up, kneel and sit up the same way in parishes all across their flat planet. The evangelists stand, sit, wail and shout in one-room gospel halls. The Baptists sit up good and straight in their mini yellow brick. But Methodists never clap or stand up in recognition, no matter the temptation. Pastor Sewell stands up and out on his own as their daily God contact.

In George's domain, never ever stand, unless you are collecting and passing the donation plate. Stick to your sitting. George preaches a power metaphor of redemption and reward. He inspires strength to lift yourself up through work. It's okay, he tells us, to use endeavour and wiles to achieve accumulation in whatever is accumulated. And George underlines the necessity of sharing our success when the ushers stand with the collection plates.

"He *picks* this path *personally* for you. Sit yourselves *up*, Citizens of St. Marys. Lift yourself *up* to the power of God!"

Although not the first to greet a local as a Citizen, he does put the "messenger of God" stamp on the brand. The Citizen brand sticks to George. Many Citizens of the Methodist persuasion will know no other messenger of God than George, due to his longevity.

George reaches out to his audience by bounding from his sermon mount, down three steps then four and five rows at a time. All heads forward not to miss this amazing leap of faith from stage to floor. Every Methodist will remember, and all heathens will hear, the stories of this first Sunday. The congregation hold their breath and wonder when the recently graduated pastor will halt all this prancing about.

Now he stops, with his index finger pointed to heaven high on the west wall; all eyes follow like those of movie-goers watching a silent horror film at the Pleasant Time Theatre.

"Behold the path to the glory of God. Behold the heavenly host."

There, right in the top panel, first stained glass window to the right, he directs his audience. On that panel a group of unknown figures march off westward on a long glass path to the grey glass clouds in hopeful glory. Only one of the travellers looks back: that hooded stranger points forward toward the unknown, the cloudy sky. George leaves his pointing hand pointed to the same spot. The messenger of God knows the proper Citizen path.

George makes the right point. The eyes of his captive parish, too, point west to the grey clouds in that upper window firmly indicated by George's gesticulations.

"Behold Citizens, your path to glory in heaven."

Even the children who struggle to stop squirming before their exit to Sunday school focus their limited attention westward-window-ho.

It's a total focus group, and all is organized in barnyard pecking order row upon row before the Pastor's flapping and flowing arms.

Up front sit the full complement of the nine Johnston family children, not forgetting Dad, Mom and the two Schneider grandparents, all turning en masse to the right point. Thirteen ducks lined up for Sunday servicing. The Douglas family with their four boys is tuned in, except number-three son David who always turns to give his buddies boggley eyes. Mr. Douglas is grateful for his front-row pew every time the Pastor bounds two or more rows past him. A harder turn to watch the action, but no broadcast booming in his ears.

At the very back are the two permanent ushers on Sunday; undertakers through the week. The Halls, father-and-son reminder of afterlife, size up future customers. All remaining eyes open westward, even the young men of modest thinking and imagination, even the few hung-over, nodding merchant-gentlemen. Part of the Pastoral charge, too, are the second-generation Innkeeper and his wife from the big hotel. Their future son will learn to mimic at the feet of an open-mic master.

The Pastor pushes his outstretched hands, further amplifies with his broadcast voice. "Hard work rewards the Christian Citizen on the *right* path. Onward, *onward* Christian Citizen." George bounds up the auditorium, landing on the dais with a clap of thunder, the broadcast voice turned up. "Volition gives volume to opportunity."

Up, up and away his voice soars. "Sit yourself up. *Sit* yourself up. *Lift* yourself up, Christian Citizens — *onward* ye shall go. Endeavour is your ship of gold."

His parishioners relish the rewards of hard work blessed by the sermon. The Johnston family, the indifferent young men, even the nodding merchant-pioneers are awakened to this richness of their messenger's reasoning. They relish the blessing by George to carry them into Monday morning.

Still, his parishioners, not a completely mindless flock of sheep, sometimes puzzle at his golden-throat jingle of reason. His metaphors of the high seas, for example, are a stretch. A train shipment of gold, or a stagecoach carrying a strong box, maybe saddlebags on a mule — these would all be familiar and plausible in the imagination of the penny-pinching group in front of him row upon row.

"If you want the flow, you have to row. Row and *row* and *row* if you really want the flow." George rows on, and on some more. "Sitting still is a fool's goal. Do nothing and it's fool's gold."

His eyes rove back and forth, row on row.

"Sit yourself up now. *Sit* yourself up in the flow of the Lord, our host, and his son who gave us most."

From that first Sunday onward, the upward lift of this right hand always points to one of the six storybook stained glass windows. Most parishioners will agree that the Pastor points most frequently to the upper-right panel of the northeast stained glass window. (George would never ever confess to a favourite, even with the repetitive point. That would make him predictable.)

A clever Methodist refers to this windowpane's characters as "the pointed ones" whereas George becomes "the appointed one."

George's program does repeat itself, and with a lot of pointing. He aims his simple script at impatient youth, the dotty blue-rinse crowd and the daydreamers. And not to forget those hungover nodding pioneer merchants.

The windbag sails on.

One given in his service: he insists on full audience participation. He points, and his audience turns again to the upper panel that features a hairy, hooded man. Amidst a gang of unknown followers, the man appears to be turning back as he points ahead to the grey clouds. Everyone assumes that the hooded greybeard is Jesus. Sweet Jesus's hand motions towards a bushier-bearded, grander Citizen seated comfortably in the clouds at the top of the adjacent pane of glass.

The congregation remains seated all stiff row after row, upright as penguins, with George-the-messenger in charge. Pastor has an aisle stance like a football tackle. His upper parts strain in motion towards the upper goal. His right hand, his great Peter pointer, frozen in the eyes of the believers on the pane … All his Christian soldiers sit themselves up straight as a cross, inspired pew upon pew … Then, as if on cue, he belts it out.

"*You* are *Citizen* Christians!"

Feel the glow. *We are Citizen Christians.*

Down in the rows and rows, the young Christian soldiers get tuned up further through Sunday school, then choir, Cubs, Scouts, Youth and Confirmation groups. And the old folks sit comforted in the knowledge that their children are receiving the same known message. Psalm 28 or "Jerusalem" — not to mention "O Holy Night" on a fresh snowy night — warms a welcome. Comfortable spirits are felt in the soul of the audience. George's message broadcast, his wall-shaking baritone, resonates for almost four generations of St. Marys Citizens. The sermon speaks to everyone from the current paperboy up to the future local merchants and mothers, acknowledged academics and too many teachers to mention, plus one scientist with a patent on air brakes for trains.

"*Take charge.* I said … take *charge.* You could stay right there in your seat. Or …" (George sucks in his breath, expanding the breadth of his gown, moving his eyes across the ready, waiting and antsy audience, and shouts it out) "... si-it you-are-self *uuuup!*"

For years to come the parishioners will palpitate with anticipation and knowledge of the script, mouthing his instructions. Pastor George Sewell waits for breathless silence, the loudest silence heard round St. Marys.

"Sit yourself up in life. Lift yourself up, Christian Citizen! Become the king of your own earthly throne."

George pauses, casting about the entire hall with jet black eyes. George practises his reach to those individuals tucked in the farthest pew. A bolt of the broadcast voice passes the father-and-son undertakers-cum-ushers to target three heathen lookee-looks. He spotted them early in the game. They tried to sneak in through the main entrance under the steeple right on the eleventh bell, when the choir's entrance might distract from theirs. From his first day, the sermon of the immediate hire, George misses nothing in his church.

His audience is set, and he nods to the small mirror over the red curtain behind the stage. The organist, Berthold, presses the right foot down on the pedal, two bass blasts in sync. George looks left, then right, at the Senior Choir, who stand dressed in white smocks with floppy red ties; the lower halves of their bodies are blocked by the carved walnut rail that joins the red curtain on each side. A mass of white & red that fills the orchestra clamshell. A flash of the organist's hand pulls at the wall of stops. The gilded pipes herald a full chorus upon high.

And then the music stops, but there is not a moment of silence.

"Hallelujah," the Pastor says.

Softer. "Hallelujah."

And then drawn out: *"Ha-a-a-ley-ya-ya-ya-uh."*

George's hand drops. Fifty angel-dressed adults sit, as George continues to stand out. "Sit yourself up, Christian Citizens."

In this moment of glory, George puts his hands up again, pausing for self-anointed effect. And then:

BAMMO!

The Pastor freezes in his point up.

The audience congregates to George's frozen view, waiting on the next point. A cascade of smashing wood and crashing brick follows the big bang. All look to the ceiling for the scattering shards of material to break through the roof.

The broadcast message is loud and under control. "Ladies and gentlemen, please remain seated. We need order. The steeple has been hit."

George moves his obvious point from the west steeple to the east side entrance. "We need to exit through the parlour door."

A dust cloud fills the west entrance. Everyone is stunned, but they follow the Pastor's instructions.

"Ladies and children first." And broadcast mode tunes it up: "From the first row first, please. Those closest to the door. Let's go. Second row …"

George nods to the Hall father-and-son ushers at the back exits. Their emergency undertaking today is like a busy funeral in reverse, with people exiting in an organized scramble instead of entering quietly. The *Journal* will exclaim at the calm and order in exit. The reporter describes George as "the Captain of a sinking ship caring for all but himself."

"Those in need of assistance, hold your hands up."

Now help comes from the three parishioner doctors, one dentist, five teachers, six nurses, a few volunteer firefighters and a taxidermist. They are quick to track any hands in need in a spirit of general military cooperation.

"I'll take Dan. He's a patient of mine."

"Mrs. Richardson, give me your hand please. Yes, take your cane."

"Linda's having a bit of an anxiety issue. Let me sit with her for a minute."

The Pastor himself conducts those closest to the dusty entrance while directing others to the far southwest corner. The Christian Soldiers slide across the pews, then march out the side doors to the outside.

"Let's move across the pews. Those in front exit to the Sunday School."

Let it be noted that today will be the only time in the soon-to-be-titled

Rev. Dr. George Sewell's historical record at the Methodist Hall that George is not the first to gain the Hall exit.

More facts that are unproven and provide years of conjecture:

Witnesses that morning claim the Pastor's finger was pointed to the very direction of contact at the moment the lightning struck. All agree to the flash of light then the big-bang blast through the steeple. Some describe how the stained glass lit up like a sunrise. The audience glowed in a moment of glory while the windows shook.

Bammo. Lights out.

All reports describe an organized, almost military exit commanded by the new Methodist minister. There are as many different descriptions of the wording of the orders from the messenger as there are witnesses.

"Everyone exit by the parish office door … first those closest. Yes, ladies and gentlemen, start with the front row."

Many have the messenger calling out to his flock.

"Onward. Onward, Christian Citizens."

A few add the absurd detail that the Pastor sang "Onward Christian Soldiers." Facts go wandering across the street.

Bammo.

The self-righteous neighbours had an automatic response to the clap of thunder. In each church, first the service stopped, everyone turned to the outside wall facing the blast, and the men stood. Not a word, but a look back and forth: *That was real close. What did it hit?*

The Calvinists and Episcopalians vacated their pews to survey the disaster. They found their neighbour topless. No time to waste on sanctimony, hubris. The cross-street congregations ran towards the litter and smoke. The Christian Soldiers ran to help their too proud and puritanical Methodist neighbours.

Methodist humility learns a hard lesson when lightning strikes; the hard-gained steeple chase is lost. The blast blew the crown off but left the six-storey foundation.

The Presbyterians and Roman Catholics are left to argue which of their spires is most prominent. The Episcopalians rest their argument on their short Norman beauty; they remind all that it was the first built. *("And we have had clarions from our founding in 1853.")*

The Methodists step back from their disaster, look up, adjust the picture with a flat top and move forward.

The half-empty cavern was brought to full attention that day, filled with spirit from a true messenger of God. Hired on the spot, George has the auditorium packed within four Sundays. Full again and again for the next sixty-five years. Pastor George Sewell's reputation skyrockets.

(*The new minister is the real deal up on Church Street, no matter how sawed-off their highest steeple.*")

The Innkeeper will be there stage east, telling the wild tale to his Monday-morning coffee klatch. Son will listen from the café kitchen hall to the well-worn tale.

A parade in downtown St. Marys, circa 1890.
People are gathered in the street near the Grand Central Hotel.
The carriageway opening on the far left will become the barbershop.

CHAPTER 2

Catching a Lift

1913

"**L**ook at the size of that dust plume."

A welcome distraction from the backbreaking work scuffling hay. Scuffle, scuffle, then stoke it for drying. The Swiss father-and-son team love their outside work when the weather is fine, with perfect heat for a quick dry job. They feel good about their bountiful efforts in the field. The Methodist Pastor speaks in easy terms in support of initiative, hard work and their reward.

The dust trail rises at the edge of the confluence of St. Marys, moving east of the Thames on the north river road. This main artery snakes north, going by the name Centre Gravel well into the next century. Confusion for later generations who will know it as a winding but smooth stretch of pavement.

Roads that lead from St. Marys in 1913 start on an assortment of hard-pack and asphalt, soon turning to potholes and odd grades, all on gravel. A summer given is the dust shooting out behind your Town exit. Often no rain for two weeks.

Blanshard Township hugs the northern boundary of St. Marys, featuring the richest of land. The Swiss father and son are late immigrants forced to settle on leftover lands with a lot of roll. Tough to plough and seed, but good drainage and great views for these years of driving dangerous.

"He must be doing fifty," the son says. "Look how the cloud curls up behind him."

The gravel always kept it slow for horse travellers in the know. Somehow the switch to a motorized carriage cuts the blood flow to reasonable driving. These drivers have no idea. They might as well be riding a bull. The father states the known script:

"Watch when he hits the Otterburn Creek culvert."

The tiny bridge has big lips, gravel to cement then back to gravel. The first hit knocks the passengers forward while the driver grips for control as the car slides to the second lip. If he can straighten out before the second lip, all might be good for a landing and off on his way. The few smart automobile owners start slow on gravel and brake for the culvert. Father's known script continues (Son knows it well. He could watch this scene all day, especially if it means a break from the hot-handed work):

"See if he gets some air and keeps it under control."

The car does not slow down. *Whomp*, there's air. *Whomp*, it lands.

Move to the right, slide, then straight. Move again to the right, jerk left for the upcoming big *whomp* into air. The dust floats past. Father and son lose sight of the car. The culvert will direct the careless driver to a soft landing in the wet cow pasture stage left. And there the car sits, while the dust slides up the concession road past the field.

"Son, see the second plume coming from the north."

Both look to their right.

"Lucky break for us," Father continues. "We don't have to walk to the phone. The other driver will stop and get help from Town."

The second plume will stop, then continue on to the hard surfaces of St. Marys. Next on the script will be a bell from the fire station.

In front of his coffee klatch, the Innkeeper recognizes all bell tones. The short single ding repeated three times, he knows, is a call for auto-motive help. (Double ring means fire response, triple is a drowning.)

Help will be soon on its way from the downtown back-alley stable. Huff & Puff wait for their harness. Their ears perk up to the specific bell tone. Silly straw hats are permanent fixtures on the donkeys' heads. This is the turn-of-the-century towing service.

These are the days of driving dangerous.

For seven thousand years the horse dominates world history — through chariot, cavalry, or the burden of a pack load or a wagon — to expand trading horizons and political boundaries. Then in the late 1700s, the whistle of James Watt's first steam engine calls forth a new age. Tracks of the iron horse run parallel to the growth in travel, first between cities, then across countries and continents.

St. Marys is a bridge point to all directions — north and south on the Huron Road to Goderich, or east and west on the Talbot Tract passing to London. All this traffic funnels over the 1860s Victoria Bridge.

Local affluence has pocket purses full. During the 1870s, St. Marys ships more grain than all agricultural transfer points in Canada but the Lakehead and Toronto. Grain by train winds the Town up to busier times, necessitating new services including liveries, farriers, teamsters, blacksmiths, additional farmhands and accommodation.

Like mushrooms of hospitality, hotels sprout up across the municipality, some small, some large. The largest of all, the Grand Central Hotel, hosts eighteen rooms on its second and third floors. That modern marvel, indoor plumbing, is shared on each floor. The Innkeeper's family live in a three-bedroom apartment above the kitchen with another bathroom. The rental rooms, though small, have tall ceilings for no other reason than to accommodate the racks of stunning six-foot windows facing Main Street. Your best face forward. Below the eighteen rooms, the Grand Central offers, in addition to a small lobby and office, a large café beside a transfer alley from Main Street to the back.

Opinions are divided about whether the train complements or competes with coach travel, but in either case the Hotel offers convenience and access. A comfortable entrance fireplace greets guests. Horses, wagons and such are moved to a livery and paddock out back. Next to the small lobby and the Hotel's central staircase is the impressive bar with all the accoutrements and an entrance that flanks the double-sided fireplace. Opposite the bar fireplace, the wall is covered by a blinding assortment of mirrors, glass shelves and coloured seltzer bottles. The *Detroit News*, *London Free Press* and *Perth Daily Courier* fan across a low round table reinforced with three embroidered sofa-style chairs. Fresh news imported by train is dropped at key front doors in Town by Dobson Delivery. The solid brass, seventeen-foot boot rail, lit up with gas lights, reflects the storefront's upper leaded-glass windows. A special spot for coffee with newspaper contemplation in the AM or a refreshment in the PM.

Enlightened news is left for the reader, but the real news is served hot and oral in the café across the hall. Or it comes raw with local detail later, back in the bar.

Dobson Delivery, two blocks over, provides those horseless Citizens with a livery service. A generation earlier, the Dobson family branched out from farrier and blacksmith work and won the contract to service the public stagecoach crossroads at the confluence of the Thames Valley. Now Kipp has two coaches, green with gold letters, standing by for schedules at the Grand Trunk station at the Junction and two Canadian Pacific stations, one midtown and the other down on the Thames River off the downtown. The single Canadian National station (rebuilt in 1908 in salmon-coloured brick) is the largest, prettiest and most central for visitors and travellers. A little traveller foresight on the correct choice of station whether coming or going can save anywhere from four blocks up to twenty, given that the Junction station is on the edge of Town. The Canadian Pacific station will take you off in another direction on a slow shuffle to Buffalo, if that's the destination. Your next stop could be New York City, but it's much more likely to be Toronto. The Junction and CN train stations access the two mammoth viaducts that enable trains to pass over the river-and-creek confluence. The third line runs flat, west of the Grand River to Lake Erie from a bumper stop behind the Great Star Flour Mill. The downtown CP station, one block back along the Thames, is a wooden mirror of the brick CN beauty. All in all, trains arriving on regular schedules create more enterprise.

When the horseless carriage lifts its head late in the nineteenth century, travel becomes a basic privilege of an expanding middle class.

The wave of progress rises to a climax in Detroit. The largest industrial complex in the world is the dream-world factory built by Henry Ford at River Rouge, two hours from St. Marys. Uni-colour Model 'T' and 'A' cars, pumped out like sliced white bread for the masses, fill football-field-sized storage lots waiting for delivery. An affordable and available means of independent transportation expands the horizon of the individual far past the ability of any horse.

Henry feeds the imagination for travel by camping with his buddies Thomas Edison and George Westinghouse. Their photos with Model T conversions in the background appear in *National Geographic*. The direct-to-customer factory feeds the hungry imagination of wannabe adventurists.

Off in the big world, a myriad of horseless-carriage model choices spring from hundreds of former buggy and bicycle shops.

Kipp Dobson was born with wheels. A photograph in the Archives shows two sisters, an unhappy friend, and smiling Kipp on the Dobson side yard. His wooden wagon is centred on four hoop wheels. The red-painted frame has a highlight banner of loose red, white and brown crepe. Kipp remembers the colours waving against, one imagines, a background of clacks and creaks from the uneven sidewalk on the path to Queen Victoria's Jubilee celebration. (The Stonetown Museum has the red wagon and original coloured bunting. Great additions to their annual Queen Victoria Picnic.)

Kipp's early love affair advances with age alongside his family livery enterprise. His father built the original livery, which now occupies half of one central block. Paddock, stable, barn, repair, storage, loading and unloading, sales and offices — all multiply under the convenience of a central location. A warren of roofs covers the whole enterprise wall to wall.

Kipp is self-educated and well-researched on the subject of Detroit the city — first, by a comfortable stop in the old hotel lobby for the luxury and novelty of a daily newspaper. Every day fresh to Kipp's eyes, the *Detroit News* takes the young country man and his imagination to the city. Kipp gets wind of Henry Ford's production capability in the early 1900s.

Seems just a few years ago he was picking up his Detroit passage on a Grand Trunk train from the Junction station via Sarnia. Within a generation, he'll be driving his Ford two-door coupe with V-8 along Lake St. Clair on Highway 2.

The new age of transportation needs a fresh start. Kipp branches out for more space. He buys dedicated land across the street but over the bridge, land he's viewed from his father's old desk in his father's old second-floor corner office. In 1912, in his thirty-eighth year, Kipp Dobson acquires the first car dealership in Town, from Henry Ford himself.

A complete design contract is signed for a custom-built facility.

Heady stuff like this gets noticed in the small Town. Kipp is building a business that services only the automobile. Air and gas pump, parts room, hydraulic lift, grease pit, wash area, and even washrooms for customers and employees all add to the wonder of the new facility.

Dobson Motors' first order comes by train, direct from Henry himself.

Henry and his young son Edsel had discussed Kipp's first purchase, cajoling the Canadian dealer with options. "Well lad, what's it going to be?"

"Well Mr. Ford, it's going to be black." Kipp got a laugh with his response; all Fords are black back in 1912. "My first vehicle will be a stake truck."

A series of letters from both Edsel and Henry at the Archives include this contract with personal notes scribbled back and forth on both sides:

Thank you Mr. Ford and Edsel,
           — Kipp.

Best of luck Kipp. Let me know how it works for your new Ford Store,
           — Henry Ford.

The first auto-merchandising tool in Town is more than a toy. The red truck (yes, Kipp had it painted) is a purpose-built, mechanized show wagon out of Kipp's own childhood memories. The *Dobson* and *Motors* are black with gold shadowing, embracing the dark blue and bright white Ford logo. Gold stencilling brackets the wood bars on the flatbed. The dressed 'T' runs as a real eye-catcher to the entire rural male population of all ages over a ten-mile radius and beyond. *("Gotta get me one of those Fords.")*

The wall space in his father's old office displayed dozens of business photographs from the Dobson family record. Kipp's new office includes his most prized wall-of-fame photograph, taken at a Detroit reception with Edsel and Henry Ford. (Kipp will later remember a very odd Mexican couple in attendance. It doesn't occur to him at the time to get a photo of Diego Rivera and Freda Kahlo.)

                                               LORNE EEDY

It's class all the way for the self-generating pioneer merchant. Kipp orders the iconic corporate-issued blue-and-white enamelled Ford logo for out front. He ups the image with the additional wrap of forged iron in three-foot letters that spell out *Dobson Motors*. The sign for the times arrives in parts by train at the Junction station, picked up by Dobson Motors' very own Model T stake truck.

The red bow border of newfangled red neon comes all the way from Winnipeg.

Before the sign goes up, or is even unloaded, Kipp has already taken advance orders with advance payments. There's not one truck in the first bunch of twelve black-enamelled coupes and sedans. The dealership gets a grip on local needs, though, converting some of the original coupes to small stake trucks. Sedans will become the preferred choice of the well-off. Farmers will show up in town in new Model T stakes.

The first twelve customer contract orders belong to a grey-haired gang of gentlemen that includes all five of the Town's doctors, one dentist, one pharmacist, two ministers, one bank manager, and Jack Rogers Sr., the richest Citizen in Town. But, last but not least, it's the Innkeeper from the Grand Central Hotel who will make the most use of the T. Collectively they are a perfect storm of unqualified motorcar drivers trained only in the art of carriage navigation. It's a vortex in the cortex when horse sense sends twentieth-century machines herky-jerky down potholed paths. With new infrastructure in paved highways the province races to keep up, but not as quickly as Henry pumps out cars. Soon Saturday or Sunday drives might take a family on a big adventure to Grand Bend on Lake Huron, a grand total of sixty kilometres.

Most of the first twelve keep their machines in repurposed barns. Now they own garage queens, impossible to drive on snowy winter roads, during muddy falls and springs, or on most rainy days. On open-season days, the dust kicks up a storm on a trip to the lake or London, necessitating hats, cloaks, goggles and scarves. Automobile drivers dressed as aliens explore a big new land. They back up their expenditure with "the adventure of it" justified all the way to their Molson Bank account down on the corner of Queen and Edney.

"Half my patients live in the country," the doctor tells himself. "What's to happen if there is an emergency birth? Think about the time lost hitching those horses against the safety of mother and child. Many families do not have automobiles, but they do have a phone."

Rev. Sewell counts enough country noggins to clarify his self-anointed need:

"Half my parishioners live in the country. What's to happen if there is a spiritual need, or a crisis? Do I expect the family to show up on my doorstep? No, I can sit up and make the move to the family in need, indeed."

The bank manager does a similar count with his rural account holders who have the use of two sub-branches. The bank manager can't make it to half his customers. You can hear the mental gears shift as he heads out on the gravel roads:

"Our branches in Kirkton and Lucan can now be easily staffed from St. Marys. I need to visit each village once a week to fulfill my responsibility for complete reconciliation at all times."

Most supplies for the pharmacist come from the city by train. He makes a long reach for a gravel drive to the city:

"I can cut the turnaround time by half with an automobile. This gives me better and quicker access to London."

The Innkeeper knows that more than half his customers need a transfer:

"Patrons can be picked up at the station in style by automobile. We can make an immediate response. One call will take care of it all."

The doctor has the final prognosis on timing and the end of horses:

"Even if the family does not have a phone, they can fetch me. Maybe my patient will be worse off if moved! I can drive straight there with the family member, get a heads-up on the problem."

Pharmacist, bank manager and richest man all agree:

"We need better and quicker access to the city. They should pave the road."

Driving anywhere proves a hazardous pastime. There's a briar patch of ruts, potholes and mud anywhere off Main Street. Main crosses James, John, Thomas, Peter, Mary, Anne and Emily, Church and Water Streets. In turn a series of narrow gravel lanes fan out from these minor streets in spokes. For Town folks, the home course jockeys around loose strays and wild-animal road kill.

For the last fifty years the open road has featured roadhouses, a total of eight thirsty stops between Town and London. These recharge spots dry up, left in the dust of road traffic that can go the distance with increased radius of travel. Three of those casualties change over to domestic use, three go derelict, and the other becomes a gas station general store. The one pony still in the game, in the village of Birr, gains life through a bit of village support, a Supertest gas pump, and a general store that picks up a busy highway convenience trade. Highway travellers love the pumpkin wagon, sweet corn, bushel baskets of apples and firewood bundles, season dependent.

Even in what will soon seem like roadworthy conditions, the automobile strains the bounds of seasonal dependability. The damn contraptions will not start in cold or wet conditions without help. Kipp's passenger-transfer livery business has never been busier. Kipp's corner office, in the midst of downtown action, offers more than a good view. If his radio is off, the bells can still be heard from the fire hall one block over.

Today, the bell tower's final *dong* echoes down the stone-walled alley that borders the rear end of the Dobson complex, to the large stone stable hidden between the fire hall and the expanded livery. Still active, the stables struggle on as survivors during the years of driving dangerous. The greatest four-legged team in Town & Country history are stand-up witnesses against the winds of change. At the bell, the team is out of the block and jingling up the back alley. Kipp smiles to the sound of a jack-ass rescue, a dilemma familiar to pioneer Citizen automobile drivers.

Kipp knows that weather conditions dictate the script directed by the over-confident reformed buggy drivers. Snow, fog, ice or a flat tire put the driver on trial. Today, in the dog days of summer, it's dust.

A research report in the Archives compares the profiles of the first automobile owners and their original horseless rides. The paper shows a near-universal occurrence of accidents, from multiple close rubs, bumps and fender-benders to full-on crashes. The most astounding fact is that the records show no fatalities, unless you count road kill. The *Journal* reports a Noah's Ark of animal fatalities, from goats, cows, skunks and raccoons to one pet snake and two pet rabbits.

In 1913, the ride is prehistoric. There are no windshield wipers. The distractions start with the driving apparel of goggles, scarves, trench coat, gloves and tight floppy hat with tie-down. The car churns on slippery gravel, on four skinny rubbers, not to forget open distractions, a long list. Cattle, gnarly dogs, a spooked horse pulling a buggy, Grandma and Grandpa gingerly out for a walk, kid on a bicycle, and vermin of all kinds, including deer in unlimited numbers, offer a helter-skelter of obstacles. A target game for years of driving dangerous. Hill and dale to London adds on the complication of train tracks that cross your route up to five times. Tracks laid pre-Confederation do not include crossing gates or flashing lights. For the first ninety years, you have the responsibility to stop, look and listen.

But not one danger on this long list matches the scary white-haired man who sits behind the wheel. He demonstrates a most singular and ultimately dangerous mindset: a breed of confidence that has ridden the pale horse of a passing century, now commanding a modern-day machine. The right foot double-clutches, the right hand pushes the knob forward to third gear, a modest reach for a little giddy-up. The right mind thinks: *Do NOT stall the mechanical beast through lack of gas.* The left foot pushes down on the pedal. The final gasp on the closing choke gives one last cough off into the outdoor adventure.

The deaf and determined driver, now in third gear, needs to wipe those goggles. Two gloved hands on the wheel. Sorry — one hand on the wheel, the other adjusts the choke. Quit riding the clutch. There's Fred Loft out for a walk. Quit waving at people. Two hands on the wheel. Head straight ahead.

One of the first twelve purchasers of an automobile is Doctor James Lane. He is mentioned in the diaries of both the Rev. Dr. Sewell and The Barber. The microfiches from the *St. Marys Journal* show a litany of appreciation letters. The writers describe a doctor who covers the needs of his patients rain, sleet or shine.

The good doctor never takes a back seat to any Citizen of St. Marys and surrounding countryside. Nor does he look in his rearview when driving into the wide open. Kipp is often surprised at the weather conditions the doctor moves through. A question in passing from a recent Café encounter:

"Jimmy, how did you ever get out of town on Sunday? That was a snow bowl."

"Kipp, I recommend the proper attire."

Kipp pauses to think about dress.

"Chains," Lane says. "I have chains. Back wheels only, too. Do not want to plough with the chains. Back chains give me all the traction I need."

Kipp Dobson will die behind the wheel of a Ford from a heart attack in 1934, a Ford man to the very end; even he thinks to himself that in such a blizzard he would be happier at home with a warm fire.

On a summer Saturday morning in 1913, Doctor is in the house. The Lane kids are waiting for a justified mini-adventure. No emergency phone call last night or so far this morning (the phone rings both in the hallway of their grand home and in the side office with separate doorway). The children are a chorus of Muses to the open roads. The eldest, Jamie, will write a bestseller on a small-town doctor's practice. In the late 1950s, the popular book becomes one of the first television series produced in Toronto with outside sets, all shot in Kleinburg. Mother makes a full breakfast that includes homemade maple sausage and buttermilk pancakes. Time to enjoy and anticipate a glorious day off. Where off to? The sedan is in the driveway, pointed to the street. The first convertible seen in Town. Father Doctor makes his prognosis a sunny question.

"Top up? Or top down?"

The kids squeal out their answer. *"Dow-w-w-w-n-n-n!"*

Then the tempo changes.

"Father, can we drive in the country?"

Sweet music for a father comfortable in his years of driving dangerous. Father may be looking forward to a drive even more than his small passengers. And no worries about the dirt: the good doctor gets Jackie Kooren, the teenager two doors over, to wash his car.

"It's Centre Gravel for the Lanes," he says.

"Father, can we go fast?"

Mother always stays at home, but "fast" catches her attention. Mother stares at the Doctor, who steps up.

"Fast?" he says. "See how fast you children can get dressed."

The three Lanes rev their car engines, spinning off from the kitchen table.

"Goggles too," Father says. "Remember your goggles."

Jamie stops and turns. "Father, the sky is blue."

"The dust, Jamie. Through and through."

The doctor shouts over his son to the girls who are streaking past. "Goggles! Goggles on, everyone."

The doctor concentrates on getting himself dressed, only to turn and find three sets of goggled eyes looking up at him.

As Mother sweeps them out the back door, her dark eyes keep to her husband. "Have a nice, slow drive everyone."

The goggled eyes push and shove to reserve their spot. Sisters align to double up on the older brother, who's trying to gain the front passenger seat by entering on the driver's side. Jamie's sisters block him. "We get the front seat."

There's room enough for two girls, but it's inconvenient for gear-grinding.

"Our turn," they continue. "You always get the front seat."

The results are always the same, because they make sense. Father returns from the back of the car, having tied down the roof. He points at Jamie. "You move over." The sisters are next. "You two. In the back."

Jamie opens and closes the back door for his sisters. He moves past the wheel to his co-pilot position. Being an older sibling has its advantages. One is the front seat's unblocked view.

All the children see, feel and remember horse-drawn transportation. A car drive in 1913 is better than an exotic palm-tree-lined vacation in the modern age. The excitement in the moment distracts them from the number one issue: the white-haired driver.

These are the years of dangerous driving.

Doctor Lane drives down Queen Street, adjusting the cough on the choke. Then he turns north on Water Street, over the innovative 1908 steel-link bridge, referred to simply as the Green Bridge. With an innovative design based on the Eiffel Tower, it narrows to a single lane over the Creek.

Jamie will be a great driver in his time. "Father."

"Huh?"

"Father. Push the choke in."

"Ohhh-kay."

Doctor Lane grinds down to second gear, putting his foot on the accelerator. The single lane is open for a quick crossing. The children hold on for the bounce as the bridge drops them back on Water Street North, which turns into River Road East, although it goes north.

"Thank God the River Road starts on asphalt," he says. "This hill would be a grind."

Jamie and the girls grit their teeth for the sloppy shifts. They can't hear a thing in all the chugging as their heads bob back and forth.

The girls' hats flop and wave through a stubby tunnel under the Sarnia train viaduct. All hands hold on as they breeze by Hillcrest Farms. The Holsteins do not lift their heads. Doctor Lane concentrates on the gears, the grade and not stalling. Asphalt changes to gravel. The Ford ploughs ahead in second gear, sticking to worn tracks.

The adventurers float downhill to a second flat stretch that ends in a hairpin turn from the edge of civilization onto Centre Gravel. Dr. Lane respects the give-and-take that this turn takes. The girls slide to the left with their nails anchored into the flock-carpeted seats. No matter how many times he's been through this bend before, Jamie's head still bounces off his father's shoulder. Father smiles, and Jamie frowns and rubs the side of his head.

Distracted Father keeps a scorecard, as if he might have preferred a career as a veterinarian. "Jamie, is that the Hereford bull?"

Jamie freezes in terror as his father points the 1912 Ford Model T convertible in the direction of the bull. Jamie knows from experience that when Father makes a point, the convertible is first to follow his direction. Years later, the popular author will paint the scene in slow motion.

Father points.

And there points the car.

Jamie sits up even taller as Doctor Lane twists again to take in the open-topped scenery. Easy does it, all's well — until Father turns to the back seat. Jamie follows the good doctor's field of vision back to his sisters while the car sails off to the right. Jamie's head is in a constant wig-wag of anticipation.

There is a lucky warning shot. The front left wheel hits a rock, which pushes the car back across the field to home gravel. Jamie hopes for the best, grips the leather seats in the worst way. His father lifts his left hand off the wheel and points into the distance with his index finger. Jamie ignores the point, focusing in despair on the one hand still on the wheel. The open car grunts and groans over the cut wheat.

Warning Jamie Lane, Danger.

With another bump, Jamie's head jerks in the direction of Father's gaze. Directly ahead in the sea of grain is a big bull. One humungous Hereford, a vast stud known affectionately by all as Johnny Come-Lately. The target has an indifferent eye to the ensuing drama. Jamie screams from his core. *"Da-a-a-a-ad!"*

Older and younger sister join the chorus. *"Da-a-a-a-ad!"*

In the chaos Doctor Lane turns to Jamie in the front, then to the horrified sisters in the back seat. One hand holds the wheel which rocks left, then right to the rhythm of the wheat. Jamie can see his father's eyes roam far off their tracks and back to the road; there is hope. There's even more hope when Father grabs the wheel with both hands.

No one has a chance to worry about their roughed-up butts. Off they all go on a no-bull tour towards the grassy concession ditch. A tailing of shrieks follows over the dirt waves of the field. *"Da-a-a-a-ad!"*

Leaving her two siblings to a duet, the younger sister cries out in a conclusive refrain. *"I wa-a-ant to go ho-o-ome no-o-owwww."*

A miracle occurs. The front wheel hits another rock, redirecting the off-road adventure closer to the ditch that makes a moat line along Centre Gravel.

An unfamiliar amusement ride ensues as they climb back up the bank to the road. The kids bump back and forth in the back seats with frothy stomachs. The doctor's heavy black bag bounces between the girls. Jamie vise-grips his seat with both hands, eyes ahead. The ditch becomes an adventure start-up with a sideways slip here and a slide there. Father grinds into first gear, pushing on the gas and letting 'er go. Bump, then another bump, as the good doctor strains to pull the rudder right, right over the shoulder. The front tires crawl, gaining grip on the road with a sigh of relief from back to front. The Doctor-Captain overcomes the worst of the ditch to re-establish control of his road boat. A little luck, with two hands on the wheel and eyes front.

But.

Father does not know best.

He turns. The man turns to his young daughters. Their eyes look back at him, as wide open as their mouths.

"We want to go home no-o-o-ow."

As he starts to speak, to reassure, his right hand leaves the wheel and bad luck intervenes. The front right tire, suffering from that direct rock hit, peels off the rim. The girls see the black rubber flap by. *"Da-a-a-a-ad!"*

For the first time in his life Doctor Lane is speechless, holding on by his fingernails. The car sags left and grabs for safe harbour, an outward edge of the rural road. Doctor Lane's hubris can't outlast his dwindling luck.

Planted in the shorn grain field, his roaming car is converted into a mechanical monument to years of dangerous driving. Johnny Come-Lately stands nearby, head down on a sweet spot of wheat stubble. The family group is jostled but silent. The doctor is steamed that the flat tire has prevented another return up onto the road. His son leans over to see that the skinny lower rim is invisible in mud. The children stand for a moment then exit the car, jumping off from the sideboards to dry grass. A message from big brother.

"There's cow pies *every*where."

The three stare from safe ground at the sunken rim of their world. A rare occasion for Doctor Lane, who needs to call on a very peculiar tow service. Before long, a second plume of dust approaches from the north. The traveller stops to call out.

"Doctor Lane!"

Citizens often recognize the driving doctor out and about. The good doctor waves. The children stand in the field, staring at Johnny, who ignores all as he munches on his wheat. The Citizen calls out, "Heading to Town. Huff & Puff?" with one thumb up.

The good doctor gives two thumbs up in reply.

The car starts off on the gravel, then disappears in front of its dust plume.

The call is making its slow way back to Town. Wait and the bell will toll, a single ring that will soon be answered by (say it as if it's one word) Huff-&-Puff. First, our thumbs-up Samaritan needs to cross the Green Bridge to get to the St. Marys Fire Hall #1.

Downtown, back off that stone-walled alley, ass heads rise up in the air with eyes a-twinkling. Kenny the teamster swears his donkey team can sense when they're needed. A regular in the Methodist adult choir, he sings his tune in anticipation of their need to help, followed by a bell ringer. It's a ditty sung to a popular tune from a Gilbert and Sullivan operetta, "The Pirates of Penzance." For the record, a few non-Methodists refer to this as Hillbilly Poetry:

> *Ding ding dong,*
> *This is the donkey song.*
> *Ding ding dong,*
> *Sing the donkey song.*
>
> *Not your regular ass,*
> *A tow job of class —*
> *With a 24-hour ask.*
> *Two asses up to snuff,*
> *Our names are Huff & Puff.*
>
> *Ding ding dong.*
> *Sing the donkey song.*
> *We have the stuff —*
> *No matter the task —*
> *Our names are Huff & Puff.*

Enough choral fluff for the asses. In anticipation of the call, Kenny hooks up harness and tackle to a unique cart with a long wooden box on the single axle. A bare hard plank of maple acts as a bench seat for the short ride. The thumbs-up Samaritan has just dropped off the request for help to Jimmy the stable mucker who relays the directions to Kenny in the back fire hall stable.

In minutes, the proud pair with silly straw hats prance out of the double stable doors, right down the narrow alley. Out on Water Street right past the shiny reverse-parked Reo fire engine. *Jingle, jingle.* Fire Chief Phil gives them a lift off with his fire call whistle. Opposite side of the block, Kipp in his upper-floor office can decipher the direction by the sound alone. The bells head west, away. As the whistle pitch from the Chief rings out, the *jingle, jingle* speeds up for a moment then slows in tempo. Kenny must be approaching the Green Bridge.

The ears of St. Marys wait for the cast-call that's familiar to all.

"Huff. Puff." His alto-mezzo voice skips up the Creek, and back down the Thames. "Huff & Puff. Up boys, up."

Even with blinders the donkey pair never relax on the metal link bridge with the no-grip wood slab floor. Neither Huff nor Puff is big on the colour green unless the item in question is edible. Kenny takes the harness leads and talks them across. With a few soft huffs and equally as many gentle puffs, the team is back on the pavement of Water Street, where Kenny hops on the hard-ass but convenient box bench.

The donkeys know the drill. Kenny cracks a long twig with a knotted rope tag for motivation for all their asses to get on up the hill past Hillcrest Farms. No swimming in gravel, no swerving on the hairpin turn; no problems with bumps or the big hump over the Otterburn Creek culvert — nothing limits the pair. Kenny sets the pace with a knotty stroke. All three are on the same steady path, a path slow enough that no dust plume is in pursuit but still fast enough to save the day.

Jamie and his sisters have finally broken away from Johnny on his spot to pick black-eyed Susans. The bull never lifts his head from the grain chaff. The entire field can hear a jingle on its way. The children play along in fun. Who can see the straw hats first? Who is Huff and which one is Puff? Today is an introduction that will continue with apples and carrots for years to come down a back alley in the downtown.

Kenny hops off before the donkeys cross the ditch. He directs them past the front of the automobile for the hookup. Kenny is not under Doctor's orders. "Jamie lad, do you want to steer?"

Jamie's out of the muck with full concentration on getting the grip of both hands behind the wheel. Kenny turns from the beaming driver to his client. "Doctor Lane. Pulling should work. If we can't change the tire, I'll tow you all into Town."

Father is about to override the tow-and-go prescription to his son behind the wheel, but Kenny interrupts the thought.

"Let the lad have his moment. No harm. You'll be behind the wheel before you know it, Doctor Lane. Let's get this harness buckled onto the axle."

Kenny wastes little time. "Now Huff, now Puff. *Huff.* Puff. *Huff.* Puff." And here's Johnny — even the bull can't resist lifting his head for the tow show. Huff & Puff torque down on the stubby pasture. The convertible twists and slides up to the hard-pack road. Kenny calls it. "Huff, now *Puff. Huff* now Puff. *Huff. Puff.*"

Heads up for another incoming puff: a puff of dust, floating towards them from the north. The plume continues on to Town, while a second black (of course) Model T sedan pulls to a stop. Out pops the Pastor with his Brownie camera in one hand. His pug Sambo, the little black pant ripper, waits behind the slobber stains on the rear passenger window. With Christian soldier motions, George parts the sea of gravel, marching over to the group beyond the raggedy green edge. God's broadcast messenger stops and stands with one hand waving and the other held high making snappy attention with the brown leather-covered box. "Good people. A photograph, please."

Kenny and Doctor Lane escape from the invitation for the photo record. The teamster settles his pair, remaining back in a shadow for the Kodak Brownie. The kids, though, line up for their revered minister, the man up front each week who points to their Sunday School relief out back.

FLASH.

Three smiling Lane siblings sitting atop the back seat can be seen above the straw-hatted heads of two toothy donkeys in the lead. A classic time capsule held in a cardboard box at the Archives. All the details fit to print in the *St. Marys Journal* in 1913 can be found on microfiche. More can be mined from both The Barber's and the Pastor's diaries.

The photograph will attain worldwide fame on the cover of Jamie Lane's first book, *Country Doctor: The Years of Driving Dangerous.* An English-language bestseller, winner of a Leacock Award — and

the fans! Fans flock to town in their imported cars and smoky SUVs
to grab their colour-photocopied map of "The LANE Path" before
zooming off behind a dust plume of their own. The donkey image gets
a first makeover in colour for an appearance in the credits of the early
CBC television series, and then a second when digitized for the Netflix
remake. Citizens can't contain the overflow discussions comparing
Kleinburg and St. Marys. All this success comes from a simple candid
camera shot, a Kodak Brownie pop-up flash on a rural gravel road.

(The self-gilding and guile by George that day in 1913 continued on
straight to the newspaper offices, where the Rev. Dr. insisted in a direct
commandment handed to Stew the Editor: "Take what the *Journal*
needs. In turn, I'll take a proof sheet and two sets of prints. I will pick
them up after Wednesday's paper." No thank-you from the man before
the door slam.)

That tiny bumblebee-coloured film roll develops into a black-and-
white winner. Stew sees *Journal* sales spike from the great front page
photo, their bathroom darkroom producing scads of matted beauties
that will become super collectibles. A crop of samples, poor exposures
and second choices, and the negatives, end up in another kraft Archives
box marked *DONKEY STUFF* ... stuck on the same shelf with two silly
straw hats.

CHAPTER 3

This Side of Seventeen

1920

During a slow news week the *St. Marys Journal* digs up some banked filler from the "Years Ago …" files. The reprint of recent history causes derision around the Innkeeper's morning coffee klatch. An irregular starts it up this morning. He holds court waving the folded copy in the air. "Who's the jackass in that picture?"

Everyone knows the photo without having to look at it. Doctor Lane's two young daughters captivate the camera with generous smiles. The girls sit up on the upper back of the padded Ford flock-seats with Jamie tipped forward on the edge. The presence of the great gusto Pastor, George Sewell, who took this photograph, can be felt in the upright posture of the subjects: *"Sit up, little Christian Citizens."*

(In years to come the Charles Wolfe Cruise Archives will care for a raft of donkey clippings and photographs from the cement plant, the lime kiln, the block quarry. Long before Town life progresses to the point of leashes and licences for cats — before those unsettling letters in the *Journal* on the loosing or leashing of animal nature — the Town is a familiar site for roaming donkeys. These misused refugees to a new mechanical age are left to free-range on boulevards and in flatlands, parks and the large, open municipal cemetery. Four-legged lawn-mowers that also fertilize.)

Today a regular comes out cautious. "Careful, it's the kids and Kenny. You mean who's the jackass who took the picture?"

That stops the irregular point. Another regular makes it clear. "The jackass did shoot a great photograph."

The group does not suffer the fool but likes to fool around with the subject. Names of artists suffer a round of the crescent-shaped counter.

"Picasso is an ass."

"Van Gogh was crazy."

"That Dali artist is a fool."

And three at the end of the counter state in chorus: "And the Pastor is a jackass."

The Innkeeper steps in. "Top-up, gentlemen? Top-up?" He motions with his head to the back. "Son, get the second carafe."

This week's newspaper passes through the gathering with assorted interest and sordid comments.

"I'll bet you Doctor Lane spits up his coffee when he sees this."

"He's got a closet full of white high-collar shirts."

"The doctor will want to shove that camera up the jackass's fat butt."

"No one ever tells how that convertible landed there. Why did they need the Huff-&-Puff job?"

"Now Huff. Now Pu-u-u-u-uffff …"

Another blows the word out his nose, muffling his voice with a napkin to a cough. "*Ph-ph-ph-u-u-f-f-f* me."

A big laugh all round for the comic. Just to be a smart-ass, he adds on, "Maybe he doesn't get any at home."

The Innkeeper holds the broadsheet page up. "Look at Kenny. You can almost hear him."

The redirection cues up a chorus of fun.

"Ding. Ding. Dong."

"Now Huff. Now Puff."

"Huff. Puff. Huff. Puff."

More laughs make a happy chatty coffee morning.

After dragging out the dishes, then getting them cleaned and stacked, the son takes the garbage out for his mother with the donkey song stuck in his ear. (In his diary that night, he will leave out the teenage kitchen detail but record Kenny's ditty word for pencilled word.) He marvels that the guy dressed in the angel robe singing in the Methodist Senior Choir on Sundays is by day the ding-dong donkey songster.

The lad packs up the garbage back in the barn. As he works he imagines his hands on the dark maple wheel of his father's new Ford V-8. He worships its twentieth-century technology with the electric wipers, fan, adjustable seats, roll-up windows, even synchromesh for second and third. The other side of seventeen is dazzled by the seventy-mile-per-hour top speed. The Deluxe 1920 Sedan reigns as the very first mass-produced flat-head V-8, a first-class replacement after the Model T held on through the war years. The Innkeeper's 'T' had become more of a donkey, running its course for Hotel customers and a budding driver. The V-8 is personal, a wheel choice for a car man.

The Stonetown Cemetery holds plenty of danger for the learning driver, with dirt cover on hairpin corners, moments of gravel, surprising potholes and the occasional free-range donkey. To top it off for the beginner behind the wheel, the single-lane graveyard paths mix and mash right-of-way options for opposing traffic.

(The latter happened a dozen times while his father was giving him lessons in the graveyard last year — whoops, incoming obstacle ahead as another car navigates the turn: "Father, do I stay to the right? Or to his left?" "Just stop the car, son. On the left. Clutch down, brakes nice and easy. We'll let them go by. Smile and wave.")

The cemetery holds other kinds of danger as well, adult-restricted. When Ralphie Nixon and his father were out practising, Ralphie swerved from a donkey on the path — only to catch a man and woman compromised behind a stand of junipers. His father pointed in horror. At first Ralphie and his father thought it was an angel statue praying to God. The wings of the angel, though, were a man's open overcoat. A lewd and nervous moment for the father, with a son not mature enough to put the gas on a detour past. Mr. Nixon whispered his blow-by-blow viewpoint to the coffee group. Ralphie told all his friends in slo-mo playback, including the future Barber.

After graduation from the cemetery, the Innkeeper moved his son onto the open roads. The V-8 ate up the miles outside Town for gravel experience, all practice paths leading to the pasty face and wire-rimmed eyes of licence examiner Andrew (Dewy) South.

All his friends including Ralphie detailed the test drive on Centre Gravel over and over: "Dewy took me north out Water Street over the single-lane Green Bridge."

Forewarned, the Innkeeper drove the lessons home with his son. "He wants to test you on the bridge's right of way. Then he wants to see you shift up the hill passing the pavement onto gravel. Slow down for the change. Somewhere he'll ask you to turn around, backing out of a laneway. After the hairpin turn."

They practised the route a dozen times.

"He wants to see you shift through the turn," Father said. "Keep it in second going in. Downshift, double clutch to first. Do not stall or he will flunk you."

The gears cried out in a heavy metal pitch for relief.

"Son. Clutch full down. Then shift."

Father's right hand traced the shift. His left hand grabbed an invisible wheel. Eyes forward. The learner leaned his right eye off the road to watch Father in motion. "Clutch out, with a touch on the gas."

Both heads went backwards.

"Whoa! A *touch*. A touch of gas, son."

Father took his hands off the imaginary shift and wheel to look at the driver. "We're on gravel. Whoa, 'til we get to Highway 7." He gave the boy a big smile. "Son, if you don't get these turns under control, it's back to the graveyard shift, eh?"

Dangerous times for the young apprentice as tires swam, slipped and slid along the loose gravel road, but life could not have been better. Gravel run, gravel fun.

He finally got his licence last month, but he would never drive their Ford V-8 off the property laneway and parking area without Father's permission. Now, in his work imagination, he's speeding along and he's not alone: his girl Wendy Moore slides under his right arm, while his left stays on the wheel. Later he will be her chauffeur for a slow ride through the cemetery. Chauffeur, that's French for personal driver. Wendy likes French class. Whoopsie, foot on the brakes. "Whoa. What's that?"

In his daydream a grey pony-sized animal steps in front of the young couple in a search of greener pastures. Any blast on the horn draws neighbourhood curtains but no attention from the four-legged jaywalker. "Damn donkeys never move off the road."

He ignores Wendy for a moment with both hands on the wheel for a sweeping swerve around the obstacle and on through the cemetery with a touch of gas.

The Pleasant Hour Theatre would be a treat with her soft upper arm up against his. Two tickets, two popcorns and two pops while all his buddies snicker three rows behind. He squeezes his imagination with both hands outstretched on the wheel of the V-8 sedan.

Long before any thoughts of barber school, the lad spent every Saturday at the Pleasant Hour Theatre. Long before scissors, he earned the twenty-five-cent admission as a dish pig in the café on weekends and days off school.

After school, the son has taken advantage of a café lifestyle throughout his teen years. With advance permission he invites a friend for the most excellent French fries and delicious thirst-quenching cherry Coke served with a smile from either Mom or Father. A solid friendship tactic alongside his solid defence for the Midget hockey travelling team.

Hockey takes the team down new pavement to exotic locations like Lucan, Embro and Thorndale. All are weather-dependent, not just because of roads, but because their ice surfaces are open to the elements. St. Marys has a covered horse barn with an ice floor. Outlying kids think they're playing in Maple Leaf Gardens:

"It's a horse barn. You can still smell the shit."

"The only shit is our team's play."

"No shovelling snow, and saved from the rain. Wow."

The Innkeeper's son has the size and reach to fight, but instead he hones his ice craft with jest and a touch of mimicry.

When he gets that look back of anger after a hard knock into the boards, he has a battery of responses: "Knock knock who's there?" "Nice knockers, buddy." "Did you wear aftershave just for me?"

If the opponent drops his gloves, the lad points behind his back. "It's your mother! She's watching you."

Other hits raise a sharper edge: "You skate like your ugly sister." "Your grandmother shoots harder."

Wendy never comes to the games. She doesn't like hockey. Wendy likes more class — especially French class.

High school comes easy enough for the lad, though no university is rising on his horizon. Higher education costs muffle a lack of strong interest. Fifty years later universities would probably feast on hockey talent like his.

Besides work at the café there's hockey practice, Boy Scouts and, until graduation a few weeks ago, homework before and after school. Sometime before Saturday date night he fits in a bath and a shave.

The rattle of a hoop score from a soup tin into the garbage can takes him out of the front seat, back to the weekend morning shift. He can hear the hubbub of coffee contemplation in the café as today's theme continues.

"Huff & Puff would be a great team for Kipp's livery," someone calls out.

All heads around the crescent-shaped counter swivel to catch a reaction from the Livery's owner. The Ford dealer is tight in his corner without a twitch or a nod — the game is on for the group.

"They're better looking than Kipp's drivers, too," someone else says.

Kipp looks over his folded broadsheet. He sips his coffee, covering a smile.

"Maybe the boss should buy some straw hats for the drivers."

"Ask the asses. They're experts on straw."

When the morning breakfast rush is over, the young dish pig hangs up his apron and takes a walk. Like mowing the lawn, fetching mail is a welcome step out from the routine life of the café kitchen.

He detours back to Jones Street then around the corner two blocks over to get the mail. The post office is a marvel of nineteenth-century Romanesque architecture that looks more like a jail. Deep indigo mortar holds stone blocks, cement cornices and brackets, and urns with a gaudy finish. The eight-foot opaque windows with matching indigo steel bars accentuate the jail aspect.

He sorts the six envelopes as he descends the wide granite steps. He needs only to see the breasts, one button undone on the sapphire Kitten sweater, to know their owner. Watching his step as he descends — what an excuse to cop a look. Wendy watches him step down. He forces his eyes to her smile. "Hey Wendy, on the mail route?"

Her eyes flash at the question as she looks at his grip on the enve-lopes. "You've got a catch there."

Wendy looks down as she comes up a step closer. Her chest pops up and out a bit. That second button is about to burst. All this commotion noted by fresh teenage eyes in seconds. The lad is wordless with a goofy smile. Wendy tilts her head with a bob forward of red hair. "Remember, dance Friday night," she says.

She didn't even phrase it as a question. She's ready for the next step.

"Can I pick you up in the Deluxe?"

Wendy settles both feet on the granite-slab step. "Daddy's letting my baby have the car?"

The wordless goof wakes up. "Well, I *am* on the other side of seventeen."

"*C'est très bon, mon chauffeur.*" Robin-smart kitten does another bob with a nod; those eyes flash. "This side of 8:30 then."

She skips up to the doors, and he stumbles onto the sidewalk, back to the Hotel in a quiet walk of contemplation over his solid pickup commitment. Worst case would be Father insisting on a chauffeur with a chaperone. That's not happening — not with Wendy Moore in the front seat.

When he gets back to the café, Father is holy rolling. "And those temperance ladies." Ten o'clock coffee has full attendance.

"No one wants to be seen drinking at the bar, let alone slip back home with liquor on their breath. Those women pop out of the cracks in the pavement if booze raises its head. A good Citizen cannot have an honest refreshment."

The Innkeeper holds his audience's attention, ready for some naming of names.

"If the God-messenger windbag wasn't empowering those people." The Innkeeper leaves little to the imagination as to who. Not this morning; he's on the edge. "If that holy spirit windbag hasn't cursed us enough, then it's that Mrs. Snoddie."

This named-name teaches English to the upper grades at St. Marys High School. The son looks up from his dish towel; that's another class he shares with Wendy. His teacher is now off the breakfast menu blackboard and onto the hot skillet.

"That Mrs. Snoddie," the Innkeeper says. "That woman grabs the mickey right out of Richie Rosen's hand. Right there on the street. *Bang.* She smashes it on the curb." The Innkeeper's right hand chops an invisible bottle on the counter's edge. "She's another sanctimonious disciple of George."

The naming continues unabated, to the satisfaction of the thirsty counter group. "Broken spirits on the sidewalk. And that woman can't stop. She has to lecture little Richie on the evils of liquor." Standing at the kitchen sink, the boy shakes his head. As the main cleaner of the café washroom, he's had to clean up after the drunk. He's amazed at his dad, who now pushes the sympathy button.

"Richie was gobsmacked by the death of his sister. Ethel, you know. You know the one, she died of consumption? That woman disrespects his time of mourning. We deal with loss in our own ways. Have some respect."

The gathering pauses to build in their minds the sidewalk diorama. The Innkeeper shakes his head and repeats. "That woman."

Richie, not a coffee regular, is getting the most attention of his sad drunken life.

"All this from that woman. All in full-monty. Right there …" (The dish pig can see his father extend both hands forward toward the large display windows. Regulars swivel on stools to follow their host in his point.) "… right in front of my Hotel. That woman." The Innkeeper looks across the u-shaped counter. "That woman. That oversized Panda thinks she can lift her leg on my front door …"

Kitchen detail has never included the image of Mrs. Snoddie as anything but a nose-in-the-air teacher. A pissing Panda?

As the boy tips a load of plates into the sink, he gets to singing along while he works:

If we sit for a fête of drinking fun,
Fingers count the beers we have done …

(*Fête* is another word from French class. It means party. French means a class Wendy loves.)

But two hands are needed to get the sum
After so many chugs, down so divine.
There's a rack of empties left in a line.

In a back upper room at the Methodist church, hidden from the

Sunday school at large, is the Confirmation Room. On Sunday afternoons, he joins up with Wendy for the Confirmation group, another class Wendy likes.

A few Sundays back Wendy stood in front of the young Christian group reciting one of the Pastor's own poems:

If we sit down at set of sun
And note to God things we have done,
And counting find
One glance most kind
That fell like sunshine where it went —
Giving light to count the day well-spent —
Then receive thy manna sent.

Wendy, in her aqua Kitten sweater, made such sweet notes out of the Pastor's dumb words. A special glow for her best boy; a showstopper for the rest of the guys. (The other girls, meanwhile, ran out to White & May's on Monday to pick over the depleted stock of sweaters. They wanted to join the tight-knit group of teenagers.)

Behind Wendy on the two-step stage, backed by the biggest of blackboards, George gazed upwards through his moustache eyebrows to concentrate on the prose. The guys focused on the figure behind the small fruit-stem podium, mouthing each word she recited by heart. The same question was on the minds of all the bad boys and too-innocent girls: *Does she or doesn't she pad her bra?*

"Sit up," came the Pastor's jarring voice when Wendy finished. "*Sit up* and take notice, young Christian Citizens, to those with success." George's moustache eyebrows reached out. "Then ask yourself: Who do I want to be? One of them?" The eyebrows rose while his head affirmed the message from God. "Or someone who just lets your parents carry you? Or worse … like, like that degenerate Richie Rosen."

What did Richie do to make the Pastor's shit list? He was a failed Baptist and a successful drunk living out of his parents' basement.

The impression got worse after class when Sewell took the Innkeeper's son aside for a private message.

"I can get you more time on the ice." The Pastor smiled at the young hockey player. The lad could look but had no time to think. "But I can't do it for a boy whose father sells booze."

An offside remark that confirmed George as Bad Pastor.

The subject never came up again, to anyone. But now the boy continues to play on his own version of the Bad Pastor's poem. Each time he comes up with a new line, better and better and round and round goes his ditty:

So gents, here's to more liquid sunshine down our throats,
From pilsener, lager and ale bottles sent,
For a golden path to our stomach coats.
Now we go … *(He motions to his zipper)* … with quality booze well-spent,
So away from the Grand Central we are sent.

The only confirmation his Sunday classes have provided is that the Pastor has taken a comfortable livelihood away from his family.

In 1920 the Hotel is sputtering along with a hangover from the *Ontario Temperance Act* of 1916. The Act will hang a rubber tire around bar business until 1927. The liquor laws are a direct hit that affects the future direction of the Grand Central Hotel.

Transportation changes have already damaged every part of the Hotel's trade other than food and booze. The Innkeeper disappears less often from the café to deliver fewer patrons back and forth from the two remaining train stations. Citizens now drive to the university city of London for just the day, passing by seven closed former inns. Meanwhile, sales representatives from the city can pack their car solid with samples, making multiple stops before they return home before dark. Although the café is at full capacity for morning coffee, people pack lunches or drive home. The Innkeeper compensates for the vacancy increase with a buffet of rentals by week or month: newlyweds on standby while they wait for their first home, single young men in their first jobs in need of breakfast and dinner, or the new bank manager building a house before the move.

Monday nights the Innkeeper draws the window curtains for the Rotary Club meeting, always with a guest speaker. The downtown merchants' association books Tuesdays for a Hungry Man Breakfast. Many businesses use the curtain approach for Christmas gatherings or special recognition of retiring employees.

(The Archives has a behind-the-curtain photograph of the Rotary's twenty-seven serious members in two rows, one seated and one standing. Curator Larry wonders if the men were grumpy-hungry or didn't like the dinner.)

The hostelry business disappears, but the Hotel's name does not. The third floor transforms into storage rooms with the enamelled room numbers left over from the hotel days. On the first floor, the Grand Central Café is known as the beehive of buzz for those who wish to be in the know. Rather than passing out keys, the Innkeeper serves breakfast, lunch and dinner along with his baker wife, a small part-time staff, and don't forget "Oh Henry" the Chinese cook. (My father tells the story of eating a burg and fries with my grandfather there as a kid and hearing, "Oh Henry, a #3. Hold the gravy.")

The Innkeeper's new routine as a landlord and café manager frees him up for extra attention on his son, who needs a firm future. With the carriage passageway out to pasture, winds of change have whirled away at the gathering cement dust and paper litter. Closing in the space, he adds lath and plaster walls with the wiring and plumbing hidden. The ceiling is a continuation of the embossed tin treatment used in the café. All is mapped out on paper to fit the magnificent seventeen-foot walnut bar backdrop, a centrepiece refurbished for the west wall that frames three huge side-by-each leaded mirrors. Father sends for a catalogue which reflects the finest in hydraulic barber chairs, a red leather and nickel-plated throne that will send the right customer invitation.

No hurry with the horse out of the barn and his son not yet out of high school. The Innkeeper has more time on his hands in afternoons and evenings to terrace the rock garden out back, expanding it over the defunct coach path. A six-foot statue of Venus appears at the far end in a trade reclamation of a bad bar debt. Soon the goddess is joined by a six-volt wire, current enough for two electrified fountains. One small fount spouts water from a large bullfrog into the bathtub-sized pond. The junipers make a back border where his wife faces bright bunches of petunias to dress the length of the garden terraces end to end. A number of unique and colourful rocks apply an attractive touch to the terracing.

By 10:45, with refilled cups, the room relaxes to the theme of weather. The Innkeeper turns his attention to the kitchen. Father catches his son with both hands in still dish water, a dirty look of wonder on his face.

"Son, how about backing the car out of the garage when you're done there?"

"Sure thing, Dad."

"Son, make your three-point turn, then back the car up to the grass. Careful of the rock garden. Put the trunk on the lip of the sidewalk."

The lad knows a delivery is a move into independence for a young driver. He smiles back to his father's wink.

"First things first are Hotel errands. Just be back by lunch, son." The words couldn't be sweeter if they came directly from heaven. The blood flow shuts down his brain, leaving only one thought remaining:

I get to drive on my own.

Okay, two thoughts:

I can drive by Wendy's house.

With engrained Methodist Sunday School intent, the lad finishes the job on the remains of breakfast and coffee. In short order he stacks the rinsed dishes on the drying rack while the mopped floor dries. He's fixated on the enamelled key fob dangling from the oak rack of cast eye-hooks. The blue & white Ford logo stands out above all. He wipes his dish-white hands, then uses the same cloth to polish up the fob. The V-8 calls from the garage.

After he loads the trunk and climbs behind the wheel, Father interrupts his dream. "Back it in when you're done," he says. "Door closed. Keys on the rack."

Delivery can wait, even if Father thinks he knows best. First the chauffeur will head straight out Wellington for a grand loop that will include a dream pass-by.

"Son, drop the laundry off first so it's ready on Monday."

"Got it, Dad."

Whatever other stuff Father throws out there, he figures, just nod and agree. If asked to get groceries, the lad will get the job done. Laundry, no problem, Dad. All becomes points gained for weekend rides.

A smart lad knows what's on first, a roll by Wendy's house. If that guard dog of her father's is not watching the driveway, then he'll toot the horn, looking for a wave. If he gets the all-clear, he'll do a practice back-up into the Moore driveway. Just a wave from the front steps will be thrill enough.

The lad has never seen and certainly never touched a female breast or female nipples. The image of a pair of grapefruit with huge navels from Paul's Fruit Market racks them up in his mind.

Zap. He jumps back as his father slaps the screen door shut.

"Son, Red & White. The food order is ready, after the laundry drop."

The lad rolls ahead now, ear to the open window, never surprised by the parental voice of repeated instructions that follow him out.

"Ring the red buzzer twice. Twice only, or old Jasper cranks it up."

Knowing that Father likes acknowledgement, he slows down and nods his head from the passenger window. "We're good, Dad."

The lad knows the reward he has in mind will come. But first a tapping on the rear passenger window. He stops again.

"Son, have you considered making the move towards barber school?"

With school finished, the future is now on a time clock.

"And what about Grade Thirteen?" the boy says.

Tick.

"Grade Thirteen," his father says, "if you are going for university."

Tock.

"What if I decide to go at a later time? Doesn't dropping out eliminate the option?"

Tick. "Consider the math, son. Grade Thirteen plus five years of University, graduate a teacher. Barber school is three months, twelve miles away. The math is easy. You're up five to six years of income, all before the teacher teaches one lesson. That's even assuming you get a teaching job."

The argument is weighty. Tock.

"Big decision, Dad."

Tick tock.

"Son, the right decision is what *you* want in life."

The Innkeeper doesn't bother mentioning his son's average grades and his pedestrian effort at assignments. From across the downtown, a bell chimes three times as the Andrews Jewellery clock winds down.

"Be your own boss. A business that you can manage as you wish."

"Dad, I'll never get to leave home."

"Do the math, think of the cash, son."

Money means one thing to the boy — a car of his own. More silence makes room for one more point. "Cash to support your own family." Wendy could have popped up here, but Father knows best to keep mum, stick to the cash. "Cash to buy a house."

"Points made, Father."

The old man leans into the open window. "I just want *you* to have a choice in continuing our business. I admit that things are changing, but it's a way for a property to remain in family hands. It's your choice."

"I *am* proud that our family built the Grand Central Hotel." Father likes reassurance.

"The best decisions for the future are always made with well-informed research."

The boy slides the column shift into drive. "Where did you say you wished the car backed up to?"

"When you get back, if it's early enough" — Father gives him a big smile, a different kind of smile — "how about driving over to Stratford to do a reconnoitre on the Barber School?"

Chapter 4

Petrified Rock

1933

The Ford 'A' Model C labours along the hard-pack path toward Arizona. The snazzy sedan outpaces a dusty tail that follows along the highway shoulder. Any fan of the Model A pedigree would recognize this model as different, something unique. Along with the Ontario plates, there's something from a far-off northern place. First indication is the sound, with a throatier muffler. Got your attention? Have a look close up, for the unique logo displayed on the side of the hood. All shiny in chrome, it reads MODEL C V-8. Charles knows that his Canadian-built model has ten more horsepower than its American-built cousin. He's a distant traveller confident in his car choice, the most modern means of vehicular transportation of the day. His lifelong friend Kipp Dobson has guaranteed it. *("Adventure of a lifetime, Charles. Sarah will love it.")*

Samples of petrified rock from the rock garden.

This is the first time my grandfather, Charles Wolfe Cruise, passes on his way from Canada south on Route 66. He was the first driver from St. Marys to visit either St. Louis or Chicago, and now he's on to parts southwest. He sends notes along the way for his loyal readership in the *Journal*. The three-on-the-tree standard shift is a short reach as he continues his big stretch for adventure. A comfortable Ford with heavily padded seats, the 'A' Model C with eighty-five horse helps him roll along in third at a fine clip. It's steady at fifty miles per hour from St. Marys to Chicago then down 66 to Arizona.

The past three winters he boarded the train on the edge of St. Marys at the Junction. Three short stops to Chicago before catching the midnight train, the California Clipper. This fourth winter brings him in the comfortable Ford sedan. He drives under the Detroit River in a tunnel, arranging for a tour of the wonder designed by a St. Marys boy, Archibald Gillies (soon Archie will venture north to help open up Timmins for gold mining). His readers will love getting a firsthand report on a local lad made good. Charles covers Detroit and the new murals by Diego Rivera at the Detroit Institute of Arts, adding up to three columns' worth which Charles will mail from Chicago before he picks up 66 to Arizona.

Charles' privileged origins in a merchant pioneer family afford him the time for a long drive south in order to preserve his health. He also needs to preserve a happy marriage.

He writes daily — columns, letters and postcards. Some of his published memories help capture a loyal readership for his weekly ramblings in the *Journal*:

A few weeks ago I told of being called up by phone one morning by a lady who surprised me by saying that she was one of my Fingal students from 1904. A couple of weeks later Mr. Fred Howell of Omaha saw my reference in the Journal, wrote to say he had gone to school in Paris, Ont. with this lady's brother George Whitten. You may remember George from …

A standout column for those who love trips down memory lane. Winter readers follow his exotic travelogue line by line. Charles loves the style of the Southwest, a neverending diorama straight out of his favourite Zane Grey pulp Western novels. He witnesses a movie shoot in Monument Valley; along with his column he sends the paper a photo of himself with director John Ford. (My father always claimed it was the first *Stagecoach* film and John Wayne shot the photo.) My grandfather writes as a Citizen witness to new worlds for the folks back home. Readers care little that his column for the *St. Marys Journal* sometimes needs three or four editions to catch up to his travels. His first winter south he was the first Citizen of St. Marys to fly in a plane. A published photo shows Charles in hat, tie and cane with a goggled man before a Gipsy Moth Biplane. A shot to the moon for his readers. Another time he meets the iconic Tom Mix, the original actor cowboy. His weekly column, "The Rambling Traveller," draws big readership year-round. The well-written log is big stuff in the small world of St. Marys.

He waits two more years to pull it all together in his sixty-page booklet. The soft cover announces RAMBLES IN THE SOUTHLAND: BY THE RAMBLING TRAVELLER. (Dave the printer, who occupies his days with draw tickets and obituary cards, is a cautious man: *"Charles, one thousand copies is a lot. We should start with one hundred? Maybe two?"* One thousand carries the day. Charles comes close, selling over nine hundred.)

Church groups, women's institutes, fundraisers, annual meetings, and most area clubs, odd orders and secret societies welcome Charles' travelogue in person. In 1935 he's a technological wonder with his portable projector and slide-up screen.

Although well read, the book never gets a reprint. (The Museum Archives has two dry boxes of them in their basement; Curator Larry would love to sell you a copy.)

Most important and unusual in the Archives, though, are the private letters the loving husband composes for his wife.

I noticed that every bit of sunshine, every fleecy cloud that floats across my vision, warms my feelings this early morning … One cloud caught the sun, though, and a shadow crossed my brow. In a flash light shone to my soul — your light, the light that gives me strength and a smile to take me through my day. I'm counting the days to your arrival, my love.

In the southwest, Charles sticks to a well-developed routine. You could set your watch by the Cortes Hotel's all-male waiters and their Charles Wolfe Cruise good morning. First, a black coffee accompanied by the broadsheet *Phoenix Sun*. The expanse of paper limits table room. Two poached eggs on brown, with chorizo added as a token to the Spanish influence. The entire hotel staff below the management — including all those in the kitchen preparing breakfast — are Latino. Sixth-generation Spanish with a few new arrivals from Mexico make up the team. Charles has no idea that his simple breakfast with a touch of chorizo could be so much better. He can't wait to show his farm-raised wife a Southwest version of sausage. The table is cleared with a coffee refill left beside his notebook and pencil. He clears his cloudy morning mind for his daily letter to Sarah, which will be sent from the hotel lobby. A seven-day deadline on his column and a daily round of activities in the sunburnt centre of Arizona allow him to pick and polish his desert stories.

Charles joins the Sierra Club, their first Canadian member. Through a series of Club lectures he learns about the region, then he joins day trips to lost pueblos, amazing Spanish missions forgotten with time. The city library has a sizeable section on local history. Sundays at the Congregational Church and Tuesday lunch meetings as a visiting member at the Phoenix Rotary Club add to his days. Collateral lunch, dinner and coffee invitations from these contacts round out his active schedule.

A photograph in the Archives shows a man wearing a straw boater hat, with suspenders pushed apart by his round belly, in the gilded glory of the open Cortes lobby. The Archives, in the same file, also has the calling cards for the gentleman in the picture. Charles Wolfe Cruise makes a special order from a lithographer in Stratford for embossed cards for the first trip. A smart-looking introduction with his St. Marys postal address on the front of the card and his name above CORTES HOTEL OF PHOENIX, and their three-digit phone number. A curious, affable traveller open to invitations to explore new sites with new

American friends. Sarah knows how well these winters have improved her husband's health. That raspy breathing is less pronounced; Sarah can enjoy a good night's sleep. Nevertheless, Charles promises this will be his final winter visit.

Sarah attended Stratford Normal School for a post–high school teaching certificate. This after acquiring her Geology degree from that trendy university in eastern Ontario. She moved out west to teach in Strathcona, Alberta. Her appointment to St. Marys High School brought her closer to home. Here she met a descendant of a pioneer merchant family, Charles Wolfe Cruise. Obviously, she has both a sense of adventure to travel out west to teach and the smarts to return as the Town's first female science teacher. Her dictionary mind, her art, her engagement in discussion — these are smart attractions for a young single man suffering years of Pastor George Sewell's blasts.

For Sarah it is the land above all that brought her back. The family's third-generation farm near Granton will always be home, and she has a keen interest in preservation, whether it's her fieldstone homestead or her church, the solid brick Wesley Methodist Hall.

Her structured upbringing, anchored by solid attendance at the Young Christian Club, marshals the lovebirds into a quick marriage — some raised eyebrows say rushed. My grandmother joked that it was love from Young Christian sight.

"He wouldn't take his eyes off me."

My grandfather countered it was the starch-collared cotton dress. "Blinded by an angel. She attempted to sing some George-inspired psalm. Awful prose, pretty pose."

Sarah was born into the Methodist front-pew drill at the red brick Granton church. In short order she marches Charles and the three small boys, not a year apart, into the Methodist Hall each Sunday.

"Charles, it's for family's sake," she says.

Charles thinks of their three boys under five as hellions, not angels in church.

Sarah grows comfortable in her St. Marys front pew where she learns to adapt to the overbearing messenger of God. Her uncle, the Reverend Jasper Longstaffe, fills in for George's summer vacation. (The ultimate irony of this family comeuppance is that George would never get a chance to witness a humble man behind his cherry podium.)

For the four Southland trips, Sarah is a messenger in her own right in correspondence to Charles:

Our old brick home, brown and sweet,
Here I wake when all the world's asleep,
Thinking of you with happy cares.

A morning glory in comforter deep,
I hold you tight, then all my prayers
In my heart I lay forever to keep.

This year she will join him. Sarah has stayed back with the children four full winters with a part-time housekeeper and full-time nanny. This year she and Charles will be the first in Town to drive home from the Southwest. Her sister, Ellen, is coming from Kingsville to hold down the fort for four weeks.

The three boys are John Calvin, Robert Wesley and Charles Wolfe Junior. The third and last son, the third repeat on the family name Charles Wolfe, still gets, even as a two-year-old, "Baby Chuck." (My father will go off to university, graduating to Charles for the rest of his years.)

The youngsters lick their lips in anticipation of fun times alone with Auntie Ellie. They appreciate the chance to have four full weeks of days with her instead of just a Saturday or a holiday occasion. The aunt writes to the boys ahead of time:

We can get Grandfather Cruise to pick us up Friday after school
for a camp at the farm. The pond is frozen for skating. The barn
will be warm enough for hay-mound jumping. If you like we can
do this twice. In Town, the horse barn arena has public skating
Thursday nights. Wax those toboggans up, boys! John, you and
Robert work on this before I come.

Knox Hill, opposite the Methodist Hall, shows off winter with a slick toboggan run. Both rink and slide are convenient to the Cruise brown-brick home. In the week before Ellie arrives, Sarah covers responsibilities for the two oldest. The nanny is given instructions for Little Chuck, who has neither skates nor a space on the toboggan. Sarah will pull the swaddled bundle with two sky blue eyes in a red sleigh. The older ones are allowed to take a run on their own with supervision. In fact, John will enjoy his first winter independence, hitting the hill with a pre-organized group of neighbour kids.

Sarah spends two days going over the routine hands-on with her sister. ("Little Donnie Marriott and Sammy Dunseith are good lads. Responsible on the hill. On time, there and back for public skating. That Corey Sadler is problematic. Okay in the group, but trouble on his own. So no Corey in a pair.")

The Canadian Pacific passenger train picks up Sarah at the Junction station at eight AM, livery by Kipp himself. The quick step chugs of the steaming pistons can be heard for miles and miles. The kind station attendant, in a worn-through cap and double-breasted but too large jacket, turns the signal to red. Scurrying out to the far end of the platform where it becomes grass, he holds out a long pole with a red flag waving the CP letters. The locomotive acknowledges him with a blink of the light. Now he runs back to help her; important passenger Mrs. Cruise needs a luggage lift to her reserved first class seat. The attendant stomps out from the jettisoning steam, a ghostly ghoul reaching for her bags.

Yes, electric signal lights, but in 1933 the toilets remain outhouses and the waiting room keeps bags, parcels and packages in transit. Ten years later the convenience of heated shelter and a warm toilet seat will be added. The station will be closed at the end of the war. At the height of the Depression, the passengers suffer through the uncertainty of all four seasons on an open platform with scant roof coverage.

The four-minute stop leads to a forty-eight-hour transportation adventure. Sarah has done her research. Not one Citizen of St. Marys besides her husband has ever taken a trip to Phoenix. He's offered lots of suggestions which she has supplemented with some library books and the *Detroit Free Press*, delivered daily to the Grand Central Hotel lobby. Finished copies were passed on to her so she could read snippets about American life.

Sarah's train brings her south in comfort. She spends most of the time in the dining and lounge car. A great read includes *Brave New World* by Aldous Huxley; a new author, John Steinbeck; something light from Agatha Christie; and as always, for the correct course, her Jasper Wilson–dedicated New Testament. The top-drawer menu offers fresh shrimp salad, an introduction to eggs Benedict, steeped tea and a succulent bison tenderloin, all of which distract her from the clock. Her first Dr. Pepper is a marvel in technology, sound and taste. Soda usually comes from a fountain, so a cap is a novelty. Even ice is not a problem.

"Mrs. Cruise, ma'am, would you like another soda and ice?"

"Most kind of you Sam, yes, please."

The young mother's first time alone in her adult life is a refresher. Her station drop in Chicago is at ten PM, giving her enough time for a walk about before the midnight departure. Charles has described a food stall with a wonderful selection of treats to tide her over on her sleepover. ("The butterscotch nougat is brilliant. Don't forget some of their homemade black liquorice for me.")

At the stroke of midnight, the California Clipper leaves for Los Angeles, with two stops. Breakfast and lunch are included in the fare. The second stop places her in Phoenix late the next evening. Her night and day of first class service flashes by in no time while she soaks up the Western scenery, all memories that will last forever.

On the open Phoenix platform (two seasons: hot and hotter) the warm glow of a Southwest sunset welcomes her into Charles' arms. The Union Station is an introduction to the Southwest aesthetic, with its mission-style rounded arches and red tile roof. The transfer of her luggage is arranged to the hotel so the couple can soak up the dry air of the evening. Their walk takes them past the Central Methodist Church where the side door opens up for an appreciative stop. No words necessary for their thankful prayers on a safe arrival. After an embrace, it's off to Donofrio's for the best ice cream in Phoenix. Alongside their spectacular flavours — watermelon, pecan of course, and even prickly pear cactus — the family also operates a flower shop. Piero has a pre-arranged desert rose corsage to pin on Sarah.

Saturday's city tour includes the native artifacts of the new Heard Museum, which has a nice café. The Victorian Arizona State Capitol is nearby, along with Frank Lloyd Wright's Arizona Biltmore which lays out an excellent high tea. Then the ghost tour at William Wrigley's mansion, and the best for last — a new movie release by Noel Coward, *Cavalcade*, is playing at the Studio, a theatre close to the hotel. Sunday, the full service at Central Methodist is followed by a special-invitation lunch in the greatest of private gardens. On Monday, the owner of the Phoenix Sun, a fellow Rotarian and Methodist, and a brother Moose Lodge member, hosts them for horseback riding at his cattle ranch with a barbecue to follow.

On Tuesday they prepare for their road trip. Charles has booked an appointment at the Scottsdale office of Sanford's Insurance South West Road Tours. Sanford's is, no questions asked, the genesis of travel information for all the Southwest as well as Mexico. All questions asked and answered by (as the gold letters spell on the storefront window) "South West's experienced travel guides since 1895." Charles questions the dates in a winking aside to Sarah.

"Kit Carson and Buffalo Bill Cody must have been customers."

The representative reviews all the printed material with Sarah, covering all significant vistas and historic sites. "That's a long way to go. Canadians, you say. Let's get you straight and correct on your path."

"Safe and comfortable too," Sarah adds.

The rep unfolds the map which has their route highlighted in yellow. His eyes appear above his reader glasses as he repeats to his special audience. "And safe and comfortable too, Mrs. Cruise."

The travel information includes all the important details for early car travel. A stress-free time on the open trails is facilitated by a folding shovel, light chains, a large air pump and a tire repair kit including patches, inner tubes and a large tube of rubber glue. One spare's on the driver side at the hood, the second is over the chrome rear bumper along with the two full gas cans and the small leather-strapped trunk of emergency gear.

Sarah will have the best in amateur guides at her side. Charles has long had their return journey all studied up and mapped out. The route is solid; it's the confidence of his wife that he has to secure. He nods his head as the security of a local insurance and travel agency calms Sarah. Knowledge is power, and silence keeps a happy wife.

The return home by car will take them direct to the Northeast on an all-pavement adventure through Albuquerque and St. Louis. Charles' first leg of his trip earlier that winter, from St. Marys to London, took place on gravel until Oxford Street in downtown London. From there, Ontario's premier asphalt Highway, the 2, takes off to Detroit then Route 69 to Chicago for 66. All solid roads from London to Phoenix and back.

Their trip will go off the Sanford's map past St. Louis. Petrol stations are marked by little totem poles on the map. There is not an abundance of totem poles.

First night takes them to the railway centre of Winslow, where Sarah passed through a week ago without stopping. Here at the corner of nowhere and double rail tracks, the Fallen Arrow Hotel and Copperhead Lounge provides accommodation without reservations. The hotel staff are puzzled by the mysterious couple, first because of their arrival by automobile instead of Santa Fe rail car, and second because of their snazzy wheels and Ontario plates.

The reader at home will relish the description of the deep-dish, oven-baked breakfasts. No one ever poaches eggs in a sauce. In the oven? What is this salsa on my chorizo sausage? Unimaginable delights to the Citizens of St. Marys.

After the hot breakfast in the cool of the dawn, the Sedan once again labours along the hard-pack path, outpacing its dusty tail. Charles sits comfortable in the knowledge that this adventure is worth the effort.

First the bouncing, heaving highway takes them through The Painted Desert. The early-start plan gives them their two stops before high noon. On the first day Sarah packed an icebox with the help of the Cortes Hotel kitchen staff; in Winslow they refresh the ice and get a fill-up to keep them in road shape. They need to make Albuquerque late the second night.

The Painted Desert and its neighbour, Petrified Forest, America's fourth National Park, are already a popular drive from Phoenix in 1933. Ancient times turned the Arizona pine forests into a Sodom frozen in the desert. To fathom the Forest's ongoing popularity, consider that in the twenty-first century, despite the vigilance of seven park rangers, over eleven thousand kilograms of fossilized wood will go missing every year.

In years to come Snowbirds from Canada, a novel concept, will follow Charles' path, driving their cars south and west along Route 66. It's a more independent and personal journey than on a train. The slow traveller stops at the new parks, novel postcard sites and cheesy gasoline stations. More than a top-up on gas, these are attractions along the way. Washrooms not at all clean — the phony teepee — goats nearby, and sometimes a bear in a rusty cage. A sandy hue of fudge stuck under waxed paper — pickled eggs in a jar — some souvenirs, all tacky — shelves of cans and an icebox with no ice. Travellers know better than to ask. (*"Ice comes on Thursdays."*)

Gas is the most important thing, of course, while any toilet break that's not just stopping by the side of the road is more than welcome.

The drab black and white of The Cisco Kid is no match for The Painted Desert. The Desert seems to Sarah to be a brown version of Ontario's white, wintery landscapes. She could imagine putting this scenery into one of those rotating-screen lamps — a few cacti, thorny shrubs and a coyote or two. She talks to herself in the moment. "That would be my choice for the scene to light me up. Maybe it needs a cowboy?"

"The Painted Desert is like wallpaper for the petrified wood," Charles says.

The pedigree of Sarah's greater family includes her farmer father, her Methodist minister grandfather, her mother the Methodist minister's daughter, two Methodist missionary spinster aunts and single Uncle Jasper at the lake. Not one member of this group would shy away from discourse, comment or debate, up to a full shout at any time, on almost any theme. Although a passenger with complete respect for her partner, Sarah drives the conversation.

"My thirst increases with the scenery, the dryness of the air, no water."

Charles enjoys the company, allowing Sarah to roll it out.

"Water, water everywhere," she goes on. "We have the pond on the farm. Then Uncle Jasper's cottage at Ipperwash squat on Kettle Point Beach."

Beach? he almost asks aloud. It's a rocky shore with little sand on that immense fresh-water lake.

"Our whole life springs from water!" she says. "In St. Marys, which is in a river valley, we can walk two blocks from our home to our choice of the creek, Thames River, the falls or Rice Lake. You and I need to appreciate our abundance of water all the more. Someday it might be gone!"

Charles wants the conversation back on track to a lighter subject. "We do have that quarter kettle from Jasper's. Nice reminder of the lake."

Sarah thinks of her uncle. Free time at the lake as a young girl was the best of growing up. His mentorship inspired Sarah to study geology at Victoria College as part of a three-year science degree. This led her into teaching high school science. This Methodist girl of modern thinking has never believed in creation, other than as a nice story; neither does Uncle Jasper, who instilled in her an interest in science through the spirit of the land, including the rock kettles.

"That's an interesting geological phenomenon," she says. "A unique form created through Lake Huron's repeated wave action over hundreds of thousands of years. Add into the mix seasonal storms, ice grinding and sand movement, and there you have it, stone kettles!"

Kettles look like two large woks joined together. (Woks are a familiar tool even to this Westerner in 1933, as Sarah's spinster aunts cook with woks after learning as missionaries in China.) The kettles litter one unique point on the entire Great Lakes shoreline, there at Kettle Point, the setting of Uncle Jas's home.

Uncle Jas attends to the spiritual needs of the Indigenous population and a number of pioneer cottagers. Forty-six Sundays a year — not to mention weddings, funerals and christenings — he commands the one-post pulpit at the small Methodist church nearby. Add a few more Sundays filling in for George in St. Marys each summer and you have full-time service to the Lord's flocks. His wonderful words pass over the sunburnt foreheads of summer survivors. Jasper would rather be the apostle at the lake than cross the sea like his older sisters. Every sunset and most sunrises the white-bearded living Moses stands with a graniteware mug of Chinese tea by his Great Lake: *"I can see you, Great Manitou of the waves, making those kettles."* The wind can hear him.

From her sunset passenger watch, Sarah feels her Uncle Jas on his shoreline looking Southwest towards her. She repeats to herself: "I can see you, Great Manitou of the waves, making those kettles."

The car shimmies, gives a shudder as it makes tracks over a sandy section. The memory of the moist Lake Huron shoreline disappears along with the subject of rock kettles. Uncle Jas is left in the dust too. Charles pulls back with ginger on the downshift as he navigates sand-covered pockets. As with his limited experience with drifting snow — most cars at this time are parked for winter — he tacks a course over each sand wave, searching for tire grip on the next patch of bare asphalt. No real worries, though, with no traffic on the roads, and there's no point paying attention to followers anyway, since he can't see anything out the browned-out rear split window. He ignores any bumps or steering-wheel shudders to concentrate on his wife's thoughts. With a slight twist he can see her face in the mirror. Charles never plays cards, but he knows when to hold and when to play. You cannot discount hubris in the first female geology graduate from Victoria College, University of Toronto. He deals the geology card.

"Amazing," he says, "the diorama of the frozen forest in stone. It appears to have been a burnt forest at one time, but frozen still."

Sarah turns to listen to her personal guide.

"Thousands of years ago these stone fenceposts were new formations. Before witnesses human or dinosaur, the rocks made their formation. Here we are thousands of years later as witnesses to the transformation. How many people before us today, here on this dusty road, have had this experience?"

Sarah lets her husband go on in his moment of geological glory.

"These prehistoric stones need to be seen firsthand on the ground." He peers under the visor. "We have a rich opportunity before us — what better time to pull over? At least before the sun sets on us."

Charles has disclosed his true agenda. As he turns to face her, he polishes up the rock idea. "A choice memory comes home!"

Sarah replies with incredulity. "We're going to pull over ... and do *what?* Did I hear you right?" The Southwest grill turns on to high.

　　　　　　　　　　　　　　　　　　　　　　　　　　LORNE EEDY

"What is this choice memory that's coming home?" she echoes. "A rock from Arizona?"

Charles is surprised by all these sudden fly balls hit to left field. "Yes, we can stop the car, find a place to park." Slow down, he reminds himself. He softens his stance. "Then we get out, just look around, together." He stumbles a wee bit in the silence. "I bought a little shovel in Phoenix, and some burlap bags …"

"*We*, Mr. Cruise? *I* would look forward to enjoying the rocks in *our* garden." The unfamiliar intonation from his wife spells warning. "Sounds like a plan for a special memory. Remember what happened with *my* family rock in *our* garden," she says. "And, I might enjoy samples of petrified wood if I didn't have to worry about that free-haircut deal!"

"Whoa, dear. That's just a joke between me and The Barber. We were just having some fun. We're friends." After mumbling out fun he barely finishes the word friends.

"That was fun? Now you think it's a *joke*? Is this what *your* friends do?"

The Barber and Charles go back together, farther than the big red & nickel barber chair. Back before St. Marys High School they were early childhood friends sharing Sunday school, scouts, choir, Central School and the Pleasant Hour Theatre (before Kitten sweaters), not to forget those complementary hand-cut French fries and fountain cherry Cokes. Now the friends are pencilled in together on the calendar hooked onto the bathroom door. The monthly appointment will celebrate a tenth anniversary when he returns.

And yet, the free haircut for the gift of a unique rock is not about their lifelong friendship — this is competition. Charles bought into the marketing deal as soon as The Barber opened up shop. He has a friend, needs a haircut and loves a bet. He was on familiar terms with the rock show long before he met Sarah at the young-adult Methodist meetings. This woman should understand that she's inherited a relationship with a haircut appointment. Charles decides to reveal all in the front seat of the Sedan:

"The Barber gave me the challenge before I left in the fall."

"Challenge? You mean a *bet!*"

"He challenged me. He bet me *two* free haircuts for one rock from Arizona."

"Gambling is a sin. With one rock, you are gambling, Charles."

"Our choice is in front of us." On a confessional roll, Charles reveals one more choice: "I made a side bet with Aaron Kane."

"Aaron Kane?"

"For a third haircut."

"What happened to the first two free haircuts?"

"Done like dinner. The second rock is our private side bet."

"Now it's *two* rocks?"

"It's all easy-peasy dear, with the lineup of choices that line the road on both sides. Quick stop, a few steps, the shovel and the bag. We're on our way before you can say Flash."

"Explain this third gamble on a free haircut?"

Charles backpedals in a fury. "Just a side-bet," he explains, "whereby *after* I get my first two free haircuts, I reveal the big surprise with a second choice rock."

"Gambling, Charles. Throwing the dice of sin again."

Her incredulous expression does not stop him. "Aaron bet that he would cover a *third* haircut if the second rock works! The haircut isn't technically gambling since Aaron would pay …" Seeing the blankness on his companion's face, he fills the space. "Sarah, this is more than a bet. It's a challenge!"

Sarah stays silent in the face of masculine reason.

"Three free haircuts, dear — three!"

"Thank you. Looks to me like suspect male intrigue between you and that barber. And shame on Aaron Kane too. Does Margie know? *You* are all still gambling, Mr. Cruise."

She pauses before introducing a dirty piece from history, adding more heat to the kettle. "And your last suitable example came from *my* family farm!"

An unconscious grind on the synchromesh as Charles gears down for the highway's grade. "Yes, but no one told me that it was a kettle."

"Kettle or not, it wasn't suitable to yank it out of the front garden of *my* family farm!"

"Your two-hundred-acre family farm has a thousand-plus free

samples in the rock department," he says. "Your father would shake my hand, anyone's hand, who helped themselves to his farm rocks. A little dramatic Sarah, 'yanked out'?" He fails to see Sarah rolling her eyes. So he rolls on. "Your father might as well have a sign: FREE ROCKS." Finally he stops to look at her.

In the moment of eye contact, Sarah pauses in reflection. She turns a little.

"Yes, your accounting of rocks in the field is many times true," she says. "But Charles, *not* out from Dad's front yard. Those are the choice pieces, not just garden trim. Field rocks from the field do not compare to the special examples in the garden. We picked them ourselves. And worse, the kettle was a handpicked gift from Uncle Jasper."

Charles makes his last stand behind the wheel. "How was I supposed to know that was a kettle, if I wasn't told the family details?"

"Ask and ye shall find, seek and ye shall know."

Sarah is about ready to kiss and make up. Day two of a long drive home, so steer for happy days. Charles seizes the silence.

"Please, my dear, I would never with any knowledge barter with anything of value from your family farm. I respect your heritage."

From the passenger side, Sarah shifts gears in the conversation. She gazes left then right, directing her glove over his hand on the shifter. A touching moment as she directs her Ontario guide to pull off the road.

"My goodness there's a lot of stone stock here, Cruise. How about this piece of land for some prospecting?"

Charles brings the sedan to a suitable pull-off. Silence inside while the approaching tail of dust in the mirror passes off into the desert.

Sarah gives him her Sunday-service look, which consists of a forbidding finger-point and a smile. "I need a promise this time round. A promise for my Charles to keep, or I will never let him sleep in peace again. *Our* choices stay in *our* chosen places, my dear."

Charles reaches for the right tone. "Rocks do flavour a hot day into a pleasant spot." And then scientific for the geologist. "They seem to absorb the heat of the day."

"Stories about *our* rock discoveries should foster a tradition in our family, great stories passed through our boys and our grandchildren. These future generations will be able to look down at these great examples, whether petrified wood or a Lake Huron kettle. Our descendants will say they came from 'our grandparents, Sarah and Charles Cruise back in the thirties.' What nice stories to repeat, dear."

"Rock solid logic, eh? Do you think they will remember?"

Sarah recognizes that small fringe of uncertainty in her larger-than-life husband. "My faith is in the process," she says. "The boys, sponges that they are, will remember enough to tune their character. In maturity with their families they'll repeat the stories to build the character of their own protégés."

Charles fills with pride at the aspect of heritage, lineage and history.

"I guarantee that the rocks will stay in place," he says. "Passing a few stories on to the boys and their children sounds super. For the here and now, our choices will keep to our garden."

"Charles, I do have to ask in good conscience: Do we *really* need to take another rock? Remember those thousands out on the farm and kettles at the lake."

"We may never do this again!"

Charles puts aside any guilt over a few missing rocks. "Arizona will always be a distant reach for the Northern traveller. No one will ever play golf in the desert. Where would the water come from? Who would take such a long, dusty drive to enjoy these natural features? Traffic will never hurt this area." He pauses in the warm car for a few cool breaths. "We have a car with a large boot! With that spade and bag ready to go!"

Feeling the cool-off, Sarah blows a fresh kiss towards Charles. "I have a special spot beside the back door for one or two." She winks. "And three, let's put the boot to that free haircut with an extra large choice."

Chapter 5

Home & Office

1942

Phwap. *Phwap. Phwap.*

"Father, let me. Let-me, let-me."

A stammer call on stuttering tiptoes is followed by the cascade of tap, tap, tapping from a seconder, ready and set. "Father, you said it would *be my turn next time.*"

Phwap. Phwap. Phwap.

Small fingers make a short sharp point in the direction of their father's rolled-up sleeve, which telescopes a fleecy arm back and forth. All eyes follow the motion in frozen concentration. The sisters are tucked back in the corner of their parents' bedroom-sized bathroom, a converted hotel room connecting parents' and children's. Victoria and Virginia are standing-room-only for a private showtime shearing by their father. Although both girls have learned how to whip and wipe the open blade across the stretched leather strap, they wait for permission.

"Vicki, let your sister have her turn please." He passes the strap end across to the younger girl. "Remember how I showed you to stand. Good." He waits. "That's right, make sure your sister has moved back a bit." A nod in that direction.

The sharpening strap has brass end-buckles with a porcelain-blue Delft swivel knob. Virginia holds one end while she gives the blade one timid stroke then another against the well-worn leather buckled up to the cherry double vanity. Only her father's eyes are visible above a steamy wet cloth that he holds behind his neck. His attention is on the strap, a Barber School graduation gift, timeworn enough that perhaps the deerskin will soon be repurposed into the cover of a book, maybe a diary.

"Here, Vicki, hold my facecloth." He drops the cloth with a big smile. All eyes look down. "Careful, it may still be hot."

Vicki giggles as the masked man turns back into her father. "Father, you look like the Lone Ranger." Her head tilts back for a look up. "When you cover your face like that."

No time for cowboy antics: his shaving brush dabs a foamy finish over his moist and warm face. The other hand turns on the cold tap. He looks down at Virginia with a hand out.

"Madame, my rapier." He turns to the mirror with chin up and pinched lips. "But, I do hope" — the blade makes contact — "that I look like Sir Joseph for tonight's dress rehearsal of *H.M.S. Pinafore.*"

Daughters are mesmerized into silence by Father's dexterity, with one eye on them and the other keeping track in the mirror. Two strokes to the lower left throat are impressive, but a careful pass over his Adam's apple? Whoa. He seizes the moment to pause on the reflection for a checkup from the neck up. The light from the chandelier reflects brightly in Father's steel blue eyes. The girls sense the release of a new feature in their private showtime when he turns half-shorn with a salute. Yes, they answer in giggles.

Tonight he's out the back door, up the alley, and left then right to the auditorium at the Town Hall for the final rehearsal of a barbershop favourite in Gilbert & Sullivan's *H.M.S. Pinafore.* Some light distraction for the darkness of the war years. The Executive of the Stonetown Players postponed the '39 production for three years.

It was Mrs. Snoddie's open letter to the *Journal,* directed to Board members and cast, that turned the stage lights on. Of course Mrs. Snoddie has a reputation as a profound letter writer; her opinions in favour of temperance and leashes for pet cats dominate Page 5 opposite the Editorial page before and after every election. This time the high school English teacher threw a change-up by writing on an unexpected topic. And her verse knocked it out of the park:

Time to shine,
Oh Town of mine.
Stage lights bright, shine the light.
Before God's might,

While overseas our sons and daughters fight,
We celebrate this dark time with
An entertaining night.
I can hear the call

To the auditorium hall:
Pinafore! Pinafore!
Sails unfold, buttons of gold,
Petticoats sweep the dance floor,

And the chorus voices soar!
Time to shine, Oh Town of mine.
Stage lights bright, shine the light.
Can you hear the call?
Pinafore! Pinafore!

Off script at home, The Barber has been playing with the operetta's subtitle, "The lass that loved a sailor." Maybe it could be replaced by a kitten who fell for a barber?

In front of the mirror now, Sir Joseph clears his performance pipes.

"But-but-but …" Winking at the girls — *"But-but-but-but …"* — Father sings bass. *"Bu-u-u-utt. B-b-b-b-u-u-utt."* He stops with the grandest smile then goes high in alto-soprano fashion. *"My, my, my … My-my-my-my little buttercups."*

He button-taps a dab of shaving cream on each nose — *"But-but-but-but-buttercups …"* — looks up into the mirror — *"I am the Admiral of the Sea."* — then shakes a finger. *"No greater Lord than me …"*

He looks back down at the girls — *"But-but-but-but, I come home to thee-e-e-e …"* — more finger dabs and giggles — *"my little but-but-but-buttercups."* Chin back up, close in to the mirror — *"But-but-but-but, this will be the reflection …"* — eyebrows and fists up, head cocked — *"of a-a-a-a-a very excellent gentleman."*

From above the remaining lather, a cough, another cough, and two winks.

"To be a true and worthy see-e-e-e-lection.
Sir Joseph to all-l-l-l your dee-e-e-e-tection.

No greater Admiral of the Sea than me-e-e-e-e."

Scrape, scrape, scrape. A nasal grip allows a close circular shave around the mouth, muffling the last of the little ditty. No limit to the bass sound for the master mimic.

"No more bew-bew-bew-beautiful …
Than my little but-but-but-but-buttercups."

The song stops over the porcelain sink for a rinse. Vicki's all smiles, knows the drill and has the warm facecloth raised up ready. Now Father becomes The Mummy. Vicki and Virginia smile along, both satisfied Sir Joseph has returned to being their father.

He's blessed — it's a wonderful wife that gives their spacious apartment in the old Hotel the home stamp of a happy family life. He smiles at the phrase his wife coined to sum up their married life upstairs and downstairs in the Hotel. Home & Office, that's what Wendy called it, even before they had graduated to a commitment ring.

The girls watch in silence as Father cleans up, lost in thought about life with his happy wife. He motions to Vicki and Virginia's bedroom — they both have homework assignments due tomorrow — as he trails off toward the master bedroom in silent appreciation. On his way he pops the suspenders over his shoulders and grabs the brass-buttoned coat off its hanger in the hall closet. From the puffy flocked armchair he grabs his wood rapier, floppy tie and, of course, the Admiral's peaked cap.

Since his first role in *Babes in Toyland* in Grade Ten, he's graduated through all of Gilbert & Sullivan, including two previous performances of *H.M.S. Pinafore.* He holds a regular gig every second Tuesday night with the Stonetown Community Players. Every second Wednesday, meanwhile, Wendy volunteers as a Brownies and Guides leader. Wendy is well-versed from her childhood experience back in the Methodist Annex, returning as a leader in the same building.

Tonight's dress rehearsal for the weekend run matches up with her night out. She's suited up to Guide away in her pressed brown cotton dress with official Lady Powell belt and a sash sleeve of badges. The Barber loves his Kitten in uniform, so she gets a hug and squeeze as he enters the bedroom. "How many badges did you earn as a kid?" He does a magician-style hand wave up and down both arms. "Looks like fifty-plus on your sleeves, plus the sash. You would need … I've never seen a Kitten with five paws. You'd need that for all those Brownie credits to fit on you." He gives her a look and a smile. "The one that I don't see is Master Bedroom Queen."

"That one's for my Admiral's private eyes only."

Beguiling, that's how he would describe her; Kitten is what he's called her from the beginning. The embrace of her Bandit perfume sends him back to happy days on a date in the V-8 twenty years earlier. He can still feel the pull of the accelerator on the hot asphalt. They had borrowed his father's car to drive to the City for a dress-fitting for her friend Betty's wedding. It was a hazy lazy day, the high corn steaming in the heat, the wheat steeping in the lack of a breeze. That day he stuck to the pavement of Highway 7, backing off the accelerator when Wendy rolled her window down. He was looking forward to that right girl-friend touch as his left hand slid the window down.

"Kitten, too dusty. No time for a car wash."

No turn, no look from the driver's side as she slid over to him all fuzzy and kitten-like.

"Let's just enjoy the ride." Her voice called him to turn as she shook her honey-red hair in the warm window breeze. His foot was off the accelerator as he soaked up the wide, wide world of her smile. The wind drowned out her words, but he could read her ruby red lips. He sees, not hears, her next words to this very day: "Plenty of time for detours."

There had been hand-holding walks home from school in Grade Nine, and then a first kiss in Grade Ten after a root beer float at the Hotel Café. Wow, Wendy met Mother and Father. The car drives started after they graduated from Grade Twelve. The young lovebirds came together on their shared flight path.

After The Barber graduated from Perth Barber School, head instructor Mike recommended his apprenticeship at Jonny's Gent Cuts, the busiest shop in the city. Jonny kept him busy, the apprentice's worn hands garnering little rubs at night from his gal. Meanwhile Wendy studied to achieve her secretarial diploma from the J. Stephens Vocational School in Theatre Town.

Most Fridays he got the day off from Jonny's and was able to borrow Father's car, so he drove her to school and back. Their Friday drives home are some of his favourite all-time memories. His buddies called the St. Catharines–built V-8 with the throaty purr "the cat's scratch," with the name always followed by a group growl. The Barber appreciated the sentiment, but *his* number-one cat was the Kitten waiting for a pickup at school's out.

Most Fridays he stuck to asphalt, a top-gun pilot on a regular beeline back to the old Hotel. (Dust was the worst evidence of a secret detour under Father's, not to mention Town, eyes.) Sometimes, though, time permitted a turn off Highway 7 in a wink, and they were off on the winding concession roads for a gravel run. That was a time when feeling lucky was the real deal. Wendy would return his smile as they pressed on the short detour. Unnecessary words had been replaced by silent signals.

From his first times driving with his father in the Stonetown Cemetery, seeing a couple parked in a car together, most often in the back seat, was a teenage revelation. He began noticing these adult remainders everywhere: off-path loose tire tracks, a white tissue or two in the wind or, no surprise, cans and bottles of the cheapest brands of beer or liquor lying about the tombstones. Soon enough the smart student gathered an inventory of private stops from the forensic inventory. Further evidence came from outside sources including older buddies, his cousin Alex, and Billy the gas jockey at Otto's White Rose. Not to exclude Mumbles from the pool hall. All liked to brag a little or a lot, but he noted one essential recommendation besides a sofa-sized back seat: private parking.

And that meant lack of traffic, a clear line of sight on anything incoming, the ability to exit with stealth, and don't forget a blanket for passenger anonymity. Mumbles explained:

"Buddies even had flashlights. The blanket covered some hot action. We just outwaited them. And had fun *doin' it*. Cold night. They gave up. We kept warm."

Over the next four years, he and Wendy found privacy in country drives along the banks of the Thames, becoming well versed in dust and encounters of the adult kind. Fun plans and seasonal surprises at Lemonade Springs, the river forge at the Trafalgar Bridge, and the blind concession in the Zorra swamp (never mention the haunted bridge there — romantic thrill killer). Quick choices closer to Town included behind the storage shed at The Flats or over the Town line in back of the closed Blanshard #9 school. Number 9 would prove a worthy lesson in parking practice many times over for short-distance Kitten contact.

Back in Town that July Saturday, he reversed the boat-sized Ford through the vast stable doors of the former Hotel livery. Wendy watched the manoeuvre from the wide parking area in front of the livery that she called an old barn, ready to soak up the warmth of the rock garden. As he followed her he popped his pack of cigs out and lit up. God love her, Wendy allowed her man a smoke from their late high school days onward, with restrictions never ever mentioned.

Hidden from the upper back porch, they passed down the flagstone path towards armless Venus and the pea-gravel pad. Wendy scuffled a kick at the shaggy growth between the flagstone joints. He would never forget the sideways Kitten look she gave him at that moment. "Your father should spend more time on the weeding than on his cigs."

The path took them out of the great shadow of the grand Hotel into the sunlight. "Nice to get an extra drive in the V-8 out of Father, to say the least."

A Kitten wink. "Father knows best. He didn't give us enough time for the River Road drive."

"Father has a lot on his plate other than big breakfasts at the Café." A sideways look back at the rear of an aging dowager. "Look, there's a lot there. Commercial and residential rentals, the Café, property and building maintenance." His turn to wink. "And a family home. My whole life has been" — he scissor-fingers a hair buzz cut — "*headed* for here."

Her eyebrows rise over an eye roll and a crooked smile. "I get it." He remembers being gobsmacked by what she said next: "I would say the Hotel is an homogenization of home & office." She looked up at the full eaves. "Kind of an old queen, gracious but well worn. The old girl has your parents in the Café, odd rentals upstairs and downstairs, plus it's your home." He felt the bouquet of the garden rise up in a shimmer from a welcome breeze. Their eyes met. "Maybe you'll need some help on the home side." He squeezed her hand yes, yes and yes.

They stood silent before a line of phlox that pointed through the cascade of rock up to the back of the Grand Central. How could he forget that call to help that tweaked his post-teen attention? There they were, the innocent, clothed pair in the garden, garnering a partner path to paradise. Their first steps past armless Venus on the pea-gravel next to the Devil's Smoke Pit just took a large leap for young mankind. He was stuck on the colour of her lips. Flash with the lashes, she eyed him up to capture his attention. With the smack of her gum, presto, a new direction dawned on him, a silent contract.

He was head to toe in love with her, from her square heels to her cotton print dress, but something new caught his attention. The sweater, so fuzzy in salmon Angora, begged to be petted. Stop. *How many Kitten sweaters does she have?*

She touched his arm. "You take care of all things shop-wise, and the Hotel of course." She looked up and back without letting go of his hand. "That's a big job." A pause, then eyes back to earth. "I'll take care of home and garden."

Oh-oh, that's a no-no, no? The first mention of that generational responsibility, the rock garden, stopped his train of thought. Wendy seemed right away to recognize his dead look, his puffing halt over a rocky section of the Home & Office engagement arrangement.

"Easy now, I won't touch the Smoke Pit." She squeezed his hand. "And, they *are* your rocks." She paused and turned back to the rock expanse highlighted through two previous generations. "Although there sure seems to be plenty of them."

The smart and silent young lad took a break from sweater inventory. Kitten was serious. He shut his gob, eyes forward with prerequisite head nods, to gain full attention on Wendy's talking points under the watchful eyes of armless Venus. This was a trick of the trade he learned from Mike at Perth Barber School. How odd it was to meet a barbering maestro with a billiard-ball head. His students would cue up for the greatest in common-sense advice. At key moments Mike would hold his lucky silver dollar up to the class.

"Lads, the customer has the dime. The customer is paying for your time, service and attention." Mike held the shiny dollar up front until the class opened up their eyes to the big point. "So shut your gobs. The customer can't nod his head, so you nod yours." Mike's eyes bulged out

　　　　　　　　　　　　　　　　　　　　　　　　　　　　LORNE EEDY

of the hairless head. "But" — another bulging stare — "the customer can talk, so let him. *You* lads just smile big, nod a lot, and shut the fuck up."

Everyone at first was shocked by the f-bomb but soon gathered themselves up. Mike was back in what the students called man-opause, staring straight out with *that Mike look,* his insect eyes catching up to the vagrants in the back row. Mike was waiting for one thing: a class response.

When the answer came, the careful listener in downtown Theatre Town could hear the barbershop harmony ring out from the second floor. The classroom walls shook.

"Yes sir, Mike."

His other source of pertinent advice in those early years was his friend Blackie Nairn, who'd been married since his last year of high school.

"All women go to the same school, buddy," Blackie told him as he looked up from the barber's chair, "making copious copies of instructional tablets." His agitated finger jabs would lift the embroidered cape up like a tent. "They all go to the same school."

Blackie jabbed the underside of the cape again and went on. "Nor do they ever reveal their sources." He switched to falsetto — *"Call me Princess"* — and then back, raising the tent again. "Witchery, if you ask me. My friend, have you ever seen the princess's castle? You never will." The finger tent pole vibrated. "Because it's the gingerbread house in the woods. Witchery, I'm telling you, witchery!"

In the rock garden behind the old hotel on that July afternoon, The Barber puffed and listened while Wendy drew up a future picture.

"You can keep Venus, too. But" — that smile — "I will manage all the plants and flowers."

He was back off Mike's great silent cue, stuck on the profile of her loose smile and tight sweater. Armless Venus stood a silent witness to a partnership built on a solid foundation of Kitten sweaters, V-8 drives and contemplation over a few puffs.

"Weeding will be your job. Plus, you must keep your men's smoke den cleaned up." Wendy caught him off guard with another mile-wide smile. "No butts about it."

The Chair & The Mayor. That was his silent sum-up of a lucky man with concrete marital direction. She had moved heaven and earth for him, from their Genesis in the Methodist Hall Sunday School to Kitten Commander in the hotel garden. A top guide in their Exodus from a single life.

He would be just fine tethered to the barber's chair with orders from the apartment above.

Apartment #2 was combined with Apartment #3 soon after their marriage, during the ten years of no kids, when mother hen ruled the roost in ready anticipation of future family expansion.

Wendy took a full-time job at the Molson Bank next door, banking all for a house down payment. He insisted that too many family members had worked in the Hotel and there was no need for one more. Molson's offered easy outside income and marital relief. "Kitten, this way you will have your day to talk about; *your day*," he told her on the day of her interview. "And not just the trailings of chitchat from off the barbershop floor."

"Yes, you can leave the chitchat downstairs; just give me a sum-up of the sordid details."

The Home & Office schedule firmed up above the most popular barbershop in Town. Wendy moved ahead with their expanded cash flow to pull Apartments 2 and 3 into a renovation show not seen in the old hotel in over sixty years, with a decorative glow of wallpaper and paint. The flocked wall coverings and stained curtains were out the door, replaced by Oriental scenes, sheers and newfangled blinds. Kitten had vision.

"Plain curtains highlight the imported wallpaper. Inspired by *The Mikado*."

He was careful to speak up, to accent the positive in an amalgamation of former Hotel rooms. "Kitten, these apartments have more floor space than a medium-sized house."

A Kitten pause with the steady index finger up. "Dear, we are wall-to-wall neighbours here. A picket-fence boundary would be nice sometime in our lives."

"There's no bigger garden on a residential property in Town." Another Kitten pause, so The Barber continued to add value. "With the smoking area so far back, you can never ever see, smell or hear."

"Doesn't stop me knowing there's monkey business about."

"Business *is* what it's all about. The Hotel and barbershop pay for all the upgrades while *we* save up for the perfect nest." He added, in jest, "And we have what must be the biggest master bedroom in Town."

"Not to mention the biggest kitchen in Town, even bigger than the Café kitchen."

As the renovations continued, the tired porcelain toilet and pedestal sink, overused by Hotel patrons, were both replaced.

"You needed a stepladder to hop up onto that toilet," she said. "And there's more cupboard space without the useless sinks. So I thought, why not new flooring? How smart is your wife, when I make a call to Steve's Plumbing & Heating and the plumber finds cracks in a drain pipe. Just think of the potential disaster in a flood. So I thought, since you're here, Steve, replace all the plumbing."

The Barber stopped nodding and stepped up to slow the cash bleed. "Kitten, the upstairs furnace is scheduled to be replaced next year."

"Just make sure we do the replacement when the floor's up and the walls are open."

He recognized that Kitten stare. "Yes, Kitten."

Wendy brought in her brother the electrician to update the wiring and replace fixtures. Mac was on a silent tour until he stepped into the living room, stopped with a scan and turned to his sister. "How could anyone read in these rooms?"

(The Barber had spent his childhood reading in the comfort of the Hotel lobby's leather chairs under a grotesque but bright chandelier, a booth in the Café with a hot chocolate, or, weather permitting, on the back upper veranda. Peek at the newspaper funnies, sneak a cig on the porch before the eventual invitation to the Smoke Pit. Not bad alone, though, under shelter of the veranda — an easy reach for his Sailor pack stash hidden in the rafters.)

Life, ten years after in the form of two beautiful daughters, would get in the way of home moving plans. Family topped the list. Like comfortable slippers, a nappy sofa, a worn sweater, the Hotel became the land of comfy. A safe port. Money spent on a nice car and lifestyle, money saved for the girls' education and their endowment, and the picket fence can wait for retirement.

In private, Wendy would always be Kitten. Kitten would be the only person other than his mother to cut The Barber's hair. He was always amazed, happy in the privacy of it all, that not one customer ever asked him, *"So where do you get your hair cut?"*

"Honey?"

Her voice pulls him out of his reverie. "Yes, Kitten."

"Put your chin up." Wendy has the Admiral's floppy tie tight under his chin. "Be still."

"Yes Kitten."

A final tug on the floppy noose completes the Sir Joseph picture.

"Honey, quit swinging the sword around!"

"Rapier. It's my rapier, Kitten."

"Whatever you call it. Call it off, please. You'd better go, you'll be late."

Sir Joseph gives an advance preview of an Admiral prance. *"My Kitten, my fuzzy little But-But-But-Buttercup, is the one to know."* His hands are out for his one-person audience. *"On with the show."* He gives her a hug. *"Your Admiral must go. To sea, to see the dress rehearsal."*

With Admiral tap-a-taps on the door jamb and a tip of the cap, he's hands up down the long hallway to the other bedroom, waving to the girls. Tonight, twenty years after he and Wendy finished their schooling days, their daughters are just old enough to be left home alone for a couple of hours. How time flies after the children arrive. The days of bedtime stories, back rubs and secret-message kisses will soon be gone, as quick as a wave out the back door from Mom and Dad. Tonight Wendy will be back in time for a tuck-in and kisses.

"See you soon, girls," she calls as she joins him at the back door, and the brown and blue uniformed pair step out on an extraordinary night.

In the spirit of the dress rehearsal, Sir Joseph can't resist a staircase chant to his leading guide. *"I'm the Admiral of the Sea, your Lord who married thee …"*

Kitten, like Juliet above on the stairs, sings back, *"You're late, it's fate, for the rehearsal you should be. Later, later, your Little Buttercup you will see."*

"I'm off, off to play my part. Yet love remains at play in my heart."

Kitten has an encore. *"Thank goodness me, the girls have their radios on. Little ears don't hear the witty ditty bitty that's off key ..."*

At Kitten's little flare for rhyme he almost trips on the last step. It's a flashback to a fall last winter, off these very same back steps. He's been careful to keep one hand on the rail ever since. Fortunately the part he accepted three years ago is one with limited dancing. He laughs to himself. Old Sir Joseph can still prance a bit.

They say goodbye, and he's stuck in a silent wave in the dark as Wendy's away to Jones Street, hidden by the poplar trees.

He does have an extra kick in his heels tonight for a favourite musical. The walk to play practice is usually one of his few chances for a smoke off-site. But Kitten was right. He *is* late. Tonight, with Sir Joseph set to lead the *Pinafore* dress rehearsal, he's full steam ahead without any smoke.

At the top of the back alley he turns left. Tomorrow night he will turn the opposite way at this corner. Every second Thursday, the Order of the Moose gather in a secret hall above the Molson Bank.

The Barber had spent four years behind the red & nickel barbershop chair when an invitation to join the rumoured brotherhood dropped out of nowhere. The messenger was a newer customer, jeweller Robbie Andrews. The Barber couldn't believe that such a young businessman from a merchant pioneer family could be a member of the mysterious organization. The minute Robbie closed the front door, The Barber flipped the BACK IN 10 sign, racing up the back stairs to tell Wendy.

That night, at seven o'clock sharp, Robbie exited his jewellery store across Queen and gave his front door latch a secure rattle. With a bare look at the waiting Barber, Robbie gave a quick point in the direction of the bank. Robbie led the way to an unfamiliar corner, a door hidden behind the upright stanchions of the iron-clad bank facade. Normal people in normal hours, plain and simple like his Kitten, use the bank's front centre entrance. But here under the cover of dusk, he joined up with the Moose herd curled along the side alley, back from the entrance. He would stay amazed to his final days that he never noticed this clandestine biweekly column. Of course, for three generations the back door of the old Hotel was the Marshalls' primary conduit — the

Queen Street door of the Hotel is too front and centre for a watchful small town — resulting in a case of main-street blindness.

Up the creaky pine steps he followed Robbie to a small door that opened up to the heavens — or at least to the vastness of a dark blue ceiling spotted with a flurry of gilded stars. The upper front wall shone on its own with a ray-spraying sun. Underneath that sun a chair, carved like a Gothic steeple, stood upright centre stage flanked by two knobby armchairs. Any leftover stage space was filled with an assortment of flag standards; any wall space had been tacked with a Moose Lodge pennant. How many Moose Lodges were out there?

Across the vast space, a moon above the small kitchen and bar smiled back with an array of shooting comets. In between sun and stage, moon and bar, twelve well-spaced rows of stencilled arrowback chairs awaited their turn.

Grounded by the greeting line of Moose, he marvelled at the odd assortment of self-anointed brothers that gather up twice a month in the fraternal rat race. There's Freddy the dreweller jeweller and Randy Randy, AKA "R-squared," the stammering bookkeeper. (Randy Randy specializes in separated women, client confidentiality and home visits.) And watch out for the vise-grip handshake of three-fingered Herb.

After his first meeting Wendy couldn't help but ask. "Are you guys called Meese or what? That is, when the herd gathers? Is it … sorry, are they … Meese?" As the years went by and she heard more of The Barber's stories, Kitten called it: "More like a bunch of animal crackers."

Now, after fifteen years' solid attendance, he lacks the hop down the backstairs when it comes to Moose meetings every other Thursday. Even going down for his likable work behind the red & nickel barber's chair gives him more of a charge-up.

All Moose activity is herd-scripted, learned by group repetition over months. Slower members take years, and some never ever learn the secret monk-like chants.

"Larry Osborne needs a crib sheet," The Barber told Kitten early on. "And he still mumbles through it all."

Most members' first order of business on arrival is the large fridge in the kitchenette. The door opens to a vast wall of one brand: Black Label. The bottle caps flip and the beer suds flow into *Moose Lodge of*

St. Marys–stencilled glasses. Many Moose hope to wash down the two lost hours. Over the years The Barber has heard confessions from other Moose brothers during rare private moments:

"Took me five meetings to get the handshakes, the costumes, the pledges, those swearing allegiances."

"And, my God, the titles. Master Moose this, Grandmaster Moose that … Took me months to get the herd straight."

"Who's who, I kept asking. I felt like an unwise owl."

One summer's meeting, the tired drama turned into a dark comedy. It was a night to remember that he never repeated into the bevelled bar mirror. That peculiar night, he had the car for after-hours errands and, running late, drove directly to the meeting. He parked out front on Queen Street, hoping he wasn't being too obvious. The rituals, time sensitive, are set in stone. "Heaven forgive me if I miss the secret handshake from my brothers," he worried to himself as he rushed to the side entrance.

Willy Graham, an ancient Moose, noted the different parking arrangement and reserved a lift home for after the meeting.

When The Barber dropped him off after the meeting, poor Willy got himself up the stairs on his own, but little did he know it was a stairway to heaven. Mrs. Graham found Mr. Graham the next morning in his rocking chair on the porch, not rocking but maintaining a death grip on his bird's-eye maple cane. Poor Willy got lifted down the porch stairs with the help of Hall Ambulance Service.

Wendy was the only audience, other than best buddy and confidant Blackie Nairn, that heard The Barber's confession from that night.

"Caught me coming in, a deer in the headlights. Punched my ticket then and there for a lift. How was I to know? Look, I did help him out of the car, steadied him on his cane. He insisted that he did not need any further help. I can hear his voice: *Think I'll sit out a bit on the porch, enjoy the summer night's cool air.*" He shrugged his shoulders. "So that's how I left him, a tired penguin tottering up the path of destruction. I even waited for him to get up the steps." The Barber shook his head. "He made it. And off the last step in a slipper slide onto his rocking chair. I even tooted the horn so the Missus would hear the drop-off.

How was I to know she's deaf? How was I to know he would still be there in the morning?"

The *St. Marys Journal* reported the death with few details: *"William (Willy) Austin Graham died peacefully at his home on Salina Street …"*

In private The Barber told Wendy, "The headline should have been *Willy commits hari-kari from Moose boredom.*"

She feigned concern. "Dear me, don't *you* die from boredom."

The final haircut-call came from Hall father or son at the funeral home. Any hairy stuff or anything unusual and morbid was kept to himself, as always. Did the family wash the hair? Comb it? A dead customer always gets a sidecut twice over with a roll to the right and a roll to the left. The unseen backside gets minimum attention. He did tell Wendy the oddest detail from his private haircut service on the body in the basement of the Hall funeral home, conversation kept outside the barbershop:

"Hall Sr. could not get the cane to release. Not without breaking his wrist. So they broke his elbow instead to get the silver owl knob up and over his tie in a most proper position."

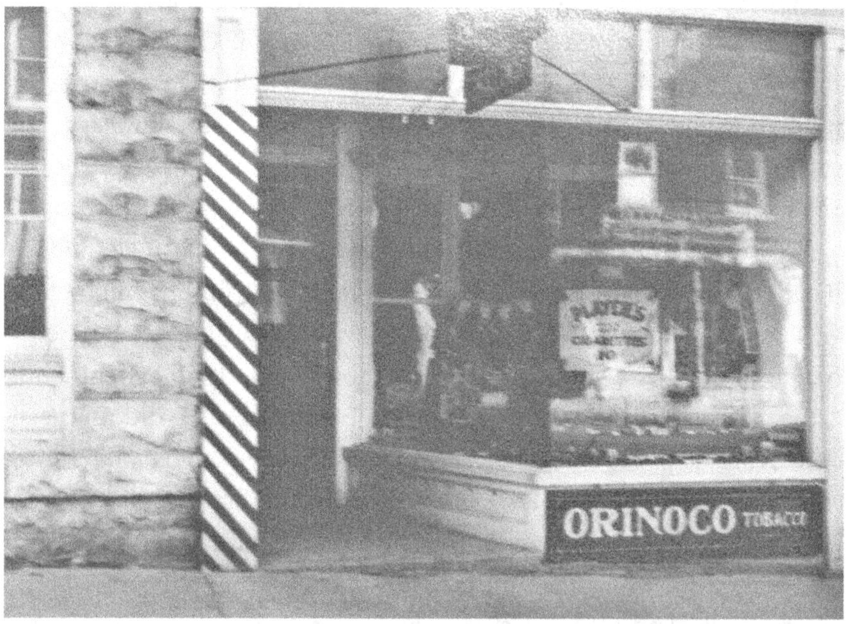

The Barbershop in the old Grand Central Hotel building, circa 1920s.

At the barbershop the stories about Willy went on and on. The Barber smiled, nodded and shut up for the most part. A great script gets greater, developing legs over a dozen years as it became known as the Rocky Mourning incident:

"His eyes were wide open."

"Covered in flies, they say."

"They say the Missus called him for breakfast, forgot, and left him to ripen up a bit in the morning sun."

"His cane, solid gold head of an owl, was buried with him."

And from his former brothers:

"Cane over his Moose tie and clip was a nice bit."

"Great Moose. Perfect attendance record."

Tonight, as The Barber climbs the incline towards Town Hall, his pace picks up with a prance in his step. "Hey Stuart …"

"Hey, if it isn't Sir Joseph."

Stuart Camp waits for him at the top of the alley at Church Street. The director of the current production, Stuart is a Community Players stalwart behind the scenes. The pair march on, The Barber's exaggerated shadow beside Stuart's short shadow facing the castle-like Town Hall under the floodlights.

"Admiral sales for all six performances," Stuart says. "Could be a sellout."

"Admiral indeed."

Town folks are ready for the rare civic show-off to brighten the darkness of the war years.

As the two march on to the Town Hall Auditorium, they're joined by some of the boys in the band. Tonight they're all in navy blue suits with an odd assortment of bowties to colour up the orchestra. The flotsam of community involvement carries on and up the back steps, with a gaggle of principals and bits, stage crew and box office, three from the chorus, and of course the real Buttercup (forget the whisper that questions her sobriety).

The crowd flow the following week will rival the greatest in Town opening nights, a date marked on the Marshall family calendar in the second floor apartment, taped to the Kelvinator refrigerator that hums.

The Charles Wolfe Cruise Archives have musty copies of the show's program. Even better, there's black-and-white cast photos digitized, and a microfiche copy of the review in the *St. Marys Journal.*

Columnist Katherine "Kit" Dell, or Kitty Litter to her lesser fans, makes special notes on Sir Joseph:

> ... a grand Admiral performance by our popular barber on Queen Street. A commanding lead of the Stonetown's best and very own homegrown talent. Sir Joseph gives a little prance too, to enhance the rambunctious dance scenes. We do remember his unfortunate fall last winter off the back stairs of the Grand Central Hotel. Well readers, slippage no more, Sir Joseph ships off on the greatest performance of G&S ever seen in these entire parts ...

Wendy posts the dislikable woman's likable review on the refrigerator, taped over the month's crowded schedule.

"That woman can sure shoot the Kitty Litter."

Chapter 6

Big Rocks

1952

I launched a smile; far out it sailed,
On Life's wide troubled sea,
And many more than I could count
Came sailing back to me.

> — Charles Wolfe Cruise, *Rambles in the Southlands*
> Charles Wolfe Cruise Archives, Stonetown Museum
> (copies for sale, see Museum Larry)

Marvin the cattle farmer tips the scales at four hundred pounds, half a year-old Black Angus Heifer. Picture him not on two legs but on two grand gateposts, a mass movement of humanity that frightens both the two-legged and the four-legged. Fifty years later, Marv would be a centre with the Argos, backed with large acreage and automated farm duty. In 1953, he's on his own to raise pure Angus beef fifty years before the term organic.

Marv practises the first half of the slogan on his childhood cap, which stated ALL WORK AND NO PLAY MAKE JACK A DULL BOY.

Marv is the third generation of a pioneer family on their Blanshard Township homestead. His father shipped off gallon cans of beef to the boys in the Great War. The general brass knows that survival at war requires full stomachs, which means the home front sells a lot of tin. Twenty-five years later Marv filled the gallon-capacity niche for Canadian Navy kitchens in World War II. Marv joked to Al, his farm-hand, "Who would've thunk it? My beef galleons sailing the seas."

Since the war Marv has built up the family farm on the bottom line of the 9th Concession into a jackpot in the beef business with a state-of-the-art canning operation in London. Someone he calls "the dude" runs the factory and fills the beef orders. Back on the farm, Marv plies, pries, plucks and picks, roaming his acres like Jason with his Argonauts.

A smart crow watching from a high perch would see Marvin using methods that he learned at the most advanced school for the farm industry, Ontario Agricultural College in the Royal City. His college training as an Aggie cuts down his breeding and veterinary costs.

School was the only time in Marv's life that he was apart from home. In a marvel of lost opportunities, he never played football. His destiny was not on the sports field — or in the medical field, although he keeps his elbow-length rubber gloves handy hung on a stanchion.

His mother did not survive his baby sister's birth. His father never saw his graduation. In the latter case, Al found Marv's old man asleep beside an uncovered well, gripping a crowbar. The hired hand approached with caution when his boss did not respond to frantic calls. Al called upon all his gumption to shake his arm, which did nothing but loosen his grip on the tool. The bar dropped, and Al ran for the phone. Doctor Lane speculated a bubble of gas had been trapped under the well's cover.

Al relayed the message to the son over the phone. "Marvin, your father did not suffer. The doctor says he would have found himself sleepy, and lied down."

The son came home to bury his surviving parent, and stayed. His modern methodology returned home too, joined by the sweat of Al the underappreciated farmhand.

Marvin can laugh at himself in his perfect small world. He has never climbed on a train, other than off to college in fall and spring for four years. The man would never fit into one of those newfangled planes, let alone agree to fly in one. Charles Wolfe Cruise's descriptions in the *St. Marys Journal* are enough high adventure for him. It goes without saying that Marv would never climb a mountain or swim in the Great Lakes. His perfect world brings homebody comfort. It's a Zen that spreads through his persona, starting with his own lavender honey on fresh, buttered bread side by side with a French-pressed coffee.

And don't forget the easy-as-1, 2, 3 work list.

Each day starts in Big Boss contemplation at the possibility of a lucky rock extraction. He works the list he pencilled down the night before. Somewhere, somehow, he will find the perfect rock: while digging fence posts, poking at foundation work, shovelling a new manure pond or dredging out the old one, or clearing up the extra paddock along the boundary line at Science Creek. The sweat and contemplation feeds the need for something-for-nothing, keeping the thought of a lucky rock at the forefront.

Marvin is able to move Al like a pawn on the plodding plot of his board game. Al works the list, wary of the Big Boss's endless numbered directions. Al tells his wife that the search makes for extra work and unwelcome sweat. Deep down, though, he recognizes the draw of the haircut-for-nothing in St. Marys. It's just that he would rather stay home on the range and use his wages to buy a more comfortable couch than make a wager over a haircut.

With his marketing approach The Barber has hit an awareness home run. Citizens partaking of neither wager nor haircut still chitchat about the storyline over a beer at the Moose Lodge, under cover with the Masons, over the fence between members of the Catholic Ladies League, even at meetings of the Daughters of the Thames, the McConnell Club or the Women's Institute. Most may never cross the threshold of the narrow barbershop. Yet every second person, from Marvin and his neighbours in Blanshard to Nissouri and London Townships, is aware in some form of a wild wager for a free haircut.

> *"A free haircut? What's the big deal?"*
> *"Are you a betting person?"*
> *"No. Devil's work. But my husband gets his hair cut there."*
> *"Is he a gambling man?"*
> *"Paul? Never."*
> *"Has Paul mentioned the wager?"*
> *"He does talk a lot about those rocks."*

Even a fool like Bobbie Binks Sr. knows about the wager. Anybody who's poking around the farm or garden is bound to think about rocks, especially in the vicinity of a place nicknamed the Stonetown.

Al thinks the silly quest has dulled Marv's mind. Most of the rocks they dig up doing all that extra work on the list end up on the reject pile behind the barn. Whenever tractor and wagon appear on the work list, Al knows he's in for a long day.

Marvin does not whistle while he works, and neither does he talk. He works the list to the final checkmark.

Late each afternoon after Al goes home, Marv approaches the Georgian rose-brick farmhouse and pushes open the wide screen door. An odd twist, the swinging door opening *into* the expansive dining room and kitchen rather than out. Before he's finished adjusting to the lack of light in the room, Goldie the Lab shoves her snout into his crotch. The house makes an odd but prestigious statement in pink brick where red is more common and fieldstone is in abundance.

He settles his giant back against a wooden chair at the kitchen table for the prepared meal out of the oven, always complemented by a large glass of iced tea.

Later he enjoys a small cigar and the glow of the sunset on his western vantage. From his corner perch on the twill sofa armchair with wood beading, his domain spreads out before him. Goldie the Lab lies on the porch near him, her ears piqued for any possibility of a head scratch. She soaks up the sweet smell of the smoky man's den. Evening in and evening out, Marv doubles up on the big, old comfy chair, a smoking-man statue in recline. He strikes a contemplative pose with his narrow-gauge licorice-dipped cigar in one hand matched by a glass of chocolatey port in the other. The closed porch keeps the winter shakes away with the help of a horse blanket and the Good Cheer potbellied stove in the corner. In a blind blizzard he sometimes skips the porch for a knee-deep walk to the closest stable for more wind shelter but less warmth. An odd combination of cow shit and a crappy cigar. In the heaviest weather he leaves the Taylor port in the kitchen; the cigar, though, never misses its role in the routine even when it's just bottom-drawer stuff from the teak humidor.

He sources the cheap smokes in Town at Dick's Groceteria. The imported luxury brands come through his cousin in the city. A parcel is sent by train for a handy pickup, prearranged on schedule — one carton of Grey Owls each month. Kipp Dobson arranges for the livery pickup of the box in thick wax paper, safe and ready to be transferred to his second-floor corner office, waiting for Marv to show up in his shark-grille Mercury.

Marv's head never hits the puffy down pillow before he's drafted and reviewed the list of the minion activities for Al's next workday. Goldie listens to her best friend with tongue out and smile on.

"I know with a little poking there's a winner. Goldie, just think — I have a rock haven with thousands of potential prizes." He gives her a heads-up scratch. "Pretty girl, there must be two thousand of them." (Head scuffle-scuffle.) "There's a lifetime of digging here."

In his mind's eye Marv hits paydirt, the potential rock count turning into a golden harvest. Goldie's heads-up to a rich vein of head scratches. Big Boss has a smile on and his tongue out for a taste of the port. "Hey girl, I bet it's more like twenty thousand than two thousand!"

The neighbours share opinions.

"Marv should have a dog."

"What size of dog would complement that giant? Needs to be a Great Dane."

"Marv has Al for his mutt. Bow-wow, Al."

All are blind to the comfortable porch pals who each night share sweet cigar aromas, a taste of port and a great head scratch.

A perfect start to every morning demands a *chef du jour*. Hedy, his Dutch neighbour, is his all-round Mrs. Service. She arrives at six bells in the morning with fresh butter from her Jersey cows. Hedy keeps the pink house Dutch Maid clean, and Big Boss likes it that way. He's up at the whistle of the kettle. She brings the dough for daily bread and the fixings for one cooked meal. Lunchtime generally falls somewhere between #3 and #6 on the work list, the menu consisting of leftovers on bread, bagged in the Igloo cooler with ice for a long afternoon in the back forty.

Every day from the crack of dawn to mid-afternoon, Hedy juggles away at cleaning, laundry and meal preparation. If the fridge is empty at lunchtime, hard-boiled eggs come to the rescue. That night's prepared dinner joins the large pitcher and gallon thermos of iced tea in the fridge. All Al has to do is pull it out and put it in the oven. Big Boss never asks how or what. He eats dinner and cleans up alone, and then all paths lead to southern comfort on the veranda. Hedy never sees the evening version of the man.

Marv's small world calls for a big mention of his love of the coffee bean. A cup of java, accompanied by Hedy's fresh toast slathered with her Jersey-milk butter and his lavender honey, starts up the morning on the right track. The duet of Marv and the bean is a first anywhere in the region. No one, not The Barber and not even the small community of Italians on and around Wellington Street, has heard of someone using a French press.

The press is a very special order recommended by his city cousin. Strange coincidence that it would come from Eaton's, a store established by a former St. Marys pioneer farming and merchant family. From a Blanshard plot the Eatons moved up the 9th Concession to Town in order to become bartering storekeepers. Soon tired of the barter, they loaded up and wheeled off for big-city cash, building a cross-country merchant empire. Two years ago the full-colour Eaton's catalogue had a Red Ryder sleigh, one-piece pyjamas, German dolls — and on page 57, lower right-hand corner, next to a starburst containing the word NEW, a tall handcrafted glass carafe with shiny trim, handle and lid in black and silver. A caffeine miracle maker in a strange and unfamiliar form. Of course, Marv would normally never look to any catalogue when The Feed Store keeps overalls in size XXXL on the shelf — nor would he ever imagine an import all the way from Marseilles — but his only cousin insisted that he turn that page.

Ever after, it's only Marv who pours the steaming water into the carafe. Mrs. Service never, ever gets to touch the glass-and-silver foreign contraption. Marv controls the entire mechanical process, from grinding and measuring to pressing and pouring. Hedy is left on the boiling brigade and the cleanup detail, never forgetting to restore all equipment to its place.

The night's porch contemplation creates the list that organizes everyone's day, human and animal. In the morning, coffee starts the engines. The aromatics! The taste that approaches bean heaven!

Hedy gets the third cup. Even if it consists of nothing but the runoff,

Hedy would never refuse her one-cup offer from Marvin. "A perfect pressed java," Mrs. Service confesses at home to husband Joe, who follows up with a tender squeeze.

Hedy thinks Marv doesn't appreciate her enough or pay her enough, not to mention that he doesn't share his honey. Marv rations his personal sideline even more strictly than he does the coffee. "Does he not realize I make the butter and the bread dough that I bring him every day?" she complains. "And my great berry preserves too. He can sure lather on that honey. Is he using it as a lubricant for his throat?"

Besides her other duties, Mrs. Service is also the Big Boss's morning listener. Marv's frequent monologues provide the background noise for sandwich fixing, mop duty, keeping up with laundry when you can only fit two pair of XXXL overalls per load, and making Ty Cobb swings for spiders and other crawlers with that goose-feather duster. (*"Hedy! Careful with Grandmother's carnival glass."*)

The one topic she dreads is last night's porch list. As she confesses to Joe: "My God, the man always has his list in his hand. He makes it into a speech. I feel like screaming it out: *It's just a job list.* Then there's the problem of something-for-nothing. Joe, the rocks change but the strategy does not. Over and over again …"

Mrs. Service finishes the breakfast cleanup, masquerading as a silent confidant in this stupid competition. All she can see is wasted time between her boss and that chain-smoking, gossipy barber in Town.

Best not to interrupt Big Boss, so she nods her head. Every four or five sentences she makes sure to add the occasional "yes." Yes, the rocks and yes, the stupid free haircut. Yes, they make her want to scream.

"Big Boss," she tries to tell him, "you could build your own rock garden. Be the envy of all gardeners with your fine stones. Your rock garden with your own handpicked rocks from your farm."

Hedy's little one-sided lectures to the boss almost never result in real debate. Most times Hedy remains silent on the coffee parade until Marv heads out the door with his list. Today, though, something's different in the morning air. Big Boss has set down the list while he savours the flavour of a new selection of bean. A rare opportunity for Hedy to direct the discourse, to take the stage as this morning's speaker.

Hedy waits for Big Boss's coffee cup to drop to the harvest table.

"You just give them away. And to that barber! All his best rocks are your rocks! Who cares about a free haircut? Once or twice a year, Boss, that's it. All that time spent on rocks that could be seen every day in *your* garden."

Marvin tunes out at the mention of free. She reaches deeper. "You could be smoking in *your* rock garden at *your* convenience."

Despite Hedy's enthusiasm, Marv soon concludes his business in the kitchen with a brush of the teeth, and caffeine carries him off to chores with an enthusiastic step. Hedy watches through the door as he follows his usual trail out to the barn.

"That Boss, his big head is going to blow its top off. All the thinking that man does." Hedy looks down at Goldie, weaving her fingers through the dog's wiry blond hair. "Goldie, there's steam coming out of his head! Big Boss spends too much time fixated on a silly free haircut. He should concentrate on the gossip. That way we could enjoy a different monologue." She closes the screen door. "Sure needs a haircut, though."

In the field, Al loads up the wagon. "Big Boss, I thought we worked that back paddock last spring?"

"Number three on today's list, Al." No need to look: the job is on the list, as clear as 1, 2, 3. "There's no need for drainage on the south side. A little levelling would do."

Translation by Al? Dig, dig, dig. "Boss, we need to move the manure pile again."

"Number four, Al. We'll leave that for last in the day. No sense smelling like shit all day."

Citizens who lived through the Depression are careful with coin but ready for some local fun. Marvin never gambles in the sense of card games with neighbours, spinning the wheel at the Moose tent at the fair, betting on the ponies, or those unfair slot machines. But he is fixated on the art of the deal. Deals are without borders, whether it's the Mediterranean naval campaign or a free haircut in Town offered by the Innkeeper's son.

Furrowing, forking and slopping give Marv ample time to meditate on strategy. In Town, The Barber sits back to watch the parade of stone stop at his front entrance. Few pass the threshold before a well-seasoned judge and jury. Boulders, rocks of spectacular size, are the entrance ticket for Marv. Each picky poke, levered pry and heavy shovel on the farm chore list may fill an order for a rock of ages. Contemplation turns to anticipation.

The concept of free jacks up the challenge like magic. The search has everything to do with farming, and nothing to do with it. The hunt moves the routine along.

Today, it's been thirty days since Marv's last haircut. Even Al notices the thickened hedge of ear-hair sprouts.

"Boss, do you think The Barber is giving any free haircuts this week?"

For Al, a surprise Boss trip to Town means extra unsupervised time on the farm. The rock quest pushes Al from anticipation toward anxiety. Will he go or will he stay?

Marv focuses on the rocks, but he also ruminates on the competition. What has that barber been offered? Who got the haircut? For a non-imbibing (albeit a thimble of port helps the digestion) dateless white-haired man with a loyal dog and a three-party phone line. In Blanshard Township, your news comes via the *Journal* once a week. When you can only get one fuzzy television channel, a dumb rock wager is as smart as rural life gets.

Today's work list starts off with a dig in the back rough for fence posts. On the fifth hole they hear *clink, clink*. Eyes are down.

"Slow up Al, let's have a look-see." The huge man leans in, out from his mushroom-cloud shadow, for a big peer into the hole. Big Boss uses his XXXL shovel to balance his contemplative look-see. Some days he uses the idle handle as a microphone and podium to impart Marvellous knowledge. "See that pointy thing? It's attached to something larger. Kinda round like."

Al knows enough about his part in the routine to drop the auger and grab the iron pry-bar. "Well, lookee there Boss, the top has ears." Down on his knees, Al plays up the find. "Attached to a round ... head? Whoa. There's more rock too ... like a body below." He's back up on his feet. "Your shovel, Boss?"

Marv is taken a bit off balance by the ask for his personal XXXL shovel. Al would rather not go all the way back to the wagon for the second shovel when he's already lugged both the post-hole auger and the pry-bar while Big Boss idles away with a free shovel. Marv reaches the handle down to Al's chest, his eyes on the hole. "Don't chip it."

"Boss, it's granite. No sense worrying about chipping solid rock."

Marv ignores Al. The hired hand ignores his boss. Al, quick to the task, has already dug a small moat low around the body of the rock.

"Al, sure looks like a dog to me."

Boss still has lots of time for a run to Town. Al sees an opportunity for an easy afternoon. "I'll get a leash from the truck." Marv stares at the hired hand. "I mean … a rope, and we'll yank him out."

Marv is in full contemplation, still under the effects of caffeine. The eternal optimist stares at the hole opening, imagining the prospects of a potential winner. Standing by the wagon with his back to him, Al can't see him lick his lips and break into a smile of anticipation.

The smart hand returns with a wide plank, which he wedges along the body to allow an easy up and out. Al ties a harness around the lower body and upper neck of the dog-shaped rock.

Big Boss quickly counts to three. Al hasn't even established a grip when Marv grabs the leash, er, the rope, with his XXXL gloves and begins pulling with his full weight.

Al has attended the travelling circus on The Flats in Town, so he knows an amazing act when he sees one. Big Boss can one-hand a rock that Al can't even lift, and with two hands Boss can singlehandedly heft an actual boulder up onto the wagon. Al sometimes dreams about a circus tent where Big Boss tosses his rocks in a feat of strength.

The harness slides over the rim of the hole and the rock plops onto the ground. Big Boss calls it: "I'm gonna name you Scottie."

Al can't help but be confident when his boss changes the designation from "it" to "you" in reference to an inanimate object. His prospects for an easy afternoon keep improving.

Big Boss touches the dog's head. "Little Scottie, we'll get you washed up. Little Scottie and Marv are heading to town."

"Looks like a winner to me, Boss. I'll load it up." He hands the shovel back. "Sorry, let me load *you* up …. Little Scottie." Al beams down as he cradles the mid-sized dog. "And get you washed up, all purdy like, before heading to town."

Marv stretches with an enormous crack before heading toward home. "I will meet you at the farmhouse."

Al knows what this means. Al will clean the rock — sorry, Little Scottie — while Big Boss cleans himself up and enjoys one last coffee.

Big Boss got a free haircut for best of show with Little Scottie.

After all, don't be fooled by all this planning and wagering — after thirty days, Marv needs a haircut, and Al and Hedy agree. Although disguised in a Blanshard Township sort of way in those XXXL pinstriped overalls, the big man appreciates a certain farmer-gentleman look when going to Town. Above the pants bib and the pressed-collared shirt shine a nice set of teeth and slicked-back hair under his burnt orange ROGER DOES IT! baseball cap. Under the brim, a swarthy complexion is interrupted by a sparse field of snow white facial hair with a top rim of eyebrow rooster combs. That hedgerow of ear-hair sprouts gets close attention by the only source of female direction in his life since his mother passed in '38.

And just like Ma did, Hedy keeps an eye out the window. From her kitchen perch, she can see him walking back, his profile small beside the massive barn. Her first thought is that it's too soon to break for the day. "Is his lunch bag already consumed?"

Goldie has ears up at the voice of the human who feeds her. Hedy checks her sturdy Bulova watch. "It's just forty-five minutes into the afternoon. Goldie girl, do you think Big Boss has found something?"

She switches to automatic mode, putting the kettle back on the newfangled propane stove before her boss swings the backwards screen and makes his first step into the kitchen. With the coffee press and necessary accoutrements all washed and arranged on their tray along with the breakfast dishes, she turns from the stove to head him off at the dining table.

"So, Big Boss looks in a hurry. Are we going to Town?"

"Yes, Hedy, off to Town we go. Little Scottie and me."

She looks over his shoulder to the screen door. "Who's … Little Scottie?"

He looks down at the tray then over her shoulder to the steaming kettle. "I need a coffee first."

For the past two weeks Mrs. Service has been drafted for occasional minor head touch-ups. So today she's ahead of the game with Big Boss during their coffee intermission. As he pours she puts her spin on The Barber's services. "That scruffy stuff around the edges gives you a pencil-neck high school science teacher look." Patience is thin from the big man while Hedy holds up the hand mirror for a look-see around his statue-sized head. "Get your barber buddy up to speed here." She flashes the mirror while the other hand mocks a feather-dust around his neck and ears. "You are all the way in Town for a proper haircut, so cut the chatter down. Tell him to do his job!"

Marv beams into the distance at the prospect of his big prizewinner fresh out of a fencepost hole. Hedy sees that look, the true meaning of going to Town. "Ah," she says. "This is what Scottie is about — it's a rock. Remember, my grandfather warned us that free anything might be worth nothing."

Marv nods his head to the beat of *How many times can she repeat this piece of wisdom?* He has faded back into the mission at hand: Town. Marv finishes his second cup than checks his watch. Al should have Little Scottie all cleaned up by now.

Hedy puts the kettle on again, then digs deep to get his attention back. "Big Boss, do the Skinny for me."

The Twist and the Mashed Potato have yet to be invented, but we do have the Skinny in Blanshard Township. The Skinny stands for straight back, tucked tummy and head up, for the proper step out, walking with one foot in front of the other. As Hedy sometimes tells him, "The Skinny condenses and firms up the body beef." Hedy learned this not from a book but from an *Amos 'n' Andy* radio episode. She only repeats what lean Andy tries to tell overweight Amos.

Marv stands up for Hedy without protest. He savours his bean.

"Let's have a look-see, Big Boss." Hedy gives him a final, full Mrs. Service checkup without the hand mirror, and Marv sucks up the female attention. "Shoulder back, chest out, gut in … suck it in, Boss."

He doesn't see her kindly eye roll, her lips silently running as she examines the neck fluff and the wheat hedge crests on his ears. Her talk finishes on the walk. "Your movement and your stature speak, telling folks a lot about you. So let's walk tall and proud like a Big Boss should."

"Hey coach, the kettle is singing."

Boss in a rush moves Hedy up the grid of importance: he pours Mrs. Service a cup at the same time as his own. Hedy savours her second cup of the day without question, knowing there must be a very special rock in the picture.

Marv savours a big win right to the last sip. As he heads for the exit, Hedy puts away his special coffee tray in record time. From the screen door she watches his departure with a send-off in two words. "The Skinny!"

Marv marches straight on out to the pickup where Little Scottie is all set and dry, sideways on the passenger seat.

Hedy stands on the side porch with Goldie behind her, all eyes on the dust plume that floats down the concession. She shakes her head at the dog. "I never did finish talking with Big Boss about that silly wager. Little Scottie — is that what he called it? Maybe I'll catch Al having a smoke behind the shed. Goldie, walk?"

Big Boss rolls into Town full steam ahead, forcing his advantage of surprise. He pushes from third gear up to second on his three-on-the-tree shifter. His Mercury "Shark Tooth" V-8 makes the first downtown stoplight on green. Clutch in, he drops into neutral for silent running through the second light. He zeroes in on a parking space for front-door arrival at the barbershop. Quality wager loaded, he slides little Scottie out from the passenger side in a cradle-hold across the sidewalk.

Marv feels it in his bones, a winner. Little Scottie will make it through the barbershop to the back door and be unleashed forever in the rock garden. Marv will end the afternoon in the Devil's Smoke Pit. Home on the farm before the Skinny he added two extra Grey Owls for any post-game celebration. Markers of confidence in two stencilled tin tubes stay concealed in the inside pocket of his XXXL pinstriped bib. Marv can taste the invitation. He savours a win and a smoke.

Marv's ability for mass movements has challenged The Barber's court of rock approval for a full score and ten years. His selection of oversized animals and mushrooms is a marvel on all tours of the rock garden and Devil's Smoke Pit.

Rule #3, AKA The Big Boss Rule, which allows Marv to drop his heavies out back, is off the table for the moderate-sized Scottie. Today's approach won't be the usual giant lift off the tailgate; Little Scottie will be chauffeured up front like the special winner that he is.

The Barber's first rule insists on a two-hand lift off the front side-walk before the rock crosses the threshold. No sliding assists, pry-bar leverage, extra hands or machine help (most farms have a front-end loader). The Barber acts as witness from his strategic position, keeping one eye on the reflection of the haircut in progress, the other on any movement on the street front. At the first sign of the waddling walk-up of a heavy delivery or even a pickup truck approaching the curb, he scampers to block the door frame. The watchful eye knows that to deliver big rocks onto the sidewalk requires a pickup or station wagon.

Marv has heard this part in The Barber's whiny song and dance over and over. "No point making my barbershop a gravel pit!"

Today The Barber stands, with seconds to spare, full witness in the doorway. It's a solid stance because yes, he's confident at home in his own court. According to Rule #4, for Marv's candidate to be successful, it must pass a quick review, the final step of approval that leads to the back door.

The Barber is judge and jury, present and future, but Marvin has a history of challenges, including the one that led to Rule #3. "Why should the barbershop drop point be outside if it's a winner?" he asked. "Recognize that size does matter. Let it go straight to the back garden. Do you really want my big'ns dragged across your parquet floor?"

After a Mexican standoff in early history over rule interpretation, one Marv boulder with off-the-scale size sat for six months in the front corner of the shop. That cornered bad rock was the impetus for Rule #2, which states in no uncertain terms: *Good rock or bad rock, The Barber never lifts.* The Judge had the cornered suspect relieved of duty without Marv's knowledge by Corey Carter, the behemoth who anchors the Zorra Highland Tug-of-War Team, in exchange for a free haircut.

It's clear this is no ordinary afternoon when Marvin, a well-known champion of the heavy weights, steps out with Little Scottie. First advantage goes to The Barber, who moves for control, blocking the threshold. "Where you going with that puppy?"

"Puppy? This is Little Scottie, best in show. Can't you recognize a winner? Great day for my free haircut."

As the hulk framing the full doorway squeezes right, the Barber holds his left hand on the door jamb. "Looks like a mutt to me."

"Looks like your butt's on the line. Call it whatever you want, little buddy." He looks down at Little Scottie cradled in his massive arms. "I'd call you Winner, but I'm good with Little Scottie." He stares at The

Barber. "And better with my free haircut." Although they are long-time friends, their shifting-about pushes the limits of Queensberry match etiquette. "A *blind* barber would see that this is a diamond I'm bringing you here."

The Barber backs up on the parquet floor, keeping his left hand pointed in the direction of the red & nickel chair. "Bet's on, Big Boss, because I still see a mutt."

"Put your specs on, blind man." Marv stops for another look down into his arms. "Careful now, Little Scottie has feelings."

Big Boss stops to inhale the mix of cheap cologne, rubbing alcohol and customer sweat hanging in the air of the converted carriageway. The Barber's eyes widen as Little Scottie is parked upright on a white parquet square.

"Sit, Little Scottie, sit. You're one purdy unique rock." Marv pats the stone head, then lets loose on his side of dog-gone brinkmanship. "Little buddy, I don't care if you call it Snowy the Terrier or White Fang the Husky. You can call it Rin Tin Tin for all I care. It's best-in-show, little buddy."

The barber chair strains under Marv. The embroidered cape stretches like cellophane. The mutt's passed over the threshold, so the bet's on. Evidence sits before the barbershop court, where judge and jury will determine whether the unusual suspect is fit for garden duty. Game's not over till the game's over to The Barber.

"This puppy won't make the grade in my backyard. Out with Spot! Bad dog, go home."

"Good dog, my Little Scottie. Best in show."

The mimic shakes a finger towards the bevelled mirror. "Bad dog! Bad dog, go home."

Marv knows half the rock battle hinges on getting over the threshold, so all is good with his Little Scottie sitting upright beside him. The Barber's perspective is less about giving out a free haircut than it is about the space behind the old Hotel. He already has a rock field popu-lated with dogs, fish, pigs, Xs and Os, a shark fin or two, warty peepers, face mask creepers and blooming big toadstools — not to mention the small rock penis he hides for a laugh in the back of the maple bar cabinet.

The Barber will never grasp the depth of his current chair competition. He assumes Marvin's the busy farmer, busy doing something or other, whatever farmers do. Marvin doesn't bring up the topic of agriculture, unless it's Al or maybe the price of beef. While in strict confidence he might explain the superiority of Massey Harris but how he does try to buy local in Roger equipment. He'll join any farmers' chorus around a mention of weather or how hard they have it.

The barbershop mimic walks a tightrope in meting out justice. His gut tells him when to tip the scales on the rules in favour of his big customers, and the biggest one now sits tight in the chair. The Barber needs two hands to unwrap the cape with the embroidered logo from the mammoth chair occupant. He shakes the cape aside. "Time for a smoke in the Devil's Pit?"

Big Boss and a select list of other compatriots all agree that smoking conversation featuring hand-rolled cigars is the most civil of inactive enterprises. Marvin performs a sleight of hand, the two tubes clinking. "Well, I did bring a pair of Grey Owls."

"I love that licorice taste."

Moments later the pair of friends, the pair of cigars, and a cradled Little Scottie are out the back door.

"Wine-dipped this time, little buddy. For me, nothing beats the taste of a free haircut."

"Blowing a little smoke up my butt, Marv?"

Marvin gears down. "My mutt smokes, little buddy." He nods towards Little Scottie, who now sits next to Venus. "Best in show, aren't you, Little Scottie?" He turns back. "I'd rather smoke it than smell it. Your ass and those bird-dip, barn-slop rules can't beat best-in-show. Eh?"

Little buddy steps back in contemplation at a rare rash moment best countered with silence. Marv, he notes, is smiling, so after two extra-long puffs The Barber adopts a lighter tone.

"Never had these before. I can taste the wine, too. Real nice."

Marv never mentions that one cigar tin costs more than two haircuts. Heady stuff for two aging gentlemen who lived at different ages through the Depression. The Barber's father was a known character who served him fries and a cherry Coke in the old Hotel Café. Smoking in back of the barbershop today is a living testament that all generational ties weave a natural web through the folks of a small town. Life is marv-ellous.

More than thirty years ago, not long after The Barber graduated, he and his father completed the transformation of the carriageway into a barbershop. The centre of attention was the state-of-the-art padded red leather & nickel-plated barber's chair, right off the train from St. Louis and dropped off by Kipp Dobson, Jr. The same day, the maple bar furniture came over from the Hotel lobby. (Right away the seventeen-foot bevelled bar mirror looked like it had always been here.) The big move necessitated help from Kipp and his right-hand man Doug Eager. Out of nowhere came Marvin with a cavalry rescue, a huge shadow that filled the doorway.

"I was just driving by," Marv told The Barber years later, "thinking about a coffee at the Café. Then I see yous skinny little guys. I ask myself, are they dancing on the sidewalk? They seem to be a hapless dance chorus. Downtown comedy?"

"That chair was nine hundred bucks in 1922. That was almost as much as Dad's V-8. The advice he gave me was, make your customer most comfortable with your top ass-et."

Puff. Puff.

The Barber laughs to himself now, face to face with the big man, as he remembers that his first impression was the backside of Marv. Those pinstriped overalls sure covered a lot of ass. He takes a deep breath as he surveys the full breadth of the rock garden. Customers and friends alike agree: *My God, it's competition for Stonehenge.*

Something obvious to the in-the-know smoker is that so many of the best specimens in the marvellous landscape lineup were dropped in their place by one special man. (*"There has to be eight humungous Marv boulders in sight right now."*)

So many of the best rocks for sitting on are Big Boss ones, too. The Barber looks down at his current stone seat, a special drop of a limestone block, a wonder. He glances up at Marv. "This one didn't win a haircut, but the seashell fossils are incredible."

Marv nods. "Sort of a crab creature frozen in there. It should be in a museum."

The stubble-faced behemoth rolls his cigar, exhaling an atomic mushroom cloud that rises and floats past Little Scottie and armless Venus. It would ascend to the great beyond, were it not blocked by the Baptist Church next door. "The magic of free." He cracks his waist-sized neck to the left. "Kinda gets your adrenaline going, right?"

"Big Boss, you *are* looking kind of ... skinny." The Barber's remark is just good-natured humour between buddies. He knows little about Hedy's town tune-up. Nor does he listen to radio's *Amos 'n' Andy; The Shadow* is more to his taste.

But Marv is sensitive today on the skinny of it all. He free-falls through an awkward pause on his little buddy's use of the word skinny. Who's been talking about the Skinny, he wonders? Al? Nope, the wife cuts the hair. Hedy? Nope. Hedy's husband? *Now where does Joe get his hair cut ...?*

The Barber watches the silent nods of a huge man in a flux of thought and presses the sensitive pause button. "Skinny looks good," he says.

Neither the *St. Marys Journal* on microfiche nor the deerskin diary in the museum's archive ever pull the curtain back on anything about a barbershop rock competition. The skinny on Marv and The Barber's particular relationship is summed up in the volume of wins; who can fathom the hundreds of losses? The Big Boss wins a record fifteen free haircuts — or more? — over thirty years. Fourteen goliath rocks, monumental winners, stand witness beside number fifteen, Little Scottie, who never moved from Venus's armless side.

One morning soon after number fifteen found its place beside Venus, Hedy finds Big Boss in a perfect evening pose dead on the porch. The tilted port glass is still in hand, the Grey Owl cigar a dark shadow of ash. Goldie sits quiet and patient at his feet. One paw on a slipper, the Lab has sad eyes up for her best friend.

The practical woman sums it up. "Thank God, Big Boss, you didn't burn the house down." She stares at him *in situ*. "No fresh bread with Jersey butter and lavender honey for you, Big Boss. First, Goldie, I will call the good Doctor Lane."

After making the phone call, Hedy returns to the porch and rubs the farm dog's head. "Well, Goldie girl, doesn't stop us from having some breakfast, does it? We's will have to wait for the doctor, so no sense getting our stomachs in a knot. Everything's in place, so let's not be of waste."

Goldie hears the high hiss of the kettle before any whistle. She knows the smell of the toaster and waits for the pop. Hedy, on cue, has one piece chopped in the dog's metal bowl topped with last night's beef chili. She sits down and spreads jam on her toast. The coffee is pressed and poured while Goldie licks the bowl right down to her reflection. "My God, Goldie. Did yous even taste it?"

Hedy resets the kitchen in time for the burgundy Ford convertible that turns into the driveway ahead of a major dust plume which drifts off to greener pastures. Hedy welcomes the doctor with considerable pomp because of the circumstances, able for the first time to offer a special visitor an imported pressed coffee and some of her baked bread. She leads him through the screen door right to the kitchen table. The doctor finds it slightly odd to ignore the elephant in the room — Marv in a permanent comfort position on the sofa chair — in favour of a hand-pressed cuppa.

"Have a fresh coffee first," she says. "Marv ain't goin' nowheres. I'll tell you about my morning."

Doctor Lane's lips have just touched the warm rim of the coffee cup when Hedy lets it roll in a blow-by-blow. "Topsy-turvy like, his evening routine, butt frozen thar this very morning." She points back to the screen door. "Cigar, all but ashes. His port glass tipped, but still on hold. Same silent spot for poor Goldie." She fades on replay. "Out thar, butt a-frozen stiff in the sofa chair.

"As I'm walking to work I says to myself, *Where's my Goldie-girl greeting this morning?*" She doesn't mention the cold-nosed crotch-sniff and the hot, wet lick. Goldie raises her head now at the mention of her name, her tongue dangling low in the middle of her golden Lab smile. Hedy reaches down to her. "My Goldie-girl knows the hand that feeds her. I asked myself why no Goldie. So I's whistles. Nothing. So I's whistled again."

Doctor Lane is silent.

"Nothing. So I's called her name. *Goldie. Goldie.* " Hedy mimes the dog's name through cupped hands, peering over her special guest's shoulders. "I could see his big white stubbled chin kind of stuck up in the air. But so weird, Doctor Lane, I sees no Goldie."

In his golden age, the good doctor has learned there's no rush in a coroner's life — take a seat when offered, and never refuse a moment to share some homemade treats. Girth has joined age in compromising his approach. Doctor Lane sucks down some toast while he pictures Hedy peeking through the doorway at the frozen man in the chair. Marv remains a perfect portrait of evening comportment; only armchair ashes and a tiny tilted glass stiff in an outstretched open hand remain.

Hedy continues. "Goldie, poor girl, had been at his feet all night. I took her into the kitchen for a bowl of comfort food. We's left all that remains the same on the porch and waited for yous to come."

Doctor Lane notices how clean and tidy is the home of this confirmed long-term bachelor; but even more striking is the status of the kitchen. There on the table is a full stable of fresh bread lined up with hand-churned butter and Hedy's prize-winning rhubarb preserves. The caramel-coloured jam and Marv's prized lavender honey look like gold at the end of the rainbow. And then his full attention zeroes in on a shiny chrome-and-glass cylinder filled with …

"Hedy, is that some sort of coffee mechanism?"

"Imported French coffee press for the best coffee in the region." She leans into the table. "Marv's big secret. Are yous ready for another cup of wonder, Doctor?"

"Yes, thank you Hedy. That's a great pour. But how does it work?"

"First, Big Boss grinds the coffee beans." She points to a cast iron crank mounted to a half-sized wooden shoebox, then gets up. "He will leave enough in this small drawer here. More than enough for our second cup, maybe even thirdsies?" She glances back. "Water's already on a boil, Doctor."

The good doctor nods in appreciation.

"The coffee is imported from darkest Africa."

Two nods and the coffee press drops to the table as Hedy's gone in a race to block the porch doorway. "It's Al, coming for the list of the today's instructions."

Doctor Lane cannot hear Hedy's quiet words for the hired hand. No matter, he jams a large piece of homemade comfort in his mouth with just enough time to double dip on the honey. Hedy returns to her coffee and toast. "We'll let the lad have a few private moments with Big Boss." She adds on with a wink, "Al will be in so as not to miss a taste of honey and toast with his coffee at the Big Boss's kitchen table. First and last supper on the Boss, so to speak."

Like most country practitioners, Doctor Lane wears a second hat of County Coroner. Waiting for the Hall ambulance transfer is an easy excuse to enjoy thirdsies on another pressed coffee. "I think that I might get one of these contraptions. Great coffee. French, you say?"

News travels fast among Citizens in the know in St. Marys. The Barber is almost the first to find out that Marvin MacMillan has died under mysterious circumstances which are to be reviewed in public after two legal notices in the *Journal*.

Many people find it distasteful that the advertisement for the hearing is delivered through the same edition as the full-column obituary and the front-page sidebar story with the heading Award-Winning Blanshard Farmer Lived a Larger Life. Others find all the information to be very convenient: *"Didn't have to buy two copies of the rag to get all the information." "Gives me lots of time to book off for the day."*

With some, nothing is ever quite right.

"That head-and-shoulders photo tells nothing of his size."

"The starched collar and bowtie were not the Big Boss."

Hedy, Al and Doctor Lane are key witnesses at the packed coroner's hearing held in the upstairs heat of the St. Marys Town Hall theatre. The facts are in and uncontested; the active farmer, although an XXXL, was considered to be in good health. The one element of Marv's death that calls in the judge to the theatre's wide stage is the lack of witnesses, besides Goldie. The sellout-sized audience fills all orchestra seats and any borders with standing space, right to the upper reaches of the balcony. Local tastes savour the prospect of any salacious details on a private but infamous large man's death.

Big Town drama in 1953 unfolds with Al first out of the front row, up the side steps to a chair on the stage. The bored judge, imported

　　　　　　　　　　　　　　　　　　　　　　　　LORNE EEDY

from Theatre Town, rolls his hands out in a silent wave towards the hired hand. Al, with all eyes on the judge, starts up from his pencil notes.

"There he sits, the perfect gent ... but a frozen corpse he was. I kinda knew something's wrong with no Goldie to greet me. His head crooked to the side. And those ashes." He reassures his listeners. "Big Boss has the most steady hands. Didn't spill his drink." Al is on a roll. "I think the Big Boss wet himself, you know."

The judge stops him. "No, the court does not need to know that detail, Mr. Morrison. Stick to ... just continue, Mr. Morrison, please."

"Yes sir. There's no Goldie, so I ..."

The judge, with little local patience, asks Al to speed it up. The upstairs Town Hall audience disagree. They want all the details in slow motion in order to absorb the full impact. Why was he single all those years? Who gets the prize-winning honey? How much money was there? Did they find the cash hidden in the walls? *("No, it's buried in the backyard!")* Did he and that Hedy have something on the go? The audience soon realizes that Al's testimony amounts to not much more than conjecture and secondhand information.

"I know something's gone wrong when Goldie didn't greet me. She always greets me in the laneway."

"Okay. Thank you, Mr. Morrison." The right hand of justice ushers him out from his solitary seat to exit stage left, then points in the general direction of the front row. "Next."

Up comes the second witness, the Dutch maid, Mrs. Service. Taking the seat on the stage, Hedy looks blank-eyed into the globe lights, turning from the silence of the auditorium to the judge who's gesturing for her to start. She nods in agreement. "Marvin had one cousin in the city. You all know how his dad died. How his mother died in childbirth with a little sister. Jayne, that would have been her name. They say the baby's head —"

"Ma'am, the court does not need to know the family history, or the size of the baby's head. Stick to the ... just continue, please."

Too late: the audience is already fixated on the MacMillan family tree. You could read their lips: *"The size of the baby's head. Whose side*

…?" And from the upper balcony, a Freudian slip too: "*Raised without his mother?*" A relative point: "*Never heard of a city cousin.*"

Hedy smiles at her Joe in the front row. "His cousin is the only relative I know of. They have contact because that's where the French press came from. Well, it came from Eaton's Wish Book, but his cousin pointed out the contraption."

Hedy nods to the stage lights. "Page 57, lower left." She turns to the judge. "Clipping was on the refrigerator for three months."

The judge is caught this time. "French press. What in the world is a French press?"

"It's from France."

"Okay. But *what* is it?"

"Well, it's a glass cylinder with lots of chrome. A chrome handle and a chrome lid. The strainer inside is chrome too. Big Boss — sorry, Marvin — would let me touch it, but only to wash it. Never let me handle it."

The audience titter at a reference to touching, washing and handling the man's *it*. The judge is tottering on the insanity of it all.

"Ma'am, please. What is a French press?"

"Sorry, sir. Makes wonderful coffee from fresh imported beans. The beans, they come from his cousin in the city. The press come from Eaton's. Sorry, your honour, the press is made in France. It's the Cham-board model. That's a city in France. Learned it on the label. Cham-board, France."

"Enough on coffee and geography, ma'am. How did you find your boss that morning?"

"In his chair, frozen there like Al said. Like Al said too, the dog was with him. All night Goldie stuck to his slippers. Poor Goldie, I pulls 'er into the kitchen for coffee."

"Ma'am, the dog drinks coffee?"

"No, I's put the kettle on boil and filled Goldie's dish with homemade toasted bread chunks with some ground beef leftovers. Goldie turned all happy again with a special breakfast. Cleaned her bowl cleaner than the Chinese dishwasher at the Grand Central Café. Her tongue —"

"Ma'am, enough about the dog — sorry, poor Goldie."

The most important witness to the inquest is the coroner, Doctor

Lane. Citizens are reaffirmed by the professional level of the affable coffee mate. "Your Honour, in my valued opinion as his family — rather, personal — doctor, he was strong as a workhorse, an active man. Never missed his annual."

"Doctor, how did you first learn about Mr. MacMillan's demise?"

"Hedy made the call. I was there in ten minutes. He was in the chair as stated by the two previous witnesses. Hedy is the only one to see Goldie at his feet. I checked all vital signs."

Doctor Lane turns from the judge to the audience. "I pronounced Marvin MacMillan dead at 7:45 AM August 12th on the 9th Concession of Blanshard Township, RR 1 St. Marys. Heart attack in my opinion, not as his general practitioner, but as the Chief Coroner of Perth County."

After a five-minute pee break, the judge rules to accept the coroner's report, that Marvin succumbed to a natural cause, his heart giving out over a large dipped cigar and a small port. The audience is satisfied with the B-movie performances.

In a footnote seen by few, Doctor Lane is kind enough to take Al aside and assure him that Big Boss had his time.

The *St. Marys Journal* in the coming weeks posts legal notices on the settlement of the estate that ripple without further words into waves of chattel distribution.

The cousin in the big city takes all the cash and investments. The Methodist Hall wins big with a substantial sum left over from the auction sale of the hundred-acre home farm. And it's a real surprise when the will turns over the canning factory to a community foundation in nearby Theatre Town. Good estate-tax move at the time; even better decades later when the need for canned beef dies and the land lives on to become a soccer field.

Marv does remember Al in his estate, leaving the farmhand all his livestock along with the second farm, consisting of one hundred well-drained acres of pasture and a massive barn to keep all happy. Al will become quite wealthy leaving beef on the hoof for a Holstein milk quota. One steer for the freezer will soon be all that remains of the Big Boss's prized Black Angus herd. (One morning while Al is preparing Marv's main farm for auction, on a smoke break behind the barn he will turn towards the rising sun, unable to face the massive pile of loser rocks hidden from the eye of drivers passing on the 9th Concession.)

Hedy expects nothing, but scores fifty thousand dollars. And she gets the most talked-about item from the coroner's inquest: the French press. The money takes her and Joe twice to visit her family in Holland. She presses on with the Chambord in her daily routine, thinking life is a wonder over the perfect coffee.

"Now mine alone." She smiles to her husband, who has become Java Joe. "Can't quite get that taste Big Boss got, though."

The cousin in the city knows why: quality. The Big Boss respected the bean by ordering his wax-sealed from darkest Africa. Hedy's beans are moderate in price and much more accessible, coming from Dick's Groceteria. Nothing takes away from her caffeinated morning moment with the fancy French press and Goldie at her feet. She savours the memories of the Big Boss even longer than Al, longer than anyone except maybe The Barber.

Back of the rock garden, next to the junipers, The Barber often has a memory puff in tribute to the Big Boss. The cigar may not be Grey Owl. He looks past Venus, with loyal Little Scottie at her armless side. Amid the bed of ivy heavy rocks peek up, silent monuments to a marvellous man, the Barber's largest and greatest customer and an even better friend.

Chapter 7

The Sharpe Kid

1955

Live while you are young, lad,
For then the songs are sung;
For too soon the boy becomes a man.
Sad, your song is almost done, lad,
So, live while you are young,
For then the songs are sung.

> — handwritten note found folded in The Barber's
> deerskin diary at the Charles Wolfe Cruise Archives.

Gunford Gregory Sharpe registers in your mind as a name above names. It's the kind of handle you might come across in lines embossed on a notary card, a brass nameplate for a corner office, or an accountant's two-colour logo letterhead. The St. Marys telephone directory lists the Sharpe family, with their unique final "e," below the fourteen Sharp families. In the Sharpe family, Gunny holds down the position of number-three son, the fourth and youngest child.

A Sharpe mention in the barbershop often begs a question:

"Are they married? Never heard about any ceremony."

"Donnellys don't marry."

"She's a Gregory, not a Donnelly. They're Orange through and through."

"Not Catholics?"

"You never see the parents. But Gunny comes for Sunday School on his own with the two brothers and sister. Where are you on Sunday morning?"

His mother named him after a Scottish icon: Gunford Castle, home to the ancient highland family Gregory.

Local wags wonder on the third name with dim knowledge on the far-off character of the Sharpe family.

"Ah, a clan of highland stock. They're either cattle thieves or murdering cattle thieves."

"Never as bad as the Donnellys."

"You are talking about the Black Irish there, lad. These Scots hold down jobs. They thieve in the afterhours."

His Ma holds Scotland dear in her heart and mind. Her father, born there, talks up a good life in the old country. (Never a word on the thievery, rustling or murder practised by the Gregory clan.)

Ma rubs her hands through the blond scouring pad on top of her youngest's head. "With a proper education, Gunford, the world can be yours."

Scottish heritage is second after English in the local pecking order — followed by Irish, whether Roman Catholic or Protestant, north or south. The families imported from Italy for the cement plant around 1900 and the Dutch dairy farmers who arrived after World War II are farther down in a hierarchy that favours the English-speaking.

On Town radar, Gunny is that kinky-haired lad from that slab house overlooking the cement plant. With the exception of his Ma, locals can't even begin to understand the lad's name, let alone its origins. They keep it simple with Gunny. The play on the highfalutin name reflects an easy specific on small stones. A Sharpe shot from the skinny kid Gunny has meaning to Citizens.

"Have you seen his accuracy? And the distance the lad can reach."

"Gunny invented the phrase, 'three birds with one stone.'"

"The Maple Leafs should draft him. They could use a shot like his."

At four years old Gunny is already a star at the Methodist Hall Penny Carnival bean toss. In the two-storey open concept Sunday School hall jammed with games, tricks, books and treats, a painted hunk of plywood with cartoon bodies and a hole for a volunteer target's head looms in the corner.

Someone yells out, "The kid cracked Danny the custodian between the eyes."

The talented windbag Pastor quickly claims credit for the church. He whispers over parishioners' shoulders, watching crinkle-head doing his thing. "Look at him. Boy has God-given skills. God blesses the poor and helpless."

Most Citizens, Protestant and Roman Catholic alike, look up to the lad as a likable natural. "Sees a hole, he hits the hole. Unbelievable for a wee kid."

Soon it's an annual thing. His calendar fills with anything target-related. From children's fundraising penny carnivals, Gunny moves up to ball toss with an adult escort along the arcade at the Little Falls Agricultural Fair. A gaggle of suspect wags tag along with the skinny kid to partake of side wagers. After two summer visits the carnies wise up and ban young Gunny, but not before bestowing a gift.

"Kid, this is y'r game. You are a ringer. The buddies here at the arcade and I want to give ya this gigantic stuffed panda."

Gunny can't believe the size of this prize. The carnie leans into him, pinching his elbow with a low growl.

"Don't fuckin' come back next year, kid. This is a goodbye present. So fuckin' goodbye."

The adult escorts, unable to hear the threat, laugh in a roar at the fat animal. "What will Gunny call it?" one of them jokes. "How about Mrs. Snoddie?"

The carnies smile back and wave at the Town group. Then they grit their teeth and step back to their games, staring straight ahead. "Panda names. What's a Mrs. Snoddie? These people are odd."

At school, practice runs a daily course, recess, lunch and recess, then back at it the next day. Sunday morning is booked for Sunday School — the Methodists take attendance, with Confirmation hanging in the balance — but there's time on the boy's schedule after Saturday morning chores for his favourite pastime. Pearly green leopard frogs fill in every empty space along both sides of the creek bank, teams of frogs walking the line in front of armed kids. The boys march to war along the creek, knocking off the frogs in a bloody species massacre in green. Gunny thinks of himself as Robin Hood from his Classic Comic.

Water puppies, turtles, wild mink, raccoons, muskrats, snakes and salamanders, not to mention kingfisher and osprey, are on a long list of off-target creatures that Gunny considers too precious. But frogs are here, there and everywhere, and for the boys it's an open, unlimited season on the pearly green amphibians.

The ritual attracts four, sometimes six boys. The gang members gather at the rattly swing bridge over the Creek, puddling along the bank trail from the upper Creek walking bridge and down the worn path to the downtown. The frogs jump to their death in droves. The morning group splits in two to follow both sides of the Creek. Opposite sides throw names of superheroes back and forth in anticipation of the matinee.

"Captain Video, can't wait to see how he escapes the Fish Men."

"Well, Superman would beat the crap out of them. Then fly away."

"Nah, Spiderman — *sput, sput* with his web."

"It's a bug, man."

They exit their Saturday subterranean world below the Wellington Street Bridge and head up to the main corner of downtown. Hunger leads to a right turn at the corner and three doors down, to Braden's Bake Shoppe. Braden Fewster doesn't need the tinkle of the tiny doorbell to tell him his guests have arrived. Every Saturday morning at 10:30 he welcomes his moist and punctual young visitors.

"Good morning, gentlemen. What will be your wish?"

The same answer could be heard from almost every seven-to-twelve-year-old on the Bake Shoppe floor.

"A Long John, Mr. Fewster, and chocolate milk please, sir."

They all hunger for the most popular snack created in the gas-fired ovens of the Bake Shoppe, a creation that comes in three variants. "Honey-glazed, or butterscotch or chocolate icing?"

Whoops, there's Mason Bradshaw with his hand up behind. Braden shifts his attention down to the smallest club member. "Now there, Mr. Mason Bradshaw. What's your pleasure, son?"

A squeaky mouse gives an upbeat answer. "Mr. Fewster, could I have the cinnamon donut, please?"

A pint of Stuart's chocolate milk washes it down. (Frances the Cow smiling on the front scares smaller children; mothers often turn the crooked cow smile around to the back or use a cup.)

Gunny stands tall in the room, his corn broom hair above all. He has sufficient grounds for satisfaction, gripping his butterscotch-slathered Long John. With two hours before the matinee, they still have the Thames at the dam to explore before that. The gang push out to the sidewalk. Braden can hear a fading song.

"Davy Crockett, king of the wild frontier …"

A squeaky voice pipes up. "Mother got me a coonskin hat."

"Who fuckin' cares, BAD-shaw."

At the Pleasant Hour Theatre matinee they settle their butts on soft warm seats, mouths stuffed with hot fresh popcorn. A cream soda provides belching noises.

Always the same chorus of uproars from the upfront seats.

From the cute girl in the class. "That's gross, Gunny Sharpe."

The older guys. "Shut up, you little pricks."

The usher. "Quiet please."

Holy Mary Catholic boys are on the same team as Gunny's group, making farting sounds from their armpits. *Fwat. Fwat. Fwat.*

A full Saturday program repeated over and over. The routine actions of Saturday never change until the forces of nature come together one day in a perfect storm. Mrs. Snoddie makes her first contact with a sure-eyed stone thrower.

The Barber has been on to the big one in mimicry for years, since way before Gunny's parents moved as a young married couple to the slab house by the cement plant.

Oh my God, each time The Barber takes the role of Mrs. Snoddie, the audience in the barbershop sit up in expectation. Behind the red & nickel chair The Barber looks down his nose to the bevelled bar mirror. He puffs up his jowels, clears his throat, and with the best of falsetto voices, the Panda speaks:

"Yoooou know, cats-do-kill-songbirds, yoooou know."

After a one, two, three-second pause he repeats a series of bird-like calls with a lisp and a cackle. *"Yoooou-who! Yoooou-who, little bir-r-r-rdies."*

"Wh-h-eat. Wh-h-eat. Ch-r-r-each. Ch-r-r-each."

Before the person in the chair can compliment his lisping bird calls, the puffball faces the other customers. *"Yoooou know, cats-do-kill-songbirds, yoooou know."*

Some say his Panda reflection inflates like a wrinkled puffball, others a snub-nosed Chinese dog or a glowing full moon with a blow hole. After it's been performed a thousand times in the shop, his audience still roars at the Panda.

Mrs. Snoddie's forty-pound pet cat is a monster feline with a grand name, Mister Master. Or his nickname, Mysta. (Mrs. Snoddie leans into her neighbour's fence to explain her two-name system: "Mister Master, as you know, has lost his male … attributes. Therefore, although the name Mister has a masculine tone, my kitty-cat baby needs a feminine touch. *Mysta.* Is that not cute?")

Mysta lies about most of the time, a kitchen-based feline. The fat cat's morning starts with his daily fix, a ten-ounce can of Eagle Brand Condensed Milk. He whiles the day away, holding court in a sunny spot on the north windowsill. His perch has a view of the newfangled electric refrigerator and up the staircase to his litter box and Mummy's bed cave. Down the steps, the back door hides the great unknown, an outside world he can see from his window perch. While digesting his prized Eagle, Mysta relishes his watch of constant visitors at the bird feeder, moving his head back and forth in Panavision. He tracks a mental mission control on bird flights incoming and outgoing while he waits for another Eagle landing.

A host of assorted piggy doves and robins gather at the buffet, along with squirrels and chipmunks, a quivering rabbit family and one beautiful-coated skunk. For seven years Mysta has watched the unknown taste of an imagined din-din, all that corn-fed meat eating at the bird feeder. If he bats a paw at the window, the bolder animals fluff up, chattering or blowing challenges and warnings. The rabbits run. The birds might look up at the first paw-bat but in general ignore the fur frosting on the other side of the glass.

Mrs. Snoddie considers herself an expert. "Cats never meow to other cats," she often tells other Citizens. "Cats only use their kitty-cat chat to talk with humans." (Mrs. Snoddie's body of obscure knowledge might bring an ironic comparison with the litany of obscure stories from The Barber.)

Each morning Mrs. Snoddie removes the plate of leftovers and cherry-picked goodies from the Kelvinator in a slide-off to the tiger-sized bowl. She tap-tap-taps on the bottom before dousing the top with the Eagle. The empty tin gets a hollow drum roll. *Ting, ting, ting.*

Mummy has her Master ditty for the grand old kitty.

"Mister Master yummy yummy,

Mysta never meows to Mummy."

Ting. Ting.

"Mysta gets his Eagle nummy ..."

Ting. Ting.

Despite Mrs. Snoddie's assertions, Mysta does engage in kitty-cat chat with the his Mummy who pours on the liquid affection. *"Meow. Hurry up, Mum-mum-mum. Mysta needs to fill his tummy-tum-tum-tum."*

Tap and ting no matter, the fat cat is at 'er. Mysta laps away in short order with belt-sander tongue as soon as the Eagle lands, his purr settling into a low hum.

Oh my, Mummy increases her volume as the fat cat hoovers down the rich topping of cream.

"Yummy, yummy, yummy.

Mysta's got Eagle in the tummy."

The cat licks down halfway before his first breath stop. Then he looks up with a kitty-cat face as if to say *Mummy, over there.*

"Me-e-e-ow-w-w. Me-e-e-ow-w-w."

Based on the tone of the meows, Mrs. Snoddie recognizes the subject of the kitty chat even before the knock on the door. Today the cat recognizes Cliff, the milkman.

Cliff is the most successful of three competing dairy operators in Town. He embellishes his status at Christmas in his custom-made, red Santa suit with real silver fox trim. Cliff has a popping stove belly and weatherworn, ruddy red face, a package that enhances his elfish style. His costume and profile make him the most popular Santa Claus for home and school events in Town history. In the Museum there's a large colour portrait of Cliff in full gear, complexion ruddy as a Christmas floodlight, squeezing a large cigar. His year peaks with his ride on the St. Marys Volunteer Firemen and Tug-of-War Team's red Lafarge Model 37 in the annual Christmas Parade. For most of the year, though, Santa lives a mundane life at 125 Huron Street with his own doughy Mrs. Claus.

In 1953 the last horse team at work in Town is a classic sight in dawn hours. Cliff is a Norman Rockwell milkman directing his team of Percheron horses. On Saturdays you might think he has three hands, the way he juggles to control the harness, load up the milk delivery, and organize a bill for the past six days. Balancing the fat change-bag and a case of bottles, he opens the back screen door with his foot and punches three knocks. No fingers left to push the out-of-reach doorbell.

Mysta has observed this routine for seven years, opening his narrow-gauge mind wide to the possibility of escape. Mysta weighs the known, Eagle life against the unknown. Yesterday's house menu of braised chicken and liver leftovers lifted his spirits enough to dull the desire for action, but nature and her need for game always take over. Mysta listens to the daily growl of his stretched stomach as he watches the fly-in at the bird feeder. His taste buds moisten.

Cliff keeps the door wedged open wide, spreading his short legs out to balance the change-bag, bottle case and notebook while he makes change. Mrs. Snoddie re-checks the balance. After seven years, Mysta has come to the kitty-cat conclusion that the door the Milkman uses is connected to the same world as the bird feeder. Now, he sees his shot at that outside-the-window world. If Mummy was listening instead of double-checking the list and re-counting the change, she would hear not purring but a whisper of Mysta meows of self-encouragement. Listen to the kitty-cat chat:

"Oh de doh, de doh, the door is open. Too de doh dah, too de doh, da dum dum. Ah, birds!"

Mysta rolls his cat eyes, grey smoky marbles, up at Cliff. He slides through the opening, two front paws out of step with the back ones, somehow avoiding contact with the Milkman. Fat and fur full forward, Mysta pushes into the biggest move of his life.

Mysta slides all the way down the steps to land between Cliff's laced rubber boots. Fat fur slides onto the cement pad with the twill welcome mat. He reinforces with kitty-cat chat. If the average Methodist credits God, the cat blesses his holy mistress first:

"Oh, Mummy dearest, too de dum dah, I off to outside." Now that blessings have covered Mysta's escape, it's down to business. *"To de birds!"*

Back in the kitchen, negotiations are complete, but a built-in Mummy emergency light switches from yellow to red. A permanent fixture — Mysta in a painted windowsill scene, the house treasure — is missing. She sweeps the kitchen and staircase perch, ignoring Cliff. He's mesmerized by her jowly head, which swivels owl-like left, then right. Mysta's absence is stunning. The alarm bells ring.

"Puss, Puss, Puss!" she calls out. "Misty? Mysta?"

Mysta does not appear. Mrs. Snoddie pushes Cliff back over the threshold and closes the door in his face. She changes to walking shoes, adds her Irish tweed jacket and proper hat with a pheasant feather shooting to the sky, and grabs her bamboo cane. Everything for the practical woman is accessible from the foyer side closet. She pushes past Cliff, who's still balancing on the cement.

"Mysta, Mysta, where have you gone?" she whimpers to herself. "What have you done, baby? Mummy gave you leftover chopped fish from Friday this very morning. Those chicken livers you love so much on Thursday."

All the Milkman can think is that the cat has a better menu than the Grand Central Café. Mummy runs the fare list into tears.

"A full tin of Eagle, Baby … the way you like it. Mysta, you are making Mummy upset."

Mrs. Snoddie, in her emergency trance, accelerates with gandy legs into a prance outside, her head turning in wise-owl guesses at Mysta's path to birdland.

Well ahead of Mummy's pace, Mysta approaches the bird feeder. The feeder crowd have seen the obese cat approaching their feeding ground. Bird brains recognize the furry beast from behind the safe wall of glass, but now that he's up close the bird brains are stunned by the size of the cat. One glance at the prance puts all in flight, no chance at chicken dinner tonight.

"Doh de doh, where did all de little birdies go?"

Mysta has never tasted bird meat, other than honey-glazed chicken with livers in his broad bowl. He has always imagined a simple greet-and-meat of fresh game at the bird feeder. Now that the meat has flown, the dumb, clawless cat takes the adventure down the garden path and further into a brave new world.

"Whoa, too-de-dum-dum, dere's one of dose bush-tailed rats. Fat too! Yum yum te-dum-tum-tum-tum. Maybe he wants to be my de-de-de din-din."

The squirrel is another member of the fur-and-feathers meat buffet that frequents the platform bird feeder. Mysta's pink tongue hangs out as he imagines the nutty taste of squirrel. Now, the rat with a cute tail heads off.

"Where's de meat going? This might lead me to his cold food box. Yum-de-tum-tum."

Mysta steps into the new world with no idea on his next brave move. He crouches under the cedar hedge on the hard sidewalk beside Peel Street.

Mrs. Snoddie is mere paws behind. Her Baby radar zeroes in on ground cover, from the garden beds over to the thick cedar hedge. Mummy mutters her monologue of self-doubt. "Baby cannot climb. Baby doesn't crawl." Her head pounds with internal debate. "Fed too well to hunt. Ignores the mice. Neither a fighter nor a lover, to the best of my knowledge. Who in the world could he fight or love? No male … attributes. Pretty puffy paws …"

She pauses, looking for blame. "Those birds. That silly little milkman." She mixes a second cat into the theory. "Could there be a hussy in the neighbourhood? A stray? Luring my Mysta from afar with cat squirts? Not my little man … with no" — she has to cough it out in tears — "attributes?"

The regular Methodist gives in to prayer. "Dear Lord. He never, ever *mo-oves from that winnn-dow!*" Perplexed but determined, she reaches for logical sense. "Dear Lord, is Baby doing his business in the bushes?"

Common sense takes over. "The Eagle Brand," she tells herself. "Baby's favourite treat. And the spoon."

Mrs. Snoddie prances in reverse, back to regroup in the kitchen. She has played the Pied Piper in a daily Eagle hit, after all. She drops her cane, grabs the empty can and a spoon from the counter, and gets back on the path.

Mummy slows to a shuffle, tapping the tin with a spoon. *Ting. Ting. Ting.* She retraces her path towards Peel. After her thirteenth step, her mind clouds in panic. "Baby has never been outside!" She revs up to full-on terror, pounding the tin for the Eagle call. *Ting. Ting. Ting.*

Mysta hears the familiar ringing sound, but everything draws him toward the possibility of newfound, exotic furry meats and feathered meats. The advance scent draws him across Peel Street.

"De-dum-tum-tum, where did that furry meat go?"

Two front paws, not quite in sync with the back set, follow the bushy tail's tic-tac-paw manoeuvre to avoid the eight snowshoe-sized hooves of the Milkman's horses. Mysta tracks the squirrel's lucky steps along the iron-edged obstacle course and into the street. Again the nine lives jump to attention as he repeats his nutty dive underneath a human car. All paws forward in an amazing race to reach the far side. Giddy-up, little kitty.

Planets are about to align for the triumvirate of Mysta, Mrs. Snoddie and Gunny. A cosmic cat collision that will replay for thirty years in a one-man show at the barbershop.

Mrs. Snoddie fails to see a bushy squirrel tail scamper up a large sugar maple with her Baby close behind it.

Ting. Ting. Ting. Mummy prances, head down, right into Cliff's lead horse. "Cliff, have you seen my cat? You know, Mister Master?"

Cliff has little sympathy for the unfolding cat incident. In fact, the anxiety of the moment is a little scary for him. Offering a little salve to move the distraught kitty-Mummy off the street, the Milkman points towards the Heber Ball house. "Mrs. Snoddie, he may have crossed the street. I heard some brake noise."

Cliff sees her face turning red. Whoopsie. Land mine. Never alarm a cat owner, Cliff. He stumbles along under fire. "Ma'am. I thought it was a squirrel or raccoon, maybe a skunk? No, not a skunk." Pause and think. "Too small. Could have been a badger or something. But not the cat."

Mrs. Snoddie ignores Cliff's monologue and hurries on ahead. "Baby could never climb a tree. He finds it difficult to climb up the stairs to his window perch." A half-dumb look crosses her face. "What if Baby is stressed? Baby needs safe shelter!" Methodist logic prevails. "A tree can provide a safe haven for my Baby's retrieval."

The panting Mummy reassures herself as she looks up — up over the little Milkman, over the two dapple Percherons, over a growing audience of a half-dozen vehicles packed on Peel amidst dozens of nosey neighbours. "My God, who are these people?"

The crowd back up to a better sight line with heads up, all pointing upwards.

A sight catches Mrs. Snoddie's eye — a large furball in the crotch of the large maple, claws spread out on the bark. "My God, what is that …?"

When the furball moves, tick, tack and paw, up the maple, Mrs. Snoddie retreats in shock. That big body up there is the same Baby that is usually curled in a spongy basket swaddled by the kitchen stove.

Mummy charges to the rescue. "Don't stress, my Baby, Mummy's got you saved."

Up in the tree, Mysta turns his kitty-cat chat frequency up to a soft siren wail. *"Te-te-de Bushy Tail, what's up? Meaty-meat-te-tum. Dum-dum-te-doh, I come and talk to little furry buddy."*

The furry meat scampers too fast up, up, up for Mysta to catch up.

"Te-doh, te-doh, up go so-te-doh. Up up Mysta goes."

Across the street, Mrs. Snoddie powers up for a virtuoso performance in front of the Citizen audience. She broadcasts the words that will become more famous in Town conversation than any George Sewell psalm or prayer. She broadcasts her message over the crowd, up the grand maple tree. The level of her crescendo is no surprise to Citizen readers familiar with the Letters to the Editor page of the *Journal*. Her Peel Street appeal to the upper branches can be heard through the entire neighbourhood.

"Be-e-elllle. No, no, no-o-o. Be-e-elllle. NO-O-O-O!"

In her stressed state she has switched from the recognizable name of Mysta to the private name, Belle, frustrating all communication between human and animal. The neighbours, later, all report the same question back to the red & nickel barber chair. *"Belle? Who the heck is Belle?"*

The squirrel, more brainless than the dumbest of cats, is nonetheless smart enough to disappear into the upper canopy. Neighbours, walking Citizens and rubberneckers close in under the great maple tree, seeming to pop up there like mushrooms.

Mysta looks down from the branch view, paws up in a bear hug. His back claws have the emergency brake on. A fat cat full of cream and kidney leftovers is in no hurry, up or down, watched by the gathering Town. *"De-te-dee-dee-dee, Mummy. Dum-de-dum-dee, I think I am stuck in this te-doh-te tree."*

As Mysta tucks in and tightens up into a final upper perch, the layers of Town activity unfold below.

The Chief of police arrives in minutes. He calls for backup from Constable Charlie, more familiarly known as Fat Charlie, a not-so-lean subject that no Citizen ever refers to as Town Constable. Big news travels fast in a slow news week. The event's political status gets a boost when Mayor Al and a few councillors appear in the foreground. The Chief and his subordinates push the lookee-looks further back behind the Pastor.

That familiar broadcast voice rings out. "People, move back to the Ball driveway. Yes Jack, the boulevard on Jones is okay. Give the volunteer firemen and the constabulary room to do their job."

With a nod to God's messenger, the Chief takes control. "Is that a 'coon up there?" he asks Fat Charlie.

"No, it's a cat."

(The Chief is already the subject of an Archives index card jammed with odd animal rescues: the toasty raccoon on the hydro pole with the pomegranate eyes, the unsettled mallard family stuck in the Park Street drain, and the badger that went grocery shopping at Dick's Groceteria. All on the record under "Animal Rescue — Odd" in the Archives' index file.)

Kitty-cat clings twenty-five feet up and stuck, still a big sight. The Chief mouths the same words as the rest of the crowd. "My God. Look at the size of it."

Speaking of size, Fat Charlie sings its praises. "Biggest darn fat cat I've seen, Chief. Looks like a treed 'coon."

"Never seen a treed 'coon in a happy come-down. Fat cat or 'coon, none treed different. Same pointy teeth, same bushy tail, out on a nose-about, causing shit, leaving shit … God help us not get bit."

"Ease up on the language, Chief." A look behind his back. "George is within earshot."

But Fat Charlie's warning has come too late. The Rev. Dr. George Sewell answers back with his message from God:

"God?" The crowd all turn from the Chief to the Pastor. "God has nothing to do with this shit. God doth create" — his righteous hand points up — "God doth create that enormous cat."

Hearing the Pastor repeat a dirty word has shamed the small group to attention. George grabs the opportunity to sermonize.

"Our Father in heaven does not create the shit. God creates the cat." Mysta looks down as if to understand that he is the topic of George's sermon below. "The cat is God's child. There is no reason from heaven for its godly girth." A few elbows and whispers translate "godly girth" to "fucking fat." Half-dumb looks are frozen onto the faces of many observers. "The responsibility lies with the Eagle. God has spoken."

The group look up in unison, searching the sky. "Eagle, what eagle?" They form small circles in confusion.

A Citizen in the know educates his circle of small boys and nosey adults. "Eagle? Eagle Brand. Condensed milk in a can. Mrs. Snoddie boils up a can every morning. That fat cat licks the bowl clean."

The Chief digresses with a mumbled pause, then gets himself back on track. He broadcasts the action to the rescuers, the entertained audience, the Milkman, the lookee-looks and Mrs. Snoddie: "Let's treat it 'coon-like, boys."

In less than five minutes, the St. Marys Volunteer Fire Department and Tug-of-War Team pulls up. Judging by their equipment they're prepared to retrieve a bear, not a fat cat. A cat will be an easy-peasy pop from the old maple. Pumper, ladder truck and emergency trailer line Peel Street to the corner around Jones Street. The red extension ladder points to the blue sky, manhandled by four heavy volunteers. They reach the maple, pushing the yellow cord on the extension up towards the cat. Mysta looks down at the experienced rescue crew.

Three men secure the mount, waiting for the fourth. Sandy, or Smiley as he's better known in Town, who will take his turn up the ladder.

The Chief turns to the mayor. "Smiley loves cats."

Up, up, up the ladder steps Smiley, who holds out his lined, elbow-length gloves for the big grab.

Mysta's dark eyes open to the horror. He remembers Dr. Scott, the veterinarian. No matter how tight Mysta holds his hips together, Dr. Scott's one hand always vise-grips while the rubber finger is free to probe. *"Human no big finger. No te-dum Mysta bum-bum-bum."*

Smiley looks at the frowning teeth, then slides closer. Mysta squeezes his every ounce deeper into the crevice of the tree. Smiley takes a moment to smile and wave at his friends and neighbours — and wow, there's some love interest from high school days in Susie Richardson at the back of the crowd. Smiley's off to impress.

The fat cat sucks it all back, avoiding any good grip. *"No stranger puts a finger on me."*

The smiling fireman calls the play from above. "The fat cat is lodged right in here." He scampers down and off.

The three volunteers reinsert the red ladder closer to the target up in the umbrella of foliage. Smiley scampers back up. Mysta has shifted deep into the clutch of the maple branch. "That fat cat is *really* lodged in there."

Under the din of cat chaos, Mrs. Snoddie shouts, "Smiley Davies! Quit calling him 'that fat cat,' you idiot. His name is Belle."

Smiley climbs down again. After a few repetitions up and down, the crowd gets vocal, an impatient posse moaning at each descent.

The rescue has lost its lustre. Smiley's friends, neighbours, family — and worse, Susie — fidget, assembled around the big maple. The vocal crowd meets each ascent with tepid applause before the encouragement changes colour to sarcasm. Finally a bit of a Bronx cheer accompanies Smiley up the ladder each time.

"Go get him. Go get him, Smiley."

"Careful, Smiley. The fat cat has nine lives. You have only one."

"Sandy, you be careful."

Smiley stops again to wave at Susie.

Six attempts later, Smiley's face sours at the antics of one precocious pussy. The crowd mood, along with that of the volunteers, remains pessimistic. Having to spend two hours on one cat draws negative attention to the "volunteer" aspect of firefighting. Desperate ideas begin to come forward.

"How about taking up some of the Eagle Brand?"

"Just take the can and bean it on the head."

"Use the fire axe to drop the branch, and the fat cat."

"Just poke it with a pole. That'll get fatty rolling."

Hearing the last comment, Mrs. Snoddie rises from her paralyzed state.

Ting. Ting. Ting. Drumming the tin bowl with the spoon, she marches over to the circle of the Chief, Fat Charlie, the fire chief, sweaty Smiley and numerous volunteer firefighters.

Ting. Ting. Ting. The circle parts.

"You will NOT be poking my precious Baby."

The Chief ranks first in protocol and knows the participants well. "Mrs. Snoddie, these are volunteers on a Saturday. This is their weekend. You know, family time. They have their own babies at home. Two hours attending a cat in a tree is not a weekend highlight. I think we should all go home." The Chief places his hand on Mrs. Snoddie's tin-bowl hand. "Let Baby come down when Baby is good and ready."

Mummy's eyes moisten up. "My Belle has never been outside in his life. He will die in that tree."

The Chief tacks his eyes straight ahead to avoid rolling them. He ignores the fact that the cat has gone from having two names to three. "Cats always come home. On the roof, stuck in the wall while mousing, even up an old maple tree, Mrs. Snoddie. Always a happy ending."

"My Belle has never been outside. My God, never in his entire life. Baby will die if Baby is left in that stupid old tree."

Smiley, as a former student of Mrs. Snoddie, tries his best. "Chief's right, Mrs. Snoddie. Mysta, I mean Belle, will be okay."

With deadpan eyes the teacher turns to the former poor English student. "Sandy Davies, you wipe that stupid smile off your gob. Get your *big butt* up the tree. Get my Baby back."

Two main protagonists in the cat incident, Mysta and Mrs. Snoddie, have driven the plot from kitchen to street and then to lofty heights on a disappearing Saturday morning. The curtain opens now to the third character, who pushes his corn-broom head into the adult circle.

Gunny, chores done, had just headed out to meet his buddies. At 9:45 as he took the shortcut through the Episcopalian Hall yard, he felt the air of anxiety three blocks away. He heard a crowd in chaos.

A detouring flood of Citizens followed in the same direction as the boy. As he rounded the corner of the limestone Hall, Gunny joined the crowd for some unclear George Sewell words, chuckling in nervous harmony with his mates.

Now Gunny and his hand-picked leopard frog stone stop the conference. "What's up?"

The Chief, Constable Charlie, the fire chief, Mrs. Snoddie and two nosey neighbours ignore the lad in his circle break-through. Smiley is still smiling, though stung from Mrs. Snoddie's verbal slap of encouragement. Smiley likes the skinny kid from the slab house at the edge of town.

"Hey Gunny," Smiley says. "Mrs. Snoddie here has that fat cat — sorry Ma'am,

I mean Belle. I mean Mysta — up the old maple tree."

Gunny will be at the top of Mrs. Snoddie's class several years later. "What's the big deal?"

"Every time we move the ladder" — Smiley lowers his voice to a whisper — "'that fat cat digs its fat arse deeper into the bough."

Smiley's notes are ignored by the circle's best, but quickly absorbed by the sharpshooter.

Gunny wants to get going, as there are leopard frogs to shoot and a butterscotch Long John waiting at the Bake Shoppe. And a little chocolate wash-down from a carton with a smiling cow on the front that looks like a cartoon. David in a Goliath situation offers up a rock solution.

"Hey Smiley, no worries. I'll take care of that fat cat." Gunny gives a boy-scout goodbye salute and then shoots away through the crowd.

Smiley half-smiles before his expression drops from a grin to a half-dumb look. He has no idea what Gunny was talking about.

While the circle plots Smiley's seventh attempt at the furry crotch of the maple, Gunny pulls out of sight, out of mind, on the far side of the maple tree. There, he positions himself at a twenty-five-degree angle in an open shooting lane to the fur cat perch.

(Some barbershop wags will claim to infinity and beyond that the term "kitty corner" originated from that cat incident. Another argument defined and refined at the barbershop:

"Kitty, right? The corner. Peel Street, Jones Street; a corner, right? Voilà, kitty corner."

Gerry the high school math teacher does the science. "The maple vertical, Heber's lawn horizontal. The lad on the west front corner of the Ball lawn. Perfect thirty-two-degree angle to target. Kitty corner.")

The twenty-foot shot is far less than his best Creek throw. Gunny imagines the arcade at the London Fair with money on the line. For once, there are no gambling chaperones in tow, nobody in the know. The skinny sniper reaches into his pocket for that special rock, handpicked and palm-sized. Gunny has packed this one favourite killer stone all week long for that special amphibian target. This kidney-shaped rock with rounded edges weighs in at about four ounces. The stone super space-saucer would be a perfect choice in the arsenal of Captain Video. Too fat for skipping but perfect for a long-range bull's-eye.

The lefty lines up. "Easy stuff. Stationary target. Here you go, fat pussy. Eat this rocket."

One eye closed, Gunny comes into focus like Ty Cobb. His windmill arm winds up, a tight spring. He rips off a strike. The fastball stone, a cold comet of granite, hits Mysta square on the cat's side, his compressed gut. Baby's hair puffs him up to the size of a sixty-pounder as he's ejected out of the crutch of the branches. Baby exhales a piercing wail, a kitty-chat scream later imitated by all gathered. The mushrooms covering the ground scatter backwards with a gasp.

Mysta sits straight up in flight, reels forward, spins twice, then deadfalls in an upside-down swan dive. Baby crawls in the air, clawing in a windmill motion. The crowd retreats further with another gasp of horror.

Mrs. Snoddie screams — *"My Bay-y-y-beeee!"* — then faints into the grasping arms of the Milkman.

The flying alien object, forty-looking-sixty pounds of frizzled fuzz, drops point blank. Witnesses will swear the cat dive was in slow motion. The crowd screams again, expecting the worst.

The crowd holds its breath as Mysta bounces off Heber Ball's solid hedge, a cedar trampoline on the far side of the maple. One cat life saved, Mysta bounces skyward. Up go the heads, looking at the flailing fat ball of flying fur coming point blank towards them. *"Aaaaaah!"*

Fat Charlie's cap flies off and lands in the dirt as he runs toward the cedars with his flabby, pasty arms outstretched. "Puss! Puss!"

Charlie could never catch a baseball or stop a hockey puck, let alone pull in a flying fat cat for a secure landing. All four paws grab for the first object on the flight path, Charlie's pronounced proboscis. Mysta's cat gut hits the vast sweaty forehead dead-on. His un-declawed back claws cling to the constable's enormous nose, the front paws doing a full nelson around his bald head.

"Aaaaaah! That hurts!" Charlie runs a cartoon-character chase in a tight circle, grasping the huge furball attached to his face.

Witnesses will claim the Chief could be heard repeating scatological slurs over and over under his breath. He's dead in his tracks watching poor Charlie run his reel. It's the fire chief who jumps into action, grabbing a pail of water off the Lafarge fire truck. He dumps it on Charlie's head, *et voilà*, the fat cat pops off like a champagne cork.

The Chief directs the Boy Scouts to disperse the onlookers then consoles Charlie. Smiley runs to the aid of the grounded fat cat, pail in hand. He grabs Mysta with the other hand, still protected by a lined elbow-length glove. He pushes the low-wailing furball into the water pail. Smiley tries to dump the pail out on the unconscious Mrs. Snoddie, but all that comes out is water. Mysta clings to the bottom of the pail.

The volunteer has no idea how to bring this cat incident to a conclusion. He gives the pail a gentle shake, and out plops Baby head first, right onto Mrs. Snoddie's bushel chest. What to say? So the fool smiles the way only a guy named Smiley can. "There you go, Mrs. Snoddie. Belle, I mean Mysta — darn, here's your Baby, safe and sound. Ma'am, let's get a little smile on your gob."

Mrs. Snoddie struggles to concentrate. For a moment she feels heaven-sent with this smiling angel helping her up. Then she pauses in confusion as she recognizes Smiley looking down at her. She searches the circle, looks from the Chief to Cliff, to the Pastor, and back into the eyes of the fool. She jolts to life. Smiley strokes the cat stuck to her front. Mummy still does not see the forty pounds of fur clinging to her camel coat. The crowd gasps as Mrs. Snoddie noddies and rises from the dead. "My Baby. Where is my Belle?"

Mysta and Mummy, both in shock, struggle to gain their bearings.

Mysta, rolled up in a ball, digs his back claws into the coat. He shuts his coal eyes and burnt mind to the outside circle and purrs.

Mummy finally opens her bloodshot eyes to her Baby-in-arms. She soothes him with kitty-cat chat. *Te Belle te-de-Mummy, te Belle te-de-Mummy."*

The fat cat purrs back in sublime relief. *"Tum-de-dum Mysta. Tum-tum-ting-ting-ting. Eagle Mummy."*

On that warm Saturday morning, Gunny's corn-broom crop just disappeared along the Peel Street hill heading down to the Creek.

The incident gets little coverage in the *Journal*. The newspaper does a "We See" on the front page — Citizen 's Cat Retrieved from the Maple at Peel and Jones Streets without Incident — plus one hundred words on the emergency response. Congratulations all round to the Chief, the police, the fire chief and his volunteers. (For the firefighters, a quote from the mayor, see Page 3. For Rev. Dr. George Sewell's letter-to-the-editor, see Page 5.)

Not a mention of Constable Fat Charlie's facial scratches; worse, nothing for Smiley. Nor is there any use for the new word kitty corner.

The rock keeps rolling.

That cat incident brings a flood of conversation. At the barbershop, a steady round of heads — the Chief and the freshly scratched Fat Charlie, the fire chief, big butt Smiley and other volunteers, a few buggy basket drivers, Cliff, and more than enough nosey neighbours and secondhand witnesses — stack on tons of detail to work that cat incident over and over again. The gluttony-is-evil messenger, the Rev. Dr. George Sewell, never darkens The Barber's door or enlightens his parishioner face to face. However, a dozen individual neighbours, along with the Milkman, repeat George's words verbatim in poor tries at the broadcast voice.

Cliff holds his horses in the red & nickel barber chair. "The horses steady through that whole cat calamity. Horns blasting, Mrs. Snoddie flapping her gums." When he gets his moment in the bevelled mirror, he winks at himself. "More brains than people, horses have."

The Milkman can't keep the lid on. "My God, that broadcast voice.

Pastor Sewell can sure blow it out that hole of his. You could hear it for miles." The Pastor even said — he looks around to confirm an empty room — "George said the shit word, three times, as if you didn't get the first broadcast."

The Barber pauses in the bevelled bar mirror for a quick laugh, and he's off. He can't help himself at this kitty corner in history. "God's fat-cat clause of exemption, redemption of the word shit and a fat cat's resurrection, all in the name of the power above. By George, he could be onto a few new tricks as The Messenger of God."

The Barber pauses on the edge of Cliff's laugh. *"Be-l-l-l-le, no-o-o-o-o."* The replay passion play always stars the distraught Mrs. Snoddie speaking out to an expanding band of Citizens. He puffs up a Snoddie mouth hole and lets it blow. *"Be-l-l-l-le NO-O-O-O-O."* Into the barbershop bevelled mirror he gathers up another Raphaelian storm cloud that rolls out cracks of thunder, Hell's bells.

"Be-l-l-l-le, no-o-o-o-o. Be-l-l-l-le NO-O-O-O-O."

The story serves up classic portions that The Barber mixes and matches. Add hot sauce from Snoddie's longstanding conflict with the Innkeeper, and The Barber will never hold back. In all the mimicking repertoire, that Snoddie woman might be the best performance — so much better when she's an agreed-upon open target. And his stand-up performance reaches its peak with that fat-cat incident. Customers eat it up, responding with stories of their own.

"I hear a shriek. It's louder than my Roger two-stroke lawnmower! I'm thinking, there's a murder in the neighbourhood. Some Belle was the victim. All I could 'ear was Be-l-l-l-le, no-o-o-o-o."

"Fred told me he was startled out of his snooze. Almost fell out of the lounge swing. He did say the same thing as the others: Has someone named Be-l-l-l-le been murdered?"

"You had to laugh just a little. Fat Charlie ran 'round looking like Lon Chaney in the Wolfman movie."

"I'm telling you, she was a goner. Amazing she could sit up with that fat cat on her."

"George's message from God: Christian Mummy, sit up! Christian Mummy, sit up!"

"It was a fire alarm. That Snoddie woman's fake flaming red hair and her face all ash. She was a burnout."

"Looked to me like an overweight version of that spinster British queen. Except it was Queen Elizabeth the Last."

"Only a one-Belle alarm. Be-l-l-l-le no-o-o-o-o."

And the one question The Barber asks every speaker in the chair? The question with the no answer.

"Did you see the kid throw the rock?"

"No."

Always no.

And lots of no's with asterisks:

"Be-l-l-l-le no-o-o-o-o, I missed that. For my part, I helped with Mrs. Snoddie. She was flat out."

"All I saw was Fat Charlie running helter skelter. Man oh man, with that fat cat stuck to his face. I peed myself."

"God is my witness, I couldn't stand another pronouncement out of the Pastor windbag. So I was out of there before he spotted me."

After the kitty-corner shot, Gunny disappeared, a slow fade into teenage-hood against the background of St. Marys. The years come and go after the first public performance of Belle and Mrs. Snoddie in that cat incident.

The corn-broom kid from the slab house on the edge of Town has kept out of the spotlight, blending into Town life with chores, school, part-time work, a .222 rifle instead of rocks.

One day, at the edge of seventeen, Gunny crosses the threshold of the barbershop with no appointment. The former skinny kid squeezes his large frame into the big red & nickel chair. Little David has grown into a Goliath at this side of six foot three. It's not often that the Barber has seen his own face reflected in the mirror with such an expression of surprise.

Gunny is quick past formality to the topic.

"You already know the story," he says. "I've heard that you tell it often. It's requested by many."

The Barber nods in a clarification. "Yes sir, a story that's become a bit of a legend."

Gunny has never been a Sir. He sits up. "Well, I am here for three reasons."

"Tell me, the kid who threw the rock, how can I help?"

"It's my birthday. I want a proper Barber haircut first."

"Your wish is my command, my young friend."

"I kind of pictured my birthday here in this chair. I dreamt about this special event in my life." He winks at The Barber. "No more Ma cuts. I love my Ma, but …"

The Barber's older experience steps up to save the young man from drowning in the chair of embarrassment. "Thank you, Gunny. I am honoured to be chosen as a cut above your mother. My goodness, a big birthday, seventeen. How else can we celebrate? Not just a hair trim but a special event." He turns to smile at his young charge. "Look Ma, no bowl." The fun has only begun. "And number two …?"

"Second, I want to hear the story firsthand, right from the master mimic himself."

"A favourite, well-practised through its popularity. Easy to repeat, young friend. And …?

"Third, I can give my perspective to that cat incident. If you don't mind my version."

"Mind? Any material" — The Barber coughs with a smile — "any detail that embellishes a fabulous story. I don't mind."

Getting right down to business, The Barber pulls on his eyebrows to stand them up and spikes up his hair. *"Be-l-l-l-le no-o-o-o-o."*

Gunny marvels at the blowfish head as the famous Snoddie comes to play in the bevelled mirror. "Super."

Super Snoddie noddies back, and blows. *"Be-l-l-l-le no-o-o-o-o."* The puckered hole blows again. *"Be-l-l-l-le no-o-o-o-o."*

As The Barber leaves the faces in the reflection, all hands on comb and scissors, Gunny settles in for his cut. He will never forget that treed fat cat, the connection to that horrible high school English teacher.

"Glad I had her just for Grade Nine," he says. "She never realized that I was the one. Her nose was always stuck up in the air. Took me half the year to figure out that she was thinking, not looking." He shakes his head. "She wasn't looking that day either." An honest look up at The

Barber. "The true story is that I saved that gluttonous thing. So fat it's stuck in the crutch of that maple tree. Were there any thanks?"

Gunny makes fun of the situation as only a kid from the slab house by the cement plant could. "Not even a polite purr from any of them but Smiley. Everybody else was too busy listening to George the pompous Pastor. He captured the full focus of the crowd when he said the word *shit*."

The Barber points out, holding one finger up. "Old Broadcast George. My conclusion from scores of recitals repeated here in the red & nickel chair is that he said shit three times." He puts fingers two and three up.

"Must have been some message. And Mrs. Snoddie flat out on Peel Street with that loud bleat."

The Barber has the beat, can't help himself. *"Be-l-l-l-le no-o-o-o."*

"I took my best leopard-frog shot from the corner lot on Jones."

"A kitty-corner bull's-eye."

"I took my best shot and was off. You see, I was a little on the late side to meet my friends by the Creek. As I ran down Peel, I kept my ears peeled, waiting and waiting for the official call, any shout-out behind me." He pauses and shakes his head. "Nothing but the wails of Fat Charlie."

"Be-l-l-l-le no-o-o-o."

"That's so perfect, you know."

"Thanks for your addition to a fantastic story."

The young man speaks up to the bevelled mirror. "You have a protocol, the well-known wager for a free haircut, do you not? I am betting on my stone."

The Barber interrupts his pocket reach. "The story alone gets the haircut. Keep the rock, Gunny. Your stone throw is already enough of a hit. De-treed a fat cat, eh?" He spreads out both his comb and scissor hands on the embroidered cape. "Show me anyways."

Gunny pulls out his fist and opens up a Chiquita-banana-speckled piece of granite. "A little beauty. Quartz veins. Look at the shape …"

Gunny passes his prize bullfrog target rock to the older man. He answers the question on his face. "Too good of a throwing rock to leave on the ground. Wasn't hard to find."

The Barber nods as he bounces the rock a few times, then squeezes it tight. "A little rock with a big part in that cat incident. May I call the cat tale 'The Sharpe Kid & The Fat Cat in the Tree,' or is that too long?"

Both smile in thought.

"Or how about 'Kitty Cornered on Peel' …?"

The young man is first to stop laughing. "But sir, a wager is a wager."

The Barber responds by circling the boy with his hand mirror. "Look at you, Gunny. There's face shadow there. I think the new man needs a hot lather and shave too. Free."

"Super, sir. Thanks so much. A two-for-one rock deal."

The older man laughs in line with the reflection of the huge smiling gob. "My son, you did go back for the rock, so *you* keep it for this very special day. I may have another freebie for you, though." Gunny turns to face the master mimic, who touches his shoulder. "Old enough for a smoke." A question put forth without a question mark. "I have some birthday cigars." He winks at his student. "They're best when shared. I feel the need to go back to the Devil's Smoke Pit."

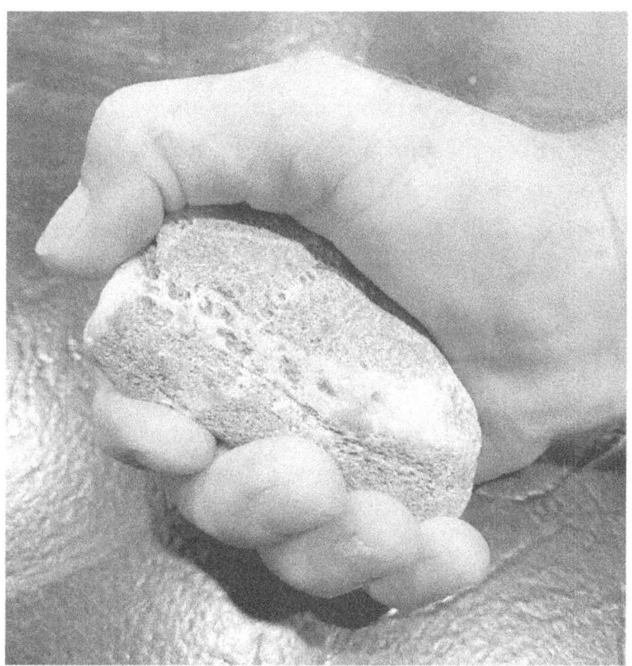

The Sharpe Kid

Gunny grasps the padded armrests in his excitement, almost pushing the nickel footrest off its socket. He could have just about popped his clutch right out of The Barber's big chair, like that stupid fat cat. An exclusive and rare invitation accepted répondez-s'il-vous-plaît. "How can I thank you, sir? And my special leopard-frog stone?"

"Not to worry, judge and jury approves. The rock is a bookend piece in the production. The finishing touch to the tale of that backward-swan-diving forty-pound Belle ringing off Constable Fat Charlie's skinny face."

Hell's bells, here he goes again. *"Be-l-l-l-le no-o-o-o."* The Barber's pufferfish face deflates and his voice turns soft and wise. "Gunny, a true *classic* chapter in our Town history." He stares up at the ceiling, razor and hot towel in hand. He tips the big chair back. "Now let's take care of that after-shadow. Tighten those lips so no razor nips."

Gunny mouth-pops a bubble out of his soapy face. "I guess there are some parts to my story that the Town needs to know. The small stone is nothing special. I picked it up by Bailey's Pond."

"Mouth closed — give me Panda cheeks."

Gunny dares not laugh. The razor is straight ahead along the neckline.

"Hold steady, steady. Shift your head right. Now steady, steady."

The Barber wipes the Barbasol from the blade. *Whack, whack,* on the leather belt attached to the back elbow of the barber chair.

"We'll discuss all details, and the little rock, after in the garden. Loosen lips with a cigar. I'll tell you how the Snoddie lady fits into the Devil's Smoke Pit. You're on time to enjoy this birthday."

The stars have aligned for a satisfactory finale to both Gunny's haircut wager and the cat incident on that kitty corner in the Town of St. Marys. Gunny follows the Barber back along the path to armless Venus with Little Scottie at her side. He directs the young lad to a seat on the concrete bench.

"You will not believe this, Gunny." He draws on his wine-dipped Grey Owl. "An economical choice for a smoke. The right price when one considers the cost of any hand-rolled Cuban cigar."

With no idea about any such distinctions, Gunny lights up on his first stogie puff.

"Our lucky day, lad. Wait and watch. We are getting the big pass-by."
He looks off through the smoke cloud to Jones Street. "Mrs. Snoddie's
on parade back from the Post Office. Her nibs."

Gunny looks over The Barber's shoulder to Jones Street. Easy for a
lad this side of six foot three. "Mrs. Snoddie? Super."

Gunny glows in great birthday fortune. Who would believe a private
audience with The Barber followed by a wine-dipped cigar? A smoke in
the Devil's Smoke Pit with an encore side performance of Mrs. Snoddie
playing herself in the live-action spectacle of his birthday. The Barber
guards his new club member, positioning Gunny between armless
Venus and himself, his back to Mrs. Snoddie.

Out on the sidewalk, Mrs. Snoddie leans up on the tips of her
sensible square shoes to try to identify the Barber's companion. She
spots two sinners in the Devil's Smoke Pit, but advantage to that gossipy
barber: the junipers are blocking a great view on this one. The Barber
doesn't even bother to turn, throwing back a cluster bomb.

"Yo-o-o-ou who-o-o-o. Yo-o-o-ou kno-ho." He throws in a tongue
birr. *"Bah-bah-bi-r-r-dzzz."* Volume is high. *"Ca-ca-cats kuh-kuh-kill
bah-bah-bi-r-r-r-dzzz."*

Gunny has never heard the full falsetto of The Barber beyond the cat
call of *Be-l-l-l-le no-o-o-o*. Does that woman hear it? He almost wants to
be a sneak and take a peek. The Barber blocks him with a huge smile.

"Be-l-l-l-le no-o-o-o-o …"

She must hear their snicker-coated guffaws under the smoke curls.
Gunny has made the right choice. "This is the best birthday of my
entire life."

Mrs. Snoddie shuffles out of the smoke scene, up the Post Office
hill, hidden by the Baptist Church, but no matter — no respect when
she's still within earshot. *"Be-l-l-l-le no-o-o-o."* The well-travelled cat
call is recognized for blocks and blocks.

A final wail blows from The Barber's puckered lips. *"No-o-o-o-o-o-o
…"*

The perfect target choice for a surefire bull's-eye is shelved in the cherry
bar cabinet next to the rock that looks like a cock. Often, when there are

no customers in the shop, The Barber grasps it over and over, swinging his right arm in a windmill. His back cracks with the perfect rotation, the exact weight in his right palm. This is the perfect pick that, with amazing grace, plucked out a treed forty-pound ball of fur in the legend of that cat incident.

The penis rock eventually does the walk to the Museum along with an assorted cast of field examples, and the deerskin diary, of course. For some unknown reason, though, Gunny's handheld prize is left behind.

Past midway point in the diary, two pages cover key points of that cat incident. The careful printed words surround a pencilled drawing of a banana-shaped rock that pops out from each side, across the stitched binding. When Larry the curator opens the diary, a bookmark note falls out. The poem somehow connected to that cat incident will puzzle amateur historians forever.

In a postscript, an internment for the orphaned stone, Terry the finishing carpenter will be tasked, thirty years later, with moving the seventeen-foot bevelled bar mirror, when off the lower shelf rolls a palm-sized granite rock. No pause in a heavy lift, no regrets at a mere stone found in the Stonetown — and the helpful hand tosses a strike out the back door into the sea of green ivy that smothers the unseen rock garden.

Chapter 8

The Knock

1967

For two years … maybe more,
Mandy first sees the worst,
For the last two years, maybe more,
He's drawn off in a four-horse hearse.

When night's curse turns to dawn's bright burst,
When black draught horses turn stallion white,
Shine on, shine on, providence first
Turns our path from strife …

After two dark years, seems a lot more,
When Mandy first sees in better light,
He calls it an epiphany.
How much stranger can it be
For any man … to first see?

> — (No signature; Larry the Curator thinks 1968–69: *"A definite Presbyterian tone of dire hellfire and in-the-floodlights redemption."* Amen to Hail Larry. This author imagines the draft took shape over a few smokes, some glasses of wine and lots of contemplation.)

Grandpa Andy Kittmer was one of the pioneers who walked to their Eden miles off the Huron Trail to stake their land. A claim north of Beechville marked on a wax-coated map. All he carried was a sack of supplies, an axe and an awl, strapped to a cast iron grate for a future fireplace. Everything ballooned out from his back under a tight canvas cover. He slung his musket so he could smoke his small clay pipe, and he walked all day and through the starstruck night to his place in the west. He knew he'd arrived when he saw the body of water corresponding to the pond on the map corner. He traced his finger along a thin blue line that leaked from the blue teardrop to the hand-scrawled X in red. He had arrived at the lushly carpeted Upper Thames Valley, one Thames Valley removed from the future Town of St. Marys.

The glacial movement that created the Canadian Shield dumped loads of a loose rock and loam mix along the Upper Thames Valley to sculpt what is now Zorra. These walking pioneers coming from the stone haven of Scotland to rockbound Zorra must have gloried in the forest cover and ample topsoil. The almighty rock facing the Highlands would have eliminated any paralysis on the job to be done in Zorra.

For pioneers relief comes first. Clearing the forest builds up the timber stock. The big stuff becomes the walls, trusses and support beams. Prettier stuff goes to flooring, door and sash. The rough stuff becomes fuel for cooking and warmth.

Rocks sourced as close as possible to the cabin become the stone chimney. The huge stone fireplace base comes from further afield, or possibly astream: Harrington Creek pops up some prime pieces of a nice flat limestone.

"Make sure you warm your cabin up before lighting your first fire," goes the usual wisdom. "If that base piece is cold, it'll crack. Best done in spring and summer." Many on their first walks to Beechville carry a small cast stove back with them.

The rich Zorra terrain is unequalled in agricultural Canada. The well-drained land with a slight roll and hardwood bush borders holds a fertile dream. But if Canada has a backbone of stone, Zorra Township is a ground-zero example. Country wags might call it a Canadian spine dressed in a Scottish kilt.

"Zorra Township, it'd be a Kittmer kilt, I tell ye."

"MacKay."

"Kittmer. They're Campbell kin. Many more of 'em."

"MacKay. Many more of 'em in Zorra, lad."

Sexual probability always enters the conversation in an eighteenth-century metaphorical way, most commonly using animal habits that cover a lot of innuendo:

"Rabbits, you be right."

A parallel point uses favourite foods.

"More Scotch eggs, laddie."

Someone always plays the Robbie Burns.

"Yes laddie, we're the food basket and stomach of our great country. The kilt covers the important parts of our country. And its genna-tilia."

The meadows will be mined of stone forever and ever. Stones never disappear, and neither does the grind of a farm life. The farm runs by the clock of nature.

"Son, you get 'em in the spring when the rocks pop out of Mother Earth. The soft ground makes it easy to pry, and the no green makes 'em easy to see."

(The Barber will learn that springtime brings a bevy of wagers. Best to guard the threshold so as not to be overrun by unspectacular examples.)

Fewer blunt obstacles protects farm equipment and allows even rows for seeding, tilling and harvesting. All that fieldstone picked, cleared and piled turns into building stone. Square choices go to house foundations. Large but nothing special? Those can face the new barn. Picks of moderate size are sent to the manure pit wall behind the shed. Massive slabs of granite stand in rows as tombstones at the Zorra Highlands Cemetery.

Scots, with an inherent love of stone, make light of their vast field yield.

"Wee exercise springs the winter out of the man, laddie."

"Gets the flab off ye, laddie."

The Kittmer clan's solid Scottish DNA was bored right out of Loch Lomond's hard-ass highland granite. Yes, the grinding personality of the Kittmers — as hard to move as the field rocks of Zorra. They came. They sawed. They cleared.

The original Grandpa Andy at the top of the tree has spread out to an orchard of Kittmer appellations in Zorra Township. A certain confusion reigns here, not just because so many have the Kittmer last name but because a reverence for the original pioneer walker stamps most sons with Andrew. Forty-five Kittmers are listed in the Zorra phone exchange, twelve with the first name of Andrew. *("Those Andys pop up like spring stones.")*

No sweat, though, as all the Andy Kittmers are differentiated by well thought-out nicknames. For example, our hero Mandy's cousin Farmer Andy is the oldest of the fourth generation. His son in the fifth is Junior. The list goes on with Fireman Andy, Auto Andy and Councillor Andy. If you need a combine, go see Tractor Andy, his nephew Massey Andy or his second cousin Deere Andy.

Our one and only Mandy is an uncle to both Guitar Andy and Massey Andy. At elementary school Mandy had three other same-names in his class, but no one from Zorra Township ever mistakes the profile of this particular Andrew Kittmer. The origin of his nickname is obvious the moment you find yourself looking up at the sheer size of this man. The name Man-dy stuck right from the birth of the twelve-pound baby. The Barber is amazed that any human being could be even larger than his friend Marvin.

In rugby, Mandy's the running flanker, a fired-up farm fuel tanker. *"Mandy mows the pitch."*

Those recent Canadian fire team champions, the Zorra Volunteer Firefighters and Tug-of-War Team, nod in agreement:

"He pulls the hose like it's a piece of rope. See him swing those ladders around, on his own. Fire monster."

And those caber tosses that move the Highland Games crowd back and further back:

"Don't be standing there, laddie."

"Huh?"

"Mandy's up, laddie."

"Moving ..."

(The Scottish games in Embro north of Beechville, by the way, boast a world caber-toss record. Who might that be?)

As for Canada's national sport? His wife Terri's interest in hockey kept Mandy in the game as an All-Ontario Midget defenseman. Terri loves a lad on blades.

And behind those XXXL gloves and size-sixteen skates is a giant heart. Mandy is a good listener home-trained by his mother, catching all the talk with a softhearted filter. After their initial surprise at the size of things coming towards them out of Zorra, Citizens come to think of Mandy as that friendly giant.

"Saw him lift the rear end of old Dr. Lane's car. His grandson stuck the axle on a piling."

"That's a Cadillac Eldorado. Heavy ride."

"Kid caught it real tight, but Mandy just lifts the car up. Two steps, swivel, and it's off."

"His tug-of-war teammates just hold on and let Mandy pull."

Terri, on the other hand, wonders about future back problems.

She and Mandy carry on as the fourth generation that calls Kittmer Farm #1 their home farm. The home farm is one of a few Centennial farms in Zorra remaining under family ownership.

Mandy was too young to remember Hurricane Hazel's ire. Life's a bitch that took a high-wind gravel run through rural western Ontario on October 17, 1927. Missing the Kittmer family home, Hazel headed on up the rise of the backyard, behind the double-door shed and up to the big barn. Hazel took a rip at the thick walls to no avail. She wailed at the walls, throwing baton javelins of strapping barn-board off into the wind. Anything loose inside followed up, up and out of the barn on the biggest chunks of roof for a magic carpet ride. In a short and thoughtful piece of windy performance art, Hazel dumped all debris in a circular pattern around Harrington Pond. The original barn, enjoyed by four generations of Kittmers, was turned to marshmallow-roasting campfire wood in seconds.

The stone walls of Old Grandpa Andy's original 1830s foundation were all that remained, holding on in topless fashion after the whip of Hazel. No longer a barn, it became a family monument, holding its position on the sidelines of the well-kept yard.

For Mandy's father, the third-generation Grandpa Andy, one barn lost was a lesson learned. "No sense having your teats in one basket." He decided to diversify by building up his milk operation.

Every farm in the Township had always kept a woodlot along with twenty or so acres of uncleared pasture. A proud local tradition of Holstein milk cows started in those marginal corners around the corn fields.

Mandy's father soon realized that by modernizing equipment he could make bigger money from the uncleared pastures than he could with cash crops. The barn on Farm #1 was no more, but Farms #2 and #3 were ready to accommodate the latest milking technology in their two massive barns. Dairy cows are hard work, so Granddad let other hands pass the parade of suction cups.

Before long, any unsold corn was helping to feed the Kittmers' quota of one hundred and fifty registered Holsteins split between the two barns.

Granddad always enjoyed an audience, whether on town trips or over a fence on a country line. "My cows only leave the barn to shit," he would boast.

That got their attention.

"Do it in the pasture. Smart as a dog, my cows."

The Kittmers' herd may not have been the largest, but it soon became the most prestigious and prodigious milk herd in Canada.

The Kittmer herd dings the bells at all the nearby fairs and beyond. From Stewart's Carnation Dairy in St. Marys to the Oxford County Fall Fair and the Royal Winter Fair — and soon to the young nation of Cuba — all agree: *"Best milk in the country."*

Their cows always make the big stage at The Nationals in Toronto. "They should put that cow on a lie detector" is a sly piece of Blanshard humour. Who would believe all those repeat championships? Easier to call into suspicion the Kittmers' ability to chart their yields.

When the Kittmer Holsteins aren't winning blue ribbons at the Royal Winter Fair, they're standing in comfort under the shelter of two ultra-modern barns in Zorra Township. The legend lives on.

"Those cows are trained to shit outside."

"No shit."

Pigs may never fly, but the Kittmers have their cows flying to communist Cuba. Starting in the 1960s, Kittmer Holsteins travel to the tropics on cargo Boeing 727s as snow cows.

Cows flying? Communist cows? You'll never stop the country wags. *"Those Holsteins are inherent socialists. It's all about the herd."*

And tropical Holsteins: *"No problem with bare teats. Cuba has topless beaches."*

"Sign me up, laddie."

With birth rates up, the Cubans have been importing milk to feed their young. Amid a US boycott of their former colony, Canada steps from the sidelines as a kind and tolerant *Norte Americano* friend. The first exports to communist Cuba are the top-of-the-line Kittmer brand. A full Zorra-bred-and-born cow harem rides in cargo coach with one bull — Mitchell the stud — segregated and sedated up front.

This larger-than-life bull story requires a larger-than-life man. Mandy travels to the Oriente region of Cuba for herd consultation and implementation.

"Old Mitch had the perfect flight pitch," Mandy tells Terri later.

"Flight pitch?"

"The key of B — bull snoring."

The Barber hears the best of his stories over Mandy's regular cut and sometimes a smoke.

"Those cows are quick at the Spanish."

The Barber battles bushy hair while sneaking a look at the big man's expressions.

"When called for milking, the cows speak any language." Mandy starts to laugh. "I sell them my best Holsteins. The Cubans call them Whol-stay-nez."

The Barber asks for a repeat on the Latin.

"Whol-stay-nez. They pronounce every syllable. Mandy works okay in Spanish. But Holsteins?"

The Barber is quick. He complements Mandy's cow call with a Cisco Kid accent. "Si Señor, Cease-ko Kid wants zum Whol-stay-nez steaks."

"Si, Señor Barber, I send zee cows. They become Whol-stay-nez *vacas*."

"Think of the cash flow, amigo. Say *adiós* to daily chores."

"Always taxes and lawyers, then death. Señor, there will be always chores on *el ranchero*."

This first Cuban cow flight occurs twenty years before the first pink-skinned Canadian tourist steps off the plane at Varadero Beach. Andy even meets Fidel Castro at a reception in the Canadian Embassy in Havana.

Andy has been quick to pick up a few phrases from the Cuban farmers, starting with *cerveza fría por favor* and chitchat about the hot climate, but he needs to prepare himself for this prestigious meeting with a few phrases. Terri can hear him in the shower.

"*Señor Kit-mar*, do you think these Whol-stay-nez will produce *bastante* milk to feed our *hijos*?"

"*Por supuesto, Señor Presidente.*"

"*Habla español muy bien, Señor Kit-mar.*"

"*Gracias, Presidente. Solo hablo de* Whol-stay-nez, *El Presidente.*"

Fidel, his brother Raul, the ranchers from the Oriente, the Minister of Agriculture, a herd of bureaucrats and technocrats, Embassy staff, and a few Russians kicking around — they all love everything about the big man from rural Canada.

"Señor Kit-mar, are there many men *muy grande* as you back in Ca-na-da?"

"Señor Presidente, Canada is a land of giants."

"*Diga que no. Señor?*"

Mandy is probably the only man in history that could wink in a conversation with Fidel Castro. "*Claro que si señor,* but they are dwarfs compared to you, *El Presidente y los Cubanos.*"

"*Señor Kit-mar, venga, venga.* We go to smoke on the garden veranda. My personal cigars, only available at *Tienda el Presidente.*"

"*Adelante, Presidente.*"

This is Fidel Castro — a lawyer and a man ahead of his time in the agricultural field — recognizing best in class in the Zorra farmer.

Mandy may not remember the hurricane, but the old foundation has never been left for ruin in his imagination. From the get-go, from childhood play to a hidden teenage smoke and his first kiss with Terri, his mind has transformed the foundation into a fieldstone stage.

Now that Mandy and Terri's two sons have both grown up and graduated from Guelph, the nest is empty and an adult vision has time enough to flourish. While walking the dogs, mowing the grass, or fetching and bending on honey-do jobs in his free time, Mandy contemplates the shadows of the past as he wanders the rise behind the shed. The quality of stone, and the amount required to produce these massive walls! All of it is his family heritage in stone to save for future Kittmers.

One night, he makes a post-dinner announcement. "I like The Barber's rock garden."

Terri hasn't seen it, but she's seen this coming. "You like that Devil's Smoke Pit. A little puff out back!"

Señor Kit-mar does know a good smoke — he's seen the generational rocks over more puffs out back than he'd care to admit. He doubles down on Town. "Even a Havana cigar is nothing compared to the beauty of his rock collection."

After dinner, Terri makes notes while Mandy talks her through the foundation's revitalization. "More than a rock garden," he tells her. "Look, there's enough rock in the walls to build four rock gardens. We need a showplace of our own. Water falling over some landscape features into a pond. Everything will be the same but different … better." Mandy fades into his thoughts. "And a statue, maybe even two. With arms. With an urn spouting water."

Let Terri make most of the choices. But definitely a barbecue in the old harness room up front, close to the propane and electricity inputs. Leave it open air. Might as well add a smoker for some of those famous Kittmer-raised braised lamb ribs.

"We need to apply a little TLC. Maybe I'll call up old Bulldozer Bob Turlock for some land levelling. That'll give access for scaffolding. Bob's Motomotion mini backhoe will be the right size for a little cleanup and drainage. He can leave the big Cockshutt backhoe at home."

Terri works his plan, by her design. "I'll give the twins a call. Joyce has a real design flare. Did you see the garden they did at the Cruise home?"

Mandy knows that Joyce and Jo-Anne of St. Marys Gardenscapes need to be booked months ahead because they just get too busy. But Terri's a magician, and a high school friend.

The twins stop by that weekend, bronzed guns in motion. Long summer hours in high-lace work boots, low shorts and T's buff up the duo. The double-J team envision a Coryphantha, the tips of its cactus flowers yellow and red, following the sun's reflection on the stone along the south wall.

"Terri, we see wisteria flowing on the east wall. A warm wash but no direct sunlight. With some wooden terracing for support, this becomes a shady place for morning coffee."

The big man puts the plan into motion with the help of Bulldozer Bob and his Motomotion Mini. Even in fading light Mandy burrows away on the idle equipment on his overtime, installing the electricity, gas lines and lights, and taking care of anything Terri wants repositioned, added on or taken away. Mandy's a man possessed to complete a lifelong dream.

One night, the late summer stillness through the open screen door catches Terri's sudden attention. Too quiet on a quiet farmstead. It's dark with no happy husband slapping the back door, no boots flipping up and flopping onto the rubber mat. Terri switches the light on, passing through the mudroom to flip on the shed floodlights. She peers through the screen at nothing. Quickly her feet fill the red Wellingtons, hands grab the wall-mounted flashlight. She runs outside, the screen door slapping behind her.

The old foundation's shadow has faded into the starry horizon. She keeps the light on her careful steps.

"Mandy! Mandy ..."

Terri wastes no more energy calling to silence. The shed floodlights fade before the dark mass of the old barn. She gathers her breath as she scrambles up the incline through the wide dark entrance, the barn door long blown away to firewood on Harrington Pond. To her right, moonlight reflects off the chrome-faced barbecue and smoker — and off the enamelled stepladder on the barn's slate floor.

Terri finds an unconscious lump up against a corner wall hugging the ladder. Mandy looks asleep but is unresponsive to her cold palm on his chest. An emergency nurse, she reverts to work mode, checking for a pulse. Relieved, she runs for the house to call the Hall ambulance service. Her second call reaches David next door at Farm #2. Before returning to the foundation she makes a last call to her mother, instructing her to meet her at St. Marys General Hospital.

The good wife grabs two lamps from the shed, dropping one by the former barn's entrance. A star to follow for the ambulance crew in an unfamiliar land. Terri places the second lamp on the barbecue. She wraps Mandy in a XXXL coat, pulling a mudroom blanket around his feet. She waits by her unconscious heap of a man, sobbing.

Two years later, maybe a little more, he's on cue for his time in the big red & nickel chair.

A very big man who fills the barber chair in a squeeze from red padded armrest to red padded armrest, Mandy has always been treated with gentle engagement, never the weighty debate and heavyweight wagers of a Big Boss Marvin. Protocol takes a big adjustment, though, after one knock of a rock.

Today Terri joins the routine for the drop-off. She pulls up the large SUV directly in front of the narrow barbershop. Before the tires are parallel to the curb The Barber appears at the passenger door for open Mandy greetings.

"Big man, welcome to the big city."

Mandy returns a smile and waits. The Barber, always an efficient host, retreats to the rear hatchback and lifts out the XXXL wheelchair. The marvel of technology unfolds before all eyes on the sidewalk. You could almost hear the *voilà*. Terri swings open the passenger door. With Mandy's upper-body help, she can shift his legs toward curbside. The Barber has done his share of lifting, between old Moose members and various dance partners at Community Players. He lowers himself to an under-arm embrace while Mandy drops his massive arms over The Barber's shoulders. Both men are up in a sidewalk embrace with a few tactical dance steps that allow Terri to move the wheelchair in for a soft landing. There's no more comfortable wheelchair, with the additional quilted padding handcrafted by Terri's mom, Marguerite. ("Thank your mother. But all those brown cows on the patches? Kittmers have Holsteins." "Mother's a Townie through and through, Mandy.")

Conversation is limited while they execute the curb-drop. The Barber pushes the wheelchair over the threshold. On their first try transferring Mandy to the barbershop chair, the wheelchair lurches backwards. Mandy weighs fifty to sixty pounds less after two years, but still tips the scales at 250-plus pounds of great pride and adjusted joy.

Big lesson learned: lock the wheels when moving the big man, so you have a fall-back position.

After the big red & nickel chair has embraced the reverse swing from the wheelchair, Terri lets out a nervous laugh. "The look on your faces when the chair swung away! Two bit players gandy-dancing with the curtain up, and no practice."

Terri turns, taking one last look through the front window as she disappears down the sidewalk.

The Barber looks at his friend in the mirror. "Mandy, have you been munching on the Hawkins Cheezies?"

The Barber knows his good customers. He is familiar with Mandy's little weakness for a classic Canadian snack. The mountain of independence has struggled with mobility and the need for help, and letting The Barber manhandle him from passenger seat to the big chair and back on haircut day is based on respect, friendship and trust. At this point in the physics exercise, great friends can rely on a touch of humour. Today, though, The Barber recognizes something more in the air, a special moment. Mandy in the chair is not just comfortable but quiet, solemn. He responds to introductory questions with the most neutral expression, not the usual Mandy-sized smile at the Cheezie cut.

The Barber has heard all the stories on *the knock*, as Mandy calls the accident. Bulldozer Bob, son David Kittmer, both the Hall father-and-son ambulance attendants, and Dr. Bob the Town's new GP have all provided details during their regular cuts. He has little time for quiet contemplation now before the tap turns on.

"When that rock moved, I was ahead of myself."

The Barber anticipates a change, looking into the mirror. Mandy's eyes focus off to the side, towards the floor. The Barber waits in silence for the next words, fussing with the scissors and comb.

"I could see everything move. Except I was at the centre, looking down from the top of the ladder." The disaster movie reel runs again. "The entire barn shifted underneath me. The ladder moved forward. Without me. Next thing I'm Rocky the flying squirrel. Surreal."

No room for laughs; Mandy sucks up half the air in the railway-car-long barbershop. "I just feel myself flying. Imagine that! First it's up in the air — look, I'm flying! — then the crash-dive down. I recall falling, collapsing to the ground. My head swung back. *Whack*. It planted on something." Big exhale of reality.

"From that point I remember nothing. Nothing more until Terri squeezes my hand in the hospital. What a surprise when I opened my eyes to find myself in City General Hospital, Room 406, Intensive Care."

Mandy inhales any energy left in the barbershop and lets it go in a torrent. "I saw this rock move, an odd piece of pointed granite. It was under the truss." He stares at an unknown point on the floor. "My ladder twists sideways, I twist the other way." Mandy shakes his head with a wry face to the reflection. "Two focking years."

The friends lock eyes in the mirror.

"For the next year, all I wanted was to get that foundation out of my mind. I honestly planned to remove it. I couldn't stomach looking at another sunrise with that monument to a knock on my head outside my window."

How could Terri have had all that patience, Mandy wonders now, with let's-call-it-what-it-is, depression? Love is always the answer. Terri thought the morning sun through the living room window would warm things up. But all he did was stare at that cherry fireplace mantel, every nook and cranny carved in his mind. The patience of Job allowed her to wait for over a year, saying nothing, until one morning she opened up over their morning cup of coffee.

"Honey," she began, sitting beside him, careful to steady the ready cup in his massive hands. "We've wasted a good deal of time and a mountain of coffee beans not picking up on the view." She turned from the window and fist-hammered his head with tenderness. "You have to get that thick head of yours turned around and face up. Yes, and it *is* face up, all uphill." He still remembers the snuggle in her bustle in that moment, the kiss on his forehead, that set him up for the key words she uttered next: "Mandy Kittmer is the man for the challenge."

Now Mandy closes his eyes, tilts his head sideways left and right down toward the floor, away from the bevelled mirror reflection. The crack of his neck breaks the silence. "Terri called our Zorra neighbours Bulldozer Bob and Alex McLean. Alex called in his extended family of masons and concrete workers. Bob showed up this time with the Motomotion Mini at the crack of dawn. All good. Bob sometimes stuck around just to talk, without any Cockshutt. A good friend knows when to go, when to stop and just listen."

Mandy's getting that mile-wide smile back. "Alex and the lads took two weeks on the concrete. Just like that, the access path was turned from steps to a smooth switchback. I said more thank-yous in those two weeks than I'd said in many years. Alex told me this is what friendship is all about. Sure, I know about friends, but Alex never even presented a bill. When I caught him alone he told me that my thanks was not necessary, my friendship was payment enough. I was stuck there pumping his hand. All he said was, you're welcome my friend."

"Nice. Does this mean you're expecting a free haircut too?"

Poker face dealt back. "Funny." He stretches into a smile. "The night after they finished, I took up where I left off two years back. Terri prepares our dinner, delicious as always, and then she cleans up. There's time to send me off up the path, on two wheels. I wheel my skinny butt around the hairpin turn of the new path." Mandy's hands push forward as his head leans into a turn. "On my own. Up, up I go in my wheel-chair." He's rolling both hands beside the red padded armrests, and then he stops. "It would just be a walk with a big loop across the rise of the hill for you or anybody else. Me, I have to stop at the switchback and catch my breath. That night I thought that the expenditure of energy wheeling up there might have created a delusion. You know, lack of oxygen."

The Barber listens, quiet with busy buzzy hands.

"Realizing that Terri was the girl for me was my first epiphany. Now here comes the second of my life."

His friend in the mirror soaks up the silence that surrounds a man in a glow. His charge has not finished the confessional flow. All eyes return to the contact point within the world of the mirror.

"I had the wrong focking rock in my head. My whole memory was consumed with two years of horror detailing one particular rock. Weird how I could paint a picture of the thing that was so wrong. Excuse the pun, but I assumed my picture was rock solid. Wrong."

The Barber returns comb and scissors to holster position.

"Knock, knock, who's on first? It takes a second knock to get to reality. My attention zoomed in on what you might think is a ghost or a phantom. But in my mind? I registered the real thing for the first time." Mandy looks down again, then returns his focus to the mirror. He sucks in a deep breath. "How could I ever miss it? There in my frame of view, there on the ground, lay the open apparition."

The Barber thinks Mandy has gone biblical.

"About two feet right of where the ladder fell, there was *this* rock. I knew in a flash that this was the real deal. I had no memory of *this* rock until that very moment. Bingo, an epiphany."

Mandy's eyes narrow, gauging the level of understanding in the reflection. The Barber picks up the look in the mirror. Automatically he intensifies his look back while nodding his head once. The silence holds.

"That night after dinner I sat in my wheelchair looking at the second rock in the corner. Two hours. I could feel the blood move through my brain. How the mind works, eh? That second rock had been lying there, hidden in memory for almost two years. Terri freaked a bit, thinking something was wrong up there, again. After two hours she came to get me. She couldn't help but wonder if there was another knock in her life. She was not impressed." He laughs. *"Paging Andrew Kittmer."* That was the first thing she said. *"Seriously, we need an intercom out here. We have lights in the yard, lights and more lights out here. But no method of communication."*

Eye contact in the mirror's reflection. "It's so simple. I just woke up one morning, click, a fresh view of life. A whole cliché experience on the right side of bed, waking up to a new dawn. The first thing I thought was how grateful I was for Terri. Next, how that stone foundation helped make the Kittmer clan. And I also woke up with a plan."

The Barber stares straight and silent at Mandy in the mirror. There are no frowns or winks reflected, not a moment of laughter between friends.

"I can do it all on wheels. I can provide for my family, for Terri, manage a farm business, have a place in my community, all with a novel landscape garden accessible to me. Turning an ancient space into a new Kittmer vista. For me, now, after two years? Life is starting to roll."

Mandy can't help acting out before the Town's greatest mimic. He casts a look to an invisible person at the back of the mirror, and then in a big man's baritone: *"Rolling … rolling … rolling along …"* The big man goes high. "Light me up a Havana, Terri dear. I think I'll take in the sunset." Then a big man's falsetto: "I'll pour you some port, dear. Yeah baby." He coughs out the final words with an armrest drumroll.

"Here I am, mobile on the farm. I'm able to inspect the project with the cement path on my own power. No more imagining, but seeing it all myself. They call me Site General Manager." Mandy puts his right hand over his eyebrows and points to the mirror with his left. "More like sight manager. I see something else that needs doing. Hey you, I see you, do that for me."

Floor look, then he comes up to the reflection. "Two focking years. Two years to get me up and mobile. I'll follow with a lifetime of physiotherapy and home care, of course. That's all good. But it took me two years to change my mindset."

The Barber stands in the bevelled mirror's reflection with scissors and comb on holster and a smiling, half-dumb look of amazement. The big man is not finished by a long stretch.

"Work on the barbecue is complete, ready for ribs. Let's eat. Listen, I want my ribs to make a sunset performance. Whoops, looks like rain, no problem. Terri added a retractable awning, a fifteen-by-ten rectangle that covers our family on Sunday or a glass of wine any day." Mandy winks, with that mile smile. "Easy and expedient access to the potty."

"I know you can stand," The Barber says. "So I assume you can whiz from somewhere? Off the edge?"

"A man's true freedom is to pee. Terri turns away."

The Barber laughs with him at the private-function reference. "Amazing grace, my friend."

"More than grace, it's Terri."

"Amazing Terri, my friend."

"All in seriousness, it's all about a certain karma. You might say stone karma, with the Kittmer family and the history of the Township of Zorra. The leftover foundation stood solid through the worst of hurricanes, and stood silent through two generations of Kittmer neglect. Karma has moved back in, fast." He pauses with a breath of relief. "Overall, I think a revived landscape strengthens my Kittmer soul."

He smiles at The Barber in the mirror. "You have to come out for the tour. We have garden lights on the path and floods showering the west wall. My McLean path has perfect pitch, a switchback laid alongside perennials picked by the twins." Mandy takes a moment to appreciate their flower choices, which include white rosebushes. Stunning. He gears up. "Providence comes from strife to lead me on this path. My contribution to the next Kittmer generation is the landscape Eden in the foundation."

"You do have the vision."

"I didn't need two legs to do the lifting. God left me mobile on two wheels with two strong hands."

"Big heart and great mind, my friend."

"The double-J's had already worked out the design plans from before, and they adapted them easily. Everyone wanted to guarantee my mobility in my special spot. It's all done now, for the most part, with some hanging details to process."

"I can see you out there, on two big wheels, puffing on a Cubano el Cortos."

"Lucky moment. The Cortos, I mean. Sent to me by my old amigo Fidel through the embassy in Ottawa." Mandy is almost lost in a proud moment. "You know that he wanted to come to Canada and visit me in the hospital? Security showed up at City Hospital. Huge rugby-sized Cubans with football-sized Mounties. Everyone had identical Raybans. Mandy whispers to the side with a wink in the bevelled bar mirror. "Never happened. I am sworn to secrecy."

The Barber is lost in the intrigue of this conversation. "Secrecy? What secrecy? Fidel didn't visit?"

"*He* didn't visit. But get this." Mandy cocks his head to the side, passing secret information. "Here I am in Recovery, now Room 257 at City Hospital. Sitting up in bed eating my lunch, through a straw by the way. I look up. Unbelievable. A voilà moment. There's my amigo Raul Castro standing there. I ask him what brings Raul to Canada? Man-day, he says …" Mandy turns on the Latino channel. " 'Señor Kit-mar, I come to see *mi amigo de Whol-stay-nez!* I gee-eve you *mi hermano*'s guarantee of a lifetime supply of hez personal *cigarrillos, muy favoritos, el Cortos!*' Here I am, unable to take my Cuban amigos for a tour of the Kittmer home farm. '*Amigo. No te preocupes. Tu hijo* David gave us the tour. Barns. *Finca uno, dos, tres, cuatro,* such *tierra rica.* You hev lots of *tierra bonita y rica, Señor. Una familia muy simpatica incluye su esposa muy bonita, Terri.'* "

Again The Barber pulls out his Cisco Kid. "*Las vacas* gee-eve *mucha leche, Señor.* Derefore I gee-eve amigo *mucho cigarrillos.*"

Being lost in translation grounds the friends in levity. Mandy reflects. "All is good on the Kittmer family farm. My revision of plans with the help of Terri and everyone else gives me a reboot on my life. Her boot on my arse. Our life — Terri and I, with the kids, Kittmer clan, friends, neighbours — all of them make up a wild bunch that I look on as abundant stars." He points up to the barbershop's tin ceiling. "More important is this rock, the right rock. My second biggest epiphany involves this rock. This morning, I bring to you *the* rock."

There should have been thunder from heaven or at least a bit of a drumroll to underline The Barber's true astonishment. "The real rock?"

"The real deal."

The Barber has listened to the details, still asks for clarification. "Not the first rock, but the second. Call it the epiphany rock. You mean *the* rock."

"Yes sir, the real deal, the stone alone. Here for you."

"Look, I have to be straight. Your story gets a free haircut on its own. Let no stone be turned in for the wager. Of course, if you want a second cut or a free shave, bet's on. But the story alone is enough for a win. The second epiphany rock makes the cut, of course, but it's not necessary in this case. Keep the rock please, sir!"

"Sir. After my two years in a fog, this … this rock is part of the process. The epiphany process means turning the stone over. Turn the stone over, turn that chapter in my life around with a simple gesture. I am moving *the knock* on. Moving on, by turning the actual stone over to you."

"That's a super big turnover. I do not need such a worthy rock. How can I help carry the load for you going forward?"

"Please, this is the load. Please take it off me, friend."

They both glow at each other in silence.

"Mandy, I will take this load of yours. I have a favoured spot in my Rock Garden. Special place for my friend's heritage rock."

"It *will* give me closure."

"Does that wheelchair allow you in a smoking zone?"

One finger points to the chair, the other points to the back door. "Light me up, Señor."

The Barber removes the cape with a practised shake.

"Terri permits me one, sometimes two cigars a week. Jesus, that Fidel is couriering me two boxes a month. I have her additional grace to bring one on a trip to Town when she encourages me to see my good friend." He gives a nod to The Barber. "As for the ample Cortos leftovers, I spread the wealth. I am Welcome Wheels at the Zorra Volunteer Firefighters and Tug-of-War practices, Moose gatherings and the Presbyterian Church chicken BBQ. Everything I offer goes up in smoke post-meeting."

Mandy cannot imagine a better finish to his confessional trip to Town. The big man stands and swivels onto the wheelchair with the wheels still locked. For a little giddyup, he pulls another little mimic on the Cisco Kid. "*Vayanos muchachos.*"

"Let's wheel on out," The Barber says. "The rock?"

"Rock's in the duffle bag."

"Cortos?"

"In the Eastern Star bag beside the front door."

The Barber reverses the wheelchair towards the threshold for the bag grab, then back through the narrow-gauge barbershop. "My goodness, it looks like a … frog? A rock toad? "Wow, this *is* some free haircut deal."

"This is not about any free other than *free*dom. Thank you. Release me from the frog, toad or whatever animal."

And our trip out back has a happy loser and a satisfied winner. The Barber pushes Mandy out the back door. "Nice-looking cigar. El Cortos, Señor?"

One thumb up. "Mi amigo Fidel, gracias." A point over to armless Venus. "Get me wheeled over here. Better view." A teamwork pull, drag and slide over the pea gravel puts the dynamic duo in position. "There's a second gift for you."

"From your contacts in Cuba?"

"The big contact himself. Fidel sent me it. His first four boxes of new, larger ring-finger-sized el Cortos." Mandy gives The Barber a sideways secret-information look before continuing in an in-the-know voice.

"Restricted admission through *el Presidente's* mark. Fidel hears about my release from the hospital. Get this …" A brief pause to counter the struggle between a puff, a breath and more words. "Get this, Fidel uses a Kittmer Holstein on the label. It's a Canadian bull, my old Mitchell, on the front label of Cuban cigar boxes. The bull logo on the cigar wrap is a sight. The four boxes labelled with a Holstein did create a bit of a stir at the Canadian Embassy in Havana. The wave stirred on in Ottawa with the insistence on diplomatic delivery."

"Cigars in a diplomatic pouch?"

"It only gets better. Fidel insisted the Canadians deliver the cigars. *El Presidente* left no forwarding address or options in delivery. He phoned Prime Minister Pierre Trudeau with direct instructions. 'Pierre, this ez *mucho grande amigo* with Whol-stay-nez. Señor Kittmer came *al principio* with the first *vacas*. He ez *amigo mio como tu mi amigo*, Pierre.' "

"Not the mailman?"

"Thunder in a bottle from Fidel. *El Presidente* spoke. '*Cubanos* buy *mucho* Whol-stay-nez so *Canadienses mandan los cigarrillos a mi amigo* Man-day! *No cigarrillos, nada vacas, nada* Whol-stay-nez.' "

"Ouch."

Mandy is tickled to his toes with his chair on the pea gravel of the smoke pit. Stranger than fiction, the tall tale relating the diplomatic incident on Whol-stay-nez.

"It must have cost them a bundle," he goes on. "They came with false pride stuck to their faces. A black Cadillac shows up at Farm #1 filled with three grumpy bureaucrats. They had tried Farm #3 before being redirected. Charging by the hour keeps their chauffeur smiling. Terri made them wait in the yard while she confirmed and rechecked the package in good order. Angus the dog growled. Terri said she could hear the limo's gravel churn on the concession road before the German shepherd sounded the alarm."

"I bet the farm dog would love the taste of civil service." The Barber acknowledges a favourite pet. "Nice and fatty fiesta piggies for hungry Angus." A question of continuity puts the pause button on the fun. "How did they get to City Airport?"

"A twin Otter out of Ottawa."

"Ching, ching and ching again."

"We the taxpayers pay for all that ching."

On a sunny, cool morning the friends bask in their special spot while the sun filters through the Cuban nightclub cloud of smoke. They marvel. They contemplate. They puff. Life happens as an unexpected interruption from a routine plan. Just then, a familiar voice booms from the Jones Street sidewalk.

"I see you-u-u-u there. I see you-u-u-u. *You-ou who-oo!* I see you there, the smoke pillar of the Devil's we-e-e-e-ed."

"Hello there, Mrs. Snoddie. Yes, we can see you-u-u-u to-o-o-oo." The Barber can't help himself, going full falsetto. First, the necessary pinched nose. Exhale. "You-u who-o-o-o. I see you-u-u-u."

Mrs. Snoddie lets the monkey-see mimic go. The two warhorses are long familiar with the field of action. Even at seventy-five-plus years, that Snoddie woman remains mobile and in a heads-up noddie. "You-u-u know it, the we-e-e-e-ed that cripples people. You, *Andrew Kittmer.*"

Mandy almost falls out of his wheelchair seat onto the ground in laughter. The Barber leans an arm against Venus for support. They guffaw in a rifle rapport. Out from the closet of the unexpected, The Barber blares a trumpet blast backwards to Jones Street, three uncontrolled farts. Mrs. Snoddie snorts under her breath and continues to climb the hill.

A good laugh energizes the friends in another round of Cuban cloud. Mandy returns to the garden at hand, pointing past armless Venus.

"Now, the important stuff. Where do we put the rock that looks like a frog?"

The Barber points to the statue's side. "Right beside Scottie there." He exhales up and away in a pause. The Barber winks at his longtime friend. "Light me up, Terri. That's the life."

Both laugh.

"Almost forgot," Mandy says. "I left a box of el Cortos on the bar shelf."

"Gracias, Señor Kit-mar. Gracias."

The conclusion here is that it's all about friends. Friends who help without question and regardless of cost, friends whom nothing embarrasses when important tasks abound.

Even after a Snoddie altercation that is moved on by farting.

Chapter 9

The Barber at his Best with Blackie

1980

Blackie needs an update,
Another hair appointment to make.
The Barber in character can make
A Town parade,
A comic charade,
A political tirade —

Does Blackie tempt fate,
When thin hair can always wait?
Not when thick lips reveal saucy bait.
Never late for a date
With The Barber's serenade.

> — The Barber, in the deerskin diary
> at the Charles W. Cruise Archives

Today is the third Thursday in the month, when The Barber welcomes a great friend to the barbershop. His oldest customer and special confidant, Eric William Nairn — Blackie to all — is up for the red-upholstered & nickel-plated chair.

Blackie's occupation takes him to a different stage on the edge of St. Marys on first and third Wednesday afternoons and most Saturdays. Behind Nairn Auctions' laminated-maple podium, Blackie is the man, the auctioneer in the huge white Stetson who hammers out his message. (*"Sold, sold, sold to the lady in the red velvet hat. That's number 51, Carol."*)

It's no surprise Blackie has a certain in-the-know stature, a special go-to reputation in Town equal to that of The Barber (absent the character mimicry). After a death, during a divorce — lose your job, move to the City — upgrade, downgrade — they all come down to a Blackie call.

Not just rocks but auctions all come with stories. "The kids in the will or separating couples? They're all about the money," Blackie often says. "No one wants the Royal Doulton figurines, the Flow Blue or the uncomfortable antique sofa."

From the moment he passes through the door in the morning to the sound of the phone's ring, ring, ring, the auctioneer is busier than a one-armed paper hanger.

"Nairn Auctions. Was that Room 3 you said? No, not 3, that's the Turner move. Yes, the Souter auction is in Room 2. You're welcome. Yes, Wednesday at one o'clock sharp. Yes, you're welcome and remember the preview is at ten. Barn wagons and basement stuff at one, yes. The W.I. will have a lunch counter. No worries, they'll have egg salad sandwiches."

He zooms his coat off to reach for another call while the free hand motions to his team, and off they go. The cast iron paper spike on the counter has the morning's pickup rounds for the unmarked cube van.

"This is a special auction," the caller tells Blackie. "Time sensitive."

Blackie mumbles a worn answer. "They're all special, everyone is in a hurry. And it's all about the money."

To the barbershop Blackie brings a full file cabinet of well-framed cast characters. One easy-to-understand mutual reference is Les Moore, with the appropriate nickname Little Les. (You just can't shut the guy up.)

Add a dash of barbershop — heck, Townwide — humour to any conversation with a Les Moore character reference.

"A little Les, eh!"

When Blackie's saddled up on the big red & nickel chair, both friends laugh at the news and nuance of their regular routine. Mo-o-o-ove on in — the two old bulls chomp the pasture over all the news worth repeating. Maybe Mull-Over Mondays dominate the public coffee klatch at The Sunriser Diner, but here at the barbershop on Queen Street it's Tattlin' Thursdays. An old-man duet of tattle and tell.

The man in the white Stetson brings 100% Grade A gossip from the world of the auction barn, well-hung and ready to bait then feed the barbershop conversation. A lesson The Barber learned bright and early in their friendship was never to discount Blackie-sourced information as less than gold standard. He scripted Wedding Girl, after all, a future classic of Town exposure and one of The Barber's best acts.

Blackie likes a bid but doesn't abide by much: no booze, smoke, swearing or betting, so no rocks for the hatless gentleman. Blackie's standing appointment every fourth Thursday at 9:15 is an excellent time for a review of the popular Wednesday afternoon sale at the Auction Barn, not to mention Saturdays, which run a full day, two auctioneers outside and in.

This Thursday's appointment has to start up on something, so The Barber tosses a crumb onto the barbershop floor. "Read the *Journal*?"

Blackie talks the line. "Yup. But it's a struggle as always, with all that unimportant church news plus wordy garden tips, odd recipes from that Kitty Litter woman, and that Nosey Parker column stretching down the front page from the masthead."

"I *see* what you mean." The Barber needs only the words "I See" to bring up the single-column tidbits and tadbits that greet your first look at the *Journal*. It's a simple fact that they're the most-read words in the thirty-two-page-plus newspaper. An erudite reader like Blackie finds nothing to feed on there, with bingo times, choral recitals, minor hockey frozen pizza sales, and the so-called meat winner Friday nights at the ANAF.

Blackie hasn't finished offing an equal share of sarcasm. "Mrs. Smith's tulips are first to bloom. Or Julia Rowcliffe reports the first robin at her crap-filled backyard bird feeder. Waste of space. And then you turn the pages. There's no news in the whole paper. Birdcage material. The only news is for the relatives of people who get caught doing dumb stuff."

"Bobby Binks locked in the Town Hall washrooms overnight. What was he doing?"

"What about Constable Lumpy McAshe and some off-the-beat flame locked in the back seat of the cruiser? We know what they were doing."

"The *Journal* only mentions Lumpy having mechanical issues."

　　

"Stupid is as stupid does."

If it's local mischief, the pair in and behind the chair probably have most of the sordid details already. Ears are up on Thursday, all ripe and ready to share a big corny harvest of small details from both Auctioneer and Barber. Their friendship has flourished from their first days in the Methodist Sunday School, seventy years ago. On these Thursday mornings, with no other ears about the barbershop, there are no secrets, no holdbacks.

The Barber snaps the cape in front of Blackie, who instantly perks up.

"Kind of snappy this morning? New arrival in the Court of Rock?"

Blackie puts his foot on the starter. "Snap up a new arrival in the Court of Unusual Rocks?"

"Yes, I be the judge."

"And jury."

"Yes my friend, and jury."

"Judge *and* jury is a dictatorship, my friend."

Blackie works towards the correct button on the barbershop jukebox to push. Of course, Leafs hockey falls naturally into the conversation any season. Or cars — the question of which local auto survivors are currently off for restoration can fill the air for public consumption. But this is private conversation, which is more interested in whose car is parked in whose garage. A top private Town topic is Bad Boy action.

"Petey Todburry." Sensing a gap in his filing cabinet on one local rascal, Blackie presses the button on the ultimate small town Bad Boy. "I haven't seen him lurking about?"

The Barber freezes in the moment, then seizes on the rare opportunity. He reverses back to the mirror, masking his surprise. "That's old news." Blackie can see a reflected raised eyebrow. "Young Petey is on to bigger things."

The Barber has the kind of delicious smile that demonstrates he has something to tell. Blackie searches his memory Filofax one more time but comes up empty.

"Define *bigger things*?"

The Barber goes straight to the scene. "It might be better said that he's on to older things. He's been dropping by the Harrison home."

There's more than enough here to set both aging bulls to a connection in the mirror's reflection, with winks and an in-the-know nod backed by a double hum. Blackie knows the Harrisons but is blank on young Petey's participation.

"*Hm-m-m-m-mm.*"

"He works the Harrison back door like clockwork," The Barber says.

"Hm-m-m-m-m-mm." Now Blackie is humming on his own. "And to be clear, what's Petey doing there, like clockwork?"

"Calling a certain young Missus Harrison."

Admission Restricted: private buddy tales of a Bad Boy legend in the making. The young or public audience may not be ready when the storyline spells out S-E-X, but Blackie is familiar with this particular young woman's, uh, profile. "Young Mrs. Harrison? You mean Cindy."

Another double-your-pleasure response: "*Hm-m-m-m-m-mm.*"

"She's got to be thirty-two," Blackie says. "He's how old?"

"He's about to turn twenty."

"I guess I've lost track of time. Petey's already *twenty*?"

Blackie's mental archive file again comes up short on Petey, with no auction activity in the Todburry realm.

The Barber ices the conversation cake. "I will give you the goods on Petey, a familiar truth known to a sordid number of ladies." The Barber gives him another wink in the mirror at the potential tale pleasure. "Unbridled fun, a mare-go-round for the perfect herd stud." The Barber stretches scissors and comb as wide as the biggest fish catch. "Have you *not* heard him called Pistol Pete?"

Answerless, Blackie shifts in the chair. "Never connected it to Petey Todburry. So, what's the pitch on Mitch?"

"Well, let's just say that Chester the Wheaton is the only dog left on the Harrison deck. Mr. Mitch Harrison is not on site, being in the doghouse."

A particular peculiar look is shared in the mirror between two lifer friends as they come together in unison: "*Extracurricular.*"

"Hard at it," The Barber says, with eyebrows raised and scissors and comb holstered. "Mitch has been studying off campus. He got caught with a young Miss Oxford Dairy Princess. They call her Miss Bliss." Blackie squirms in his seat at the role currently in play.

"Mitch had his way with her, in public at the frigging ploughing match, doing it right behind the Flying Farmers' Pig BBQ tent."

Blackie reflects on the annual agricultural gathering, which attracts rural folks from every corner of North America. The auctioneer knows about the risky business that goes on there, behind those giant yellow combines and red four-wheel-drive tractors, or hidden by tent posts beside competition furrows. Even the decent man can be overwhelmed by the scents of fresh popcorn, newly manufactured cabs, fresh manure and sweaty animal testicles. Going up country, Mitch notches up big numbers. The hunk humps away on a belle steeplechase through South Perth then across Highway 7 to Oxford County. Delivering oil, lubricants and diesel takes him down a loose gravel path scattered with farmers' daughters and isolated wives:

"You look good in that apron, Ivadelle. Ever thought about just the apron?"

"Mitchell Harrison, you have a dirty mind."

"Nothing more beautiful than just you in that apron, nothing underneath."

"Let me finish with this pump. I'll show you my big nozzle."

"Well shame on you, Mitchell Harrison."

In Town, meanwhile, all good lads continuing on the active ladder of life up to the age of eighty hang off Mrs. Harrison with rare observation, discreet distance and respectful admiration, only mentioning her upstanding profile in private conversation. The best that most men and boys can hope for is to catch a glimpse of her on her daily routine:

"*If you stand on Water Street down from the Post Office steps before eleven on weekdays ...*" (pause to imagine the descending profile on a staircase) "*... and then after that, she checks the glamour mags at Dick's Groceteria. She bends over to review the lower rack ...*"

"*Don't be stalking her, buddy.*"

"How long has this been going on?" Blackie asks.

"Since Cindy and Petey sat in the back seat together after a night out at Summerfest."

Everyone in Town or on the rural routes has Summerfest (known in local terms as the Beer Tent) on their calendar.

"Whose back seat?"

"Icky and Mads Patrick."

"Icky and Maddison, Cindy and Petey, all in the back seat?"

"No, Blackie. The naughty couple in back. The married couple in the front."

"Okay, tell me how they got there?"

"The Patricks were giving Petey a lift to the Sunriser, after the Beer Tent closed, and Cindy joined in."

Blackie waits with patience in the red & nickel chair, ready for the private sauce on that hot and fateful storyline one July night, heavy in the Chevy when Petey meets Cindy.

"Cindy hops in back for the ride of her life. There he is, Petey splayed out across the back seat of that big Chevy Biscayne." The Barber is full steam ahead. "The best-laid-out package of local ingredients. The search is over. A boy toy doll, pull-the-cord ready."

Blackie sits smothered by all the spicy sauce. The Barber pokes both comb and scissors at the bevelled bar mirror. "Sources say …" He gives Blackie a knowing look and a wink. "They say there's more grit in this back seat escapade than on a beach picnic blanket."

"Stop the train. What happened to Icky and Mads?" He knows Icky's parents, Bob and Barbie Patrick, from the Moose Lodge.

"Got the straight goods from Icky. He drove ahead with Mads cuddled tight beside him. Icky had the right angle on his back mirror to glimpse the dangle action." He gives a confidential lean in and a whisper. "Petey's the prey. He feels the fuzzy sweater sidle up to him, topped off by pouty lips up on his cheek. At thirty-two Cindy definitely seems older to Petey, but not mother old, maybe older-sister old. He moves right past age to a handheld appraisal. Meanwhile, the unattainable Everest of a married woman has climbed onto trouser peak."

The Barber has scissors on his hip, his comb pointed to his lip, as he prepares to summarize the Petey rumours Cindy has heard from her girl pals, often in euphemisms based on yard care.

"Wow. The kid really mows a lot of lawn.

"Lower the mower, big guy.

"Cindy has thought it through, heard it all, discussed it all, so nothing holds her back. Her ascent starts with a descent, a reach for the

　　　　　　　　　　　　　　　　　　　　　　　　　　　　　　　　　　LORNE EEDY

peak." The Barber stops with a point. "Remember, Cindy Harrison is *not* shy. Remember that mink coat incident?"

Blackie remains in the back seat. "Huh?"

"The mink coat incident."

As one bull tries to hook his bull friend into this short but familiar tale, Blackie pleads time to the judge and jury. "Jesus. Petey's hanging out of the holster, you've got the nicest profile around, and you want to repeat the fur coat story?"

To be clear, Blackie has a blue-label file full of his own top-rated tattle. He's charted the best stories during years of haircuts: the rector and the organist's wife; Jack and the mobile coffin; Serge and Helen getting locked in the back seat; and how about Hap Heavens and Candy Barr under the Trestle?

The Barber points his scissors in reflection. "Come on, Cindy freaking naked and loose in a fur jacket ..."

The seated old bull steers the other bull back. "Save the furry stuff. Let's get back to Cindy in the back seat."

The Barber lets the best of the big details come from Cindy and her girl posse. "*My goodness, girls. Something ... something that big ... something that abnormal ...* Cindy can't help herself after a few beers. She reports the back to Marie, the Town operator."

Blackie pulls his head back from scissor and comb with a half-dumb look. He has to ask. "That's a dirty storybook. Where in heck does a barber get this type of information from a telephone operator?"

"Marie is Dispatch. And The Barber never reveals *all* his secret sources."

While Blackie silently reflects, The Barber continues. "My friend, I do have a better view on the, uh, profile — confirmed by a googling gaggle of goggled lads."

"Talk about phooey, what the heck is a googling gaggle of goggled lads?"

Suddenly the cape is off and Blackie is being swept clean from the neck down.

He looks up. "That's it?"

The Barber holds his hand out. "A buck and two bits, please." Funny guy.

Blackie has both hands up. "That's it? Story robbery."

Any accusation of larceny is foiled by a musical ditty from The Barber. *"If Blackie needs an update ..."* Both hands are on his hips, his head cocked. *"Another appointment he needs to make."* One hand up, he gives his friend a finger shake. *"Or he will never confirm the profile take, that the googling gaggle of goggled kids make."*

Thirty days later and thirty minutes earlier, The Barber throws out a grand smile as Blackie once again settles in beneath the Grand Central cape with its raised embroidery.

"Sit back and relax, my friend. Open your ears and eyes to a goggled gaggle of kids."

Both old bulls know that the whole darn Town watched Cindy Gerow bloom into full figure, a car-stopping profile. Cindy was first made famous in 1969 when she showed up at the Swim Quarry in one of the first bikinis seen in Town.

Blackie, though, has a thin file on Cindy, one empty of swimwear. While The Barber was riding his CCM bicycle to the Quarry as a youth, Blackie was ploughing fields in a rotation with his dad. A farm boy might dip his bare feet in a back-forty pond or in a boundary stream, but he never wades in up to the waist, let alone dunks his head. Sure, Blackie knows about the "profile," but to him a quarry is just another name for wild game. On the flip side, most Town boys have no affinity for farm work or animals — it's all just a bunch of manure shovelling and rock picking to them.

The Barber picks up the tale. "The story starts when pubescent lads arrive by bicycle with their swim goggles around their necks, fins wrapped in ratty towels, with surfer-style trunks. Of course no kid in his right mind has a Speedo. *Who wants to look like a sissy with a shrivelled weenie? You want your privates shrink-wrapped? Nya nya, Andrew's dick is an acorn.*"

The Barber educates Blackie, the farm-reared kid, as the young lads get prepped for Dirty Flipper underwater on the Table Rock. "The lads wear their fins and goggles to dive down to this huge flat rock about sixteen feet below the surface, ten feet off the small diving board."

The high dive stands on the Water Street side of the pool, while the small dive peers out from the opposite corner of the concrete deck. Blackie can picture the kid klatch nibbling at the water's edge.

"With their goggles up, the lads dive off in hope. They go down …"

A farm boy can barely fathom swimming in an abandoned quarry, let alone diving. "How deep?"

"Down, deep down, Waylon Jennings–deep, down …"

"But they're little kids. How do they go so deep?"

"… At least sixteen feet deep, down, down, to sit on the Table Rock."

Blackie is stuck scaling up his six-foot frame by a factor of two and a half. The Barber sizes up the endeavour for the Blanshard native.

"That's a difficult dive, trying to sit upright under water when the body wants to float up. Their swimsuits balloon up around them as the lads try to be lead sinkers and wait. The lads rush for five or six seconds of underwater exposure focused by summer tanlines. It's busy and anxious work for the lads on their day off, from the relaxation of watching cartoons in the AM to the deepest, darkest depths of sea-view action all underwater off the Table Rock in the PM."

Swimming at the Quarry in St. Marys.

At the surface, a pre-scoped female prospect walks to the fibreglass plank of the small dive. The goggles are up as they watch her shimmering form in wait for a loose swimsuit off the diving board. Blackie is stunned by the depths Town swimmers will go to. The Barber lays on the scene.

Diving is merciless and unforgiving for a girl whose bathing suit is baggy or mis-sized. In between dives, the lads are lizards in the sun, off in the corner of the deck. They stretch out in the warmth while their eyes shift back up the grass looking for the next target, tongues wagging on potential prospects. They are oh-so-quick off the mark.

"There's Carrie Conn."

A geographic correction. "Flat as Saskatchewan."

"A real loose suit, though — you can see nipples."

A base chorus shuts off any deep-water interest. "*Flat as Saskatchewan.*"

A wise kid speaks. "How do you know Saskatchewan is so flat?"

"My grandparents have a farm there."

A chorus of agreement shuts down the subject.

"Look, boob snobs, Cindy Gerow's here." More important business redirects the boys' squinting eyes. The head of the goggled googling gang is a smart lad who looks back at the group with caution hands held out palms-down. "Nonchalant, boys."

One dummy has a gear stuck. "Nonchalant?"

"It means shut your mouth. It means look *anywhere,* anywhere" — his hand jerks randomly back towards the entrance to the snack bar — "*except* at the hot girl."

The Barber is a genius at expanding the mishmash into a great tale. "Every lad knows that Cindy's custom-fit bikini is a five-star target sliding across the grass infield. The gaggle of goggled boys are huddled in their shallow area right of the small board, looking anywhere but left. The goggling gang stay alert, prepared to launch, and then they dive, dive, dive. They're like goggling sun-golden caimans, sliding under the surface towards their bottom-row seat on the limestone triangle table."

The gogglers, ready in the water, steady eyes by the ladder, wait in vain for their prime-time diver to take the plunge.

"But upon her plunge into the quarry, all is kept bundled, as tight as the swaddled Baby Jesus. The goggled eyes fixate on the skimpy bikini, trying mentally to loosen it, but only in their imagination. Cindy dives down, down, then sidles up and easy next to the goggle set schooling on the Table Rock."

Blackie makes an unnecessary interruption. "So what does she do?"

"Sticks out her tongue, makes a monkey face, aping the lads. Cindy's a five-star catch, a difficult fish that outmanoeuvres these one-star mini-crocs, then and *always*."

That day the boys duck out of the park on simmer, stuck in frustrated grease. Hot bicycle seats parked by the fence near the gravel lot give cold comfort. They curse the girl, her mother Cathy, even that Hudson's Department Store in Detroit.

"That goggle google strategy never works on Cindy. That little black bikini top never comes off on the small dive. There is a rumour, though …" (Blackie is still lost in a deep swim, adjusting unfamiliar goggles. The Barber waits for him to come up for air) "… that her bikini bottoms dropped once, to her ankles. No witnesses, but rumours are they came off on the high dive."

Blackie has never been a butt man. Bottoms could fall off on the high cliffs of Acapulco and Blackie wouldn't turn to look. "But, you did say it was all about the profile, right?"

"*That* took five more years."

And just like that, Blackie is out of the chair and standing in the reflection of the bevelled mirror. His haircut is finished. He will never confess, to friend or wife, that he can't get enough of this alien world of unrequited pubescence at the Quarry. "My God, a third haircut?"

"Well, it did take five years. What's one more Thursday?"

"You're telling me that *Another appointment date, Old Blackie will have to make, For any hope in getting to the final update*?"

Now The Barber is the one swept away by a canny feat of oration. He can only smile back at the depth of his friend.

As he departs, Blackie holds on to the latch of the front door with a fresh breath of patience for things to come.

Four weeks later, he's bright and upright in the red & nickel chair.

The Barber is ready to shine a light on Blackie's tale fixation. First he covers the known details. "Five years later, Cindy is out of college, working in the city. Cindy returns in July and August on odd weekends."

The Barber holds all the delight in hand with his pretend phone to his ear. *"Two weeks, Mom; yes, time flies. I need a little Cindy TLC: a tan, and your lasagna and cured ham. Make sure Braden's Bakery has the order so I can make garlic toast. I love you Mom. See you Saturday morning."* He lowers his falsetto down to alto range. *"Love you too, Doll. Don't forget to bring your book. Make sure you wear your seatbelt. Please, drive with the top up."*

Blackie was already confused enough about swimwear, but now there's car care, too? "Top up?"

"Her car. Triumph Spitfire in British racing green."

"Okay, top up." He rebounds, now that he has learned a bit about bikini wear. "What about top down?"

On those hot weekends, Cindy takes her next-generation (still black, but much skimpier) bikini to the Quarry. She's discreet, taking her reading material, beach bag and towel to a flat, grassy area seldom used by swimmers. The Barber ramps up the story as he vamps up a cautionary Mother Cathy. *"Doll, there's not a lot of coverage in that swimsuit. Are you sure it's suitable for the Quarry? The local swim scene?"*

As if any mother knew anything about the googling goggled gaggle by the small dive.

Cindy calms the home waters. *"I'll avoid the diving board."*

Mother pauses and punches out one final cautionary note. *"Off the ladder, doll. There will be no equipment malfunctions."*

The Barber sets the stage at the Quarry where a line of lads, both teenagers and adult men, are strung along the retaining walls above the concrete decks that border the grass.

"Forty-plus pairs of eyes follow a bronze Venus in a black bikini bouncing onto the cement pad that follows the water's edge. All eyes count the most beautiful twelve steps to the ladder. She turns to her audience, who take a nonchalant look anywhere else, and then she pushes off in a breaststroke. She floats off from the ladder, witnessed only by the Quarry's few green sunfish and brown smallmouth bass."

After her swim, the girl profiled in the black bikini heads to the grass to stretch out on a swimsuit-clad James Bond on the *Dr. No*–inspired beach towel exclusive to Eaton's in Toronto.

All the lads have seen the great movie.

"I like the towel."

There's a reader among the lads. "What's her book?"

"Shut up."

Week after week the lads have memorized the routine by peeking around the back corner bushes of the change rooms, careful not to be obvious and creepy. First, the lads know that when the 007 towel comes out, the bikini will come off.

The barbershop talk is hot. "From afar," The Barber explains, "the randy reptiles soak up the heat from her city-style choreography for obtaining a strapless tan. Undercover, she has a private change room, for your eyes only. The visible straps of the bikini top disappear, and the top makes a seamless move down her front and then reappears at her ankles. The boys all imagine having hairy chests, James Bond stuck chest to chest with Cindy."

But something more is about to happen in the grassy picnic area at the Quarry.

"It was strapless Saturdays at the Quarry." The Barber cocks an eyebrow in an illumination of things to come. "Yup. Pistol Pete in primal pubescence has graduated from the kiddy pool to the Quarry."

The story at the Quarry gives spark to the legend of Petey Todburry on that hot Saturday afternoon in July.

"Even the older guys can't help but stare at the gruesome sight of his undress in the mouldy change room. Petey doesn't make a measured swimsuit choice from Detroit or Toronto. He suits up in XL adult trunks from the Simpson's catalogue. His mother shortens the waist."

For a farm boy, all of this is unfamiliar dialogue in a foreign country. But even Blackie can sense that it was a pivotal moment in Town life when, on the wet floors of the Quarry change rooms, the nickname came out and stuck.

"Looks more like a pistol — Magnum 45."

"Pistol …. Pete."

The lads chorus the nomination in a parody of squealing girls.

"Pistol Pete."

"Piss-toll Petey."

Petey takes the shot, shoots back. "Standing tall, guys, and swinging free."

The clever twelve-year-old has strategized an out-of-the-pool, off-the-grass strategy to tackle profile exposure. "Lads, listen up. Here's how we can do it. I'm calling it The Can Do Plan. Yes we can." After five years of failure, this tactic provided by a twelve-year-old who talks like a general is worth a try.

Every wet swimsuit in that change room stiffens up at the mere mention of Cindy Gerow. The lads would definitely be able to smell the musky testosterone if not for the live mould masking everything.

The Barber aims the spotlight back outside. "Get this, Cindy's on her front, her back exposed."

Blackie soaks up the scene, silent as a sponge. The Barber pauses in reflection. The master mimic is about to set the table in the grassy picnic area.

"She looks up." The Barber has both hands spider-walking the scissors and comb across the mirror. "A picnic table appears, coming across the grass from the pavilion, closer. Closer. Carried by twenty feet. Closer, to land ten feet in front of her."

"The lads are moving a picnic table?"

"Yes sir, twenty little feet. A portable grandstand."

"Portable grandstand?"

"Right. One row sits up front, one sits behind on top, a third line stands on the back bench seat."

"How many?"

"Dozen or more."

"Maybe twenty kids?"

"Less, no more."

Both laugh a little more on Les Moore before The Barber concentrates on the theatre. "Let's say there's three rows of goofy grins, staring down at her."

"So does she notice? The manoeuvring?"

"Better than just notice, she *watches* all the manoeuvring. The happy little chappies smile while they work, and clueless about their secret mission, Cindy smiles back." The Barber takes on the full breadth of the situation. "That Petey's a wizard. Cindy never did see him then or ever after, for seven more years." He gives another wink. "Not that she would even recognize a twelve-year-old Petey all those years later."

"Maybe if he left his XL swimsuit off."

The Barber motions with scissors and comb: on with the story. "Petey comes right out of the change room in a flash across —"

"Flash? As in flashing?"

"Stop it. Okay, he races out of the pavilion, racing across the lawn. And he's all steady-Eddy with a tall cup balanced in one hand." Eyebrows rise. "A tall cup of ice water." Rise again. "She does not see it coming. Petey races up from behind, opposite side to the grandstand lads, and throws the ice water on her bare back."

"Whoa, continuity? Where does the kid get ice water?"

"Okay, sidebar — because twelve-year-old Petey has asked a much older woman, eighteen-year-old Janet Heron at the canteen, to keep the tall cup in the canteen freezer."

"Now, why would a university girl pay any attention to a kid, let alone Janet do this kid that kind of a favour?"

The Barber has both the comb and scissors hands out front and waving in a fluster at this hair-splitting. "Look, Blackie, are we talking about Janet Heron, or on with the story?"

Two Blackie thumbs up under the Grand Central cape. "Story."

The needle hits the groove again. "Cindy jumps up like Skippy the Seal at Fairytale Gardens. She exposes all." The Barber goes biblical. "There in the nakedness that God gave to Eve." Then classical. "She's one pissed-off Venus." And medieval. "Lady Godiva is ready to ride."

Blackie's imagination basks in the hot reflection of an incredible moment. He's a ready mould for the master storyteller, like jello in seated form.

"Cindy's up, wound up for a chase. She thinks that she'll catch these little buggers. But then …" The Barber turns on the falsetto. *"Oh, my God."* He looks down at his embroidered apron pocket. "Cindy realizes that her pride and joy are out and already exposed." He has his index fingers twirling into the bevelled mirror. "They're pointing, pointing straight at the little smug and snuffling buggers on the picnic table, or rather the grandstand. She's exposed to the entire Quarry audience on the grass and around the canteen."

The Barber jiggles scissor and comb in front of his chest, hop-hop-hopping back and forth on alternate feet. He stops and looks, and Blackie listens. In deep falsetto The Barber continues with words the boys have never heard from a lady's mouth before that Saturday at the Quarry. *"You fockin' little pricks. I'm calling the fockin' police."* The Barber has his hands over his ears. "Their little ears tingle from a quick simmer to a full-on burn. Their wet butts are in flight, retreating in an irregular detour every which way and loose for the exit to their bikes along the tennis court fence."

The Barber lifts the needle from the groove momentarily over questions on context. "You have to wonder how much the little buggers even got to see, considering there were only a few seconds of exposure before all eyes started searching for any exit to save their skinny butts. Plus the shock of Cindy's dirty mouth — foreign language from a lady, no matter how hot."

Then it's back to the story. Off to the shrubby back boundary of the Quarry run the terrorized lads, looping back to Water Street and their parked bicycles, home free. Cindy covers herself up with one arm while she takes a few catch-up breaths, which gives the culprits a head start. With her free hand she points at the disappearing butts, sending cannon shots of threatening words. Her screams are heard by the Quarry audience, two sets of tennis players and a baseball practice at Teddy's Field. *"YOU fockin' little pricks. I'll fockin' cut your NUTS off."*

Petey, meanwhile, circles the shorter distance to the pavilion exit, past the musky washrooms, then out with a little wave to Janet Heron, who has just tuned into the screams. Janet will never know her role in providing the freezing prop for The Can Do Plan. He tucks himself outside in the shade of the eaves as the rest of the googling gang escape with wet arses, mixed emotions and immature male humour.

"Look, Freddy pissed his shorts." Boys know boys.

"Bobby has ass rash, running with his wet swimsuit."

"He'll get nut rash, riding on that cheap CCM rubber seat."

A touch of kindness in the rush: *"Bobby, you should walk a bit, dry out."*

　　　　　　　　　　　　　　　　　　　　　　　　　　　　　

Cindy catches the flash of bare legs spinning down Water Street. Feeling the horror of Town exposure, she lets it all out.

"Fuck you! All of you have teeny weenies!"

The Barber has watched the legend build in the eight years since, with over forty suspects claiming to be the guilty wet-bum culprits on hot seats that July day. Many so-called witnesses have Petey not hiding under the eaves but riding on a bicycle that leaves:

"Petey and I rode our bikes home from the Quarry."

And with unrealistic embellishment: *"Petey treated us to Dreamsicles at Dick's Groceteria after."*

The fruits of fantasy become sweeter with age: *"Cindy's nipples were so dark, like Jersey Milk chocolate."*

"No, they were puffy red strawberries."

And the anachronistic. *"Her left nipple was pierced."*

Blackie is lost in imagination. The narrator snaps his figures, landing his attention.

"On that hot Saturday in July 1972 when Cindy bared all from a young spitfire's iced-up water-bomb, she had not the least inkling about the future role of Petey."

Blackie, with three haircuts now under his white Stetson, is pulling the pieces together for the complete diorama. "I heard something about a ruckus in the park."

"You know that risky business can catch up on you." Big pause, deep breath. There's obviously more to this story.

Before Blackie has the chance to ask for some explaining, the Barber offers his familiar refrain. "That'll cost you another buck twenty-five, my friend." The Barber pauses again. "Until next time."

For the next twenty-eight days, Blackie head-scratches at an informationless itch. It's a wonder there's any thin hair left to cut at the end of the month. Heaven would open before he ever admitted that he did not have the goods on a major Town happening. He keeps mumbling — heard by Honey at home and his helper nephews Ron and Allan at the office — something about the Park by the Creek.

On the fourth Thursday, the Barber cuts right to the chase of how and when. "The Park Incident sure has got Town traction."

"How so?"

"So, any time a meathead estranged husband catches up to the guilty party" — a serious look — "the Town will sit up in interest."

Blackie can't help but notice that he's on the edge of the red padded seat.

"The first interested party was standing back and waiting, caught Petey on the way home from the pool hall. Petey's regular shortcut takes him down by the Creek, where the jilted cuckold caught up to the unsuspecting lad, sneaking out from behind one of the Lego stone trestles. Mitch blocked him before he could cross the Swing Bridge."

On the edge of the Creek, Blackie jumps in. "Damage?"

"Petey was lucky to leave with a broken nose. His … big part remained unharmed in a brouha-ha-ha of the highest disorder."

"Ha-ha, ha?"

"Well, it did slide from worse to farcical."

Behind the red & nickel chair, The Barber sets up the donnybrook, the brouhaha, the incident in the Park by the Creek.

"Dumb Mitch and young Petey exposed themselves to all in an incident first noticed by Mrs. Mousie Cook on her back porch."

"I know Mousie. She looks like the Granny from *Beverly Hillbillies*."

"Her ashtray sits on the white wicker lamp table beside the portable GE phone, which lies next to the Z57 police scanner flashing a red bar. Don't forget the can of Tab off to the side."

Blackie interrupts in the role of taste police. "How can anyone drink that? Tastes like crap."

The master mimic has his cheeks sucked in, pinched up and pointed out in a cheesy way. *"Just the right taste with my first smoke in the morning."*

Mousie blows out smoke from thin grey lips locked on the cig, blue eyes open and alert, for nothing clouds her view. The quilt-padded white wicker rocking chair is aimed at just the right angle for a dangle over the rail. She pulls a pair of binoculars on a lariat over her hooked nose and her large pointed ears. Thin, flame-red hair hides under a Maple Leafs toque.

(Never dissed out as a rat, she's a loveable Town mouse, this a-birdie-told-me character with scanner and binoculars in house.

"A Mousie nose for smoke, a head for fire."

"My goodness me, those ears, those mouse-like ears."

"Mrs. Mousie never stops hearing.")

The Barber cooks up the incident with Mousie as the first witness. *"That's Mitch. He's having a pee. Or is he … Someone else catches her eye. Whoa. That's Petey Todburry."*

Alert eyes widen to fire-alarm mode. Her cig hits the ashtray as she moves the phone to her apron lap, binoculars up. "Whoa."

Mrs. Mousie senses the brouhaha in the making. No ha-ha here, but a handy phone call to Marie for some emergency response. "Marie. Mrs. Cook."

Marie is the operator and dispatch for Municipality and Town Constabulary. She's the conduit and cog for official St. Marys communication, the gobsmacked gossip who's honoured to be the first on a fresh Mrs. Mousie report.

"Marie, bet ya nothing's on the scanner yet, eh? You need to make the calls."

"What's happening, Mrs. Cook? Describe the situation."

"My God, it's no situation, it's an incident. Mitch has grabbed little Petey. They're down. My God … they're rolling. Rolling in that goose-shit-covered park. My God. Marie. Marie? Are you …?"

Marie hangs up. No time to get hung up on Mousie fine detail. Marie springs into action, pressing the com button on the radio mic. "Echo. Echo. Dispatch to Russ."

The Barber rolls out the fun. "That Marie. Girl's *quick*. She knows how the situation *sizes up*." The Barber has his friend busting stitches on second meanings. "You see, Marie is Cindy's best friend. Marie has climbed Petey's trouser peak of no return in her tiny Volkswagen back seat. Marie raided the randy seventeen-year-old right out of high school — Grade Twelve, my goodness."

Scissors and comb back on the hips, he serves up all sides of the conversation with a little spiced falsetto. *"It was in Theatre City. I had dropped some paperwork off for the Chief at County Court. There's Petey on the corner."*

"It didn't seem like a bad sign that the lad was standing near the courthouse?"

"I just asked him if he wanted a lift."

"A lift from the city?"

"He had a lift, but hopped in anyways. We took Downie Road 9 for some loose-gravel fun. What a run that was. Next time it was the cemetery …"

The Barber transitions from the crypt back to the script. "From the moment of Mrs. Mousie's phone call Marie has flashbacks to those indiscretions. First things first. *My God, if Petey gets kicked in the treasure trunk …?*"

The Barber charges up his mimic mode again. His scissors are up to his mouth, while the lower hand dials the comb. He hams up a CB radio call with all the handles as Marie tries again to reach the appropriate authority, Supercop Russ on duty. *"Echo. Echo. Russ, are you focking there? Calling all cars. Calling all cars. Calling Supercop Russ."*

The Barber then churns both scissor and comb to the sky, twirling them above his head. Blackie follows his gaze with an amazed expression. Blackie can see it, the arriving calvary with cherries blasting — just look at the choreographed twirl of hair tools.

The Barber waltzes ahead. "Supercop Russ shows up."

The master mimic makes the necessary pause for Blackie to gather up all the information that expands the big stage of Petey and Mitch. Blackie's eyes are on The Barber.

"Supercop Russ is slurping a coffee outside the Goal Crease Café, parked in idle. Without a sloppy stain or dangerous drip on the console, the second he hears the character lineup, he's ripe & ready, off in a race" — scissors up — "for the brouhaha. He knows the two different actors, but nothing about the shared plot being exposed in the Incident by the Creek. Both of his cagey fish, long-sought-after catches, are in the same net. Petey Todburry's Quarry escapade brought him under the official radar scope. And Russ summed up Mitch as an entitled bad act in local adult entertainment all 'round. Russ practices strong intent but weaker intellect as he charges into action without the Chief's supervision. A confident but lone-ranger response in his role as Supercop Russ."

The brouhaha rolls on, on the brown-fringed carpet of turf. The messy struggle pushes into the gathering crowd. Everyone's a spectator. Dog walkers, nosey neighbours and rubbernecker drive-bys all get on over for a stopover at the improv by the Creek. The crowd flows out from alleys, off from the street and down from neighbourhood homes.

"Supercop lands his lit-up cruiser in the Park by the Creek right up front, live on the public stage. The flashing clown-cop car slides across the shit-covered grass, pushing the crowd to a safe position back from the shit-covered duel. Heads down, the pair ignore the pop-up constable. They have their one eye on the fight, the other on the shit — same for the audience."

A look of crappy horror from Blackie in the bevelled mirror. "Those geese. They shit like poodles."

"Yes, but poodles don't shit in flocks," The Barber nods. "The crowd adjusts back as heads turn to Russ, who throws the door open and springs onto the brownish turf. He's on target towards the rolling conflict with his flashing cherries behind him. All audience heads turn to a rodeo-clown rundown. All eyes see Petey and Mitch, down and brown on the ground."

Blackie eyes his friend for what could be next. The Barber winks. "The crowd backs up further. Their eyes watch Petey, Mitch, and now the rodeo clown. All heads turn to the flashing-cherry cruiser, rolling on, on its own. You can read their lips: *It's moving!*"

Across the Creek, The Barber mimes Mrs. Mousie leaning forward on her porch, absorbing all the action through her binoculars. "You can read her grey lips as the cig falls into her apron. *That cruiser's moving.*"

The Barber holds his scissors in an X across his brow. "Problem, problem, problem. The cruiser's moving." He stretches on his tiptoes, pretending to get a bird's-eye view of the Park. "Oh no! Russ forgets to put the cruiser in park. The car plays its own clown part."

The Barber gallops on as Russ hops out of his flashing cruiser answering the call of duty, a booty dispute, with hopes up for a hustle-up on two wanted dopes.

"Russ is a-riding his stubby legs across goose-poop park. A cop who thinks he's home on the range. What's he roping, heifers? Russ rides for a stampede opportunity honed from his Blanshard farmboy skills. Giddyup. Chase it down. Catch it. Time to reel in the sheaves on those prized dopes.

"Russ runs straight ahead, full speed ahead, damn the goose shit. If

Russ could nab these scallywags, that would be a big catch by the Creek." The Barber catches his breath and rallies on. "The crowd watches. It's cowboy cop behind in the rush, his clown cruiser ahead in a crawl that's picking up speed to the Creek."

Oh my God, his scissors and comb have changed into waving bullhorns.

"The cherries are blasting. And the clown cruiser rolls, and rolls faster, and rolls a little faster again. It's rolling downhill, picking up steam, down to the Creek. Now it *sails* towards the water." The Barber points both scissors and comb toward a distant surface in the back of the mirror. "Echo. Echo. Clown Cruiser Zero on the target."

On the cue, the scissors shift to his John Deere belt buckle while his comb settles back onto his right rump. His butt starts a-hopping, his head a-bopping, in a hobbyhorse motion. He stops to rear up his hands, calling upwards, calling through a make-believe megaphone. "*It sailed …*"

Blackie can see the painted picture in the mirror's reflection, the clown cruiser airborne, destination The Creek. Blackie watches the scissors pick out the exact imaginary target. The Barber comes to attention for a scissor salute in a goodbye reflection.

Things get even more complicated for Russ in the barbershop now, as his character gets a harelip — a mimicry tool The Barber calls upon to ratchet up the humour, also handy with his vast repertoire of lisping-midget jokes.

"*I g-not you, Petey Tah-burry. I huv you 'ow, Petey.*"

The scissors go from ear to mouth, playing microphone to the unravelling action. The Barber adds in play-by-play announcer Jim Buck Sr.: "Petey and Mitch stop. They laugh, wrapped together, plastered in goose dung, for a real shit-fit show."

Russ is pulling out the cuffs, failing to see the dual dopes pointing behind him. The crowd is stunned into silence, a strange hush that Supercop fails to notice.

"Russ is caught up in the rundown. He sees them pointing. So he points back at them." Official finger-pointing in the mirror. "*No, I've got you. Yes, I got you now.* The local lads continue to point back, now in convulsions."

The Barber and Blackie are having good fun on the chase and catch. "By the time Russ turns back around, it's up the creek. His ride has rode, or rather slid, off into the Creek." The Barber leaves nothing to question. "Rolling. Ro-l-l-l-ing. It rolls with enough momentum to launch into the water. The cruiser seems to skate on the surface as it floats off, but soon, down, down it goes with a *glug, glug.* The water-line overflows the floorboards and up to the open windows. Glug, glug, glug. The blasting cherries are up like a periscope."

The Barber lifts one hand to his lips. He pretends to guzzle from a glass. "*Glug. Glug. Glug.* Those cherries churn and churn in a pathetic death throb. Throbbing over the paddle-less motion of the sinking cruiser."

This time round, The Barber has both the scissors and the comb above his head, making helicopter twirls. He sways side to side in cruiser sympathy.

"The cruiser rocks back and forth, back, forth … and settles dead in the mud of the creek bed."

Blackie sits up. His haircut is over. The panoramic sinking image of double cherries bob-bob-bobbing along in the Creek takes a few breaths to absorb. Blackie can't help himself, he just has to know. "Where did all this information come from?"

"Get this, Petey and Russ *both* came in to wager a free haircut."

"With rocks?"

"Well, Russ showed up with the most unusual rock, a Rock of Ages. He chose a small, two-tone —"

"Ton? A two-ton rock for the ages?"

"No, two *shades*, two tones of granite. The piece is shaped … like a penis."

"A penis?"

"Right as rain, a granite *penis.*"

"But what about Petey's rock?"

It's a rare moment. After months of Cindy, she's suddenly relegated to the back seat of conversation.

Blackie turns on the barbershop threshold. "His rock. A winner?"

A wave from the back of the shop. "Next time, Blackie."

Chapter 10

The Polar Twins

1985

The Polar Twins, Ned and Jed, are even more famous than Amos and Andy, at least in the annals of Town history.

Their father, Jack Roger, is manufacturing scion of Roger Fabricating, Inc. His two hundred workers — along with their hundreds of family members and their neighbours, which pretty much takes care of the entire Town — know him as the Boss (never to be confused with the Big Boss, Marvin). The Roger enterprise produces a mix of hand and power mowers, bullocks for rototillers, sputtering two-stroke engines and the most rude-looking chainsaws. All are sprayed in an odd shade of red that's somewhere between robin-redbreast and blood orange.

Any farmer for country miles and most Town yard fanatics note the particular red.

"Jack calls it fire engine red. Not a bright red, I'd say. But a dumb choice."

"And those ugly little chainsaws. In that colour ..."

Kipp Dobson Sr. and Jack's grandfather August competed as pioneer merchants in the livery business. The Dobson family branched into the automotive, with the livery morphing into the school bus business. The Roger family dropped delivery to take a different direction into manufacturing, starting with buggy building. A generation later Jack turned up the fire, working up to those burnt-red small farm implements which are not to be confused with the Massey Harris line of farm products from nearby Bell City. That was then, when the hometown boy could hold his own against the competition from fellow scions Dick Massey and Brian Harris. The Roger shade looks even more of a blood orange next to the M-H cardinal red.

The eighteen-foot-by-seven-foot handcrafted sign proclaiming ROGER DOES IT! that adorns the factory's front entrance was unlike anything seen in town, until Kipp Dobson's neon Ford logo appeared in 1911.

Roger Fabricating's reception area, lunch room and washrooms all feature expansive illustrated art of the entire factory in pen and ink. In the portrait, fabricating workers in suspenders stand shoulder to shoulder on the factory floor, looking up at the artists beneath a red-and-gold sign that reads ROGER FABRICATING SINCE 1857. The inside job kept local artists Ken and Meggie Fletcher under a roof through the height of the Depression. Smaller print versions of the art adorn all the plant management offices. (The pieces also stand in as a standard gift for retirement presentations, always dedicated in the Boss's hand-writing. *"To our friend Mike K, thank you for 46 years of loyal service. Jack A. Roger, President."*) The Boss keeps the originals at his King Street residence, strung along the wall behind his massive cherry desk. In all the reproduced art, the Roger logo jumps out in gold letters shadowed in that odd red, screaming ROGER DOES IT!

Down on the factory floor, worker *schadenfreude* is a perpetual undercurrent washing back and forth between the four side-by-each factory buildings. Scandal school goes to work on the south edge of Town by the cement plant. His employees snicker straight up from the floor at the Boss in his neat custom suits doing his factory walkabout.

"Watch him. The Boss isn't wandering. The Boss is wondering *about Judy* Westman."

"Can Roger do it?" (Wink, wink. Nod, nod.)

Despite all the gossip, only God herself and a few close associates know about Jack fooling about with an attractive line worker named Tory in the old-stock storage room in Building #4.

The fourth building is a field of play for the ruddy boss ram with a fleet of prototype lawnmowers as silent witnesses. *L'eau de barnyard* breeds with the rich aroma of fresh grass stuck to the experimental equipment. Tory confides to a few choice girlfriends.

"My goodness, Boss could be a rutting billy goat. Go all day, ram, bam, thank you Tory."

Her line mates could wait all day for an ounce of Roger-doing-it details.

"He did hand me a monogrammed hanky to wipe myself."

"A hanky?"

"Monogrammed. Hangs on my dresser table mirror. Reminds me Roger does it."

"On your table mirror?"

"I'll never wash it."

In 1937, when Jack marries Maxine Polar, daughter of a regional bank manager, his new wife keeps her maiden name. This is pretty heady stuff, especially coming from the Polar Queen, the best the Town has ever seen. During her father Max's short term as the local branch manager, he sat as a regular in The Barber's red & nickel chair. Max somehow was an instant Moose Lodge member; maybe it came with the job. Jack, the Town's most eligible bachelor, didn't miss a thing, observing the stir of Maxine's arrival here in her adolescence, then tracking her until graduation from that snotty private school in the Big Smoke. Jack was quick to stake his territory. With his snazzy convertible he played the part of school chauffeur for weekends and holidays, serving as her escort for both prom and graduation ceremonies. Maxine got caught up in the Errol Flynn Jr. whirlwind of a blue-ribbon romance. Those in the know say it is a marriage made in heaven. The Rev. Dr. George Sewell writes in his diary that his blessings made the day:

"A royal wedding of our merchant prince and his princess bride deserves the message of nuptials from God's voice on earth. The day, bluebird bright, while the full moon shone blood orange that night, added to my glorious time …"

His parishioners present a more grounded view, with shorter words. Not unique among small towns, St. Marys looks for scandal everywhere, even right there from their sanctimonious perches in the great Methodist Hall.

"If his family name isn't good enough, then 'Roger doesn't do it' should be the slogan."

Many remain mired in ignorant speculation. *"Is it something European? Her French background, do you suppose?"*

The truth is like butter compared to the margarine of fiction:

"She lives in that big house of Jack's, cocooned all inclusive in a luxury life, if'n she's not off in the city."

"Jack pays for it. Can't she take his name too?"

"Maybe he'll drive her over the edge."

This last is a nasty reference to an earlier incident when single, drunk Jack did it, then went over the edge on a gravel back road south of St. Marys. Most locals use Lover's Lane, a single lane of privacy beside the southwest boundary of the cement plant. Couples seeking more privacy head further off the path to Lemonade Springs, a loose gradient four kilometres along the Thames River. Jack, distracted by his mono-grammed-hanky panty reach, slid down into the ditch. The woman, some serf employee's wife, did the walk of shame back from Lemonade Springs all the way to Town for a phone. Constable Fat Charlie showed up for a few tears on his shoulder. She held the soiled monogrammed hanky in her clutch as evidence of contact.

Fat Charlie's point-by-point on the fall from grace never got filed; the Chief covered up his golfing buddy's indiscretions. (Jack golfs with a big slice, much to the delight of the lower-class audience. Everyone is a better golfer than the Boss. *Big Jack, big hack." "Even millionaire balls can't buy you a decent golf game."*)

The Polar Queen, in her first action as regent after the royal pioneer merchant wedding, accompanies Jack to the Roger company Christmas party. His employees can't get over his performance on the dance floor.

"All over the young wives!"

"What about Marlene Dietrich?"

"Who?"

"Maxine, dummy. The mystery woman. Did you check her dress out? In the back light you could see evvvv … see it all."

"Back light?"

"The hallway light was shining right through her dress when she headed to the powder room."

"Yeah right. She saw 'it all' on the dance floor and that was enough of Jack. She was heading for the exit."

"Every man in the room wanted to escort her home."

"The smell of her French perfume filling the car would be enough for me."

"I would never clean the seats."

Maxine's role at 3:15 AM after the annual Christmas party is to provide open arms. The drunk Mr. Roger drops into the front hall. Maxine is Girl-Guide-prepared as she steadies him up the stairs to plunk him on the bedroom wingback chair. There she pulls off his custom-made Dack shoes. Up she balances him so the silver-buttoned suspenders come down with the pleated and cuffed pants. While the tipsy Jack tries to balance, down go the Stanfields boxers, the sole Town purchase. With one push he lands in the wingback chair, Maxine landing on top of him. His wife is ready, topless and bottomless, wearing only a silk *robe de chambre*. Maxine grasps the collars of Jack's loose monogrammed shirt. Her breasts flop in counter-clockwise rhythm across his hairy chest, complementing his thrusts. A few pokes, some snorts, and she has him off in a final groan. She's able to leverage a swing up left, right, then left again in a three-step duck shuffle to the canopy bed. By 3:37 AM, twenty-two minutes after Jack arrived home, Maxine has re-established order for the 1863 Roger Manor home.

Maxine switches to the single bed in her dressing room. "Now two people can get a good night's sleep," she says to herself.

Jack burns the Z's like one of those ugly Roger chainsaws. Maxine loves a good night's beauty sleep more than anything else. Separate sleeping arrangements, however, never limit the use of the second boudoir bed for Jack to mess up the sheets in an occasional brief conjugal visit.

Growing up across Western Ontario on a banker's circuit, Maxine is the only daughter of a banker, the only grandchild of a doctor. After elementary school she attended the swank Bishop Stewart Private School as a boarder. The expensive school was a given, given that both mother and grandmother were former students too. Even so, the Roger family gives her a step up from the moderate but mobile affluence of a bank manager's family. An aura surrounds her which locals mistake for snobbery, which in turn is easily mistaken for French. Maxine certainly looks the part. She graduates to wearing prêt-à-porter custom-ordered from Toronto. Maxine could be a live model parading the streets of Town. The wagging tongues go deep to invent details of her life.

"They send an agent out from Toronto to show her the French catalogue in person. Anything she wants. They take custom measurements."

"She walked the runways as a young model in Paris. That's where the Boss met her, in Paris, France."

"Yes, you're right. I can see it. The way she marches down Main Street."

"Marches? That may be a strong word. I like sashay. Her entire body moves in a rhythm."

"Who has ever seen her march, or shall I say sashay, on Main? I live on Main and I've never seen Maxine walk anywhere. She has a driver who carries stuff for her."

"Driver? That's Richie Rosen, their gardener! Hope he washes those hands."

The prospectors dig deeper, showing no mercy.

"There has to be something hidden in her background."

"Model in Paris, you say? What type *of model, eh?"*

"Jack's no fool and neither is that woman. It's a partnership made by the Devil."

The inventors stick to the image of Paris, but the truth is a little more boring.

Maxine shops at the Robert Simpson Company Little Room — not in Paris but in Toronto's top private boutique on Simpsons fourth floor, corner of King and Yonge in the city centre, blocks from the train station. Easy out, easy back. Yes, all clothes are Made in France, very expensive, very classy. But off the rack. Robert Simpson provides a livery service to a small, select group of Ontario-wide women on an unlimited budget. (The current Robert Simpson, a second-generation proprietor, always greets Maxine in person at the station. The Simpson family had their start in Newmarket as pioneer merchants. Mr. Simpson respects his roots in rural Ontario with the easy task of greeting this radiant young lady.)

In St. Marys, Maxine reigns from her throne at 52 King Street South, the sweetest and grandest of a long line of Town Georgian homes. She rules without spoken words, her commands passing into the community at large by means of embossed invitations in hand-addressed envelopes.

Her pride of wives, neighbour ladies and social wannabes all line up to wait for the green light.

"Did you get your invitation to Maxine's Tulip Tea Party?"

"No, did it come by mail?"

"No, it was hand delivered."

"Who by?"

"I don't know, since I found the envelope under the front door."

(The hard-to-see grimy fingerprints left at the scene mean the gardener did it.)

Top Town ladies count on at least one invitation each year to the Boss's Big Four of public events, all managed by Maxine: the Tulip Tea, Holly Tea, Pumpkin Tea and Wisteria Tea parties. Maxine is too smart to let the locals ply themselves with her husband's high-end alcohol and allow loose, boozy lips to sink ships. At the fall event Maxine always recreates her family's exotic pumpkin-and-allspice mixture. (The recipe can be found in the *Eat At Our House* file in the Museum Archives. Curator Larry claims this recipe is the most frequent download off their website.)

Maxine knows little, cares less about her husband's hanky panky. Their housekeeper just assumes Jack has one big runny nose. "That Mr. Roger sure seems to go through those monogrammed hankies! Why not just buy them at White & May Dry Goods? Packs of three for twenty-five cents." Mrs. Graul, known with affection as Growly by the Roger family, keeps her nose down, never assumes, never contemplates. They pay her more than Roger Fabricating pays any female line-worker to keep all within the halls of 52 King Street South.

As for The Barber, he practises caution. Jack does not make The Barber's mimicry casting, period. The Barber makes only the rare comment about Jack, leaving his customers to take their own bites off the Boss. Jack will on occasion show up for the Innkeeper's morning coffee klatch, however. And a weekly dose of Roger Does It, whereby the Innkeeper tends bar for Jack and a few buddies late Friday afternoons. The Boss needs a snort of courage before the weekend face-off at home.

He confesses to the Innkeeper. "Maxine has never accepted the bridle."

The Innkeeper sticks to a neutral nod. "Can't push or pull a thoroughbred. They need to lead. You need to shut your mouth, smile and nod." The Innkeeper, an experienced coach, helps douse marriage flames and preserve the pioneer merchant fortunes of Jack Roger. "Jack, she's off to the city tomorrow. Relax, you have the whole weekend on your own. Do a few rounds with your new clubs."

Father knows best about when to pass the essential ingredients on to his son two doors down; the Innkeeper is cautious about sharing information that may well get the mimic's treatment. Floor rules, however, are not so gracious — whether café, smoke pit, livery or barbershop. As soon as you're gone, the talk on you remains, carried on by the present so-called friends. The conversation sips into gear over java, and quicker with liquor.

"Jack has some fortitude — he has to face the power of that woman."

"Get used to it. That whip goes with the marital package."

"Just deserts. He whips his workers all day."

Sip, sip, let it all slip.

"I'd take a whip stroke or three from Maxine."

Time marches on through the dark clouds of the war years. For the Roger business, the war is heaven-sent manna with three shifts running on the assembly line. The assembly line changes over to produce thousands and thousands of chocolate-brown hand grenades. (The Stonetown Museum has uncharged examples along with the casting moulds.)

By the time the postwar era dawns with two royal weddings and expanded production of burnt-orange yard equipment, Jack Roger does it once again by securing the family dynasty with the arrival of Ned and Jed. For once the Town talk is stunned into silence, but only very briefly. Still, the Town sings a different tune with an heir in place.

"Jack be nimble, Jack be quick, and Maxine sure did jump on to his candlestick. Light me up, Jack."

"Roger did it."

And from the ground zero of the assembly line: *"She probably has her own set of monogrammed hankies to wipe herself off with."*

As the twins mature, even a Town fool could see that they are polar opposites. The twins untwine on opposite paths: one minimum and the other maximum. While Minimus disappears under the radar, Maximus climbs to the stars.

"That Jed sure is full of himself."

"He clocks less than 10.5 seconds in the one hundred."

"Toronto University will give him an academic scholarship."

"Harvard will give him a sport scholarship. They love smart, rich, sporty lads. Daddy will cover the rest."

Maximus's sails get some wind from the likes of the Rev. Dr. George Sewell. The ancient messenger relishes having a Roger twin star in his Confirmation class. Underneath the old fool's fluttering eyelids in the upper choir practice room of the Sunday School annex, Jed takes a biblical view of the girls' behinds, while Ned melts into the middle seats.

The Barber, though, mentions Ned in his deerskin diary but never Maxine, Jed or Jack. He can tell a man from his haircut. Ned demonstrates the class of his pioneer merchant grandfather Jasper Allen Roger, reconfirming next month's visit with the busy haircutter on payment and always including a fifty-cent tip.

Jed cares little for protocol, walking through the door at any time. Maximus can pirouette quarterback-style and backshift out the threshold to the sidewalk if he faces any opposition lineup. If the chair is available, Jed sits down no questions asked and talks football, with every game rivalling Horatio's exploits at the bridge. The Barber has little interest in football or the vanity play from this overconfident lad, but a great barber does know something about customer treatment after forty years behind the big red & nickel chair.

"Jed, big game coming up against the Theatre Town Totems on Friday?"

The Barber does it with a fisherman's skill, casting to the lad's sweet spot: his ego. Jed catches the hook without hesitation, jumping into a lengthy monologue that monumentalizes Captain Horatio's latest successes.

"Danny Snider can catch, but I have to tell him *the exact X-spot on the field.* Danny thinks too much. Thinks he's not open enough. Thinks he's not fast enough or the other guy is just too fast but also too tall, has too-long arms or too much skill. Thinks. Thinks!"

The Barber nods his head to the mirror, but the lad's gaze remains on his field of glory. Who's he even talking to?

"Keep it simple with Danny." Jed continues in a barking voiceover. "Danny. Just move to the spot, the exact spot."

If the haircut went a smidgen longer, Jed would grab the ball and run on and on into overtime. Paying with exact change and no tip, Jed takes off in a star-of-the-game strut toward the great possibilities of the upcoming Friday Night against the Theatre Town Totems.

"Totem annihilation for those cast-outs." Jed never leaves any doubt as to his cleverness. "*Totem* annihilation, eh?"

In contrast, his brother ranges wide and far in discussion, even reaching out into the universe. Ned and The Barber buzz about the show *Space Opera*. Ned watches on his parents' television, the first colour in Town. (The Barber sneaks over to the Café for his television fill in black and white.) The Roger family buy not only the very first black-and-white and colour TVs but the first heated swimming pool in St. Marys.

"The Buzz Corbett sets are just wild. I can't believe they shot it live."

With Ned, the questions need to be intelligent and specific to ignite the thoughtful lad's response and never patronize him. The conversation flows from one welcome question. "What shows do you watch in colour?"

The Barber always enjoys the well-researched TV guide of Ned's classic tours.

"*Captain Video*. It was the first in colour." And the flow goes on. "Mother gets me these Dan Dare comics out of the UK. Bought them on a business trip with Father last month. And it gets better. CBC will run the Dan Dare cartoon show next year."

Then there's the clothing choices, another deep contrast. Jed dresses the part of the jock with his St. Marys High School red-and-white team jersey in fall, winter and spring. (He covers up with the SMHS-crested football jacket in winter.) In summer he wears a short-sleeved SMHS shirt, again with crested right-side logo and on the opposite side an oversized C, leaving no doubt as to who's the captain of the SMHS football team. In the summertime he smartens up with lighter wear — tennis whites, runners and a short-sleeved jersey with a small red reminder of who's in charge, an embroidered Cover his heart. For the sake of Maxine's home report card he follows Jack in style for public appearances and on Sundays, sporting her approved dress uniform for the family's command appearances in the Roger-family-reserved third row of the Methodist Hall.

As for Ned, he keeps it simple with Growly service: a white shirt ironed by Mrs. Graul and a black leather tie. Leather is as odd as Ned gets. He has two pairs of corduroy pants for the winter and two pairs of Lee jeans, one black and one beige (never blue), for spring and fall. All chosen by Maxine at Robert Simpson's Young Man's Shop in Toronto. (White & May, though, have begun selling Lee after Maxine brought her boys into the store on their twelfth birthday, setting up separate charge accounts.)

Graduation year at St. Marys High gives most seniors a little extra swagger in the months before convocation. Jed in his C-embroidered open-neck sweater begins the fall semester with an A+ in attitude. At home, he starts up on the brother lecture while he catches the passed lunch bag from his mother. "Does the guy always have to wear the same lugubrious stuff? It's like my brother's a vampire, maybe a funeral director. Stays up all night reading then shows up for breakfast pasty-faced. All wrapped up in his crumpled white shirts and black ties. Sorry, black *leather* ties."

The Queen speaks on her home court. "Jed, never let Mrs. Graul hear you say that. You'll get a taste of real Growly, sleeping in the same sheets for weeks."

"A well-ironed Dracula, then."

Mother presses a finger on the Captain's coffee cup. "He has his own look. Just as you have your own look." Maxine waits for Jed to look up for eye contact, and then, *a-la-kazam*, she about-turns on one foot with the bell ring as pop goes the toaster. A footnote for Jed left in the air. "*Vive la différence!* Such good-looking young men."

Jed leaves his viewpoint in a mutter. "A bag of bones dressed in a mortician's suit."

Mother always hears and sees more than her children think. "You'll wish that you have your brother's physique when you are your father's age."

This slight comment carries no weight for Jed, the beautiful superstar, captain of the St. Marys High School football team. "Jack's let himself go. Too much booze mixed with sugar sodas."

"Jed, careful with that thought. Have a look at the photo of your father on his high school graduation. Graduating top athlete, may I add."

Jed goes silent, and Maxine changes her tack. "Father is the person you should be concerned about. He's still the Boss at Roger Inc., so if you have any family business interest, you need to ask your father out for a round of golf."

Growly pushes through the back door to break the kitchen silence. "Good morning Mrs. Roger, Master Jed." With longterm family experience she cuts to the chase. "Ma'am, I'll start with the young gents' bathroom."

Growly is off, and so is Jed with a hallward point and a peck on Mother's cheek.

"Thanks for breakfast. School."

As Ned enters, Jed blocks him in a hallway squeeze.

Ned is silent in one thought: *He's not my brother, he's just an asshole.* He squeezes past the fraternal indiscretion for a double kiss on Mother's cheeks. *"Au revoir Maman, je vais à l'école. À tantôt."* Another double set of kisses. *"Je t'aime Maman."*

Ned is neither fish nor fowl, neither Captain nor Boss nor a funeral director, but the real deal, through and true, a charmer.

Jed stops his twin in the foyer with a sideways smile. "Ned, there's an Arthur Lismer feature at the Art Gallery of Ontario."

Ned is somewhat surprised at his opposite's suggestion. He knows there are barely seven Citizens in Town who would recognize the name of the great Canadian painter Arthur Lismer. He never needs an excuse to feed his need for culture: the ROM, Chinatown, the AGO, maybe even the CNE in September. Maxine needs even less of an excuse to book a driver from Kipp Dobson and a call for a double pickup to Mr. Simpson in Toronto.

Jed can see the question on his face. "In *The Globe.* Ned, you know there'll be a pool party this weekend. Invitation is open. You're welcome to hang around."

Ned raises his yeah-right eyebrows.

"Shopping with Mother in Toronto? I could never handle that. But we can really let loose with Mother out of the house. Dad will be drunk after eighteen holes with his golfing buddies, sleeping in his office chair." Ned's twin gets nose to nose, lowers his voice. "That's when things get hot; maybe some topless, maybe bottoms off if we're lucky. Count on Kristi for a hair-raising show. Whoops, she's bare down there." Two winks and a point to where *there* is.

Ned's had enough already this morning of Jed's bluewater plan. Who cares if Mother hears him. "Fuck off, Jed."

And Jed does just that in seconds, waving his third finger behind him on his way out the Georgian maple doorway and finishing off with a cracker of a slam goodbye.

A warm September morning has Jed making the Captain's grand entrance at school with the red & white sweater perfect around his neck, holding an underachiever's leather school binder with the embossed Roger logo. He struts the parade line. "Hey Margie. Nice sweater. Wool, or can it be felt?"

"Jed, can I feel an invite to your pool party?"

Catching the attention of Margie's smile, Jed casts an eye over her shoulder with a finger point to his #1 guard. "Hey Al. Can I bum a cigarette?"

Jed welcomes a means to an end-pass by Margie's cute butt. Or maybe, later in the pool, the quarterback sneak for a bottomless play on the squeeze. Margie doesn't smoke, so no need to ask her anything until swim time. Nevertheless, he receives a big smile on the silent pass-over. Margie bubbles over to her locker mates.

"Jed's having a pool party and *he* asked me."

Farther down the hallway the football teammate division line up in agreement.

"Captain throws a big score party."

"Big C dives in first. It's his pool party."

"He even goes out of bounds to invite an occasional round of city girls."

"Those Totems love the heat … of the pool."

"I just go and hope for a pass-off."

Out of the pool, off the gridiron, Jed's handpicked naughty girls get the most exclusive smoker club next to the Devil's Smoke Pit. The high school fence behind the storage barn serves as Jed's exclusive puff domain. Pool-party wannabes pick up this invitation even though they never smoke, progressing from locker conversation to cafeteria lunch seat, to standing by the school fence to pool hanky-panky. The sacrificial lambs bleat away about their chance to join Jed's dream team.

"Jed asked little ol' me for a smoke."

"Susie, you don't smoke!"

"Who cares? What a hunk."

"So what happened behind the barn?"

"Nothing serious, but Jed's a dirty boy."

"Dirty talk, then?"

"No talk. All tongue."

Ned's walk down the high school walkway stands out in a different way, with his pressed white shirt and pencil-thin black tie, and the double-flap, twin-handled briefcase of a serious student.

Margie has her cute butt stuck out of her locker. Ned, though, only notices that her Home Ec assignment has dropped on the floor.

"Excuse me Margie, you dropped this." And the great student is off with a smile. "Have a great day."

Margie confesses to Kristi. "I almost wet myself when I turned. Thought it was Jed. But I paused and thought how sweet, how courteous. Jed would never bend over for anyone."

Kristi has thought a little about the opposites. "Ned talks to you as a real person, with eye contact and sincere interest. Jed stares at your boobs."

Ned's friends are waiting near his locker.

"Hey Ned, Chess Club after school?"

"For sure, Ken."

A small group gathers. "How's the science project coming, Wes? Dog crap as a fertilizer, right?"

Big group laughter, somebody asks for the project's name.

"Does Doggie-Doo Do?"

Ned steps in. "How are the results?"

"Dog dirt is strong. Burns the shit out of my tomatoes."

"I can have a look at your solution strengths, and help with the graph math on the, uh, shitty results."

The group laughs together.

Even the small group of friends in Chess Club, Science Club and Yearbook Club fall prey to weakness, though, in their backwater dreams of a Town god.

"If'n Jed Roger was my brother? I'm not stuck on pride. I'm hanging in for the leftovers at his pool party."

As if the teenage depravity of Ned's Polar opposite wasn't enough, now his friends are crying for false baptism in the holy heated pool. "Do you know how dumb those girls are? They're so stupid they don't even understand the game of football. They think the tight end is a nice butt."

"Ned, I can play dumb too. I'll take a little leftover tight end."

"Great, Tommy. Kiss his butt enough, you might make his fan club. Bring your chapstick. Just remember, it could be your sister on the dream team."

The brothers were born as identical twins, Ned older by three minutes. The difference in their personalities was obvious as early as their second birthday, when it came time to choose a cake. Guess who picked devil and who picked angel? Ned hears the Jed references day in and day out.

On Friday evening, while Jed plays God on the field, his brother has the house on King all to himself with Mrs. Graul. She serves him up her special chicken pot pie while she irons the week's supply of white shirts, smiles at her favourite son, nods you-don't-say, and listens.

Ned loves his Growly as a silent sounding board that's as comfortable as warm slippers.

"Growly, I do sleepwalk sometimes you know, to the bathroom. That prick Jed follows me and turns me at the right moment, tries to confuse my aim."

Growly nods with new clarity. That scenario might explain that smell from time to time, as well as the over-the-edge backsplash and the yellow stains on the white tile floors.

"I know he uses my towel. Wipes his ass with it."

Growly is heads down over the ironing board in shock with too much information to launder.

"Farts in my pillow, too. Thinks that's funny. But the laugh's on him. I switch pillows when he's in the washroom."

The housekeeper will never look at the boys' towels and pillow slips quite the same. She makes a mental note to wear new rubber gloves the next time she cleans the stained bathroom floor. The old ones are out with the trash.

On the field at St. Marys High School, our false god relishes the potential point spread with a thrashing in front of the home crowd. Even Jack has skipped the last round at the country club to catch Jed's performance from the corner of the pitch. The stadium is jammed with converts rocking the plank bench seats. Rival fans fail to make an impression on anybody, including themselves. Their pine planks wobble off-kilter with any fan momentum. The tempo dials up to a din of praise from all sides.

Ned will never surpass the glory of tonight's big game against the city rivals from Theatre Town, the Totems. On team huddles he's a pulpit preacher calling to his minions to sit up and listen up. Maximus's minions work the plan with gutsy legwork, head knocks and bone-shaking blocks. Jed takes the glory in fist pumps and a full strut down the field with the game football pointed up in the air to his audience.

He sends two ball jabs to the fifth row, upper right. "Chelsea, for you."

Kristi, two rows down to the lower left, unable to sit for this slight, stands up. "Hey Captain. Over. Here."

Jed knows the call of the wild, sends three ball jabs in full stride back to Kristi, who gives him an instantaneous flip. For his eyes only she flips her pleated skirt up, revealing herself to be all bare, not a stitch of hair. Six Totems players look back, all fall flat at the flash. A roar from the back benches and beyond.

"Jed! Jed! Captain Jed! Mess 'em up, them Totems there! Jed! Jed!"

Maximus victory is a foregone conclusion.

At the same time, one classy lady and her attendant, a smart-looking young man in a pressed white shirt and pencil-thin leather black tie wait for the 8:15 on the Grand Trunk station platform. Her son carries the matching Louis Veille belt-strapped leather suitcases. Mother carries matching makeup case and shoulder bag.

On the train, Ned gives fewer lurid details than during the ironing-board confessions with the housekeeper, but this twin, for once the same as his opposite, does not lay off from his point of perception. "How in the world can anyone deal with Jed? Bad enough to have him as a brother, even worse that he's my twin." Ned progresses from home and school to how the Roger family does it. "How can I trust him enough to work with him as a business partner? I have too much experience with him."

Maxine keeps family first. "Your father is a wise man when he deals in relationships. Employees, services, government, even neighbours, plus his big customers like Simpsons and international people like Allan Dhingra."

The Dhingra industrial conglomerate in India has international designs that include Roger. The windmills they export to Latin America incorporate a Roger five-horsepower gas motor, and the ugly blood-orange rototillers are a small-plot hit in south Asia. The proof of a profitable relationship is a tall stack of slate crates in Building #4. Ned has met Allan, who has visited Town on numerous occasions, including regarding a proposal for a joint fabricating venture in Kerala.

"Your father is not stupid. He knows your brother, sees his actions. He will make it right for both of his sons."

"Mother, I am not interested. No matter how Father stitches it together. No matter how smart, how fair, how transparent he tries to be, the Boss will not always be able to make it work when Jed can put a master spin on things."

Maxine takes a deep breath looking out the window, but she doesn't see the green scenery. The train and Ned roll on.

"Mother, it's a train wreck. Maybe not today, next week or next year. But it's a train wreck in the making."

She turns to her son. "Well then, follow your path, Ned." She squeezes his hand. "What is that path?"

He places his other hand on hers with a squeeze. "Business school at McGill, Mother."

Maxine turns squarely to her son and places both her hands on his shoulders with two squeezes. "And not return to your family business?"

Ned understands from those direct eyes how Maxine draws fresh air into a room. "I want to become a chartered accountant. I need a new beginning in life. I understand how Roger does it. Now I need to learn the other ways."

"So it will be a true Genesis for my son."

"McGill has offered me a scholarship."

"C'est une bonne chance."

"Une bonne chance rendre sa visite à Montréal."

A unique path to an esteemed university in a distant city with a French accent will separate the twin paths forever.

"Mother, business is business. This is my time. And this is the only time when I can make my own deal with Father. Remember, I know first hand how the Rogers do it. For once in God's life this will not be Jed's deal." Ned puts his hands on his mother's shoulders. "Otherwise Jed will have the advantage over me for the rest of my life."

Those eyes shine bright on her son, but she holds onto the family light. "You wouldn't even take shares in your family's business, Ned? Not continue in the fourth generation of the Roger lineage, even as a board member?"

Minimus is steaming ahead, as fast as the locomotive that carries them off to the city. "That cheque each month would feel like a yank on the chain. Plus the threat of a board meeting would remind me of that asshole. My direction is to avoid assholes and move on. This particular Roger will do it somewhere else."

"Son, such language from a Roger. How you forget your manners with your mother."

"Sorry Mother, the worst of Jed does not bring out the best in me. And my identical twin happens to be a sociopath." He squeezes her hand. "Mother, my decision includes a family buyer discount. I just want out."

The conversation ends with a flip of the Veille custom cosmetic case on her lap, for a makeup refresh. A driver from the Park Plaza Hotel will greet them at the station with a creamy white Rolls.

Back down the tracks, the taxi squad picks up on the pitch at 52 King

Street South. Pass-offs and completions featuring randy roosters and hussy hens play out by the heated pool. As the night winds down, the crowd thins to a few shortlisted bucks, outnumbered by wild does. The big buck gets into position behind his favourite would-be receivers. Jed's pool craft dictates the first move: the bikini-top flip. He gets his receiver's attention by motioning to her skimpy top. "Kristi, free swim time."

In a flash, she's off. Kristi jumps topless into the dark pool, laughing but unseen in the milky blue waters. She may be frisky, but the Captain knows it's risky in open waters. She vanishes, a wet dream, but no worries — there are lots of others on his team.

After one too many beers, she is leaning against a lamp post, lapping up the pool action. Jed approaches her from behind.

"Hey sweet cheeks."

Taking advantage of her distraction, Jed plants his swimsuit, up like a tent, over her bikini butt crack. Chelsea stumbles, too drunk to balance. She goes down, out cold on the stain-resistant lounge chair. Her beautiful buttocks have landed starward in an awkward downward dog. The taxi squad drool over a lost pass, out of bounds. The master of indiscretion does not stop here, however. He surveys the pool table.

Luckily Jed has a Hail Mary pass, a special leftover for a sure score on a late-night swim. Jed turns to a former first-round draftee who has yet to make the cut.

"Heather Vuyk, looking good. Pool stays open late for you."

Heather stands out at a swim party in cut-offs that graze the lower side of the only pierced navel in Grade 13. A sleeveless white shirt covers her braless tank top. The attractive girl has waited poolside for two summers to score this private invitation. This time she left the swim cover at home. "Captain, your shipmate didn't bring a swimsuit."

Jed pulls her towards him. "Pool's ninety-two degrees."

Jack likes it hot. The Boss figured heating the pool was cheaper than taxes on a Lake Huron cottage.

Two naked bodies hit the dark blue surface.

When he and Maxine return from Toronto, Ned manoeuvres a private office appointment with his father. Maxine offers strategy, cautioning

Ned on the careful choice of words. *("Talk about 'value' and 'deals.'")* Before Jack can even say anything, Ned has already punted the ball with a typed-out, point-by-point succession plan.

"Father, this is the one time in my life that Jed and I can come to a deal. Jed is the one to make the Roger family do it."

Jack finds himself in a nodding mode, a proud father agreeing to a smart plan. Then again, sobriety is a morning infliction.

"Father, you know Jed is the son to do it. The Big C can quarterback the Roger family into the next generation. My talents and ambitions will take me on a different, more distant course. I *will* do it, but in accounting." Ned shuffles the chair closer. "And somewhere out of Jed's shadow."

Jack is a dealmaker with a sharp pencil, even sharper after a Mrs. Graul coffee. Father paints the good family together in an economic future. "Son, if you take back some financing, the deal stays in the family, all private like the Rogers family prefer to do it. Otherwise, with the kind of money we're talking about, your family will have to look for outside financing."

The senior salesperson waits for his son to react, then adds, "We would start with the Molson Bank."

Jack leans over the big cherry desk and taps the glass top with his reading glasses, a head closer to Ned than he's been in years. "Family business stays within family business." The tapping stops, and he's back in the chair with raised eyebrows. "A nice big cheque would come in the mail every month. Not an ounce of sweat to pay."

Did Ned's father just wink at him? No, it's just that his right eye is quivering from the lack of alcohol. He points with his glasses. "Four percent a month. Nice piece of change, son."

"Father, I would be sweating month to month worrying about Jed and his cheque. I can't help wondering when he'll tire of licking the stamp every month. He will not be the hand that feeds me."

Jack gives Ned a cloudy look. "Now son, that's not fair. He's your brother, Ned. Born identical boys to the Roger family. The fourth generation."

"Father, I want to move on. I only wish for your and Mother's happiness." The classy son knows when to polish the family apple. "I wish Jed the very best too. This succession plan for our family will only work if I move on. And with a big family discount on the sale."

Jack sees his son Ned for the first time: a Roger doing it.

"Father, any Roger would know that the money needs to be up front, sealed and delivered. This is a win-win for the Roger family to do it for the next generation. Father, you know that's the only way it will work."

The meeting finishes in a flurry when, unannounced, Jed bursts into Jack's office, knocking the rock doorstop across the hardwood floor. As Jed moves right up to the big desk, Jack figures it's best to let him rip. Jack stays silent with one quivering eye.

"Ned can keep his share of the business," Jed announces. "I'll guarantee him a cheque every day of his life."

Jack speaks up to address the then and there. "Ned doesn't want a cheque. Ned wants to deal. Your brother has made an attractive offer."

"So seal the deal," Jed says, after a Roger family stare-down. "Pay him out, Jack."

With Ned away at university, Maxine and Jack watch Jed quarterback the Roger empire. He certainly has the genes for the trade shows. He visits all the big customers, following Jack's tracks like a canal horse. He sets aside calendar time for the Royal Winter Fair and summer's International Plowing Match, with Jack initiating him to a few of the hot spots in an old dog's life. During these events he sells Roger's shocking burnt-orange rototillers and even uglier chainsaws to farmers and citiots. At the Royal Winter Fair snowblowers replace the rototillers.

Jed has inherited a marketing strategy that does it, for now. "Country folk buy their chainsaws in the summer and early fall," his father tells him, "no later than the Plowing Match. Trimming and cutting is better without leaves, but the quest for firewood continues all year. City folk eat up the chainsaw special at the Royal Winter Fair."

If the audience is country folk, Jed can lay it on. "You know" — *wink, wink* — "city folk *need* a chainsaw at the cottage." The rural audience's snickers turn to guffaws. "That's a lot of chainsaws. A lot of chainsaws that never get a pull-job."

Jed knows that whether it's the fair, Simpsons, or Crest Hardware stores, a few November flurries and those snowblowers will sell like hotcakes. His bright and ugly lawnmowers follow him to all events, selling year-round.

Unbeknownst to Jed and his father, though, two death knells are about to ring for small-town manufacturing. First, new shopping malls are springing up with big department stores inside them, including the Toronto institution Simpsons in its fourth generation. This generation forgets their pioneer merchant rural roots. Big business is big business. These Simpsons anchor their department stores around parking lots at the edge of cities.

The second bell rings when the Simpson family strategy insists on its own Simpson line of lawnmowers, snowblowers and rototillers, a garden lineup stamped with the *Simp-licity* logo. Simp-licity products are green and white, which is a tart-up on Roger, whose products are stuck with their ugly for-the-birds colour.

While Jed convinces himself sales are up with his on-the-road efforts, Jack is slipping down into poor health. His two shots with the Innkeeper stopped long ago. Jack takes care of a fifth of excellent Scotch each day (a direct importation from distant relatives in Inverness) at home behind his forest of cherry office furniture. Maxine's frequent Toronto shopping trips are now made with an easy extension to Montreal, where Ned stays on as a graduate accountant. As high school fades into the past, Jed's dream team doesn't do it for him anymore. With no local score, Jed draws on roadshow attractions away from the wagging Town tongues. The road distraction masks the reality unfolding in the state of manufacturing.

Father can still do it, talking it up as the business grinds down. "There will never be a name on a Roger product other than our own Roger name in red and gold!"

Jed has both palms spread, wide open to the possibilities. "Father, who cares if it's our name! It will be our profits from the products sold."

"Roger name or no name."

"Big companies have their own warehouses for hundreds of stores. One buying office, one invoice and one cheque are real handy, Father. Think of how the Simpson business has transformed."

"They can Simp-plicity fuck themselves," Jack replies with hands spread, wide open to no possibilities. "The Roger logo goes on. They can do it with our product name, period. Or they don't get it."

"Father, you are the one that's not getting it. If our name is not on the unit, we're not limited in who we sell our products to. Look, we can sell our unnamed products to six different companies, all with the advantages of dealing with one big source. Just change the colours, re-design the fairings, seats, exhaust … and we can sell to anyone."

"Our name or no name, Jed. That's the only choice. How can we be Roger if we can't keep our name on our own product? And let's not fuck with the family colours."

Both father and son miss the boatload of generic imports appearing in the big department stores. Jack doesn't watch TV so he misses the SIMP-licity advertisements and, my goodness, their sponsorship of *Hockey Night in Canada*.

Meanwhile, Roger's workers toil half-hearted on the floor, looking up to see no new hires, no new products and a half-filled warehouse Building #4.

That November Jack and Jed attend the Royal Winter Fair with their monster robin-red and gold Roger booth. While they're heading to the washroom, the pair stumble across a booth a quarter the size of theirs. What catches their eye are lawnmowers made in Japan by a company called Mota.

Jack can't wait to unzip in the men's room in a sarcastic pissing match. "Sounds Italian to me. Do they make scooters too?"

Mota will soon produce the fastest café motorcycles in the world. Their sunrise-red Motomotion M4's will dominate the Isle of Man circuit. The big department stores are ahead of the deal. Simpsons and others have partnered with Mota in the last year.

Jack dies in ignorant bliss that Christmas. The *St. Marys Journal* runs a front-page obituary with a photo of the Boss holding two golf clubs.

The young Pastor Harlton gives one of the first great sermons of his ministerial life. He seizes the opportunity to bury any doubt as to whether he'll be able to replace George the messenger as the new voice behind the cherry podium. Before him, the best auditorium in Town overflows with the curious, the cultured and the corporate. Roger staff with blank expressions, given the day off, help pack the hall. A few real mourners are left standing at the entrances. The Sunday school auditorium holds the overflow crowd, boosting the broadcast by Pastor Harlton on the loud, but old and scratchy, cone-shaped speakers. Any side comments in attendance are split between dead old Jack and the new pastor.

"It's not a send-off, it's a jack-off."

"Harlton is blasting for gold, looking for a big Roger donation for the church."

"He should have got the message. The cupboard is bare. Roger isn't doing it."

"Check out the sand wedge and the three-wood in that photo. Couldn't hit either straight."

"Jack had the hack."

"Ball contact was not good."

"His balls hit targets all over Western Ontario."

The best of bad occasions brings back Ned, twenty years absent, to The Barber. He returns to St. Marys the way he left, by train, the only passenger to step off the 10:45 arrival that morning. Who would guess that the man in the cashmere overcoat is on home turf? Kipp Dobson, a fellow pioneer merchant great-grandson, does recognize a high school compatriot.

"Welcome back, Dr. Professor Rogers. Let me grab that bag." Smile and handshake. "Or rather large briefcase?"

Ned passes off the square double-handled case. "I figured you were the man for a pickup and delivery."

"Loved getting your call. It's been a few years."

"Seems like yesterday when it's your hometown. Can you pass by the house? I need to do a quick pick-up, then you can drop me off at the Town Hall."

An easy walk from Town Hall down Queen Street to the barbershop at the old Grand Central Hotel. It's his second stop of a long day, and his first time for a cut without the appointment made one month in advance. Who would have thought the first person he saw would be an ancient version of The Barber? Mother, brother and father can wait. Ned needs a haircut.

The Barber is past eighty now, some sixty-plus behind the red & nickel chair. He never forgets the notable customers, who get the better stories in his deerskin diary.

Looking out the window, The Barber smiles as he spots an incoming celebrity, kitty corner at Harris Electric, crossing the main street. He drops the *Journal*, scampering to the threshold and down to the sidewalk.

"Welcome home, Mister Ned Roger, welcome home."

From Ned's vantage, nothing has changed but wrinkles and white hair. A fine specimen of an elder man, coiffed and smart from head to toe behind a starched and pressed white apron with the original embroidered lettering. Ned could swear it's the same bowtie he marvelled at during his first haircuts. Older eyes detail The Barber's polished Oxfords and matching sculpted black belt. My goodness, pants with cuffs. St. Marys' most polished gentleman holds the door open in wide welcome.

"I'm so sorry that it took your father's funeral to bring you back. I am so glad to see you."

Ned is genuine in turn, stepping onto the black and white parquet floor. He has little time to reflect on the similarity to a floor that his wife, at great expense, picked for their kitchen. Nothing has changed inside the shop.

"Thank you, I'm surprised you even recognize me."

And The Barber gives a reminder, a reintroduction of the half-dumb look. Ned stops in his tracks, looking at this particular facial expression unique to his hometown.

"I remember your first smoke back in the rock garden. Your graduation from high school."

"Well, you never invited me before my seventeenth birthday. I bugged you for years. From at least twelve years old I wanted to have a smoke back there."

"For a nerdy kid you sure were fixated on having a smoke 'out back.'"

"Are you kidding! Every conscious male wishes for an invitation to the Devil's Smoke Pit."

"Not so many as you may think."

"I could see you guys smoking when I walked to the post office for my mother. I made sure I passed by. I could only think about how much fun you guys seemed to have."

　　　　　　　　　　　　　　　　　　　　　　　　　　　　　　　LORNE EEDY

"Fun? A gaggle of gabbing old guys scratching and hacking — that's an attraction to a kid?"

"Seemed so neat at the time. Maybe just a rebellious reaction to my parents."

The Barber nods. "I have never seen your mother smoke. Jack would have an occasional puff, but only with my father under the back porch." He pauses to catch up to the moment. "Ned, I believe you now teach. A professor of business, no doubt. Living the comfortable lifestyle in Montreal."

"Life is good, right. I confess it was good from the beginning." He tells The Barber about the lump sum payment he received from the family empire. "I took my father's payment to a recommended investment broker. When I look back, Walter had the vision to buy into IBM, McDonalds, lots of bank stock, and ironically, Canadian Tire stores. I cut my lawn with a Motomotion lawnmower."

"How about the teaching at McGill? That's a university with lots of history."

"Correction. I haven't taught in the past few years. I'm more administrative."

"Head of a department, I understand."

"Some days I think I'm a college secretary." Ned pauses for an eyebrow trim. "I'm Dean of the David Oliver School of Business."

"Impressive."

"Thank you. For your ears only, but it's even more impressive that our business school is world ranked at number eight by *Wealth* magazine."

"Young Mister Roger, from the old neighbourhood, does it."

"It's a good gig for the local kid."

"A fourth generation of a great St. Marys family." The Barber pauses, then smiles into the old bar mirror. He catches Ned with a wink. "Those smoking days would be long gone now, I suppose?"

"I jog now. I do have something time to time, but nothing more than a finger-sized cigar."

"Now tell me, Mister Roger, what would be better than a nice hand-rolled Cuban in the rock garden?"

Even for the young whiz with an established reputation, a Cubano takes all bets off the table for a smoke-free day. Or does it, Mr. Roger? "I take it all is in good order out back," Ned says.

"Yes sir, it is."

"I have something that could be even more surprising. Even more than me showing up for a haircut."

Ned reaches for his square brown attaché case, nothing brief about it.

"Okay, surprise me."

He taps the top. "I am packing a significant rock. Are you still doing that marketing schtick with the unique stone?"

"Always. But it's not schtick, it's a wager. What are you offering to wager?"

"I'm here to get a haircut for a funeral service, nothing more. But I *do* have a rock."

Ned catches a look from The Barber in reflection. The Barber, of course, would never admit surprise.

"Let's call it a wager for the sake of history. A rock that Jack cannot wager on.

But his son will. This rock comes right out of Jack's office."

"I will take it as if the rock came from Jack himself! But I can tell you, it's most definitely a surprise."

"Both a surprise and a mystery for myself, also. He used the stone as a door stop in the entrance to his home office."

The company photos show a home office filled with a cherry orchard of hardwood furniture. The wood for the furniture is believed to be the same used for the four-foot chair rail and three-inch-thick doors. After Jed took the original factory drawings to decorate his office at work, Jack smothered the walls with his favourite artist, Ken Fletcher. Fletch had a far-off love for the ocean, and Jack's office was flooded with his paintings which depict oversized neon-coloured tropical fish. In the photos in the Archives, Jack's office looks more like a seafood restaurant than the command centre of the Boss. Foggy drifting by Scotch for the good ship Roger.

Ned flips the double flaps of the case. He needs both hands to pull the rock out.

The Barber has never seen anything quite like it. "My gosh, it looks like a shark fin."

"Jack liked the killer image. Remember, Father always wore those Greg Norman coral or green golf shirts. You could see him three tees away. I swear that he glowed in the night after returning home from his game." Both laugh at that sight. "The way I imagined it, it would take three showers to get that glow out."

As the light remarks fall away to silence on the barbershop floor, The Barber picks up the conversation.

"Kind of ironic, don't you think? You bring a stone from your father's office when he never crossed this threshold for a haircut. My father knew him over morning coffee and a Friday-afternoon snort at the bar. My father kept lots of secrets never to be repeated."

Ned smiles as this ancient version of the Barber he knew reaches for the soft neck brush. "I have to tell you, Jack did know the deal. The free haircut wager caught Father's attention. Business was business, an art to Father. He loved the game and the subsequent strategy to win. My guess is that he heard lots of stories through your father. Jack liked hearing Town news."

The Barber pauses with a serious face in their otherwise lighthearted cut and trim. "There is terrible gossip that makes the town into kind of a toilet bowl. That kind of crap is only supposed to go round in circles, but sometimes it sticks."

The Barber's brush does a round of Ned's pinstriped shirt and black leather tie. Ned watches the finish in the mirror. "Father never let on that he listened to that stuff. He left the dirty business to his lesser subjects. Jacked supported happy days, which is good for the lawn-mower business."

The Barber takes his turn in silence, thinking of his father running a business that managed lots of talk in a daily coffee klatch. Now Ned picks up the dialogue, returning to his father. He dangles a mystery on Jack's haircut.

"I can make a sure-bet wager on one thing you don't know. Where did Jack Roger get his hair cut?"

The Barber has never spent a lot of time dabbling in The Boss's choices in life. "I assumed on the road. Jack did travel a lot."

"Wrong. Maxine cut it."

"Are you serious? With all your dad's money?"

The shark fin rock doorstop from Jack Roger's home office.

"Yes, my mother."

"What a surprise, having your mother do that work!"

"Opposite. Maxine insisted on doing it. She held firm views on style. With Maxine it was head to toe. Shoes, belt and haircut, she did it her way. She had some talent, as my dad never complained. Jack liked the mirror. Jack never tolerated fools unless they had young plump titties."

The Barber's expression is a surprise look in the mirror.

"I confess that's the most …" He pauses for Ned to look up. "That is the most ever I've heard anyone in this chair or otherwise say about your father. Jack was a subject verboten."

"Let's be honest; Jack was Jack. And the chip off the old block — Jed is Jed, too. Why hide it when from all the gossip, some things will stick, true or imagined. Still, whenever Jack was leaving for a show or a sales run, she never let him let him do it without a style consultation."

Having heard enough salty references to Jack and the Roger family, an experienced Barber moves the conversation along. He's already swimming in new information. "Never would have guessed. I usually get a call from Junior at the funeral home. The family likes to have the deceased trimmed up a bit. Never got a call for Jack. Never gave it too much thought."

"Maxine did it."

New information makes the room silent again as The Barber digests the facts.

Ned catches his eye in the mirror. "Tell me, sir. What did you learn living in Town all these years? The Barber who has seen thousands of heads."

"Life is what happens after you make plans."

"I'm looking for something more personal."

"Life is too short to spend with assholes."

"Wow, that's personal, and gritty. How about something more philosophical from the first of all Town barbers?"

"My best advice for living in St. Marys is to remember it's a community, and consider yourself blessed. City people live in boroughs, neighbourhoods, above and below highways, and above in the clouds near God in their tall buildings. Here, we are one and all citizens of St. Marys, grounded in a true community sense."

Jed can only smile at the wise perspective found in a small town barbershop.

The Barber never sees the well-known Dean of Business from Canada's oldest English university again. He does see life's lessons, hears the repeated tunes, all off Queen Street. Inside, reminders are there to be seen for those who look. The shark-fin rock joins the barbershop as a doorstop for the closet-sized washroom. It will be one of eleven distinctive rocks that The Barber will drop off at the Stonetown Museum before his death. These winners will line two rows of wrought iron shelves on the exterior of a small storage barn. Floodlights will show off their particular vein and shape at night to observers of the garden landscape. Hidden from view, their select stories wait within the deerskin diary, deep in the Charles Wolfe Cruise Archives at the Stonetown Museum.

EPILOGUE

No story with rocks
from Rockton, right?

St. Marys, Ontario, 1996

"I roamed afar and often
Where rarer blossoms grow,
But never one among them
Has ever charmed me so.
The rock garden cherished,
Where a child returns carefree,
To revel in the hard beauty
Who softly smiles back at me."

— Virginia Marshall,
Mrs. Snoddie's
Grade 11 English
assignment on poetry

The rock garden in 1990.

ON a dank, dark night, I am standing beside the old rock garden, with the final sale in three days.

My buddy Paul, a common-sense talent, has joined me with his truck.

Shovel, pry bar and sweat have created an eyebrow-shaped opening. The granite slab underneath doesn't move an inch. The gash in the emerald isle of packed ivy keeps a tight lid on the rock.

Paul and I cut, dig, pick, shovel and pry, widening the view of the huge rock. More prying on the dirty mass and out it pops. "Pop eye," one of us says. Some sweat humour.

In the past week Paul and I have mined forty rocks out of the tight green blanket. We follow an established routine. Shake, rattle and roll from the ivy-covered rock line. From the pop-up, the rocks are rolled and positioned with duck steps until they're tipped onto the rusty wheelbarrow.

Handy directions from Paul. "Tip it sideways, keep it that way. We slide the wheelbarrow tight, parallel to the tailgate." He makes a roll with both palms outstretched. "So the rim catches right …" His hands grapple the wheelbarrow into position. Paul motions me to the front side. "1, 2, 3, lift. Stop. Now steady." Four hands balance the wheelbarrow on the lip. "Wolfe, we need to plan the drop. Contemplate home delivery off the tailgate."

He nods for the tip. The rock plops off and once over. "Keep 'em parallel, and not too far on, buddy. I need them tight to slide 'em off just right." Big smile. "Rack 'em and stack 'em," my delivery buddy concludes. "It's easy-peasy."

I nod with a few deep breaths at his super strategy for the hefty stone prospects. All the planning on this end gives us a no-effort backup to the exact drop for Jane's marked stops. "Don't work hard, work smart," I say with a chuckle, remembering how Scrooge McDuck advises his grandnephews Huey, Dewey and Louie.

Poke. Poke.

Another stone buried by ivy, ready to be plucked. Life takes, life gives. I have given all I can to a tired historic building. Now a sale with a short closing leaves little time to move an unknown quantity of quality rocks. I tell my friend Paul, "There's more buried, and more in that ivy. Doesn't matter where I poke — bingo. And bingo again. Each one is very unique."

On Sunday the leftovers will be as good as thrown out. The new owners have little interest in rocks. (Don't feel bad. I had little interest in them twenty years ago.)

In the final days, the deal closing faster, what's left in rocks seems to have got bigger and bigger. I punctuate every boulder with gigantic curse words.

"That's one fucking dead weight." Pause and big breath. "A fucking contender." Big breath and contemplation. "How in Hell are we getting that one tipped on the wheelbarrow, let alone tipped onto the tailgate?"

Paul wonders at the size. "Ice Age marbles if you ask me."

I wonder at our size. "Have to be a Neanderthal to lift them, if you ask me."

Most stones of this colour and magnitude have to represent a free haircut, I'm sure of it. Each one has to be a match for a wonderful story. Paul, too, is fascinated with The Barber and his wagers from sixty years in a former carriageway.

"Wolfe, all your research. Should be a book. Rocks and stories."

"A barber betting on odd rocks? People would think I'd lost *my* rocks."

"Your rocks, add in some stories. You're so full of shit. You could do it."

The rock garden, touchstone for four generations of the Marshall family, has touched Paul too. Now we reap what others have sown.

The great-grandfather laid out a garden alongside an adjacent property wall. The grandfather closed off the carriageway to make a barbershop. His son introduced a pile of new stone product for the family garden with his wager scheme. Virginia the great-granddaughter, a merchant who also lived on-site, dressed up her garden with a pond and fountain next to armless Venus and Little Scottie. A platoon of scattered dwarfs and gnomes and a Bambi fawn replaced The Barber's smoked-out buddies. (The former set of creatures have all gone under the hammer at Nairn's Auction Barn.) She spent all her time and profit as a successful single businessperson to help keep things up-to-snuff for building appearances. At least for as long as she was able; then came the cane. Life for Virginia, unable to do those stairs, became dependent on good neighbours or phone and delivery.

Over these last ten years as sole stewards of the property, Jane and I have picked a rock here, a stone there to fringe our borders at home. A slow parade has made its way up Jones Street from the remnants of the Devil's Smoke Pit. The group of eighty line up in amazing zoomorphic forms: the Scottie Dog, a rat, a Shark Fin, Sweepy Weepy, The Penis, ET and Darth Vader, The Meteorite, The Pig, Yoda, a hippopotamus and at least five mushrooms.

Smitten with all the variety, I once placed a call to Western University's Geology Department. I found myself blathering on about stones and their character. Some of the rocks have been rendered digital, so I offered photos before any possibility of a future visit. As Mr. Small-Town-Congenial, I always offer a great cup of coffee too. "And we'll take a quick look around the garden."

The Department of Geology never offered City hospitality. The message taker didn't even ask for my email. "Professor Corby deals with rocks. I will leave him a message. He's very busy. Thank you for calling."

Click. The geology guy never returned my call. The line of communication to the academic world went stone cold.

The rocks file along the Wolfe and Jane Cruise gardens of the Cruise family's five-generation, pioneer merchant home. It's not a rock garden landscaped in a concentration like the one at the Grand Central Hotel, but spread here and there throughout. Three pieces of petrified wood dress up veranda posts at the entrance. Off the flagstone sit the pig, the Scottie dog (Venus is left downtown standing alone) and a hippopotamus. Above, a Grande Allée–style trellis fills up with a wall of wisteria flanked by bushy magnolias. On the left, bird feeders attract a dinner crowd in flight. Opposite side, your visual frame follows right along the board & batten coach house with an edge of annuals. With so much beauty and fowl action, most people ignore the array of stone mushrooms and animals in rock disguises, not to mention the petrified wood. All will walk by, as Jane and I walk by many times a day, the hidden stories.

Initially it was hard not to keep pointing out the obvious. "This one looks like a penis." See Jane give that look, so change subjects. "How about the shark fin here?"

Jane's an art history graduate with an undergraduate degree in sciences, and a backup smile. "Help me, Wolfe. Are both mushrooms and a penis zoomorphic? One is fungi. The other, is it not something? Something that big, attached to an animal?"

Semantics. I ignore the oblivious and keep it obvious. "Whatever they are, they sure are treasures."

Penis: Everyone in the know has heard and repeated the story of the sinking cruiser in the Park by the Creek named after a fish that does not exist.

Shark fin: The Cruise family home is one block from the Roger family home; old Mr. and Mrs. Roger were always around when I was a kid. Talk about story alignment, I once tripped over his shark-fin rock doorstop. Old Jack invited me into his cherry-lined office when I was collecting for *The Globe*. Never saw the rock on the floor. I was mesmerized by Jack Roger inviting me in, into his grand old wood-lined office.

The petrified wood under the trellis, with birds incoming and a cappuccino in hand, often brings Charles Wolfe Cruise into contemplation. While my grandfather's *RAMBLE IN THE SOUTHLANDS* has tie-ins with The Barber's diary, I couldn't find any solid connection to the petrified wood pieces at my home office or Archives, in oral pass-me-downs or the microfiche of the *Journal*.

"He did ramble on." Jane loves beating the windy path of a story. "My God, the guy wrote tomes on the Southwest."

Sometimes the sun dances through the wisteria, drawing us out to the bouquet of side perennials with their trim of rock. I love the big granite and quartz pieces at the bottom of the driveway.

Any one of those could have been handpicked by Marvin. And how about the giant toadstools? They can't be anything else but free-haircut material. The Barber's deerskin diary does describe the shapes of some of these boulders. It falls just short of providing stories for them, though.

In the ten years she was my tenant in her vast apartment that takes up two-thirds of the second floor, Virginia mentioned the free-haircut deal many times. She mentioned the existence of stories from the rocks, too. She even pointed to the Archives, and her father's diary. But I was distracted by life, and I never asked or had a look.

"I feel bad, but what am I to do?" I would tell Jane. "Talking with Virginia all day doesn't get the job done. Nor does it pay for anything."

Being a landlord is the easiest job in the world. Until the phone rings. And rings. That Mennonite-replaced roof developed small leaks; oh look, someone's leaking on my front steps; there's the dirty hallways, unwanted cats, eloping raccoons and MIA rent.

My standard landlord rant: "These tenants all have better cable than we do. HBO! And ..." (pause for a breath) "... and they can outsmart you on not paying the rent."

Virginia hadn't done any maintenance in years. The gardens had gone ivy league in a wild state. I gravelled over the grass paddocks, which eliminated a mowing expense and increased revenues with paid parking. But the costs kept coming. The building needed a new air conditioner. And those leaks! Maybe a second new roof. My respect for heritage and preservation encouraged me to keep things as they were — or maybe I was just cheap and lazy and the place was in disrepair.

I got a soft introduction to renting with my first tenants, Virginia and Pearl the retired postie (later replaced by the Minister's mother). Then my tenants changed. Old ladies were replaced by young couples saving for their first home. My prospects dimmed as my renters became outside smokers and inside tokers, cat owners with full litter boxes, and hungry singles always out on the lookout bringing back drama, trauma and more cigarette butts. In between they watched HBO on their big smart screens. Any stories from the past — whether poetic, bitter-sweet or hilarious — now wore on as a waste of time for the distracted landlord and this rent-dodging crowd. What I bought from Virginia is an income property, not the stories about some barber and his rock garden.

How could I admit to never even giving a thought to recording any of Virginia's stories? The distracted landlord was further embarrassed that he could not remember anything of note, the who, when, which and how of these rocks. What customers, what special characters made the haircut wagers? So it was with a touch of guilt that I shook the sands of time off those oodles of stirring stories from the Archives. Still occupied with real life, I slid snail-like through piles of paper, stacks of files, and those blinding microfiches. Over time, the loose threads of all those notions and ideas began to be sorted and stitched into a recognizable fabric.

And so I find myself standing behind the Sold sign in a warm evening rain by the Jones Street entrance to the Hotel. I'm just waiting for Paul to bring his pickup around to the street, when out of nowhere I hear my name.

"Wolfe. Wolfe Cruise, is that you?"

My neighbour Cathy Jackson — she lives two doors up from me and Jane, across from the former Roger home — approaches under cover of an umbrella. "Wolfe. Just coming from the Post Office. Thought it was you."

I'm a wet, nodding observer to Cathy's undercover approach.

"Rocks you're moving, then." She looks over my shoulder. "Lots of rocks, I would suppose."

I am still nodding.

"A memory of Victoria would be nice for us."

I am dumbfounded at her mention of Victoria, Virginia's younger sister. A memory of Victoria? I wonder at the possible connection between the last surviving Marshall, who's eighty-plus years old, and the fiftyish Cathy. How does Cathy even know there's a rock garden, let alone rocks on the move?

Nod your head, smile and wait for her justification.

"A memory?" I ask.

"A memory for my great friend Victoria, for my garden."

Part of me thinks a friend's memory in Cathy's garden seems fine, especially when there's more than enough memories left and too little time while Jane and I have picked our fill. My logic tells me to favour neighbour relations with the right flavour. My grandfather always recommended a good-deed-first move, no matter the character.

And yet, something seems off. I have never seen this woman out in her bushy garden, and I know from outside advice that Cathy is someone to be treated with caution as a well-known tongue wagger. Slippery Seale, the ancient wrangler in all things real estate, has experience on this local player.

"Half right she is," he told me once. "The real problem is figuring out which half. Which half is the right, which half is left to guess as wrong." The Seale put a stamp on Cathy with a laugh. "I'd rather be a questionable half-right than fully half-dim." And the godfather of in-the-knows doubled down. "Save that role for her husband, half-dim Dan."

Cathy nods her head towards the rocks, which are out of sight behind the building. "Victoria would be so pleased to sit in our garden, and see her memories."

I nod and turn my head at the absurdity. She brings me back with her chin close in. "Victoria would love it. The rocks … in *our* garden."

I step back behind the Sold sign. It seems like a stretch that after my twenty years of ownership there's suddenly all this interest in a bunch of rocks. I have to ask. "*Your* garden? Doesn't she want something for *her* garden?"

"Victoria loves the idea of putting the rocks in our garden. Special rocks resting in a special place."

I must have a question mark smacked across my face. Cathy's face gets red as she continues. "And that special place, it's in *my* garden. Rocks from Rockton for the house."

Stop that train of thought in its tracks. Rockton? The abandoned limestone quarry north of Royal City, a haven for motocross dirt bikers? Cathy's raised eyebrows are furrowing back at me. I blurt it out. "Rockton? What do the Marshalls have to do with a motocross track in an old quarry? In Rockton?"

"*That's* where the family went every weekend. To pick out special ones. Victoria told me all about it, how they brought them back."

Cathy is 100% reaching. Rockton never came up in the conversation with Virginia, never.

"Cathy." My inner voice now screams *No, no, and no, do not speak,* but like a bad old dog, I do it anyway. "Cathy, remember it's the 1940s, 1950s. Families did *not* jump in their Buick Roadmaster" — the furrows on her forehead are waving, twitching back at me. I'm 100% in — "and go for weekend jaunts to Rockton."

A hundred percent in danger, that is. She grounds my goofy grin with her frown. "I am most *certain* they did. Go to Rockton."

"Cathy, most of these rocks, the biggest and most interesting, came across the barbershop floor of the old Hotel." I double-focus on her eyes through the dripping rain on my clear safety glasses. My God, her pupils are darting flames at me. They seem to swivel counterclockwise.

"Now Wolfe, you *do know*. Your story is not the real story."

"I know how individual and unique these rocks are. Look at them,

Cathy." I make some feeble hand motion. "They did *not* come from one place." More eye-darts flame me away from the edge of the cliff of absurdity to a possible lifeline of compromise. "Heh, maybe it's both. Like two stories into one: Rockton and The Barber."

Cathy throws it right back. "That is *not* the story."

"Come on, it's rocks with a story. That's the story."

My half-effort response hits a full nerve. "Are you calling Victoria a liar?"

"Tell me, Cathy." Full speed ahead over the cliff of absurdity. "Who did I buy the building from?"

"Virginia."

"Who owned the rock garden?"

"Virginia."

"Who sold me the building with the rock garden?"

"Virginia."

"And who told me the story about the rocks?"

Cathy draws the line with a waggy finger holdup. "You *are* calling Victoria a liar."

She's trolling with that finger pointed in my face. I should take the bait, bite her fishing finger. Just take a chomp.

"Listen up here, Wolfe." Her words take on an eerie sameness in pitch. "If you were not my friend, I would not be telling you this." She's clearly perplexed by my half-smile. "You have insulted *me*. I am telling you this as my friend. Your version is *not* the story."

With her right hand up, jabbing her finger at my left eye, I can't help but step back. No biting, so I make a feeble attempt at light humour. I am a generational non-combatant and a great deflector.

"Come on, Cathy." Dig up a nice smile. "You sure are *ruining* a really great story."

"I'll be back with My Nick."

As she turns half-right to cross the laneway, Paul beeps her from his path with a touch of horn. Let's just say she almost lost her umbrella.

As Paul and I drive back to my house for the drop-off, Cathy has left us with lots to laugh about.

"You know, Wolfe, if Cathy has Backhoe Nick in tow, that is serious business."

My goodness me, Paul is right. Nick owns a front-end loader just primed and ready to pop these puppies out. Paul and I are limited to a pickup, pry bar and wheelbarrow.

"I better be there," I tell Paul. "You can drop me off."

A note to the reader: Take your God-given free will to choose whether the half-right woman's wrong or the good landlord writes with a poison pen. There's nothing recorded in the Archives on the fourth generation of the Marshall family. There isn't much on Virginia or Victoria in the deerskin diary, or in any of the shreds of correspondence.

I had heard all about Victoria for years, though, from her older sister.

"That Vicky," Virginia would say. "All she does is wait. Wait for me to drop dead. Then she gets it all."

And more on lesser family members. "And her kids! Vicky parades them through my home. They paw at the few remaining things that I have left. They never quit telling me, *Oh, that's nice, Auntie Virginia.* Well, old Auntie Virginia has the final word on nice. They are not getting their say on anything. Nothing until the will is read. That's how nice old auntie Virginia is."

As a witness never called upon, the landlord heard about a long list of family transgressions. In the end, I had just hung up the phone after receiving the sad news from the coroner when Vicky called me cold for keys.

"Hello, Mr. Cruise. May I call you Wolfe? Wolfe, it's Victoria Marshall calling."

I had never met this younger sister.

"You have been so supportive of my sister. God rest her soul. So supportive of her through the years. All so nice of you. Wolfe, you understand all this legal stuff. By the time we wait for the lawyers it will be months. The funeral is Saturday, the kids are back. It would be so much more convenient to organize all that stuff while they're here. We need the keys."

She could hear my silence on the line.

"Virginia," she clarifies. "My sister was always there. There was never a need for the convenience of keys. You understand, Wolfe?"

I do understand. I understand that I have never seen you visit your older sister. I understand that you and your daughters want more.

"Wolfe, we are her only family. We just don't have keys."

"That Vicky" never did confirm the instructions of the will, and the letters of the executor never appeared. I complained to Jane, the only one who listens.

"I could have insisted on the fine details, the departed official instructions. A hold up but it's Virginia's only family. So I held out the key. The solitary woman did mention the whole gang in her will. Everybody had an eye for something or other, but something or other ended up being slim pickings."

Virginia got the last laugh. She mixed up the take, with wrong names for wrong items. Those sleazy siblings sizzled. Virginia's will, I suspect, will keep the Marshall family feud going on for another generation.

After Paul and I drop off eight beauties at Jane's direction, he drops me off at the Hotel. Three bodies huddle in the light rain behind a five-ton dump truck. Number one steps out, wary of Paul's dangerous pickup.

"My Nick and Katie and I have selected these ten rocks."

Marked with fluorescent stakes, her choices are not stones, not even what I would describe as rocks, but massive granite boulders. Marvin-sized winners, landscape goliaths. Cathy's ten is more like sixteen, too.

I remind myself that Nick charges by the hour, not like my friend Paul. On this warm but super crappy night Nick steps out from the truck with three pairs of gloves, three shovels, three picks and one pry bar. He himself does not wear gloves — tough guy keeps it all hard. Mother and daughter are gloved and ready to get dirty. Nick shoves the third pair of gloves towards me.

He might be My Nick, but he's not *my* Nick. I'm supposed to help? I donate the memories, I give up my free time, and I'm supposed to pick up a shovel too?

Nick seems to hear the mind of a draft-dodger rumble. He gives a gobby grin to the ladies as he holds up the gloves. "Lookee-see, quick hands for a fast job."

I tug on the gloves, and with the clock punched Nick is off to the farthest orange stake. Rock and roll ensues, all handpicking to Cathy's jig-a-jig on the dig. Daughter and hired hand follow orders in the heist, as boulder after boulder is hijacked to an unrelated garden. I'm sure neither Cathy nor Nick nor Katie has any clue about the Hotel's history or even the existence of a barber, let alone all those stories.

We follow Cathy's point while the hired hand pokes and pries along. "Great, Nick — this one next."

Nick gives Cathy and Katie a smile. "And a 'ittle wiggle here, and a 'ittle wiggle there. Let's not 'ave a muscle tear." My word, that Nick's a cheeky lad. His light words fall with another heavy roll onto the lawn. "Wolfe, use the maple stake and get them close to the tailgate."

The hydraulic tailgate is a smooth operator for the heavy lift. All the rocks roll smartly along, ramping up onto the tailgate with a double pry. The hydraulics cry a little under the strain of a triple lift.

Nick identifies four rocks for us to leave to last. "They'll need to go up one at a time."

Finally, with a 'ittle wiggle and some big pushes, the parade lines up across the stainless flatbed. Cathy's choices are tip-top, top-of-the-chart rocks that tip the scales. As I stare at one whole lotta of weight spread on the back of the five-ton truck, opportunity knocks for a little rain on Cathy's light logic.

"Wow, they are brutes," I say. "Sure must have weighted down that car of theirs."

"Car?"

"Their car trips. Every weekend to Rockton." My inner voice again shouts *no, no, no,* but I hear myself say the words. "It's a wonder."

"A wonder?"

"A wonder they could lift these. Even if the whole family helped."

Cathy gets in the dump truck and sticks her face out the half-open passenger window. "We shall return."

No thanks, no goodbyes, and the dump truck does a shimmy, shake and rattle over the sidewalk up the Jones Street hill.

An hour later, Cathy returns. "Victoria loves my picks. She would like to see more."

Nick is quickly off in a poke through the ivy jungle. *Clank.* Rock and roll each boulder over to push, push it up past the grass for a quick flip, tip over the lip, and onto the hydraulic lift. At least this time I am left standing with my gloves off.

Unapologetic and silent, in minutes Cathy has what she wants. Nick

     LORNE EEDY

can punch the clock on the delivery of eight more massive examples of free haircuts.

The rocks bang, rattle and roll over the curb. Nick grinds up the grade in second gear, high beams shining through the messy, dank night. He feels the heat of my glare through the half-open window on his side, gives me a thumbs-up flash. Cathy simmers in the right side of the cab, out of the summer rain.

Poor Jane hears all the sordid details later that night, and then for weeks and months to come.

"Who does she think she is? This was no memory quest, this was a grab-fest. Where was the Free Rocks sign, anyways?"

Jane can always put these difficult people in perspective. "It's been a big week, dear. The Hotel is gone, and we have all the rocks we want and no more tenants."

"I ate the bullshit sandwich she served up. *My older friend*, ha. *You are my friend*, ha. Ha. Ha. Ha."

"Be grateful for what you have, that's what your grandmother Sarah would have told you."

"I will have to look at twenty rocks in her yard."

Jane puts two fingers on my lips. "We've never looked before. Nor has she paid any attention to us. We will ignore her, just as she has always ignored us."

"Unless she wants something."

Finally I bring myself to change the subject to the weather. "Hey, love the rain out there." A wink for Jane. "Puts some relish on eating her dust."

"Correction, dear. You did call it a shit sandwich."

With two days left before the close on Sunday, there's one last call I have to make. Uncle Raymond Rath is not an actual family relation, but he's a wonderful friend of the Cruise family. I had promised old Uncle Ray his pick of the rocks ages ago, and he tagged three Goliaths. Out of respect to Virginia, he let the stones lie for many years.

I call his farm in Ebenezer, two concessions over from Marvin's former family farm. Uncle Ray is a ripe old age, but right on to the call display.

"Wolfe, g'day."

"Building is sold, Uncle Ray. Do you remember those rocks?"

He replies without a second's hesitation. "You bet I do! Raymond never forgot his rocks. I've been waiting. Sorry, Virginia." I can just picture Ray's non-phone hand pointing to heaven, and then back to Earth. "I picked three out, right?"

Put a checkmark beside that senior memory of Raymond's. When it comes to recollection, he has all his rocks. Ray has hearing aids, though, so I do have to speak louder.

He himself is loud and clear. "I paid good money for those garden rocks at the Moose Lodge auction."

In the auction listing I described The Barber, the free-haircut wager and the old rock garden, under the heading ROCKS WITH A STORY. The existence of a barbershop wager that fills up the backyard with odd rocks fabricated fun over a charity dinner. Most marvelled at the concept of the converted carriageway where Angie Daylrimple now does nail care. Those few history buffs at the Moose auction are among the few who are aware of the faded gilt letters spelling THE GRAND CENTRAL HOTEL across the high eave over the mass of yellow brick. (I do my share on the street to the accidental passerby. Up I point, up past the bevelled glass and past the mass of yellow brick. Does no one in this Town look up?)

Two or three rocks auctioned for the Moose Club always got two hundred bucks or more in bids.

"The building sale closes this Sunday," I tell him now. "Understand, that's two days. If you want 'em, come get 'em. *Now* is the time."

"My congratulations come to you, young man." The consummate gentleman: respectful, classy and affable. "Give me time for one call, and I'll be back to you."

"Sorry for the last-minute notice. My buyer wants a quick close. Real quick."

After I hang up I turn to Jane. "Uncle Ray even remembers Marvin as a kid."

Jane, having listened to the phone conversation, predicts that Uncle Ray, a known procrastinator, will lay off one mañana too late, and the closing will pass before he crosses the backyard. "That Raymond Rath is the only gentleman I know that makes shit sound like saddle soap leather polish," she says.

Raymond Rath, at eighty-seven, has twenty-two years of seniority on me. He lived and worked the formative parts of his life in the environs of the old Grand Central Hotel. And smoked out back, too. His haberdashery was located across from The Barber's front door. On his slower days, Raymond would get a great sampling of who and what crossed paths on Queen Street. His store also sheltered a big round table out back where conversation made the rounds. Nothing open range like the Sunriser: this was a by-invitation group of Citizens in-the-know. The locals called it The Round Table, simple and clear.

"The Round Table, you say? At the back?"

"Behind the draw curtains. There's the real action."

"I thought that was where Ray did his tuxedo-rental measuring and pants alterations."

Behind the curtains, closed-door politics, unprinted *Journal* news, scandals of the down-and-out, legal notices and the court reports did the rounds. Slippery Seale, the Chiefs of both Fire and Constabulary, the Town Clerk, the Mayor, the Presbyterian minister and a select bunch of vintage St. Marys who's-who would never miss their weekday confab at ten on the button. Styrofoam cups, real creamers and a sugar shaker complement the Theatre City daily, a boring inventory of Canadian magazines, and as always, the most recent edition of *The St. Marys Journal,* all spread across the solid pine tabletop. All conversations began with *Did you hear, Did you read* or *Did you see.* (In-the-know people never say I, always you.)

The Barber could have skirted across the street for a reverse view with Raymond, but at ten in the morning he was too busy. But Raymond was always good for a smoke, a regular haircut, or both. He never made an appointment. He would scoot over when he saw The Barber looking out of his narrow window beside the striped barber pole.

Over my umpteen pants alterations, Raymond has never mentioned a wager or a free haircut. On the flip side, there isn't much on Uncle Ray in the deerskin diary.

Raymond once told me he had The Barber as a Sunday School teacher.

"He did a great Moses throwing the stone tablets around."

Had his first smokes right there in the rock garden.

"The haircut was alright," he said. "But nothing beats a Sunday School teacher who invites you out for a smoke. As a teenager I didn't say much in the Smoke Pit, but I couldn't help take note of those rocks."

The Rath family has lived for generations on their Blanshard farm, but third-generation Raymond Rath changed uniforms from overalls to suits. After becoming a clothier he was also a part-time farmhand, with his land rented out to his oldest, Grayson Senior. In his later years Ray's help is limited to light barn activity and serving as backup combine driver at harvest. He doesn't garden but enjoys a smoke outside with something to look at. Raymond wants a sunset memory of his life to take home, something with good substance to reflect on when he's having his smoke.

Contrary to Jane's prediction, in less than an hour Uncle Ray lands there in the Hotel's backyard with his hulking number-one grandson, the man-boy Grayson.

I have set aside and marked the three Marvin-sized examples chosen way back when. "Cathy Jackson couldn't contain herself, asking whose were these rocks."

Ray is always quick to the point on his vast experience with Town characters. "Wiry hair." My half-dumb look expands the point. "The Barber would tell you that the more difficult the hair, the more difficult the personality."

Meanwhile, Grayson — or Amazing Gray, or Junior, or just Amazing — grapples and grips the stone choices alone, rolling them along to the waist-high tailgate. A bigger man than My Nick, in the class of Big Boss or Mandy Kittmer, he stands quad height to the tailgates. The rock lineup somehow looks smaller with him towering over the lift.

Gray stoops to conquer with a grapple, grip and heave. And that gapping grin. "Nothing like a little practice for the Downie Tug-of-War Team."

The Rath lads accept an offer to toss on a few more, size permitting. Later I tell Jane that I could watch Gray lift boulders all afternoon. His arms, heavy guns, are vise-grips fine-tuned by years of rock picking in Blanshard Township. It's not a surprise that Amazing Gray is number-one grip on the line for the Blanshard Tug-of-War Team, a CNE champion. Gray the Gamebreaker is the envy of the Nissouri, Zorra and St. Marys Tug-of-War Teams.

Under all the cover of achievements, he's a fun guy. With a twinkle in his eyes, Grayson leans his butt on the tailgate, and the truck's rear end sinks four inches. "Heh," he says. "I *always* go for the hand job."

My ears go crimson at the Blanshard humour. Not to be misunderstood, Junior gives a double eyebrow-raise. "Eh?"

Raymond looks to Grayson with his bushy eyebrows raised. "You *do* have the grip to get that job done." The apple apparently hasn't fallen far from the tree.

A big guffaw all round. I stand back to watch Gray roll his huge neck side-to-side. He stretches to the sky with a crack of rolling thunder down the back. Without a word, the last rock goes heave-ho with a bang, a bump and a bounce onto the truck box.

Gray stops and turns. "You know, I used to work for Virginia back in my high school days." Virginia never mentioned help. "Raymond introduced me to part-time work in Town twice a week. He took me across the street to meet Virginia, and that was that. After school."

Raymond is stuck in a comfort lean on the side fender. "Lad needed to learn independent responsibilities. Virginia wanted a strong arm around."

Gray has a smarty-face look about him. "Raymond," he says. "The truth is it saved you guys from paying an allowance. When the job started, farm chores continued, but the pay stopped. Nice move, Raymond."

Gray gives Raymond a reflective smile. "I would wait till six for Raymond to close the store. I remember that. Do my homework on that round dining table. When Raymond needed help on the harvest or bailing, he was waiting in the parking lot at the high school. Anyways, outside cash money helped. So I mowed her lawn and weeded the garden."

Grayson could be a witness for the prosecution on my recent neglect of the dowager. I stand guilty as I consider the majesty and magic the garden must have held. All I can say:

"It must have been a beautiful spot?"

Grayson stands by the tailgate with a distant expression, a reflection of pride. "Sure was, Wolfe. I loved that rock garden." But there's nothing judgmental in his tone. "Virginia would have it looking good. My sweat, her direction."

Gray winds back to a pleasant time, back to high school in St. Marys. A job after school was his first bit of independence after slopping pigs, chasing chickens, milking cows and grooming his sisters' skittish horses. Nobody to account for the lad buying his cigs from Dick's Groceteria. Puff on a few behind that goofy dog rock beside the armless statue. Further independence while Victoria concentrated on her fine-ladies-clothing-and-funky-gift store. He had a few haircuts, even preschool stuff, from The Barber.

One horrible skinhead cut in Grade Five finished Gray on The Barber. Gray remembers how all his friends were going for a buzz cut. Mothers lined up their little lads for a summer poodle style, a cut for hot weather, but every kid hated a mommy-chosen lid. It was Gray's fault completely; The Barber had given him fair warning: "To me, that looks more like something you would do for a flea infestation. Beware what you want, son. You might end up with it." No surprise that Gray followed a parade of local lads getting a bad haircut for independence.

Gray moved on, choosing Sonja's Beauty Salon around the corner, an easy recommendation from his older sister. Sonja hires super-pretty apprentices. "My goodness, Xanya was so cute. She was in my sister's class." I can relate — my choice as an independent customer would eventually change to the very cute young ladies at Kut 'n Kurl, and forever later with The GGs on Water Street.

Grayson savours a wonderful past as he puffs away in the here and present of the long and narrow rock garden. Raymond and I wait on the pause.

"Yup." *Pf-f-f-fff.* "I remember having my first smoke here."

Quiet contemplation understood in a smokers' circle. Gray remains in static thought.

"I think *a lot* of citizens did their first turn" — *Pf-f-f-fff* — "smoking out here. And first haircut."

The sweep of his vision leaves a trailer of smoke.

"Think of it. The Devil's Smoke Pit." Gray calls up a full hand of image cards from his memory file. "All these super neat rocks from Mr. Marshall. Everyone calls him The Barber. You remember him, right?"

Remember him, right. My first haircut, my first independent appointment, my first buzz cut, but never a smoke. Today I am learning so much more. I keep it simple, not referring to my research record. "My grandfather went to Arthur Meighen with him. That's when the school was up off Wellington Street."

"So he knew The Barber?"

"Grandfather Charles was a customer for thirty years. I'd say he was a buddy. Father too, like me and you, he got his first haircut here. Dad continued on once a month right to the end. Until The Barber had that stroke."

"Those cigs were going to catch up to him."

A wind gives the Junipers a shimmer and shiver. *Pf-f-f-fff. Pf-f-f-fff.*

When the haze from smoke and memories lifts, I've got one thought on my mind. "Gray. You did say rocks from The Barber?"

Pf-f-f-fff. "All organized like. Organized in his rock garden. Kind of like a library."

"A library?"

"You know?" *Pf-f-f-fff.* "Rocks *stacked*, like books. Each in an order, with their own story."

The brakes are on in my mind. I stop, stone deaf in the moment. I breathe in to focus on Grayson. "Did you say stories?"

Pf-f-f-fff. Grayson is caught in his fond memories of wonder years. He doesn't have a clue about Rockton. "Yup. Every one of these stones, many are boulders. Yup, and each one has a special story."

Grayson's two thumbs run an inside path up the stretchy straps on his pinstripe overalls. His fingers do a drum roll on his upper chest. *Pf-f-f-fff.*

"Yup. Rocks with a story."

Author's Note

My family told stories.

For over a hundred years the Eedys were the owners and publishers of the *St. Marys Journal*.

A lot of news made its way around the Eedy kitchen table, including those characters' stories that never made it into print. ("You mean the ones who never got caught," comes the clarification from the coffee regulars, all nodding their heads.) These not-fit-to-print stories are what I remember and need to share.

My great-grandfather covered the American Southwest, all his adventures detailed to faithful readers three weeks later in the newspaper. He was the first St. Marys resident to drive to California and the first to ride in an airplane. He also met Tom Mix, Hollywood's first big Western movie star. All of this was big stuff before our small world today. When he returned home, he retold his exploits for the church and service-club dinner circuit, where he sold his book *Travels in the Southlands*. (The Museum Archives does still have a box of copies.)

My suffragette and temperance grandmother, Grace, taught in Alberta pre-WWI with Nellie McClung, and they were friends for life. Any questions on grammar or spelling, Grace got the call. Off the record, she told of summers with her Methodist minister grandfather at Kettle Point or her minister father in Kingsville, who was friends with legendary conservationist Jack Miner. On the record, her tales of ear-pulling encounters with local drunks were epic.

My mother, a war bride from the west, followed in Grace's footsteps with a newsy column that ended in one, maybe two recipes from known households. Her best stories were from the pre-war years when she was a teenager in the "frontier" town of Prince George, BC. My father carried on the tradition with his column "The Rambling Reporter," top right of the editorial page each week in the *Journal*. Father also had an off-the-record battery that included "Honest Herb and the Crooked Cow," "Saturday afternoon at the Pleasant Time Theatre," and "Tom and the Cacklelator," the story of a boy who responded to a pronunciation correction with, "Cacklelator, that's what I said, diddle I?"

Then there's my Uncle Jim, who lived one block over from us. He whipped up after-dinner entertainment with a casting call of odd St. Marys characters that gave us all a review of life in the 1920s. He told us about his father, a country doctor reared in the horse-and-buggy age, behind the wheel of his Model T. And he had one story about a sharp little kid who knocked a fat cat out of a tree with a toss of a small stone, in front of the entire volunteer fire department and with the entire town as an audience.

But my stories come from more than just a career as fifth-generation publisher of the *Journal*. When I purchased the Grand Central Hotel in downtown St. Marys, that property came with four generations of history and the rock garden behind it. The previous owner became my tenant, and I did not listen to or ask about the real stories of her barber father — a failure about which I am embarrassed to this day.

There was no deerskin diary. The rocks are real, with over one hundred on display at the Eedy family home.

The stuff about the years of driving dangerous is all true, and Dobson Ford was a real local business. There was no Huff & Puff tow service, however, nor a population of loose donkeys wandering about town; I just love the image of loose donkeys. Driving lessons — and life lessons — in the cemetery are part of local lore.

Holstein bulls were indeed sold to Cuba from right here in St. Marys — from two farms that are now subdivisions. The rest of the Cuba stuff is "bull" shit. (My university education is Latin America pre-1748, with Cuba a sub-specialization.)

The story of Hurricane Hazel is true, although I've changed the year. Someone did fall off a ladder working on an old barn foundation. Mandy Kittmer is fiction, but not the vast numbers of Kittmers in Zorra Township.

A final note: All the characters in this book are fictional, whether they're based on a real person or an amalgamation of personalities. I've named the characters after a mix of friends and family, so that I can give as many as possible affirmative answers to the question, "Am I in your book?"

All the stories are based on true events, tweaked for good substance and great entertainment.

And check out my previous book, *Gay Cheese*, for my favourite tale never to make the newspaper — "Wedding Girl," a titillating vision of couture.

Acknowledgement

Lorne is proud to still stand before the dowager of yellow brick — whether behind, looking towards the 60-foot-wide veranda, or in front with eyes up to the faded blocks of gilded letters: GRAND CENTRAL HOTEL.

And, my heart goes out to my best friend, my long-standing wife, Nancy.

www.ingramcontent.com/pod-product-compliance
Lightning Source LLC
Chambersburg PA
CBHW061231210726
48293CB00003B/728